I'LL BE
WATCHING
YOU

CHARLES
DE LINT

WRITING AS
SAMUEL M. KEY

ORB
A TOM DOHERTY ASSOCIATES BOOK
NEW YORK

FOR
WILLIAM GOLDMAN,
WHO DOES IT SO WELL

I'LL BE WATCHING YOU

This edition edited by Patrick Nielsen Hayden.

An Orb Edition
Published by Tom Doherty Associates, LLC
175 Fifth Avenue
New York, NY 10010

www.tor.com

Library of Congress Cataloging-in-Publication Data

Key, Samuel M.
    I'll be watching you/ Charles de Lint, writing as Samuel M. Key.—1st Orb ed.
        p.   cm.
    "A Tom Doherty Associates book."
    ISBN 0-765-30435-X
    1. Stalking victims—Fiction.   2. Divorced women—Fiction.   3. Photographers—Fiction.   4. Abused women—Fiction.   5. Strangers—Fiction.   I. Title.

  PR9199.3.D357I45   2004
  813'.54—dc22

                                                        2003061253

This book was written under the name of Samuel M. Key, originally published by Berkley Books in January 1994.

First Orb Edition: March 2004

Printed in the United States of America

0 9 8 7 6 5 4 3 2 1

I'LL BE
WATCHING
YOU

INTRODUCTION

Sometimes the darkness calls, and I find myself approaching it. Not because it has any sort of appeal to me, but to try to understand it.

One of the ongoing themes of my work is the effect that preternatural encounters have on the ordinary person. Mostly, the darker sections of my novels arrive from the human psyche, with the magical elements playing against that shadow. But the Otherworld contains as much darkness as it does ambiguity and light, and to ignore it entirely strikes me as only telling half the story, hence the books I wrote under the pen name Samuel M. Key.

I'll Be Watching You originally had a working title of *Deadlock* and was the last of the books published under the Sam Key byline. At the time of its release, it was my only published novel to date without a preternatural element in it. Since then, Subterranean Press has done a limited-edition hardcover of my P.I. novel, *The Road to Lisdoonvarna*. Like *From a Whisper to a Scream*, *I'll Be Watching You* is set in Newford. In it the meanness and spite, as well as the redemption, came wholly from human hearts.

When my first "horror" novel, *Mulengro*, appeared in 1985, readers picked it up expecting the usual de Lint novel. *Mulengro* has many of the elements that readers have come to expect in my work, but it also contains somewhat graphic descriptions of violence and its after-effects, which some readers found disturbing. I can well understand that some people prefer not to read horror fiction, so one of the reasons I decided to create "Samuel M. Key" was so that readers could differentiate between the types of fiction I was writing. The Key books would be the darker ones. No secret was made of the fact that the pseudonym was mine, since it was merely a device to let readers know in advance that they could expect a darker story between the covers.

If you'd like to know more of the origins of Sam Key, please visit my Web site at www.charlesdelint.com/faq.htm.

The Sam Key books are dark, and at times, graphically rendered novels, *I'll Be Watching You* as much as any of the others. Though ultimately they reach for the light, the journey to get there becomes both arduous and harrowing in places. Much like life itself, really, reminding us to take care of each other along the way.

—Charles de Lint
Ottawa, Fall 2003

THE TRUTH IS BEAUTIFUL, BUT THE
BEAUTIFUL IS NOT NECESSARILY TRUE.
                        —TIMOTHY FERRIS

EVERYONE THINKS OF CHANGING THE
WORLD, BUT NO ONE THINKS OF
CHANGING HIMSELF.
                        —LEO TOLSTOY

FRANK

ONE

A thunderstorm was raging in Rachel Sorensen's sleep. She was in an old barn, somewhere up north, far enough away from the city that the swaying trees outside the run-down structure could be called a forest. Rain came in between the old gray boards of the wall she was crouched against, splattering her face. Or were they tears that wet her cheeks? Because she knew she was hiding again—not until the bruises went away, but so that he wouldn't add to them. Her shoulder still ached from where he'd wrenched her arm from its socket, two nights past.

A sudden thought came to her, and she looked frantically around the barn with the next flash of lightning. What if he was in the barn with her? What if this time, when he rammed the pistol up under her chin, he pulled the—

The thunder woke her.

She sat upright in her own bed, in her own apartment. The ache in her shoulder was just a memory. Her cheeks were damp—crying in her sleep again. But it had just been a dream, nothing more. One more false memory to add to the collection of real hurts and aches and bad memories that she was still trying to put behind her.

She looked out the window, hoping the view it gave of the park would calm her, then realized that it wasn't raining. The sky was clear. Stars could be made out against the city's light pollution, which rose for miles into the sky above the streets.

The thunder came again.

She turned her head once more, this time to the doorway of the bedroom.

It's the door, she realized.

Her gaze went to the clock beside the bed. The digital readout told her it was past three in the morning. She shivered.

Please let this just be a dream, too, she thought.

Because she knew who it was at her door. Her therapist had explained it to her: no matter where she went or how well she hid her tracks, if he was determined enough, he would find her.

"You have to be prepared for that," Dr. Caley had told her, sympathetically.

But sympathy was no help right now. She started to reach for the phone, but knew it was futile. By the time the police came, he'd be gone again, leaving her to deal with their endless questions. By the time they came, she could be dead.

He was here *now*. Pounding on the wood with his thick knuckles. Hands once gentle, turned hard and angry.

"We just haven't got the manpower to put a squad car outside your building every night," the detective had explained to her, apologetically.

Apologies were no help either.

There was a lull. He'd stopped his assault on the door. But now she could hear his voice, muffled by the door, but all too familiar.

"I'm your goddamn husband!" he shouted.

She buried her face against the pillow.

"No, you're not," she whispered.

He was nothing to her now. He should be the past, lost, forgotten, but he wouldn't let her give it up. *He* wouldn't give it up. There had been times when her body was a road map of bruises, the time he threw her down the stairs and broke her collarbone. It could have been her neck. Times, all those times, too many times, and then he was so sorry after, so sorry, he'd go back on his medication, he promised he would, he didn't know what had gotten into him, because he loved her, he really did, and she, God help her, had believed him. Time after time, she had believed him.

She left him twice before the divorce, and both times he tracked her down and brought her back. And showed her how much he loved her with his anger and his shouting and his fists and finally the gun shoved up under her chin.

Such a calm, kind man, it was hard to believe, their mutual friends told her when she left the third and final time, ran to a shelter for battered women, let them hide her until the court date. But they didn't know about his condition. They didn't see him when he stopped taking the medication, when his easy good nature slipped away like the loose mask it was, and the depression began, and then the paranoia, and then the anger.

No one could understand. Not their well-meaning friends. Not her own mother telling her that it was just the pressures at his work, Frank really loved her, marriage could be a bumpy road but they'd get through the hard times.

Rachel's body was healed by the time she went to court, but she had the pictures to prove what he had done to her—photos taken by Sarah Bell at the shelter. Thank God for Sarah. Thank God for Frank's doctor, who explained, yes, Mr. Bedley did have an unfortunate condition; it could be controlled, unless he refused to take the medication that had been prescribed to help him deal with his problem. Thank God for all the kind strangers who believed and helped when those in her own social circle—Frank's friends, she'd learned all too painfully—and even her own family hesitated, looked awkward, kept talking about reconciliation when all Rachel wanted was freedom.

There were three locks and a safety chain on the door, but as Rachel lay there, listening to her ex-husband pound on the door, they seemed a very flimsy defense now. Trembling, she got up from the bed and crept down the hall toward the door.

It shook as he began to hammer against it again.

She looked around her untidy living room for something to shove against the door. Frank would hate this room. A coffee mug and a plate full of crumbs still sitting on the side table beside the chair where she'd been reading last night. Piles of magazines on the coffee table. CDs scattered across the top of the stereo cabinet in a disorganized jumble. The jacket she'd worn home from work last night still tossed across the back of the sofa.

Cause for a beating—if this was their home, if they were still married. But it wasn't. The room belonged to her. The apartment was hers, and he had no right to be outside her door, still tormenting her.

There was nothing to put against the door. She wasn't strong enough to move any of the furniture on her own. And that was the problem with being a woman, wasn't it? They were all stronger than you, all those men with their fists and their anger. Every day she read in the paper about the horrors husbands and fathers forced upon those they claimed to love.

Because they were stronger. Because they could. Because they had pressures and stress and it was understandable, wasn't it, that they needed an outlet? It's not like they meant to hurt anybody, was it? It's not like they reveled in their power with their boyish grins and strangers' eyes.

The pounding stopped again.

"I know you're in there, Rachel," he said, his voice calm, so calm, so *reasonable*. "Please let me in. I just want to talk to you, that's all. I just want to explain things to you." She heard a heavy thump as he leaned against the door. "I've changed. Things'll be different this time. I promise you."

Rachel stood in front of the door, hugging herself to stop shaking.

"Rachel, honey. Please."

There was a time when she would have believed him, but she didn't know that person anymore. That woman she had been—that poor, gullible woman, frightened of her own shadow—had finally grown stronger. She remembered all too clearly how his whispered promises turned into her screams. She remembered walking on eggshells through so much of the time they'd been together, making sure that she did nothing to anger him, that Tuesdays they had pork chops, and steak on Fridays, that she folded his underwear in two, not three, that she was always waiting for him when he came home, that she did everything he wanted when they were in bed, even when it hurt, even when it left her with an empty gnawing ache inside her, because her body remembered a time when he'd cared about pleasing her.

She'd had to fit the image of her that he'd created in his mind—that kind and considerate mind that had changed three months after their marriage, when he'd forgotten to get that simple prescription filled. He'd come home late, and she'd forgotten to pick up his suit from the cleaners, so he hit her, an open-handed slap that was still hard enough to knock her from her feet, and then he was so sorry, God he was sorry, but not so sorry that it didn't happen again. And again. An endless spiraling loop of apparent and very real pain.

He didn't know her. He had never known her. He'd never tried, never *cared* to know her. Why would that have changed now?

"Rachel?"

His voice still soft, a little boy's voice, knowing he's done something wrong, desperate to make amends. It meant nothing to her now.

A light tap on the door.

"Rachel, please?"

She made no reply. Dr. Caley had explained it to her. He was just pushing buttons, looking for the one to give him leverage back into her life. Fear. Pity. Need. Compassion. Whatever it took.

"Jesus, Rachel."

He thumped the door suddenly, and she jumped as though he'd hit her.

"Open the goddamned door, Rachel, or I swear I'll break it down."

And he would, too, she realized. One of these times, he would. He'd just break it down and drag her away again, back to that house that he owned by himself now because she hadn't wanted anything from him, just her freedom. It was her lawyer who had insisted on negotiating a hefty divorce settlement.

"These days, money *is* freedom," Marian Prusakowski had argued when they met in her office to discuss strategies. "He owes you that much. He owes you the chance to get your life back on track, and you won't be able to do that without the freedom from financial worries for the first while. We won't go for support—just a straight settlement."

Frank owed her a lot more than that, Rachel had realized in the months after their divorce was finalized, but he wouldn't even give her breathing room, court order notwithstanding. She'd come to understand all too soon that the restraining order was just words on paper, devoid of real meaning or bite. The only way the police could enforce it was if they actually caught him in the act.

By then she could be dead.

He started to hammer against the wood once more, and then Rachel heard another voice in the corridor outside her apartment.

"Could you keep it down?"

It was her neighbor, Rob Carter. He lived two doors down. A sweet, gentle man. She felt safe talking with him, having him over for a coffee, or going to his apartment for one. He was gay.

"Mind your own business," Frank told the man.

"It's past three in the—"

"I don't give a shit *what* time it is. I'm trying to talk to my wife."

Please, Rachel thought. Just go back into your apartment.

"She's not your wife anymore," Rob said.

They'd talked about Frank before. Not the first time they met. Not the second or third. Not until Rachel felt safe with him, not until that time she was coming home from work and saw Rob walking down the street ahead of her, arm around another man, and knew that it was only friendship that he wanted from her.

"I guess someone's looking for a fat lip," she heard Frank say, his voice moving away from her door.

Rob didn't cut a very impressive figure. He was a slight man, with thinning sandy-colored hair. Not like Frank, with his beefy shoulders and arms, courtesy of his workouts at the health club that he kept as regularly as he did everything else in his life except that one simple act of taking his medication.

"We'll see what the police have to say about that," Rob replied.

Rachel heard his door slam shut, locks engage.

"Now see what you've done?" Frank shouted at her door. He hammered on the wood, shaking the door in its frame. "Are you happy now?"

He slammed his fist against it one last time, then Rachel could hear him move away toward the elevator.

"Her own husband. Won't even talk to her own goddamned husband. . . ."

Rachel sank to the floor, still leaning against the wall, arms still wrapped around herself. She listened for the arriving *ping* of the elevator, for the doors to open, then shut, and then finally it seemed as though she could breathe again. But she wouldn't be able to sleep. Experience had taught her that.

She huddled against the wall for a long time, until she finally got mad at herself for letting him get to her this way again. She stood up, ran a hand through her tangle of blond hair, then turned on a light and went into the kitchen, where she put on the kettle to make herself some herbal tea. It never calmed her enough to get back to sleep on a night like this, but it helped take the raw jangling edge from her nerves.

She was never sure when Frank would show up at her door. Sometimes a week or two went by; sometimes he came two or three nights in a row. She'd moved twice before to get away from him, but he always tracked her down.

This apartment was the most expensive yet, because it had security. A doorman. She'd have to talk to the realty company again. She didn't know how Frank had talked his way past the doorman, but she could guess. He was so kind and considerate, wasn't he? Such a charming, genial man. Who wouldn't trust him?

She'd changed jobs once as well—not through choice. She'd been fired because Frank kept showing up and frightening the customers. Standing in the door of the gallery, yelling at her until someone called the police. That was when her lawyer had asked the judge for a restraining order against him—he wasn't allowed to come to her building or where she worked—but it didn't seem to make any difference. It never made any difference, not to her, not to any of all those other women in situations similar to hers.

At least he hadn't found out where she was working now. She hadn't told anyone, only Lily.

TWO

He had to choose soon.

There were so many ugly women in the world. Porcine nightmares with smothering bodies and others so anorexic they looked like AIDS victims. Some with mustaches, some with hairy legs, some with both. Downtown streets at lunchtime were a swarm of gaunt features, close-set eyes, double chins, fat butts. It got to the point where it seemed like it didn't matter which way you turned, there was always some fat cow waddling down the sidewalk toward you, or some weasel-faced little loser giving you a hopeful look.

Perhaps more depressing were the ones that were just plain. All those dowdy, forgettable women with their thick ankles and varicose veins, mousy hair and washed-out complexions, dressed in drab off-the-rack clothes that were often years out of fashion. The gaze slid right over them, caught by neither beauty nor blemish. There was a whole shadow army of them, on the streets, hidden away in frumpy apartments, toiling as clerks and secretaries and housewives, young and old, invisible, discountable.

The beauties—the real beauties—were few and far between.

You had to appreciate them while you could, because something always came up. They moved. They got married. They got ugly.

He remembered a time when he was living on the East Coast and there'd been this perfect little Oriental woman, but he'd waited too long and she got hit by a truck. When she was finally released from the hospital, one side of her face was immobile, her legs were all withered, and she was confined to a wheelchair. She wasn't beautiful anymore. Looking at her, it was as though someone had played a cruel joke on him. He could still see where the beauty had been, but it had all been stolen away.

He'd narrowed his choice down to three this time. They all lived in the building opposite his. The buildings were paired. "Sky Towers," the neat blue-and-white sign said as you pulled into the entrance to the parking lot. His apartment was on the fifteenth floor of B. His beauties all lived on the west side of the Tower A, their windows facing his. That's how he picked them.

He sat up by his window with the telescope that brought them in so close they might as well have been in his lap, and watched them, one after the other, whoever was home, whoever had her curtains open. His own sheers showed just enough sky to let him peek out. Usually he used the telescope just to watch, but sometimes he set up the camera with its massive 60mm telephoto lens supported by a tripod, and then he took pictures, auto-winder whirring—*shrr-snick, shrr-snick*—as he shot frame after frame of his beauties.

He had his own darkroom set up in the bathroom, did all his own developing and printing. You couldn't trust commercial photo developers. They got scratches on the negatives, dust spots and less definable blemishes on the prints. They didn't care, about either the art or the perfection of the subject. And besides that, they liked to report people to the police.

That was how he got caught, the first and only time.

The walls of his apartment were papered with the fruits of his labor—images of his beauties, moments of time trapped in chemicals and paper. The photographs started out as black-and-whites, but he painstakingly tinted each one until it matched the true colors of its subject before he tacked it onto the walls beside the others. Because you couldn't trust color film either; the colors never seemed true.

There wasn't much you could trust at all in this world, only beauty, and you had to catch it while you could, or it, too, slipped away and spoiled like bad fruit. Perky breasts sagged. Lovely slender thighs thickened with fat. Chins doubled, tripled. Perfect cascades of hair became thin and brittle. Sweet innocent eyes grew clouded with age, surrounded by ever-deepening wrinkles.

But not these three. Not yet. They were still all so perfect; he just couldn't decide which to choose.

He'd hacked his way into the realty office's computer to get their names and where they worked.

Caroline Wells lived in 1512, directly across from his own apartment. She was the redhead, built for pleasure, if a woman ever was. Her skin was like snow, lightly freckled, hair cut short, eyes so green they could have been jade. Long legs, flat stomach, firm breasts. She worked for the City Parks Commission, overseeing the department that organized the parks' recreational activities. Single, and didn't have a boyfriend. At least not one that she brought home. Sometimes he wondered if she was a lesbian because the only people she ever had over were women.

What he liked best was watching her do her aerobics, first thing in the morning, every morning, usually stripped down to just bra and panties. She always drew her curtains when she was getting ready for bed, but he had one precious series of photos from a roll of film he'd shot on a night when she'd forgotten. The one TV show she never missed was "L.A. Law." Sometimes he tuned in to the show at the same time as she did and pretended they were watching it together.

Lisa Hawkins was the slender black woman who lived in 1216. Her skin was the color of coffee with a dash of cream, her dark kinky hair usually drawn back from her face in a cluster of tiny braids that hung down to the middle of her back, little beads on the end of each one. He loved the wide set of her nose, the fullness of her lips, the dark mystery of her eyes.

She was a model, signed to the Charlene Grace Agency, which didn't surprise him. Her every movement was elegance, and whenever she stopped, it was like she was posing—but they were natural poses, gloriously unaffected. He could watch her vacuum her apartment for hours.

He scoured the fashion magazines to augment his own private collection of pictures of her, following her career with eager interest. He even had a video of her being interviewed on a local cable network show, *In the Studio with Clark Addison*. She had a boyfriend, but he didn't think it was too serious between them, because he'd seen her going out with other guys as well.

She was the most unapproachable, though, because of her profession. She would know him immediately—by his work and by his reputation, if not by sight—and it was anonymity that he required. That he craved. Without it, the perfect moment was cheapened and made common.

The one thing he was not was common.

He thought his favorite might be the woman who lived in 1414. Her hair was long and curly, and naturally blond—unless she was dyeing it down *there* as well. She had a face that was a soft, perfect heart, with pouty lips, pale blue eyes and a perfectly shaped nose. She had a fuller body than Caroline, but it didn't run to fat. She also had a better fashion sense than Lisa.

His walls had the most pictures of her. His favorite was a print he'd blown up to life size. She'd been standing at her window looking out, arms folded across her full breasts, hair drawn back into a loose bun, her features so wistful. It was almost as though she'd been looking right at him as he shot the photo, yearning for him to touch her.

He knew she was recently divorced and had been the assistant manager of the LaBranche Gallery in Lower Crowsea until two weeks ago. She hadn't told the realty company where she was presently employed. He'd tried to find out at the gallery, but since he had to be circumspect about that sort of thing, he hadn't had much luck.

What he liked best about her was her air of vulnerability. When he looked at his photos, when he watched her through the telescope, all he wanted to do was enfold her in a protective embrace, and he could sense that she was waiting for someone just like him.

He was still awake, looking out his window, when the light went on in her apartment late that night. Unlike the others, she rarely closed her living room drapes. He aimed the telescope in through her window, zooming in on her as she made herself a cup of tea. He tried to read the brand, but couldn't focus on it quickly enough. It looked like an herbal tea.

He got up and heated water in his microwave, then brought the cup back to the window, a bag of lemon-mint tea steeping in it. When it was ready, he sipped at his tea, sharing the experience with her. He watched her sitting in her favorite chair by the window and focused directly on her face, marveling at how gorgeous she was, even without makeup, even this late at night, with her features all sleepy and obviously upset about something.

"Rachel Sorensen," he said softly.

God but she was perfect. No airbrushing needed; just a natural beauty.

He thought that maybe he'd made his decision a long time ago, the very first time he'd idly panned his telescope across the side of her building and trapped her image in the lens of his viewfinder. They didn't get a whole lot better than her.

THREE

Lily Kataboki stretched languorously in her lover's bed, then cuddled closer to him. She had a small-breasted, slender figure, black hair cut close to her shoulders, bangs so short they hung an inch above her brows. Her eyes were the deep blue of a Caribbean lagoon, her complexion almost ghostly white. She trailed a hand over Tom's chest, smiling at the scramble of freckles under her fingers.

Her first impression of him had been red hair and freckles. He was a good head taller than her, but then most people were taller than her, so that wasn't what had drawn her gaze. No, it was the clutter of him that had first attracted her. Red hair all cowlicks and tangles, the jeans and the T-shirt with the faded Broken Hearts logo under a cotton sports jacket far too casual for a gallery opening. And the freckles, carousing over every bit of skin that was showing.

His apartment was much the same. Nothing where it was supposed to be, everything in disorder. You were as likely to find a tube of paint in the medicine cabinet, as the toothpaste propped up on the shelf of his easel. It wasn't the clutter of someone too lazy to clean; rather the bemusement of one too preoccupied with the task at hand to remember to tidy up after the last project.

It was the direct opposite of her own apartment, her own life, and that, she supposed, was what she really liked. Thomas Downs brought a sense of chaos into her own orderly life—not enough to derail it, just enough to keep her slightly off-balance. And interested.

"Which do you like better?" she asked as she continued to trail her fingers across the road map of freckles and fine curly red hairs that covered his chest. "Before or after?"

Tom turned his head slightly so that he could look into her face. "Before or after what?"

"Sex."

He smiled. "What kind of a question is that?"

"Before." Lily went on, "it's all anticipation and quivering and great big warm coils of energy uncurling inside you, but after it's like nesting, deep and warm and floaty, where nothing could ever hurt you. I just can't make up my mind."

"Does your boss know you think like this?"

Lily worked as a teller at the Unity Trust on the corner of Yoors and Williamson, just this side of Chinatown, her days filled with the systematic debiting and crediting of her customers' accounts.

"Of course," she said. "Why do you think he hired me?"

"Think he'd let you take an early lunch?"

"Probably. Except I've already planned to have lunch with Rachel."

"How's she doing anyway?"

Lily sighed. She sat up and leaned against the headboard. Snagging a pack of cigarettes and a disposable lighter from the nightstand, she shook out a cigarette and lit up.

"I wish you wouldn't do that," Tom told her.

"Me, too. I'll quit tomorrow."

It was her standard response. She hadn't known Tom all that long—it was just six weeks since the opening of his one-man show at Le Gallerie Corbeil—but she appreciated the fact that he was gentle in his disdain for what she knew all too well was a bad habit. One day she'd surprise him and she really would quit, but thinking of Rachel always made her reach for a cigarette.

"Are things sliding downhill for her again?" Tom asked.

Lily shrugged. "I wish I knew. Sometimes it's hard to figure out just what's going on behind that pretty face of hers." Rachel's beauty was a perfect camouflage for her distress—most people didn't try to look any further—just as her fashionable wardrobe had hidden the welts and bruises her husband had left on her body when he beat her. "But I always expect the worst."

They had met at a self-defense course sponsored by the Ferryside Women's Co-op. What Lily remembered the most about that evening was how hot it was in the community center, but there was Rachel in stylish slacks and a blouse with full-length sleeves. She looked great, but out of place for the session; everyone else was in a tank top and sweats, or something equally casual. It wasn't until they got to know each other that she'd learned about the abusive relationship Rachel had just escaped. The long sleeves and slacks were to hide the discoloration of ugly bruises that were only just beginning to fade.

"I can never understand how a woman could stay in a situation like hers," Tom said.

That was a male response, Lily thought. For all that Tom was about as liberated a man as she was likely to find in her own age group, he still carried around the baggage of his male-oriented upbringing.

"It's not that simple," she said. "You have to imagine a situation where you're entirely dependent on your husband. You have to ask permission for the simplest things—going out, money for groceries, things you take for granted if you're the breadwinner in the family."

"But you could always just leave."

"And do what? Go where?"

Lily stubbed out her cigarette. She considered lighting another, but forbore and felt momentarily virtuous.

"If your whole life has become tied to your husband," she went on, "everything from the structure of your social life to his paying the bills . . . it's just not easy. Life outside the family unit seems so foreign and impossibly complicated. Rachel got married while she was still in university. She's never really had to look out for herself before. She had no work skills or job prospects. When she left her husband, she had to learn how to cope with all the basic responsibilities that you and I just take for granted. For her, it was as though she was learning a foreign language."

"It doesn't seem right."

"It's not."

"Not just what happened to Rachel," Tom said, "but that she wouldn't want to understand those kinds of basics while she was still married."

"Don't blame Rachel; blame society. We're brought up to think that the man's going to handle it all for us. Most men don't *want* their wives to have any sort of independence outside the marriage. Even if the woman works, he still wants to handle all the finances, the planning, everything. It's a power thing, Tom." She'd almost said a male thing, but that wouldn't have been fair to him. "It's all got to do with control."

"I suppose," he said with a touch of doubt in his voice.

Lily forgave him. Growing up male, he just couldn't know. And at least he tried to understand, which was more than you could say for most men with whom it had been her misfortune to get involved.

"The men in this city," her friend Susie had intoned mournfully while they were commiserating with each other over recent breakups a few months ago, "can be divided into three categories: married, gay, or creeps."

She'd agreed until she met Tom.

"Let's talk about something less depressing," she said.

"Like what?"

Lily looked down the length of his freckled body.

"I've got a better idea," she said.

She threw a leg over him and sat on his chest. He slid his hands up either side of her, thighs to torso to shoulders, so that they met each other at the nape of her neck. Then he pulled her upper body gently toward him so that their lips could meet.

"Let's not talk at all," she whispered when they finally came up for air.

Tom's fingers trailed shiveringly down her back by way of response.

FOUR

I'm not such a bad guy, Frank Bedley thought. I'm not some monster. So why does she keep treating me like I am?

He sat in the kitchen of his two-floor bungalow in Woodforest Gardens, north of the city proper, considering breakfast.

He just had his ups and downs, that's all.

He couldn't remember much of last night. That always happened when he stopped taking his medication. But taking the pills seemed to mute everything—colors, sounds, *feelings*. Sometimes he just couldn't deal with it anymore. He'd be feeling good, normal, standing at the bathroom sink, vanity door ajar, the little plastic container of prescription pills sitting there on the shelf, and he just wouldn't be able to take them.

This time he'd manage, this time he'd fight the way everything just started to distort and go crazy on him.

And he would, he really would, for a couple of days, or a week, or however long it took until something would set him off. He'd even know as it was happening that it wasn't real, nothing to get worked up about, it was just his condition, but he wouldn't be able to stop the depression, the unreasoning fears, the black rage. . . .

Last night, he'd started for home, but stopped off at a restaurant for dinner. Then he'd—what? Gone by to try to talk to Rachel again, but the details were a blur. It wasn't like he'd blacked out or anything. It was just all a little fuzzy.

But it was clear, too. He knew that everyone was conspiring against him, that nobody *wanted* him to get back together again with Rachel. What he didn't know was why. All he wanted was for things to be normal again. He wanted to fit in.

Up and down his street, dozens of other men and women were getting ready for work, just as they were doing on every other street in the subdivision. Sure, it was a pain, fighting the traffic into the city every morning, and back again at night, but it was worth it. Where else could you get a place as nice as this, in such a peaceful, *safe* neighborhood? Green sculpted lawns and gardens, not a single run-down house. Good neighbors. No real crime problems, beyond the odd break-in. None of that urban blight. It was a perfect place to live.

So why the hell would she want to leave?

An image flashed in his mind: Rachel falling down the stairs after he'd hit her, tumbling down the flight in what had seemed like slow motion, finally slumping at the bottom like a marionette with its strings cut. She'd broken her collarbone. It could have been her neck. His own voice had haunted him, following him down the stairs as he took them two at a time to reach her where she lay: *Don't be dead, please God, don't die.*

Frank shook the memory away. That had been an accident. An aberration, plain and simple. He didn't beat on women. He liked them, respected them, believed in women's rights and equal pay and all that other stuff. Hell, hadn't he let Rachel take night courses to get her MA after they were married? But he also believed in the sanctity of marriage vows. She was supposed to be there for him, no matter what happened.

Everybody he knew had agreed—the breakup hadn't been his fault. Even her own parents had tried to convince her she was making a mistake. He'd paid for the house and covered all their expenses. He'd never cheated on her. So he had his ups and downs—didn't everybody? So they had a few arguments. Christ, there was no such thing as the perfect marriage.

He saw Rachel lying on the floor in the kitchen, pressed up against the corner cupboards. He was sitting on top of her, one hand gripping her face so that she had to look up at him, the muzzle of his .38 pushed up under her chin while he screamed at her. He couldn't remember what had got him so angry—not now, not even while it was happening.

He squeezed his eyes shut until the memory went away and all he could see was bright stars flashing against the backs of his eyelids.

That hadn't been him. He hadn't *meant* to do that. And while he couldn't remember what had set things off, he did remember what had led up to the moment. She'd been driving him crazy, dinner late three nights in a row while she was taking some stupid art appreciation course at the community center, the laundry not done, the goddamned bed still unmade. Christ, who wouldn't get mad?

But dragging it all out in court, up there on the stand where everyone could hear and it made him look so bad . . .

He finally decided against breakfast. He poured himself some orange juice, then carefully washed the glass, dried it and put it away. Time to get to work. Some people still had responsibilities. Some people kept their word, did what they said they were going to do, didn't jump ship just because things seemed a little rough.

He stopped in the bathroom before he left the house, put an eyedrop in each eye to clear away the red, then went out to the car to join the lineups leading into the city.

"Women," Colin Featherstone said. "Go figure them."

He and Frank were sitting on a bench in Fitzhenry Park eating the lunch they'd bought from one of the vendors' carts that lined Palm

Street. It was a perfect summer's day, temperature in the high seventies, not a cloud in the sky. How could you not want to eat your lunch outside?

Colin had a soft drink and a couple of jumbo hot dogs; Frank was having deep-fried zucchini, a small salad and a carton of 2% milk. He preferred to bring his own lunch from home, but there was no one to make him one now that Rachel was gone.

"What about them?" he said after he'd swallowed a mouthful of lettuce and cucumber.

"What exactly is it that they want?" Colin said. "I listen to the rhetoric and it seems to me like they want it all. They want equal pay and equal job opportunities and for us to share the responsibility of taking care of the home, but they also want us to baby them and buy them flowers and Christ knows what all."

Frank just shrugged.

He and Colin both worked as systems analysts for the Daco Systems Corporation. They shared an office on one of the two floors the corporation leased in the Kessel Building on Bunnett Street, which also housed the offices of *The Newford Star*. Colin and his wife Janet had a condo right on the southern edge of Lower Crowsea, which put them one subway ride away from work. Janet had her own interior design business with an office directly across the street from the Kessel Building, though she and Colin rarely took lunch together. Janet was always meeting with a client.

But Colin didn't mind. "You need time apart," he'd told Frank once. "Gives you something to talk about when you're together."

They made the perfect yuppie couple. They were both attractive, dark-haired and lean, neither showing their encroaching age. All the trappings were in place: they had the condo with its state-of-the-art electronics and jacuzzi, contemporary decor and art investments; they owned a silver Porsche, had the right circle of friends, were members of the correct health and beach clubs.

Rachel had never liked either of them.

"Take your wife," Colin went on.

Frank wished he wouldn't bring up Rachel. He'd had the misfortune of the divorce trial coming smack-dab in the middle of a bad week for news, and sometimes it seemed like everybody he knew had been following the two days' worth of coverage. A year later and the secretaries at Daco were still giving him the cold shoulder except for a couple of the new girls.

"Rachel had everything," Colin said. "A beautiful home, great clothes, no worries, and what does she end up doing after you guys split up? Working in the back of some framing shop like some uneducated immigrant where she can't be making more than a couple of hundred a week before taxes. Now who in their right mind makes a trade like that?"

Frank put down the piece of zucchini he'd been lifting to his mouth.

"She works where?" he said, trying to keep his voice calm.

"You know," Colin said around a mouthful of hot dog. "At Heartworks. It's just a few blocks north of our place, in the Market. Janet bought this new Etoile print at a show a couple of weeks ago, but she didn't like the mat that the artist used. So Janet took it in to get it redone. I was picking it up when I spotted Rachel working in the back. She never did come out to the front of the shop. I don't think she even saw me."

Frank nodded casually as though he were just remembering something fairly unimportant. "That's right," he said. "I'd forgotten she was working there."

"Now, what kind of a job is that for a bright lady like her?" Colin asked.

It proved to be a rhetorical question, for he immediately launched into a rather confusing tirade that equated poor-paying, service-oriented careers with the country's current lack of decent representational government, but Frank wasn't really listening anymore. He kept repeating the name of the place to himself, over and over again, like a litany. Like a promise.

Heartworks, Heartworks.

He'd go there tonight, right after work, but this time he'd play it cool. He'd scout it out. Keep his distance. Wait a bit, maybe even give it a day or two before he made his approach. No more of this embarrassment of being thrown out like some kind of bum the way he'd been treated at the gallery, or trying to talk through a locked apartment door with some fag neighbor threatening to call the cops. He'd wait until he could get her alone so that he could have a decent conversation with her, face-to-face, heart-to-heart, husband to wife, without all kinds of interruptions.

Heartworks.

Oh, Rachel baby. Don't you know you can't hide from me? We were meant to be together. God was our witness, honey. We got married in His house, with His blessing. Some little piece of paper signed by a secular judge doesn't mean a thing compared to the vows we made before God.

FIVE

Rachel felt better in the morning. Where last night her apartment had seemed to serve as the flimsiest defense against her ex-husband, now it felt like a haven again. Her own place, four walls to protect her, and she had the only key. Until she left Frank, she'd never lived on her own, going from her parents' home, to a dorm at college, to living with Frank. She'd been surprised to find that she liked it.

She put on some coffee and turned on the radio, then took a shower while the coffee was brewing. Toweling her hair, she paused as WKPN's morning DJ announced the day's weather. She'd planned on wearing her usual: conservative slacks and a short-sleeved blouse, or a midcalf-length summer dress like the one she'd bought last week at Morning Glory's, with a pair of low-heeled shoes. But she didn't have to, she realized. She didn't have any bruises to hide anymore, and her new job didn't require her to dress to the T's.

She hesitated a moment longer, then laid out a pair of baggy cotton shorts, a bright red T-shirt and sneakers—the kind of things she only ever wore around the apartment or at her exercise class at the Y. She knew she was going to feel vulnerable walking out on the street dressed like that, but she had to start living like a normal person.

The weather promised to be too beautiful for slacks today. And lots of women wore shorts downtown.

"For God's sake," Lily had said to her once. "There's nothing suggestive about dressing in shorts and a T-shirt. You don't hear men being called tramps because they're walking around in shorts and muscle shirts, do you?"

No, Rachel thought. But men didn't have to walk a constant gauntlet of suggestive remarks and stares every time they were out in a public place the way a woman did. It didn't matter how you were dressed; shorts, tight jeans or miniskirts just made it worse.

But she was going to do it anyway. She was going to be comfortable for a change. She was going to be herself—or at least as much of herself as she was able to find. It got a little confusing trying to figure out just who she was these days. All her life she'd lived under someone's shadow—that of her parents, her roommates at college, her ex-husband. Trying to fulfill society's expectations. It was time she got out from under all those shadows to see if she could cast one of her own.

Sometimes she was afraid that she was going to discover that she didn't have a shadow to cast, that she would have to spend the rest of her life being no more than the sum total of other people's perceptions. She was an almost invisible presence, even in her own life. But it didn't have to be that way.

It starts with making choices, her therapist had told her. Her own choices, made for and by herself. "Start small," Dr. Caley had said at one of their recent sessions, "and work your way up to the big ones."

With her bathrobe wrapped around her, she got a cup of coffee, then returned to the bedroom to put on the clothes she'd laid out. Dressed, she made toast and took it out onto the balcony, where she alternated bites of her breakfast with putting on her makeup. Light mascara, a trace of eyeshadow. When she was finished eating, she added a touch of lipstick, blotting most of it off onto a napkin. She combed her hair with her fingers—it was too thick for a comb, and it would lose all its natural curl if she used a brush—and then hurried out of the apartment to run for the bus.

She had one bad moment leaving the apartment building—the sudden fear that Frank was lurking out there, waiting for her—but the only person she saw was a homeless man on the curb outside the Sky Towers' parking lot, looking for empties along the grass border. He had a two-wheeled shopping cart half-filled with empty bottles and cans that he dragged along behind him as he peered under the flowering shrubs. The rattle of the bottles and cans against one another made an oddly pleasant sound, almost musical.

She just made the bus, settling in her seat near the front and trying not to grip her purse too hard. She'd been all too aware of the considering look the bus driver had given her as she came up the stairs, and then the man in the business suit three seats down who gave her a slow, appreciative once-over as she made her way to her seat.

Her legs felt naked. She had to stifle a giggle when she realized, well, of course. They are naked.

She wasn't sure how it had happened, what brought the change, but at that moment the day turned around for her. She found that she didn't really care about how the bus driver or the businessman had eyed her, didn't even care about still feeling slightly self-conscious. She sat up straighter in her seat and looked out at what was turning into just as perfect a day as the DJ had promised. She found herself looking forward to going to work. Maybe she'd even get herself a ten-speed and bike to and from the shop.

Rachel was almost grateful to Frank for making her change jobs. It's true she missed the gallery. The show openings and meeting the artists when they came in with new work, the social life that she never quite joined, but which she loved to be on the fringes of, the sheer pleasure of being surrounded by the fruits of so much creative energy. It was inspiring. And, in some odd way, therapeutic.

But there was also something therapeutic about working with her hands the way she did now. She and Helen were busy in the back-room workshop all day, not making any creative decisions, or helping customers with theirs, just completing orders. Heartworks had enough of a steady clientele and walk-in trade to keep them both busy full-time, as well as employing two other people to work the floor and deal with customers—Amanda Gray, the owner, and Tami Razzell, who sometimes helped in the back when it was slow out front.

Rachel liked the idea of an all-women workplace. It fostered a sense of safety; here was a place she could relax and not have to worry about men. She wasn't sure that she was ready to give them up or any-thing, but experience had soured her on the other half of the human race. Frank. Frank's lawyer. The judge. The police. Not to mention all those men who weren't a part of her life, with innuendo in their eyes when it wasn't spilling from their lips.

"Hey, babe. How about you and me . . . ?"

"Check the front load on this one."

"Wrap those legs around me, honey, and I'll think I've gone to heaven."

She was no longer shocked when she heard something like what Lily had told her about how she always flagged down a cab and took it from the bus stop to her apartment if it was after dark—even though it was a ride of only one-and-a-half blocks. It was hard to explain to a man how it felt to be living in a state of constant threat. Rachel hated the idea that every man was a potential enemy, but all she had to do was turn on the news, or see the faces she passed on the street, to have the truth hammered home.

"You can't trust any man," Helen, an avowed lesbian, told her when they were working that morning and Rachel brought the subject up.

"I've got a neighbor who's gay," Rachel began.

"In some ways," Helen said, "they're the worst. They live com-pletely outside of a woman's influence."

"But what if they're *like* a woman?" Rachel said, still thinking of her neighbor Rob. "What if they were just born in the wrong body?"

Helen paused in the middle of cutting a mat for a gorgeous print of Monet's *Water Lilies, Giverny*. The piece always made Rachel feel calm, with its bright swirls of color turned all ghostly.

"I'm not sure if I believe in that," she said after considering it.

"But what about . . . ?" Rachel's voice trailed off.

"Me?" Helen finished, smiling as she spoke.

She was a tall, striking woman, with handsome rather than pretty features, short brown hair, almost androgynous. Her wardrobe, at least what Rachel had seen of it so far, seem to consist mostly of jeans, cowboy boots, men's shirts and sports jackets.

"I love being a woman and I love women," Helen said. "I've never wanted it to be any other way."

"I used to want to be a boy," Rachel confessed. "They always seemed to have more fun."

Helen nodded. "When a boy's rambunctious, he's just being a boy. When a girl wants to act a little rough and tumbly, she's called a tomboy and her parents work harder at keeping her in a dress."

"Mine succeeded," Rachel said.

Helen smiled. "Needless to say, mine didn't."

They worked together in a companionable silence after that. The piece Rachel was framing was a large print of Leger's *Disks and Town*, a cubist wonder of color and shapes. She didn't agree at all with the wooden frame the customer had chosen—it stole away some of the stark sharpness of the images as far as she was concerned—but there was nothing she could do about it.

"There was one time I wanted to be a boy," Helen said suddenly. She paused in her work again, her voice pitched low, reflective. "I was in love with a girl in my English class. I didn't quite understand who or what I was then; all I knew was that I couldn't approach her the way I wanted to. I had to be a boy to be able to hold her and kiss her."

She shook her head.

"Funny the things we remember," she said as she went back to work.

Rachel looked at her for a long time before returning to the Leger print. She wondered what it was like to hold a woman, to be held by one, but the thought woke no sexual urge in her. Neither did thinking of a man.

Sometimes she felt like some weird sexless creature, transplanted to a world where everyone but her had their life in order, someone to love, someone to love them.

Maybe she should get a pet.

"I'm only twenty-six and I feel like my life's already over," Rachel said.

Lily, three years her junior, smiled and lit the cigarette she'd just shaken out of her pack.

"Hardly," she said before she looked back at the menu.

They were sitting at a table on the second-floor back patio of the Templehouse Cafe in the Market. The patio overlooked the river and was filled with a bohemian lunchtime crowd. There were more artists, poets, musicians and freethinkers per square Market foot than there was in any other part of the city. Lily had been impressed to see how casually Rachel was dressed. Definitely a step in the right direction, and in this crowd, she fit right in.

"You know what I mean," Rachel said. "I'm just drifting. I don't seem to have any purpose in life."

"Give yourself time."

"It's been over a year."

"Yes, but . . ." Lily laid her menu down. "Is it Frank? Has he been coming around again?"

Rachel nodded. "But it's not that. Or not just that. I feel unaccountably . . . restless."

"Maybe you're just feeling horny," Lily said, smiling at the expression that came to her friend's features.

Shock was too strong a qualifier for the look. It was more like a child hearing a forbidden word. For all Rachel's sophistication in certain matters, Lily thought, she was so very naive in others.

"I don't think so," Rachel said. A slight flush had risen to brighten her cheeks. "I mean, I'd like to have a relationship, but . . . oh, I don't know. I don't buy into the idea that who we're with defines us, but somehow being by myself makes me feel closer to a homeless person than a regular member of society. Sometimes it feels like everybody's got somebody except for me."

Six weeks ago, Lily could have commiserated, but she couldn't anymore. Now she had Tom. Still, she knew what Rachel meant. It wasn't just sex. It was having someone with whom you could share all the little events that made up your day, the good and the bad. Someone who knew you well enough to smile and empathize in all the right places. Someone you trusted.

She hadn't seen as much of Rachel recently—not nearly as much as she had in the months before meeting Tom. Realizing how hard it was for Rachel to get close to people, Lily thought she now understood what was bothering her friend. It wasn't just her libido. Rachel was simply lonely.

"I've got a friend who just got back to town," she began, but Rachel was already shaking her head.

"Please, Lily. I appreciate it, but I don't want to be set up with some guy no matter how nice he is. I don't think I'm ready."

Lily wondered if she'd ever be ready, but she kept that worry to herself. She took a drag from her cigarette, blowing the smoke away from Rachel.

"She's not a guy," she said, quickly adding, "and she's not a lesbian either like that woman you work with."

"Helen's really nice."

"I'm sure she is. No, this is a woman I used to know in college. She just got back to town, and I was thinking of introducing the two of you anyway. Her name's Jessie McKay, and she's an artist, which made me think of you, because even if you don't work that side of the trade, you're still really interested in art, right?"

She paused, noting the odd look that passed across Rachel's features.

She thought back on what she'd been saying, but couldn't see what might have called up that look.

"I don't have to introduce you," she began.

"No, no," Rachel said. "I just got distracted for a moment. I'd love to meet her. What medium does she work in?"

"Watercolors, mostly. She's been living in New Mexico for the past few years. She's had a few shows and a company down there's using her work on a line of note cards, but she said she was ready for a change again, so she's moved back."

"I remember the name now," Rachel said. "You gave me a box of her cards for Christmas. Desert scenes with armadillos and coyotes. They're all deep red and brown tones with impossibly blue skies. Her work's lovely."

Her voice was wistful as she spoke—almost envious, Lily realized with surprise. She hadn't seen the envy before, but she was familiar with the sadness, though it wasn't until this moment that she had ever considered that it might have its origin in more than the breakup of Rachel's marriage.

Lily wanted to follow up on it, but then the waitress came to take their order, and an opening never arose in the conversation again, where she could ask without feeling as though she were putting Rachel on the defensive.

They both had Caesar salads, Rachel ordering iced tea, while Lily decided to hell with calories and had a nonalcoholic piña colada. Lily brought up her friend Jessie again after she'd paid their bill and they were about to return to their respective jobs.

"Maybe the three of us could get together on the weekend," Lily said. "For Sunday brunch?"

"That sounds like fun. Thanks for lunch, Lily. It'll be my treat next time."

Lily put a hand on Rachel's arm before she could hurry off.

"Are you going to be okay?" she asked.

She knew it was an inadequate thing to say. Who could be okay, coming out of what Rachel had? She was still in therapy; her ex was still hounding her. But Lily felt that Rachel understood the concern behind the deficiency of the question.

"I'm working on it," Rachel said.

"Call me if you ever just want to talk," Lily said. "If you can't get me at home—do you know Tom's number?"

As Rachel nodded, Lily felt dumb, like a name-dropper, except here the dropped name was pointing out what she had, and Rachel didn't, rather than anyone's brush with fame. Talk about rubbing salt into a wound. And Rachel *had* been calling her. She'd been trying to get together with Lily for over a week. Today's lunch was the first free time that had come up, and that was only because Lily had made an effort to keep the time free. It just seemed that she was always doing something with Tom.

Lily didn't like the idea of having to choose between Rachel and Tom, didn't like the idea that she was neglecting a friend just because her hormones were in overdrive with the first bloom of a new romance. Rachel and Tom got along well enough, but only on the surface. They seemed to rub each other the wrong way, though Lily could never quite pinpoint how. Anyway, threesomes almost always got awkward after a while. It was too hard giving equal time to both persons, and you ended up giving them both considerably less than you would on a one-to-one basis.

And then Lily realized something else. Tom made time for his own friends—he had his baseball on Friday nights with guys at the pub where he used to work, the odd night out with other friends, usually Ian Jackson, with whom he sometimes shared studio space when he was working on a particularly large project.

But she, Lily realized, she always seemed to wait to find out what Tom was doing before she organized her own schedule. The knowledge bothered her. And it was her own doing, too, not something that Tom had pushed upon her.

"We'll make a day of it," she told Rachel. "Like old times."

Rachel smiled. She had a smile that was like a beacon, like the flame calling moths, Lily thought, not for the first time. With her looks and that charisma, which was all too often shuttered away behind self-consciousness, it was no wonder that her husband was still trying to win her back.

Someone should tell him that bullying wasn't the way back into Rachel's heart. Someone should just tell him to bugger off and die, when it came right down to it, because after all he'd done, a woman would have to be a fool to take up with him again.

Lily knew that Rachel might be shy, even a little naive, but she wasn't a fool.

"So," she said. "What do you say?"

"I'd like that," Rachel replied.

"Then it's a date."

SIX

He couldn't believe his luck, the way she'd just fallen asleep in the chair, mouth slightly open, long lashes lying against her brows. He'd shot two whole rolls of film through the telephoto, squirming with delight when she shifted once and her nightshirt fell open to reveal most of one softly rounded breast. He'd taken three close-ups of it alone.

A moment like this could never be staged, he thought as he ran the last print through the fixer and then rinsed it in the sink. He switched on a light, turning his darkroom back into a bathroom, and clothespinned the print to the line strung between the top of the window and his shower head, where it could dry along with the others.

You had to just take such moments when they came to you, seize the opportunity. That was what separated the artist from all the common photographers. The artist was always ready; the artist instinctively *knew* when the moment was at hand.

He stood back to admire the finished prints, already looking forward to tinting them. This was world-class art—as good as any of his published work that got such glowing reviews from all those critics who sometimes seemed to spend more time inflating their own limited sense of self-importance than discussing the work at hand. Better, really, because they were his, his alone, not to be shared. Because no one understood, not even his subjects.

He owned them. With every photo he took of a subject, he owned that much more of her beauty, her spirit, her soul. He was like time itself, the unforgiving and inevitable evener, except the beauty he stole was preserved in his work. It didn't vanish into wrinkles and fat and bony protrusions. It lived forever. Here, in his albums and file folders and on his walls.

It was something he had to do because the beauties didn't, or wouldn't, or couldn't. They let themselves be ravaged by the years. They let breasts sag, thighs thicken, hair grow brittle and gray. They let eyes, which once shone with the understanding that the world owed them for their beauty, grow milky and cynical and hesitant. They became drones, cows, fence posts. Inevitably, all they had been was forever forgotten. Except by him. Except through his work.

When he looked at a photo, it was like traveling back through time. His eidetic memory clicked in, and he could remember everything about the moment, what came before, what followed, his film speed, F-stop, lens, sight and smell and sound. He captured the moment, froze it for eternity. He was like God on a small stage, the director, utterly in control in the few square feet of space given to him to work his magic.

It was a gift, and he kept it secret, because there were always those who wanted to steal an artist's vision. Who would claim he was nothing but a peeper, spying on people's hidden moments, invading their privacy.

There was no privacy in art, except for the private moments between creator and subject, and even then it was better that the subject remained ignorant as well, for they could never understand either. No one could. No one knew him, no one understood him.

But he accepted that. It was all a part of the secret compulsion that drove him. He was alone in his mission, called upon by a higher power to preserve Beauty. And protect it.

He'd always had secrets. He'd been a gawky kid growing up, a real nerd, all arms and legs, as likely to trip over an obstruction as to avoid it. It wasn't until he reached his twenties that the mismatched size of his features all settled together and left him with the rugged good features of, if not a leading man, then at least a model such as the Marlboro man. But the benefits came too late. By the time he'd lost the physical attributes of his nerdishness, the person he was to become had already been shaped by his formative years.

His sisters had called him a sneak, claimed that he was always slinking about, spying on them. The other kids made fun of him because his gangly form couldn't adjust to any kind of sport that needed coordination, because he never seemed to talk much, just looked at people from a distance, because he was different.

Photography had saved him, beginning with that small hand-me-down Kodak 35mm camera that his parents had given him for his twelfth birthday. His first developed roll of film was the catalyst for an epiphany. When he held the prints in his hand, when he realized what he could capture with lens and film and photographic paper, his whole life turned around.

He got a paper route. He did yard chores throughout the neighborhood. He read every book on photography they had in the library and begged, borrowed, or stole photography magazines from the corner drugstore. He scrimped and saved until he put together his own crude darkroom for black-and-white prints, and then finally got his first telephoto lens—nothing fancy, just an 80mm—and life changed for him again.

What he liked best about the new lens was that he could now take pictures of people without their really knowing what he was doing. The girls hanging around near the entrance of the mall might see the camera pointed in their general direction, but they'd have no idea that in his viewfinder he was close enough to count their zits.

He was still the nerd, but people sort of liked him now because of his pictures. He worked for the school paper and the yearbook, and everyone got used to seeing him with that camera slung around his neck. But their friendliness just seemed to drive him deeper and deeper into himself. He could forget nothing, so how was he to reconcile the smiling face of the jock, so pleased with the shot he'd taken of the boy's touchdown, with the mocking face of the same boy, bullying him the year before?

More and more, he began to live on the fringes of, first the social circles at school, then society at large. Nights would find him prowling about, not knowing what drove him to creep through backyards and alleyways, until the night he saw Sherry Jane Palmer undressing in front of her open bedroom window. It was the cause of this third flash of life-changing insight, but it proved to be his downfall as well.

The roll in his camera at the time was color. Because he didn't yet have the facilities to develop it himself, like a fool, he took it into a photo store to be developed the next day.

That night the police came to his parents' door. They had an envelope full of the pictures he'd taken of Sherry Jane—perfect, gorgeous Sherry Jane. His pictures. Their fat thumbs on her beautiful small breasts as they showed the photos to his parents.

It was so obvious that she was unaware of his presence. That they'd been taken from outside her house.

The names they called him—not so much the police, but his parents and sisters. Pervert. Peeping Tom. Deviant.

He fully expected to go to jail, but he was only fifteen at the time, so he got off with a stiff warning. That wasn't the worst. His parents took his camera and developing equipment away. His sisters spread the story around school. He was sent for psychiatric evaluation and then therapy.

Normal life forever ended.

But oddly enough, he didn't mind. He still had his secret store of photos that his parents hadn't found, and now he knew that he had a mission to perform, a real purpose in life. He understood that he'd been given the gift to appreciate and preserve the private moments of beauty to which others would not allow themselves to be privy because they stepped across the bounds of decency.

He became two people: his hidden self, the secret artist who knew he must be patient to begin his life's work, and the repentant teenager who slowly won back the trust of his parents and therapist, if not his siblings. There was never a boy so dedicated to good grades and decent behavior as he became.

He took up physical fitness, exercising every morning, jogging, enrolling in judo classes, then more esoteric styles of martial arts. Though his features were still a nerd's, he slowly developed a sense of coordination and physical well-being.

When his photographic equipment was finally returned to him, he made no mistakes with it. He ignored the urge to stalk beauty in the night. Instead, he pretended a vague disinterest in camera and developing gear, shooting a few pictures at family occasions, but otherwise leaving the equipment to gather dust on a shelf in his room.

It wasn't until he went away to college that he finally came into his own.

He smiled now, remembering those first heady days of freedom from his parents, convincing them to let him take a small bachelor apartment off campus, the way he went mad with this camera, shooting roll after roll of film, day and night, private moments captured forever as only he could snare them, the long nights in the darkroom. And somehow he'd kept up his grades as well.

It was a wonder he hadn't made another mistake, he thought, as he took the dried prints down from the clothesline and spread them out on his desk. The only thing he regretted was that he'd never been able to keep those pictures of Sherry Jane. Who had those photos? he'd wondered over the years. Where were they now? Moldering in a police file back east? Thrown away?

Years later he'd tracked down Sherry Jane and caught her in his camera, but it wasn't the same by then. She'd still been a beauty, but the perfection of her youth had been eroded away by a bad marriage and the simple passage of years.

He glanced up from the fresh set of prints to his favorite of Rachel where it hung on the wall, looking back at him. He couldn't believe that such perfection could be found in this city. How could someone walk its grimy streets and still retain their innocence?

He cocked his head as though listening to a question.

What had happened to Sherry Jane hadn't been his fault, he assured Rachel. And he loved Sherry Jane still, just as he loved all his beauties.

"But not as much as I love you," he told the photo.

SEVEN

Rachel knew nothing of the man watching her from the apartment tower opposite hers, but like him, she had a secret. Hers, too, involved imagery, and she carried the existence of it wherever she went, but unlike him, she was no longer able to consummate hers. She hadn't been able to do so for years.

Where does it go? she'd asked herself far too many times as she sat staring at a poorly executed drawing, or worse, a blank sheet. How could something that was once so much a part of her life simply disappear?

She had considered herself an artist once, but the description no longer fit as it had when she was in high school, and later, in college. As if she were finding the clothes she wore as a child, hidden away in an old chest in an attic, she could look at her old paintings and sketches, she could remember how it had felt to create them, but she could no longer wear the designation as she had when she was doing the work.

The ability was gone.

She stood now in the room that held the simple equipment her art required and felt again the old familiar yearning and regret. If only she could talk about it to someone, she sometimes thought, but to do so without hope of actually producing work made her feel too much like a pretender. She'd heard far too many customers in the gallery remark, "Oh, yes, I'm quite interested, but I just can't find the time," as though time were all it took. As though art were something anyone could do, if they just had a few spare moments.

The truth was they hadn't the skill or talent and probably not even the inclination. They just liked the *idea* of it, wanted the glamour they perceived to surround an artist without actually having to do the work.

Rachel once had the skill, talent and inclination. What she lacked now was inspiration. And the courage to discuss it with anyone. Barely able to cope with the shambles of her marriage, she couldn't face offering up another side of her life to public failure.

She sighed as she moved through the room. Having lunch with Lily had made her realize just how much she'd been missing her friend lately. It was like rediscovering a forgotten pleasure. But it had been awkward as well. She'd been all too aware of Lily's circling around the source of her melancholy, had seen Lily's sudden understanding that it wasn't based just on her escape from an abusive relationship, but ran deeper, was more secret.

But whenever Rachel tried to speak of her art, the inside of her mouth felt like a desert and the words simply dried up and blew away, turning end over end like dusty, windblown tumbleweeds. She hadn't been able to share its existence with anyone—not for years. Not even with Lily.

She kept her paints and brushes, her old sketch pads and paintings in her spare bedroom with the door locked. When Lily and Rob had asked about the room, she'd fended off their questions with a nonchalant remark about using it for storage of this and that, and had obviously been successful, for neither of them brought it up again.

But as she stood in that room now and stared at the blank pad of watercolor paper that sat neatly in the center of her drawing desk, she wondered why she had ever even bothered. Her therapist had told her that she should find something to fill up the hole that her broken marriage had put in her life—"And preferably not another man," Dr. Caley had added. "At least not immediately." Taking up her art once more had seemed the perfect solution.

Except it was gone. She remembered the mechanics of how she used to work, but the gift that sparked inspiration to move from mind through hand to paper was gone. She felt like a blind person suddenly regaining her sight, only to find herself trapped in a colorless, windowless, unfurnished room.

What paintings she did seemed either grotesque Bosch parodies with none of Bosch's dark luminosity, or empty, flat images, clichéd and poorly executed. Her choice of colors always seemed wrong, the images were undefined, the water bled into the pages and made the colors run. Her pencil sketches had no life. The more lines she put down, the further they took her from the images she was trying to capture. She would look at her earlier work and mourn the loss of that talent, for once she'd been good. Before Frank got her to give it up— "You want to know the truth? It embarrasses me, looking at these nude guys and women, okay?"—she'd had a real gift, which had atrophied through disuse.

Neither her parents nor Frank had ever taken her work seriously. Little humorous cards for birthdays and other such occasions—that was fine. That was "Oh, isn't this cute? You're so talented, Rachel." But serious work made them uncomfortable, and she'd ended up buying into the idea that life drawing and nude portraits were not quite proper. She'd taken a few art appreciation courses, just to maintain her interest, but the less she kept her hand in doing real work, the more it became merely information that she stored, rather than emotion she felt.

She'd given up her art to save her marriage, never realizing how

much her art had meant to her or how ultimate its loss would be. She
hadn't even known that she'd made the choice until long after it had
been made.

The process had been gradual. Whenever she'd worked, she'd felt
guilty, because she knew how much it bothered Frank. Eventually, her
sessions grew shorter and shorter, tapering off until she'd stopped
altogether.

She'd been an artist, then she was Frank's wife. The two had appeared
mutually exclusive. But divorced as she was, without Frank, without
the guilt, she'd been honestly surprised at how elusive inspiration had
become.

Sometimes she thought that part of the problem in trying to paint
once more might have come from working in the LaBranche Gallery.
The work Hans accepted for the gallery was incredible. Every moment
she was there she was surrounded by so much assured artistic expression. Paintings, sculptures, wall hangings, mixed media. The gallery
always seemed to hum with the vibrancy of the work shown in it, she'd
thought whenever she came into work in the mornings.

Sometimes she would just stand in front of a piece and it would literally take her away. She would begin casually studying the artist's
style, the effect gained from his brush stroke, that combination of
colors, only to be startled by Hans's hand on her elbow.

"A little less admiring and a little more work, perhaps?" he would
say, with an understanding smile to take the sting from his words.

All that art, she thought, and then all the time she'd spent talking
with the creators of that work—she couldn't help wondering if the
overload of talent had been inhibiting.

But it hadn't always been so. Once, the better the art was that she
experienced, the more it inspired her. But going home, night after
night, to work in her own little makeshift studio with only painful,
aberrant results had worn away at her confidence.

Other times she felt that she was just receiving her due. She'd given
up the art, abandoned it the way some people abandoned their pets,

and now she couldn't get it back, even when she wanted to. Her art had died in a ditch somewhere. Struck by a car. Or suffering from malnutrition. Or perhaps someone had found it and taken it in, cherished it, loved it.

Abandoned by her, it was theirs now. It would never return.

Rachel sat down at the drawing table. She picked up a brush and flicked the soft sable back and forth against the tip of her finger before setting the brush back down again. She stared at the blank page on the top of the pad. It was the same page that had been there for the past week. The others, the ones that had preceded it in the pad, had all gone out with the trash on Tuesday.

She thought of Lily again, how nice her friend had looked in her black satiny jodhpurs with the white blouse and black sandals. If she closed her eyes, she could see Lily's features with perfect recall, the way the breeze had fluttered her bangs, the startling pallor of her skin, the impossible blue of her eyes. Lily almost seemed as though she'd just stepped from the CD jacket of one of those British bands that played what the press called New Romantic, or Gothic, music. The image was so real, the possibility of her realizing it in graphite seemed so close, that she almost reached for a pencil to put it on paper. But then she just sighed.

Who was she kidding?

She got up, after compulsively centering the pad on the desk.

Maybe that was what was wrong, she thought. This room looked like it belonged to Frank. Everything was so neat and tidy, everything in its place. Tubes of paints snugly arranged in their wooden box, pencils lined up in a neat row, brushes in the tall clay New Mexican pot that she'd found at a flea market, reference materials shelved in alphabetical order close at hand. Her old studio when she was in college—just a corner of a bachelor apartment—had always looked like a cyclone had just hit it. This, even with the carefully chosen prints on the wall— maybe too carefully chosen—was sterile.

She stepped forward, bent, then swept her hand across the top of the desk. Paint tubes, brushes, pad went flying to the floor. The pot holding the brushes broke, and sharp clay shards skidded across the floor. She stared at what she'd done, aghast for a moment, then she tugged at a book until she could get her hand in behind the whole row of them. She pushed them all out onto the floor as well, spines cracking, books falling open, heavy art stock creasing as the weight of one book mashed the pages of another.

Her eyes began to blur with tears. An unfamiliar rage burned in her chest. She kicked at the books, once, twice, knocking them across the room, where they crashed into the scattered debris of her art supplies. Her cheeks grew wet, and she could barely see for the tears. She tore the posters from the walls, pulled off the framed prints and threw them to the floor. Glass shattered, frames came apart under the sudden stress. With a grunt of effort, she knocked the drawing table over onto its side, then fled the room.

When the tears finally ebbed, she just went to bed. To hell with dinner, to hell with her art, to hell with life. She didn't think she'd ever be able to fall asleep, but she nodded off almost immediately and slept straight through the night.

She surveyed the wreckage of her studio the next morning, leaning against the doorjamb with a cup of coffee in her hand. The mess gave her an odd feeling, both bitter and uplifting. She wasn't sure what she really felt. She just knew that a tightness seemed to have eased in her chest. It was like taking off a bra that was too constricting when her breasts had grown swollen due to her menstrual cycle. The same sudden sense of relief, although it wasn't simply physical.

An inner pressure had lifted as well.

After a while she just closed the door and went about getting ready for work.

EIGHT

Frank stopped off at the McDonald's on Highway 14 on the way to work. He stood humming to himself as he waited in line to give his order and had a smile for anyone who happened to look his way.

"You bet I will," he told the young woman behind the counter when she handed him his breakfast and told him to have a good day.

He walked over to a free table, balancing the tray in one hand, holding his briefcase with the other. The briefcase was about a pound and a half heavier than usual this morning, the extra weight the result of a piece of hardware that Rachel would have recognized with dread.

"Hello, Mr. Smith & Wesson," he'd said earlier this morning as he took the handgun from its storage place in the bottom left-hand drawer of the desk in his study.

He wasn't going to hurt Rachel with it. No, there weren't going to be any more accidents. That was one of the promises he was going to make Rachel when he saw her this afternoon. He wasn't going to slap her or push her or hit her or even get angry, not ever again. He was in control now. But he did need something to persuade her to get into the car with him and go for a ride.

So that they could talk. Just that. Talk.

He'd put the gun back into the briefcase as soon as they were someplace safe where they could talk. There was going to be no repetition of that time in the kitchen.

He frowned, his good humor faltering as the image rose up of her sweat-stained face, hair matted against her head, eyes almost blind with fear as he drove her into the corner, up against the cupboards where they met below the sink. He'd put the gun up under her chin, the cold metal against her flesh, right there, where the skin was so very soft and tender.

He blinked fiercely, willing the image away.

Maybe he should've taken a pill this morning after all. But he'd wanted to have a clear head when he talked to Rachel, and the pills didn't allow that. They put a gauze across the world so that everything sharp lost its edge, sounds and sights were muted, feelings were . . . diminished.

Why the hell did he have to take them anyway? He was a bright, normal person. He didn't have the problems some people did. He wasn't an excessive person. He didn't have an addictive personality. He wasn't a drug addict, or an alcoholic like his father had been. His father hadn't needed any excuse for a drink—or to take off his belt and teach a two-year-old Frank what happened when you weren't a good boy and did a jobbie in your diaper when Mommy wasn't home to clean it up.

He rubbed at his temples. Jesus, he'd been feeling so good. Why'd he have to remember that? It had happened so long ago and his father had done worse to him in the years that followed, but that always stuck in his mind. He should have been able to put it behind him by now.

He supposed it was because it was unfinished business. He'd never had the opportunity to confront his father, never had the nerve. And even now . . . his father was ten years in the grave, but every time

Frank thought about him, he could feel his scrotum shrivel up and try to vanish into the arch between his pubic bones.

He hated feeling so . . . so inadequate.

He made himself concentrate on Rachel. Not Rachel in the kitchen with Mr. Smith & Wesson snuggling up against her throat, but the real Rachel, the way she'd smile when he explained everything to her, when she'd say, "Yes, it was all a mistake, honey. I want to come home." She'd be all soft and dewy-eyed, eager to please. Lowering her gaze, she'd add, "If you'll have me back, honey."

He could feel the corners of his mouth tug as he smiled, and the good feeling slowly came back.

God, wasn't it a great morning? It was going to be another perfect day. The best. Everything was going to be so good because they were going to be a family again.

He took a bite of his Egg McMuffin.

Tomorrow morning Rachel would be in the kitchen again, cooking his breakfast, sending him off to work with a bagged lunch, fulfilling her God-given role while he fulfilled his, just as they'd sworn to each other that they would when they got married.

He didn't know how he was going to be able to wait through the entire day until she got off work.

NINE

Lily was sitting in front of her vanity, putting her makeup on, when Tom appeared in the doorway behind her. He leaned up against the doorjamb and took a sip from his coffee, red hair standing at attention because he hadn't brushed it yet this morning, jaw and cheeks fuzzy with a light stubble. He wore only a pair of boxer shorts, and that was more than he needed to wear, she decided. If she hadn't been already late, she might have been tempted to just say to hell with it and jump back into bed with him. Instead she smiled at him in the mirror.

They'd spent the night at her place after going out dancing, which meant that they hadn't been here for more than about nine hours, but the bedroom and kitchen had already taken on the tousled look of Tom's apartment. Clothes dangling from chairs and one of the bedposts, breakfast makings and dishes cluttering the kitchen counters and table. He hadn't hit the bathroom yet.

"Did you ask your sister if we can borrow her car?" he asked.

"What for?"

"To drive up to Isabelle's this weekend. Remember, she invited us?"

Lily shook her head. "You never mentioned it."

"Oh. Well, we're going up to Isabelle's for the weekend. She says that the field of cosmos behind the farmhouse is just starting to bloom. Wait till you see it. It's like a Matisse brought to life, just an incredible sweep of radiant color. It always reminds me of that scene in the movie version of *The Color Purple*."

Lily laid down her eyeliner and turned from the mirror to face him instead of his reflection.

"I can't go," she said. "I'm seeing Rachel on Sunday."

Which reminded her, she hadn't given Jessie a call yet.

"You don't want to go?" Tom asked, the surprise plain in his voice.

"It's not a matter of wanting to or not; it's just that I've already made other plans."

"But Isabelle's expecting us—it's all arranged."

Lily shook her head. "For you, maybe. You should have told me sooner."

"You just saw Rachel yesterday."

"And you just saw Isabelle last week."

"That's not the same."

"Oh?" An odd sensation woke in the pit of Lily's stomach. Don't let's have a fight, she found herself thinking. They hadn't had one yet, and she didn't want to break that six-week record. "Why's that?"

"I don't think Rachel much cares for me," Tom said after a moment.

Lily started to relax. Okay. This she could handle.

"She's just wary of guys in general these days," she told him. "Besides, you don't have to worry. You don't have to see her. It's just us getting together with Jessie for the day."

"But—"

"You can go on ahead to Isabelle's."

"It won't be the same. I really wanted you to come."

He said it in such a pouty way that Lily felt herself getting irritated. Well, you should have told me about it sooner, she wanted to tell him, instead of just assuming that I'd be doing whatever it was that you wanted to do this weekend.

But she took a steadying breath and simply shrugged.

"We'll just have to plan things better in the future," she said, keeping her voice mild.

"What about spontaneity?"

Lily sighed. "How would you like it if I broke off something we had planned to do, just because something else more interesting came along?"

"But that's exactly—"

"No," Lily said. "That's not what's happening here. I didn't know anything about going out to Isabelle's farm until five minutes ago."

"But you know now."

"That's true. But it doesn't change the fact that I've already made other plans."

"With Rachel."

He said her name in a way that reminded Lily that it wasn't Rachel not liking him that bothered Tom, but rather that he didn't much care for Rachel either. She started to ask him why, but then she remembered a tirade he'd gone off on with one of his friends at a bar during the first week they'd been seeing each other. He and his fellow artist considered art dealers, gallery owners and the people who worked for them to be nothing much more than vultures, feeding off the artists, taking forty to fifty percent and for what? For doing nothing more than providing the space to hang canvases and hold shows. They were nothing more than middlemen, reduced to their commercial pursuits because they had no creative talents of their own. They were leeches, sucking away at the heart and soul of art, simply for the money.

She remembered thinking of Rachel as the two men spoke, and she also remembered the coolness with which Tom had accepted the information that Rachel worked for Hans Schaale at the LaBranche Gallery.

Not all artists felt that way about the men and women who helped bring their work before the public eye—at least not all the ones she had met—but she supposed there would always be those like Tom and his friend who resented their existence. She didn't quite understand their attitude herself. Sure, there must be unscrupulous art dealers, but there were also so many others who were in the business for the love of the art itself. When she thought of some of the small struggling galleries in Lower Crowsea . . . there *had* to be better ways to make a living. You could only struggle like that if you really cared about what you were doing.

But none of that was Rachel's fault.

"I can't help it if you don't like Rachel," Lily said, trying the words on to see how he would react. It was important for her to know that she wasn't going to be put into the position of constantly having to choose between her friend and her lover. She'd already decided yesterday that she wasn't going to let that happen.

"I never said I didn't like her," Tom replied, not really answering the question. "I just don't know why you have to spend so much time with her."

"Because she's my friend. And actually, I've spent far less time with her since I met you than I ever used to. I feel like I've been ignoring her and that's not right. She's my best friend."

Tom put his coffee mug down on the dresser, right on the wood, where it would probably leave a ring, and started to get dressed.

"So fine," he said as he tugged on his pants. "Go and spend your weekend with her."

How can this be happening? Lily thought. Ten minutes ago I wanted to take him back to bed. I thought his messiness was endearing. Now all I want to do is give him a good smack because he's acting like a spoiled child.

"Let's not fight," she said.

"Who's fighting? You're just telling me that you'd rather spend time with Rachel than with me, that's all. What am I supposed to do—like it?"

"I . . ." Lily began, but then she just shook her head.

It was as if they were balancing on the top rise of a roller coaster and all it would take now was one wrong word to send them roaring down with the brakes gone. Their relationship was still so new—who knew if it would survive a major blowout? And that was exactly what she felt they were on the edge of.

Tom was dressed by now. He paused at the door, hair still tousled, still unshaven, but the image was no longer endearing. He seemed to be waiting for her to say something—for her to tell him she'd changed her mind, she supposed—but Lily kept quiet.

Better to keep silent than to say something she'd regret.

"I guess I'll call you later," Tom said.

He waited a moment longer, then turned away. She listened to the door of her apartment slam, and he was gone.

Wasn't that just wonderful, she thought. What a horrible way to start the day. Why did he have to be so pigheaded about such a simple thing? It was the first time that she'd put a dent in his plans for what they were going to do, and the fact that this was the result did not bode well for the longevity of this relationship, she realized gloomily.

"Shit!" she cried suddenly.

She picked up her hairbrush and flung it across the room. For a long time she stared at where it had fallen, then she got up and put it back on her vanity, setting it neatly into place between the matching comb and hand mirror.

She couldn't even talk to Rachel about this because Rachel would just feel all guilty about it, when it wasn't her fault, but Tom's. But Rachel wouldn't see it that way.

Lily sighed. She glanced at her wristwatch where it lay on the vanity.

"Shit," she said again.

And now, on top of everything else, she was going to be late for work.

TEN

It was so simple, he didn't know why he hadn't thought of it before. All he had to do was watch her through the telescope until she left her apartment, and that wasn't hard at all. It was combining business with pleasure, because he could watch her for hours. She didn't have to do a thing. She could just sit there, reading a book, and he was mesmerized. Today, however, he had to keep it all in perspective. If she left while he was in dreamland, then he'd just have to start all over again tomorrow morning—a pointless exercise because he'd already put on the suit.

When he saw her head toward the door to her apartment, he stood up from the telescope. He straightened his tie in the hall mirror, picked up a briefcase to add to the veracity of the image he wanted to project, and went down to the bus stop himself, just another businessman in a two-piece suit, heading into work.

He reached the stop a few minutes before she did—his building was closer—and had a bad moment when he saw the number 3 approaching, the bus Rachel usually took, but Rachel wasn't there yet.

He turned to look for her and smiled with relief when he spied her running down the sidewalk from Tower A, toward the bus stop. He held the door so that she wouldn't miss the bus.

"Thanks," she said, flashing him a smile.

He felt as though he'd been struck by lightning. She'd spoken to him. She'd smiled *right* at him. Not out the window of her apartment, thinking of God knew what, but right at him. Really *seeing* him and smiling and saying thanks.

He let her precede him onto the bus, admiring the smooth turn of her calves as she went up the stairs ahead of him. He'd never been this physically close to her before, and the effect was like discovering her all over again. His heartbeat was a jackhammer pounding in his chest. He felt weak-kneed as he got on behind her, following in the wake of her perfume, and was barely aware of dropping his fare into the box.

The bus driver gave him an odd look, and a warning signal went off in his head. The first rule was Don't Be Noticed. Try to be invisible, and if you couldn't be invisible, then be the next best thing: so innocuous that you simply didn't register.

He straightened his shoulders and forced himself to act normal. The seat he took was across the aisle from hers and one seat back.

The trick was to drink in her beauty, here in the flesh, so physically close to him that he could just reach over and touch her if he wanted to, but without ever appearing to pay the slightest bit of attention to her. It wasn't easy—particularly when the man directly in front of him kept turning to look at Rachel's legs like she was some kind of public property.

He felt like grabbing the man by the hair and smashing his face against the back of the seat ahead of him, until his nose broke, until his head cracked open, until his own mother wouldn't recognize him. Then he'd grab a pen and puncture the bastard's eyes, pop 'em both, one after the other, like they were grapes, that'd teach him, but he breathed slowly, forced himself to remain calm.

When the bus turned down McKennit in Lower Crowsea, and Rachel rose from her seat, he was ready to disembark as well. He got up, timing the move just right so that when the bus lurched to a stop, the edge of his briefcase banged into the head of the bastard who couldn't keep his slimy eyes off Rachel.

"Oh, God, I'm so sorry," he said to the man, who turned angrily around to face him.

He didn't know what the man saw in his face, but the guy went a little pale and quickly looked away.

You got off lucky, he thought as he hurried to get off the bus.

Rachel was already striding back down McKennit to where the bus had turned off Lee Street. She wasn't hard to keep in sight, not with that swing in her walk and that gorgeous mane of hair. It looked like spun gold in the morning light. He couldn't understand why everyone on the street didn't just get down on their knees and worship her as she went by. God knew he would if he didn't have this job to do.

She was like a goddess, and he'd do anything for her. Anything.

He was surprised when she reached the corner and almost immediately stopped in front of a store. She rapped on the glass door and waited for a response. He kept on, walking right past her, glancing up at the name of the store as he went by. "Heartworks," the sign said, and below it, "Custom Framing."

A few stores past the framing shop, he paused as though to look in a window and surreptitiously checked what she was doing. The store's front door opened, and she was let in, then he heard the lock engage once more.

That was where she was employed? After working in that gallery where she was a more beautiful masterpiece than all the pathetic works of art in the place put together?

It didn't make sense.

There was a restaurant across the street with a small sign that said "Breakfast Special" in the corner of the window. He crossed the street and went in, taking a booth by the window from which he could watch the front of Heartworks. He ordered a coffee, took some papers out of his briefcase, and pretended to study them.

At nine-thirty a woman he didn't recognize unlocked the front door of the framing shop, but this time it was left unlocked. She flipped the "Sorry, We're Closed" sign to the side that read "Come In, We're Open" and disappeared back into the store.

Rachel never came out.

She really worked in there, he realized. Unbelievable.

He finished his coffee and paid the cashier for it after having left a tip that was neither too large nor too small. The waitress barely looked up at him as he paid, which was just the way he wanted it. Once outside, he crossed the street at an angle, then turned so that he could walk past the framing shop.

He paused at the window and looked in as though studying the framed prints in the display. He saw two women inside, neither of them Rachel. One was behind a long counter that ran the length of the store at the rear. She was busy with some sort of paperwork; the other was dusting.

Behind the counter he could see a door leading into a back section. Where they did the framing, he realized. The sign above it said, "Employees Only."

That's where Rachel must be. Working in the back. Framing prints.

He shook his head and walked on down the street. She deserved better. And now that he'd settled on her as his choice, he'd make damn sure that she got everything she was entitled to.

The streets were starting to fill up with people. He found himself enjoying the bustle, especially when he got down to the farmers' market. The square rang with conversation and bargaining and the sound of a fiddle that drifted through it all from where the busker stood on a corner playing, with his fiddle case open at his feet.

The air was filled with every imaginable scent, heady and rich and of the earth, as though the city with all its vehicular exhaust didn't exist. Colors ran riot across the vegetable and flower sellers' displays, a rampaging canvas just waiting to be captured on film. He imagined the photos he could take, the pleasure he'd get tinting them, capturing all that remarkable hubbub of hues and tones from memory.

Except he hadn't brought a camera.

Nothing stopping you from going home to get one, he told himself.

He could make a day of it. Shoot a half-dozen rolls, close-ups, wide shots. And then, when the day wound down, snap a few shots of Rachel leaving work. He could even ride the bus back home with her.

Well, why not? he thought.

Decision made, he walked down the block to the stop where the number 3 would pick him up on its return journey back across the river into Ferryside. On the bus he opened his briefcase and took out a piece of paper and a pen. Using the briefcase as a desk, he began to make a list: (1) Study habits away from Sky Towers. (2) Check out friends. *No losers.*

He underlined the last sentence twice. Beauty like hers had to be complemented by companions who were at least attractive. You didn't display a rose in an old tin can. Not that Rachel would be able to find friends to match the quality of her own beauty, but he should at least do what he could to weed out the real embarrassments. (3) Instigate friendship with the woman in 1216 or 1512? he wrote, then added: Maybe with both?

He wondered if that was even possible. Probably not. The logistics of his pulling it off so that it seemed natural were far too complex. But what an image that created in his mind: Rachel bookended by Caroline on one side, Lisa on the other. A queen with her ladies-in-waiting.

His penis began to harden, pressing against the soft fabric of his suit. His briefcase hid the swelling, but he still glanced nervously about himself as though his fellow passengers could sense from his features his body's betrayal. No one was looking his way.

He scratched out the third entry on his list, and wrote in instead, Arrange meeting? How? For photo shoot?

No, that was too obvious.

The bus pulled to a stop, and he glanced out the window to check its progress. Coming up on Kelly Street. They still had to cross the bridge to Ferryside. He had started to look back at his list when his attention fixed on the man boarding the bus. He turned the piece of paper over to the side with a phony business report and willed himself to be invisible, but it didn't help. The man came down the aisle, pausing beside his seat.

"Harry?" the man said, looking down at him with a smile. "Harry Landon? Is that you?"

Harry put a puzzled look on his face and shook his head. "I think you're mistaken. . . ."

But the man wasn't that easily put off. He looked incredibly pleased to see him, which pissed Harry off to no end.

Of all the people to run into this far from their hometown, it would have to be Buddy Elman. Elman had treated him like dirt all through high school, but now that was conveniently forgotten. Now it was two old pals reuniting after too many years apart.

"C'mon," Elman said. "You can't fool me with the modesty bit. It's Buddy—from Jackson High. How you doing, guy? Better yet, *what* are you doing in this place? I thought I read in *People* magazine or somewhere that you'd relocated to Europe."

He had moved to Paris for six months, but not through choice. He'd had to go because of a little problem that had arisen with his beauty of choice at the time, but that wasn't something that had come up in the article Elman was referring to.

"I like it better in the States," he said, relenting.

"Who wouldn't? Shove over a bit and let me take the weight off my legs."

Harry moved over in his seat so that Elman could sit down. The man had put on weight. He'd always been chunky, but that helped when you were a linebacker for the school team. Now he just looked sloppy. He had one of those ridiculous short brush-cut mustaches that just made the square shape of his head seem all that more pronounced.

"I tell people that I know you and they never believe me," Elman said. "I mean a guy like me—I'm in the car business now, you know—where am I going to meet a famous photographer like you, right? But I tell 'em, hey, the guy and me, we went to school together. He always had a camera, until—well, I don't tell 'em about *that,* you know." Elman nudged him in the ribs. "Hell, she was some looker, wasn't she? I'd have paid for a picture of her with her hooters hanging out in a minute."

Sherry Jane Palmer, Harry thought. The great childhood indiscretion.

He'd been open about it with interviewers, but for some reason it didn't really interest them, which never made much sense to him, the way the media usually treated anyone unfortunate enough to come under their scrutiny. Instead they wanted to talk about his ability to make the rich and famous appear like everyday people, without robbing them of their glamour. They wanted to know what the stars were like. Madonna. Tom Cruise. Kim Bassinger. Film stars, rock stars, famous models. They wanted to know how he could afford to work only a couple of months out of the year—check out the royalty statements on any one of the coffee-table books he put out every couple of years, he'd felt like telling them, but he'd murmured something about research and the photographs requiring a lot of preparatory work before he ever had the subject in the lens of his viewfinder. They wanted to know why he preferred anonymity to fame.

They wanted to know everything except for the only real bit of dirt in his life that was public knowledge. He'd only ever seen it mentioned in one article, as a kind of humorous sidebar to illustrate his long love of the medium, and that reporter had made sure to repeat verbatim Harry's avowed regrets about the situation.

They wanted pictures of him, as well, but there he always drew the line. When he did allow them, it was with his face half-hidden by a camera. Usually he just had them run one or two of his more famous portraits with a piece.

Harry Landon wasn't interested in being known as a personality, in being recognized on the street, or in a restaurant, or when he was going about his *real* work. No one knew even what city he lived in, let alone country; not even his agent. All his business transactions—rent, utilities, bank accounts—were run through corporate names.

The last thing he ever wanted was to be placed in a city where some unfortunate . . . incident might occur. His life's work was to refine, to protect, to preserve, but sometimes, through no fault of his, complications seemed to arise.

"Did you ever hear what happened to her?" Elman was saying.

Harry shook his head. "No. She got married, I guess."

"Well, yeah. But then some sick fuck took a knife to her and chopped her up into little pieces. It was all over the papers back home. Happened just before I moved out here."

"God, that's awful."

"Well, yeah. But they ran a picture of her in the paper and, man, had she let herself go."

"Really?"

Elman nodded. "Hey, I'll bet your snapping those pictures of her was the high point of her life, you know what I'm saying? It's got to make a woman think she's pretty hot stuff, to have something like that happen. She probably knew you were out there and was just putting on a show."

"I suppose. . . ."

"So tell me, Harry. You ever get to boff any of those babes in your books? The wife's got three or four of them—bought 'em because we used to hang out together as kids, you know? Sort of like, hey, we know somebody famous."

Harry fantasized smashing his briefcase against Elman's head, not just a tap as he'd given the man ogling Rachel earlier, but driving it into Elman's face, again and again and—

"I'll tell you, some of those broads"—Elman shook a hand in the air between them—"oo-wee. They are *hot*. You've gotta tell me, do they come across?"

Harry shook his head and replied with far more patience than he felt, "It's purely a professional relationship."

"Christ. What a waste. So what're you doing in Newford? Do you live here? This is so weird, meeting you on a bus like this. I thought a guy like you'd be chauffeured around in a limo, you know? Wait'll I tell the wife. She's never going to believe me."

Harry sat up a little straighter in his seat. "Actually," he said, "if you've got the time, I've got some special photos that never made it into the books that I could let you have a look at if you're interested."

"You're kidding me, right?"

"Not at all. Of course, I'll understand if you're too busy. . . ."

"Too busy? Hey, this is great. It'll be like old times, checking out the latest pictures, you know?"

That was right, Harry thought. Elman had been one of those who was always interested in seeing Harry's new pictures—mostly to see how many of them he was in himself.

"Just like old times," Harry agreed, wondering how Elman could forget the way he'd treated Harry, treated him like he was no better than some kind of bug when the whole business with Sherry Jane had come out.

He reached up and pulled the bell cord that ran along at the top of the window.

"We'll have to get a transfer, though," he said. "I'm staying in a place near Foxville."

Elman gave him a plainly disbelieving look. "Foxville? That's like a ghetto, man—all those niggers moving in there from Haiti and the Caribbean. I thought for sure you'd have yourself a penthouse downtown, or a place in the Beaches."

"I like to keep a low profile," Harry said. "Here's our stop."

The bus pulled up on that side of the Kelly Street Bridge. When

Elman saw that Harry was serious, he got his bulk out of the seat and led the way to the door, where they got transfers from the driver and disembarked. They crossed the street and were just in time to catch the number 16 heading up Lee Street into Foxville.

"You ever think of riding the subways?" Elman asked once they were seated again.

"I get claustrophobic down there," Harry told him.

"Hey, me too," Elman said, as though that just confirmed his feeling that they were really brothers under the skin, two old pals, hanging out together again.

He maintained a running dialogue the whole way up Lee Street, jumping around from subject to subject without rhyme or reason. Harry gave him his full attention, made Elman feel as though he was really something special. It wasn't hard to do. Like most people, Elman was already primed to think of himself as the headlining star in the movie of his own life. Harry just helped to confirm that.

It was something he was good at. Many of the subjects in his books had egos the size of dirigibles. Harry had learned how to stroke them, just so, a very long time ago.

As they neared MacNeil Street, Harry pulled the bell cord again.

"Listen," he said as they got off the bus. "So long as we're here, I just want to check out the viability of a location shoot. You don't mind, do you?"

"Whereabouts?" Elman asked.

Harry pointed to the ruins of the old L & B sawmill that fronted the river at the end of MacNeil. Its lot had overgrown until it was almost like a small forest, surrounded by a chain-link fence that had fallen, or been torn down, in long stretches. Across the river, a line of deserted warehouses leaned shoulder to shoulder like worn-down bums waiting for a soup kitchen to open. The whole area had a lost, deserted feel about it.

"It's for a new book I'm working on," Harry said. "Beauty set against the urban blight. I don't know how it'll play in the Midwest, but they'll eat it up on the coasts." He gave Elman a grin. "I'm trying to stretch a little. The reviews were all good on the last book, but I could tell the critics were sensing a certain sameness in my approach—maybe because I can feel it."

"Hot women in places like that?" Elman asked, waving a hand vaguely in the general direction of the ruined mill.

"Sure. Why not?"

"You're one weird dude, Harry."

"It's how I stay on top."

Elman grinned. "Can't argue with that."

"Anyway," Harry said, "the reason I want to go have a look today is that I'm a little nervous poking around the river down there on my own. You see a lot of rough characters in this area."

Elman's chest puffed up a little. "No *problem-o,* pal. Let's check it out."

It was as simple as finding out where Rachel worked. When they got down by the river, Harry had Elman check out the depth of a deep shaft that was used for who the hell knew what in the old days when the mill was still running. It had to be thirty feet deep. Someone had tried to board it over at one time, but the wood had all rotted and fallen in by now.

When Elman bent down to have a look, Harry picked up a rock and brought it down on Elman's head. The surprised *ooph* that escaped from between the man's lips and the crunching sound as the bones broke played like a fine wine on the palate of Harry's mind. He stood carefully back, so that the blood wouldn't spray him, and hit Elman a couple of times more just to be sure.

He stopped when the skull was caved in, gray matter oozing out with the blood. Looking down at the mess, he really wished he'd brought a camera with him today.

"You should have just walked on by," Harry told the corpse. "I gave you the chance, but no, you had to talk to me. You had to force the issue so that you could brag to 'the wife,' didn't you?"

He pushed Elman's corpse into the shaft. Looking down, he couldn't see a thing. He checked around the edge of the shaft, tore up some sod that had blood on it and tossed it down as well. Then he scuffed up the ground so that what he'd done was no longer so obvious. A few hours under this sun, and the dirt would be so dry you wouldn't be able to tell a thing.

There'd be the stink of the body, of course, but it was pretty far down, and who'd come down here to stumble over it anyway? Kids drinking, or shooting up. Bums. Not exactly the kind of people to go to the police.

Elman's wife would report him missing, but in a city this size, where people went missing all the time, the police had enough on their minds without trying to track down something like Elman's disappearance—especially when there were no leads. Because no one was going to put the two of them together, no one would really have noticed their meeting on the bus, coming up here, even walking down MacNeil from the bus stop.

That was another thing about a city this size—people minded their own business. And there were two kinds of people they ignored. Loudmouths, because if you didn't pay attention to them maybe they'd just go away, and a nondescript person such as himself who had made such a successful study of blending in with his surroundings.

Harry picked up his briefcase and followed the river down to the next street over. He took that to Lee Street and walked across the Gracie Street Bridge to where he caught the number 34 back home. He didn't think of Elman at all—it was as though the man had never existed. Instead he went back to his plans for the day.

Change, he thought. Get a camera. Head back to the Market.

He was going to make a real day of it.

ELEVEN

It wasn't until she got to work that Rachel realized the implications of what she had done last night.

She was cutting a piece of glass for a poster of a local band that a customer had brought in to be framed. The design harkened back to those old Filmore West posters in the heyday of psychedelia, and if the name of the band—The Crashing Bores—hadn't been on the work order, she would never have been able to figure it out for all the confusing loops and swirls. She hoped for the band's sake that they didn't measure up to their name.

The current fascination with the sixties—she'd missed them herself, but had no regrets from all she'd read and heard—filled her thoughts as she threw the trimmed pieces of glass into the recycling bin. She froze at the sound it made. The glass breaking at the bottom of the bin brought last night back to her in a sudden rush:

Her sterile studio.

Her sudden rage.

The destruction.

The odd sense of peace that had followed.

But now she could see it all from a new perspective.

My God, she thought. She was emulating Frank. Frank with his fix-ations, his sudden rages and the gentle calm that followed them. She was twinning her relationship with her art with how her relationship with Frank had gone. From the studio with everything in its exact and proper place, so regulated it was almost anal, to the way she'd simply let a red wave of anger wash over her, to the ensuing calm that had let her sleep through the night without disturbing dreams.

She stared down into the recycling bin, the jagged shards of glass blurring in her sight, and felt sick.

"Did you cut yourself?" Helen asked.

Rachel looked up, startled. Nothing seemed familiar for a long moment. Not the workshop, not Helen. Not her own hands gripping the edge of the bin, knuckles whitening.

"What . . . what did you say?" she asked finally.

Helen finished clamping the frame she was working on and moved over to the glass recycling bin where Rachel still stood.

"You've gone so pale," she said. "I was asking if you'd hurt yourself."

Rachel shook her head. "No, I . . ."

Helen's fingers were light on her hands, gently prying them away from the edge of the bin. She held onto Rachel's hands, worry creasing her features.

"Rachel, what's the matter?"

Rachel reclaimed her hands from Helen's grip and wrapped her arms around herself.

"I . . ."

The worst of the sense of dislocation was starting to pass, but what had brought it on wouldn't go away. She felt as if she had to take a shower, but how did you clean away an ugliness that had lodged inside you?

"You know how when you're growing up," she said. Her gaze fixed on Helen's mouth because she couldn't quite raise it to the other woman's eyes. "How you're always afraid you're going to turn into your mother?"

"Tell me about it."

"Well, I think I'm turning into my ex-husband."

Helen gave her a blank look.

"I know," Rachel said. "It sounds weird. It's just . . ."

She finally raised her gaze. There was such a look of genuine concern in Helen's eyes, such empathy, that Rachel found herself telling Helen about the previous night. She talked around the specifics of her stalled art and the studio itself, but still managed to convey the upshot of what had left her feeling so lost and upset.

Helen sat up on one of the worktables, legs dangling, while she listened.

"They're all the same," Helen said when Rachel finally ran out of words.

That was something Rachel liked best about talking with other women: they were more prone to sympathy. Men always wanted to put forth facile solutions to a problem when all you really wanted was to have someone listen, really *listen*.

"I suppose," she said.

"He was never very supportive, I'll bet," Helen went on.

Rachel nodded. "Although it never really occurred to me until I left just how much I gave up for the marriage. Ever since the separation, I've kept thinking I'll be able to get back to the way I was before I met him, but it doesn't seem to work that way."

"It takes a long time to get back what they steal from us," Helen said. "I learned that the hard way from my own ex."

"I didn't know you'd been married," Rachel found herself saying, realizing even as she spoke that there was a whole world of things she didn't know about her coworker.

"Oh, yes, I made the big mistake just like all too many of us have," Helen said. Her eyes took on a hard look, and she grimaced with exaggerated distaste. "But you learn. The way I look at it now is, may the bastard rot in hell—along with every other man."

Rachel didn't know how to respond to that. This kind of conversation always made her uneasy. She felt the same sort of inadequacy now that she had when Sarah had taken her to a feminist study group one night while she was living at the shelter. Rachel had understood the other women's bitterness, but even with the bruises of her marriage still discoloring her skin, she hadn't quite been able to connect with what they were saying.

The trouble was, she was pretty sure that she was still attracted to men, or at least to the idea of a man, in her life. She didn't hate them; she was just scared of them.

"Sorry," Helen said, reading the mixed emotions that were playing across Rachel's features. "I get a little hard-line whenever that particular subject comes up." She hopped down from the workbench. "We'd better get some of these orders done or Manda will start paying us per picture framed instead of at an hourly rate. Hit a slow week and we'd be out on the street and starving."

Rachel nodded. "Thanks for listening."

"Hey, that's what we're here for—to take care of each other, right?"

"Right," Rachel agreed as she headed back to finish mounting the Crashing Bores poster.

She'd been lucky, she knew. All the women she'd run into since she left Frank had been so supportive. But maybe she'd been depending too much upon their largess. Maybe she had to strike out on her own for a change. Maybe the reason she found herself becoming like Frank was because that was all she'd known for too many years. The strange play between violence and tenderness, the preciseness of everything in its exact proper place, had become so familiar that normal behavior seemed odd.

She remembered something that her favorite prof had said about creating art, how the creative impulse couldn't exist in a vacuum.

"You have to delve beyond the common boundaries of what you normally experience," he'd said. "You want to paint, fine. But don't ignore sculpture. Don't ignore literature. Don't ignore the photo on the front page of the newspaper. You have to make an effort to experience everything—from gallery art to graffiti, poetry to symphonies. You must always keep your eyes and ears and nose open for new sights and sounds and scents and tastes. It's only through a wide variety of experiences that you'll grow as an artist. Diligent practice isn't enough. To that you must add the greatest effort to experience as much as you can from what life itself has to offer."

She could almost see the words before her, transcribed in her notebook from his lecture and reread often.

It didn't apply to just art, she realized. It applied to how you lived as well.

She knew so few people, she received so little in the way of external input from real life. She read, she watched TV, her pursuits were all solitary because she was afraid to take a chance, afraid to step out on her own.

I live like a nun, she thought.

She stared down at the bewildering spin and loop of the words on the poster, feeling as lost as sense was in their swirling colors.

Just like a nun.

But God help her, the idea of doing otherwise left her just about paralyzed with fear.

TWELVE

Lily got the call just as she was starting her lunch break. When Tracy told her it was Tom, she was tempted to just ask her to tell him that she'd already left for lunch.

She was still fuming over the argument they'd had this morning, to which had been added the aggravation of her finding out that she'd been passed over for a promotion. She'd really been counting on the move to a lower desk job in Customer Service Administration—not because she disliked working as a teller, but because she could use the extra money, rents being what they were. She just couldn't seem to save money; when the end of the month came around, her balance was always hovering at around three hundred dollars.

But, no. Even with her seniority, she'd been passed over and Sheila Thompson had gotten the job. She didn't want to point the finger or anything, but she wondered how much the way Sheila flirted with the manager had to do with her getting the position.

From where she stood, Lily could see right into the manager's office. He was sitting behind a polished brass nameplate that read

Brent Cameron, looking out the window at all the women going by in their summer skirts and shorts. The slime bag. Lily had made it pretty clear to Cameron from day one that she was strictly interested in maintaining a business relationship. He hadn't said a thing, though his gaze had roved over her body and then he'd raised an eyebrow as if to say, Baby, you don't know what you're missing.

She might joke to Tom about Cameron's sexist attitude, but that was just her way of dealing with it. The truth was that it was an irritation that rose at least a half-dozen times a day. Sometimes she had to just clamp her teeth together or she knew she'd say something that she'd regret—not from a moral standpoint, but from a financial one.

She needed the job. But where the hell did a guy like Cameron come off, anyway?

"Are you taking it?" Tracy asked, her finger poised over the flashing button where she had Tom on hold.

"Why not?" Lily replied. The day couldn't get much worse.

She nodded her thanks to Tracy as she took the receiver from her, and sat down in the chair beside Tracy's desk.

"Hello, Tom," she said, her voice heavy with weariness.

"Are you all right?" Tom asked.

You can ask that, after what happened this morning? Lily thought.

"Sure," she said into the receiver. "I'm just dandy."

"Oh. Well, I . . . I just want to apologize for what happened this morning. I had no right to get angry with you just because you'd gone ahead and made plans on your own. I wasn't thinking, I guess, which isn't much of an excuse, but it's an honest one at least."

He paused, but she didn't fill in the silence.

"I never realized that you were feeling the way you were," he went on after a moment, "that you felt we were just doing things that I wanted to do. I just assumed that if you had something you wanted to do, you'd tell me. But I was thinking back, after I left your place this morning, and I see you're right. I'm not really sure how it happened."

Another pause.

"Lily, why didn't you ever say anything?"

She sighed. "I don't know. I guess everything was going so well, I didn't want to make waves. And then I kept thinking things'd change, but we fell into the habit of you making the choices and . . . well, it's hard to explain exactly. It didn't seem really wrong or anything, because most of the time I wanted to do the same things anyway, but it just ended up getting to me."

Now it was her turn to leave a hole in the conversation, but unlike her, Tom immediately stepped in to fill it.

"I'm really sorry," he said. "We've never had an argument before, and I really hate the way it feels. The sun's shining outside, but it's like I'm walking through a miasma that's just turning everything gray. It doesn't help that I've felt like a heel all morning for storming out the way I did."

"Yeah, I'm not having that great a day myself," Lily told him, but then added, "though it's not all your fault."

She told him about losing out on the CSA position.

"Are you just going for lunch?" Tom asked.

"Yeah."

"Why don't I come by?" he asked.

"I don't think that's such a good idea," Lily told him, "but it's sweet of you to offer. I've only forty-five minutes left, and by the time you got here, we wouldn't even have time to order before I'd have to go."

"Then can I meet you after work?"

"I'd like that," Lily said.

They talked for a few minutes longer, then Lily hung up and went out to pick up a ham-and-cheese sandwich from the deli down the street. Maybe, she thought as she sat on a bench outside the deli, the day wasn't going to be a total loss after all. She was still pissed off with Sheila and Cameron, but it didn't seem quite so important anymore.

Instead, she sat thinking dreamily of Tom and what a genuinely nice guy he was. Too bad he didn't have a brother that they could introduce to Rachel, she thought.

THIRTEEN

By quitting time, Rachel was still brooding about how much her actions of last night resembled the way her ex-husband had treated her. All those stories she'd heard of married couples becoming more like each other the longer they were married came back to haunt her. Had she and Frank been married long enough for the worst parts of his personality to bleed into hers? And if they had, why hadn't he acquired anything of her?

She refused to accept the idea that he was stronger than her. Physically, yes. But not where it really counted. Her will was her own now. She might still be messed up, but she was never going to fall back into the same trap that she had every time he'd expressed remorse in the past, and she *wasn't* going to let him influence her, change her, control her. And she *certainly* wasn't going to emulate him.

But God, what had come over her last night? . . .

Throughout the day, she had busied herself with the various prints and paintings and posters for which she had work orders, but without any of her usual interest in the subject matter or the customers' choices of mats and frames. Functioning purely on automatic, she mechanically went through the motions until the minute hand of the clock above Helen's worktable slowly climbed through the last half hour of the day, reached the twelve, and it was finally six o'clock; time to go home.

Not that home held any appeal for her. Not tonight. Not with that mess waiting for her in her studio.

If she were smart, the first thing she'd do when she got home was clean it up. Deal with it immediately so that she could work on putting it behind her. She just had to tell herself that she wasn't like Frank, she never would be and what had happened last night was merely an aberration that was not going to be repeated. She wouldn't *allow* it to be repeated.

But if she were really smart, an insidious voice whispered cynically inside her mind, she'd just toss out all of her art supplies and turn the room into the spare bedroom it was meant to be. Throw out all her old paintings and sketchbooks, too, because all they did was make her feel crazy, reminding her of what she could have had, but would never regain. She had to face the fact that she was never going to be an artist again. Any talent she might have had, she'd allowed to just dribble away. There were no second chances. There was no recapturing the past.

Rachel recognized that voice. It was the true legacy of her marriage to Frank. It was the voice that agreed with him. The voice that told her, yes, she'd been wrong, so she deserved to be punished. Yes, she was worthless.

She hated that voice more than she did Frank, because it was inside her. Its betrayal hurt so much more because it was a part of her.

No, she told it. She wasn't going to give up. Giving up was what Frank and her parents had made her do once. If she gave up, that was letting them win once more, and she didn't think she could go through it yet again.

"How're you doing?" Helen asked as Rachel was putting away her tools.

Rachel was grateful for the space that Helen had given her today. She hadn't tried to talk, she'd just let Rachel go about her business while she'd gone about her own. The only sign that there was anything different today from every other day they'd worked together over the past couple of weeks was that Helen had switched the radio from the soft rock station they usually had on, to one that featured interviews and commentaries.

Rachel had learned fairly quickly that Helen loved to talk. She was that rarity among gregarious people, though, in that she also loved to listen. She always liked to have a conversation going on around her, even if she wasn't a part of it.

"Okay, I guess," Rachel replied.

"Do you want some company tonight?" Helen went on. "Maybe just go for a beer before you head on home?"

"Ah . . ."

"It's not a come-on, Rachel," she added, "in case that's what you were thinking. Just an offer of company." She grinned to take the sting from her words.

That was exactly what Rachel *had* been thinking. God, she thought. Did I look that obviously uncomfortable? And why should she feel uncomfortable anyway? She'd already accepted Helen's sexual proclivity. Perhaps it was because she hadn't really defined her own yet. She wasn't attracted to women, but she was scared of men—so where did that leave her?

The image of C. A. Collins's *Convent Thoughts* came into her mind, the nun in the garden behind her convent walls, holding a book in one hand, looking down at a flower. The water at her feet like glass, the folds of the nun's habit motionless, everything still, static. The nun might as well have been a statue, there was so little sense of motion about her.

Rachel refused that image of herself as well, though it seemed so apt at the moment. She knew she had to make a break from how she'd let her life close in on her, but she wasn't quite ready to do so tonight.

"Maybe tomorrow night?" she said.

"Sure. Whatever. But promise me this, will you? Don't just sit around and brood tonight, okay? Rent a video, have a friend over, or just get out of that place and do something—*anything*—to get your mind off the track it's on right now. I don't want to sound like some pop psychologist, but half the trouble we get into, we bring on ourselves. If you're feeling depressed, the less you fight it, the worse you're going to feel. It starts this downward spiral that just gets harder and harder to pull out of. Trust me on this, because I've been there."

"I look that bad, huh?" Rachel said.

Helen smiled broadly. "The one thing you never look is bad, Rachel, and you can trust me on that as well."

Rachel felt a blush start up from the back of her neck, then spread to her cheeks. As though sensing that this time she *had* stepped over a line, Helen gave her a quick good-bye and quit the workshop to chat briefly with Tami out front before she left the store. Once she was alone, Rachel took a deep breath and composed herself, then went back to tidying up her work area.

She made a haphazard job of it. Manda didn't like things to get too chaotic back there, but Rachel's heart simply wasn't in the task. It reminded her too much of the work desk in her studio before she'd set about wrecking the place.

"Are you almost finished back there, Rachel?" Tami asked, poking her head into the back room.

Tami Razzell was the least conservative person Rachel had ever met. When she and the store's owner were together behind the front counter, they were a striking study in contrasts. Manda was blond, like Rachel, but her long hair was straight and usually pulled back in a ponytail. She dressed in tailored skirt and jacket combinations and wore sensible shoes.

Tami's appearance, however, varied from day to day, depending on her whim. She might come in wearing a black leather micro miniskirt with fishnet stockings and impossible heels, or conversely in jeans torn at the knees and a baggy sweater, sleeves rolled up to her elbows. One day last week she'd looked just like one of those tricolored popsicles—long blueberry T-shirt, white lace-trimmed leggings and hot pink sneakers. Today she looked like a grown-up version of Pebbles from the old *Flintstones* show—fake leopard-skin dress, dark hair tied up in a wild knot at the top of her head, complete with a plastic bone poking out from among the startled stray locks.

"I'm about ready to lock up," she added.

"Be right with you," Rachel said.

She fished her purse out from a tangle of mat scraps that had fallen beside her workbench. She'd throw them out tomorrow. Right now she had to get out of here. The sooner she got home and faced her studio, the sooner she could start the healing process.

Now who's acting like a pop psychologist? she thought as she joined Tami by the front door.

"Got any plans tonight?" Tami asked.

They stepped outside, and Tami locked the door behind them.

Rachel shook her head. "I'm just going to stay in and clean up around the apartment a bit."

Tami smiled. "Don't have a date for tonight either?"

Rachel liked Tami, and they'd talked some, but she hadn't exchanged many confidences with her the way she had with Helen, mostly because she didn't work in such close quarters with Tami. So Tami couldn't know how uncomfortable her breezy comment made Rachel feel.

"Something like that," Rachel said. She had to work at the smile that she managed to find.

"My dream," Tami told her just before they parted, "is to have a cleaning lady. I'm the *worst* housekeeper in the world. It's my theory that we were born to live in a mess—you know, like magpies or something, nesting in a clutter of whatever tickles our fancy."

Rachel thought of Frank, raging at her because she hadn't replaced his high school swimming trophies in the right order when she'd cleaned his study. Tami would drive him insane.

"I don't exactly keep the tidiest house either," Rachel told her, "but I'm learning to keep it in perspective."

"Right. There's a zillion more important things to do in the world, but when that white porcelain starts going gray, even the laziest of us has to get out the soap and a brush. See you tomorrow."

Rachel returned her jaunty wave, then set off for her bus stop. She noticed a car parked in the No Stopping zone where the street widened slightly for the bus stop, and something tickled in her memory. It was a Chevy Nova, four-door, black with a narrow red stripe on the bumpers and doors. There was something about it . . .

Her gaze dropped to the license plate, and it was as though her heart just stopped in her chest.

It was their car, the one they'd had when they were married. Frank's car now. Oh god, let it just be a coincidence that it was parked here. Don't let him have found out where she worked.

She lifted her head to look around for him, ready to duck into the nearest shop's doorway, even if it were closed, just to hide her face, if she saw him. The only person she saw watching her was a man at the bus stop wearing an AIDS awareness T-shirt. There was something familiar about his features, but he wasn't Frank.

And then she had no more time to try to place the man at the bus stop because there was someone behind her, something hard stuck into the small of her back, and his voice, Frank's voice, that hated voice, was in her ear.

"Now don't panic, honey. I just want to talk to you, that's all."

She thought: He's got his gun. He's out here on the street with his gun. He's gone crazy. He's going to kill me.

"We'll just get into the car," Frank said, "and you can drive us to someplace where we can have a nice calm—"

No more, she thought. She didn't care how many guns he had.

She twisted away, turning to face him. Her hand rose defensively the way the instructor had taught her in that course on self-defense where she'd met Lily. He'd also told them not to argue with someone pointing a gun at them, but Rachel didn't care.

She was past caring. Past being afraid of Frank. He represented everything that had gone wrong in her life. He *was* everything that had gone wrong in her life.

Hit the gun hand, she told herself. Knock it to one side. Kick him in the shin.

But as she was turning, her heel caught on the edge of the sidewalk where it joined the street, and she stumbled. She clawed at the air, but she was too unbalanced. She saw Frank, the gun in his hand, the muzzle lifted, aimed at her.

"He's got a gun!" someone cried.

I already know that, Rachel found herself thinking.

Everything seemed to slow down. She fell out into the street. In her peripheral vision, she saw a car coming straight for her. She heard its horn wail, the screech of its brakes. She knew it wouldn't be able to stop in time.

FOURTEEN

It wasn't supposed to happen like this, Frank thought as he watched Rachel fall in front of the oncoming car. We were just going to talk. We were going to get back together again.

He heard someone cry out that he had a gun, and he looked down at it, the muzzle pointed at Rachel, as though seeing it for the first time.

What was he *doing* here?

The car bearing down on Rachel swerved to the left, smashing into a cab that was in the farther lane.

Frank wanted to throw the gun away, but all he could do was point it at Rachel, tracking her as she hit the pavement, his finger tightening on the trigger.

It was her fault.

It had always been her fault.

He caught a flash of motion from the corner of his eye and saw a man lunging for him. He registered the blond hair and sunglasses, the AIDS awareness T-shirt, the camera bouncing at the man's side with a lens that seemed almost a foot long.

He brought the gun around from where it had been pointed at Rachel to aim it at his attacker.

On the street, the cab was pushed into the oncoming traffic and hit a delivery van head-on, which in turn was rear-ended by the vehicle behind it. The air was filled with the sounds of tearing metal, smashing glass, people's screams.

Frank's finger tightened on the trigger, pulled it before he'd brought the weapon completely around. The sound of the gunshot cut across the cacophony already filling the street. The bullet hit the pavement, then ricocheted off into a store window. The sound of the plate glass hitting the pavement only added to the chaos. The recoil of the shot made his whole arm feel numb, and he almost lost his grip on the gun.

And then his attacker was upon him. The man's lips were pulled back in a grimace that showed his teeth.

"How dare you!" he was shouting over the hubbub. "You fucking monster, how *dare* you!"

Frank tried to bring the gun around again, but his attacker seemed supernaturally strong.

He's such a nothing looking little guy, Frank found himself thinking. How can he be so strong?

The man caught Frank's gun hand, and twisted it effortlessly so that the muzzle was pointing at Frank's chest. Frank fought the man's grip, but it was like he was a child, powerless. The man closed his fist around Frank's fingers and exerted pressure. Frank tried to stop himself from doing it, but the man's grip was forcing him to pull the trigger.

The shot seemed muffled compared to the previous one. His wrist felt as though it had been broken, and there was a sudden flame of pain in his chest.

I think I'm having a heart attack, he thought. Someone please call a . . . call . . .

The man let him go, stepped away. There were sirens in the distance. The gun fell from Frank's hand and bounced on the sidewalk.

People were screaming and shouting all around him. There was a sharp cordite smell in the air, stinging his nostrils, and the smell of something else as well. Blood.

Frank bent over, arms hugged around himself, gaze spinning. He could feel a wetness seeping the front and back of his shirt and jacket. He took a breath, and it was as though someone had put a blowtorch to his lungs and fired it up to full power.

Then he stumbled to his knees, turning as he fell. He was looking directly at Rachel, who still lay on the street, just starting to rise herself.

"I . . . just wanted to . . . talk. . . ." he managed before his mouth filled with blood.

Then he fell the rest of the way to the pavement. He was conscious enough to feel the sharp pain that rocked his skull when his head hit the road's surface. He'd never known there could be this much pain. That anything could hurt this much.

When the black wave rose up, he was so grateful, because there was no pain in it, just a spot of light at the far end of it to which he felt himself drawn.

He let it take him away.

FIFTEEN

Harry shot a half dozen exposures when Rachel and her coworker stepped out of the closed store. Three of them were of Rachel, one of the pair of them, Rachel in profile, and two of them of Rachel's companion. He liked the look of the girl. She wasn't a true beauty, but she was certainly entertaining. Too few women had a sense of humor when it came to fashion. Too many men did, only with them it wasn't deliberate.

He was bringing the zoom back into a close-up of Rachel's face when motion on the sidewalk to his left caught his eye. It was the man who'd parked his Chevy Nova in the No Parking zone directly in front of the bus stop where Harry was standing.

What an asshole the guy was, to park illegally as he had and then just wander aimlessly up and down the length of the block like he was some kind of panhandler. He seemed to be waiting for someone. Harry hoped it wasn't Rachel's companion. She looked too charming to know a loser like that, who couldn't even respect a simple thing like a No Parking sign.

Harry hated people who broke the law.

He brought his camera down when he saw Rachel and her coworker go their separate ways. Ah, the other girl did have some taste. She wasn't going anywhere near the loser. Anybody wearing a sports jacket on as beautiful a day as today had to be a loser. Maybe he needed to dress up for work, but for Christ's sake, the day was over now. Lighten up a little, guy.

The man had turned and was studying the menu of the little food joint where Harry'd had his coffee earlier this morning.

Yeah, go in and have your dinner there, Harry thought. It's about your speed.

He looked away from the man as Rachel crossed the street. He wanted to admire the clean lines of her figure in motion for a few moments before he had to pretend indifference to her. What if there was a seat free *right* behind her on the bus? He could sit there and drink in the scent of her. Maybe the window would be open, and if he leaned forward, her hair would be blown against his face. Maybe—

His gaze was suddenly drawn back to the man by the diner. Rachel had stopped to look at the car in the No Parking zone, dismay washing over her features. Behind her, the man was coming up fast. He took something from his pocket that flashed metallically in the sun for a brief instant, then Rachel's body hid it. Whatever it was, he'd stuck it up against her back.

Not a knife, Harry decided. A gun. The loser was trying to mug Rachel.

As Rachel's eyes widened with shock, Harry burst into motion. He slipped his arm in through the strap of his camera so that it would hang out of the way at his side and closed the distance between them with the lithe gait of a panther running down its prey.

"No!" he cried as Rachel tried to fight the man and fell back into the traffic.

He saw the car swerve away from Rachel and hit the cab that was in the lane beside it. The air was suddenly full of noise—people screaming, the crash of the first impact followed by subsequent ones as the cab was pushed into the oncoming traffic, brakes squealing.

The world disappeared around Harry. His attention narrowed to a fine focus. All that existed were three things: Rachel, in danger. The man, who'd put her there, with the gun in his hand bearing down on her. And he, himself.

He was supposed to be protecting her; instead he'd let this pitiful excuse of a human being attack her. If she was bruised, if she was at all damaged . . .

He was screaming something as he bore down on the man, but he had no idea what he was saying. The man took a shot at him, but he'd fired before he'd brought his arm all the way around, and the bullet ricocheted off the pavement to smash the window of a store behind Harry. And then Harry was on the gunman.

He didn't bother to use any of the martial arts skills that he still so regularly maintained since he'd first taken them up as a teenager. He wasn't interested in breaking an arm, in disabling, in merely stopping Rachel's attacker.

He wanted the man dead.

Plain and simply, the man had to die for daring to touch her, for threatening her, for risking her precious beauty.

He caught hold of the gunman's hand and twisted it around until the bore of the weapon was pressed up against the man's chest. The gunman tried to beat him off, but his blows were laughable. Harry just kept on exerting pressure on the fingers of the man's gun hand until there was the satisfyingly loud report of the gunshot, the man stiffening, the blood welling from his wound.

Harry stepped back, gaze traveling to Rachel who was looking directly at him. She didn't seem to be able to focus on him.

The red rage subsided in him. She was alive. She was safe. She was unblemished. He wanted to reach down and help her to her feet. He wanted to photograph her there where she crouched on the pavement in all her endearing dishevelment, but the sound of approaching sirens killed the beauty of the moment.

He bent over as though about to retch.

"Oh God, oh God, oh God," he mumbled, stumbling away.

Someone patted him on his back.

"It's okay, man. You had no choice."

"Going to . . . sick."

He was helped away from the dead man on the pavement, from Rachel. His body language was remorse, shock. It said he was sick, racked with nausea for what he'd been forced to do. He let the man lead him to the edge of the crowd, then turned to him, eyes desperate.

"I . . . I'll be okay." He leaned against the wall. "Help the . . . the woman. . . ."

His benefactor hesitated.

"Please . . . they're . . . they're frightening her. . . ."

As the man turned to look at the crowd that was pressing in around Rachel and the dead man, Harry slipped away. He moved quickly, but not so quickly as to bring unwanted attention to himself. He wanted there to be as little as possible to be remembered about him.

"Hey!" called the man who'd helped him.

Harry ignored him. He went around the corner, the sirens sounding far too close for comfort. As he moved, he pulled his arm free from his camera strap, brought the strap over his head. Holding the camera in his hand, he ducked into the first alleyway he came to.

He glanced behind himself as he stepped into the alley, but his benefactor hadn't followed him around the corner. Rachel and the dead man were far more interesting and must have won in the contest between the man's being a Good Samaritan and his being just one more gawker.

The alley ran between two stores for some thirty feet or so, then met another at a T intersection. Harry turned right, away from the block where all the commotion was still under way, and stopped. Looking to his left, he could see the edge of the crowd gathered around the dead man and Rachel.

Harry stepped back into the first alley, where he laid the camera at his feet and pulled off his blond wig. Removing his distinctive T-shirt, he wrapped camera and wig up in it. He ruffled his short brown hair where the wig had flattened it, then stepped into the new alleyway, turned right and set off down to where it opened up onto the street running parallel to Lee, but one block over.

Five minutes later, Harry had worked his way around to the bike path that followed the river and was just one more jogger, out for his daily run. Cradled under one arm was the bundle of his camera and wig, wrapped up in the T-shirt, but it didn't look particularly out of place. Many of the other joggers with whom he shared the path had knapsacks or were carrying their spare clothes under one arm, making their trip from office to home a healthy endeavor.

He let his thoughts travel back over the past half hour as he followed the path north.

She was fated to be chosen, he decided. Why else would he have been there at just the right moment to rescue her?

But it had been close. Far too close.

He'd have to make sure she was never in such danger again.

TOM

SIXTEEN

It took two weeks before the shock of Frank's death finally wore off. Rachel went through the days numbly, in a haze of tranquilizers. She dealt with the police, with the concern of her small circle of friends and coworkers, with the bitter accusations of Frank's mother, who kept phoning to tell her that she'd killed Frank. Lily, who was over visiting one of the days that she called, told her that if she didn't stop harassing Rachel, they'd call the police. Then she hung up on the woman.

Frank's mother didn't call back.

What Rachel found the worst was dealing with the guilt. She knew she'd done nothing wrong, but she couldn't help feeling responsible for Frank's death. If it hadn't been for her, he'd still be alive. For all that she'd feared him, for all that he'd made her life hell, she couldn't stop thinking of the man he'd been before they had married.

She kept going back over the years, scrutinizing what she'd done, how she'd treated him before she found out about his medical condition and the violence had begun. When they were first dating, there hadn't been even a hint of the monster he could become. And then, even when he had begun to hit her, it had taken Rachel the longest time to realize that nobody could be expected to stay in the kind of relationship that hers and Frank's had become.

She'd wished him dead any number of times, but had he really deserved to die? His condition wasn't his fault. Should she have stuck it out, tried marriage counseling again, tried harder to believe that they were just "going through a rough patch and everything would get better"?

It took her two weeks to be able to respond to that guilt and say no. They had no longer been a couple. The door should have stayed closed on the past. But Frank wouldn't let it go. And if she had gone back to him, if she'd let him into her life again, she'd have been the one who was dead.

Lily was a godsend through it all. She and Rachel's neighbor Rob took turns looking after Rachel, with occasional visits from Sarah and Helen, but Lily was there the most. She was the one who convinced Rachel not to go to the funeral.

"The only reason you want to go is to make sure he's dead," she'd said to Rachel, "but you don't need to do that. You were there. You saw him die. He's never going to hurt you again."

The police were gentle, though insistent that she go through the story over and over again until Rachel's lawyer decided enough was enough and put a stop to it.

"My client never saw the man before," Marian told the investigating officers. "She didn't even see him that day. I won't deny we're relieved that the threat her husband represented is no longer hanging over her, but Rachel had no more to do with Mr. Bedley's death than you did."

"But—"

"You must have twenty witnesses who actually *saw* what happened," Marian said. "Why don't you spend some more time interviewing *them.*"

But of course the information from the other witnesses was the same as it always was in such cases. Vague. Contradictory. And ultimately, useless. The man who had killed Frank, the man Rachel saw as her mysterious rescuer, had seemingly vanished into thin air. Two weeks after the fact, the police were no closer to apprehending him than they had been on the day of the murder.

Which suited Rachel just fine, because now, when her head was finally clear of the tranquilizers that Dr. Caley had prescribed, she realized that he had given her a gift more precious than anything she'd ever been given before.

Freedom.

Freedom from fear. Freedom to truly begin her life over again and never have to worry about Frank showing up at her door, at work, lurking around a corner.

She wanted to find her rescuer as well, but not to help put him in jail. She'd come to think of him as her guardian angel, and she wanted to thank him for what he'd done. If the police ever did apprehend him, she'd be the first to come to his defense.

He was never far from her thoughts. She had only to close her eyes to call up that brief flash of features that had seemed so tantalizingly familiar just before Frank attacked her. At night, she dreamed of him more and more, and lately, those dreams had taken an erotic turn.

She knew that Sarah and her friends would be horrified at the idea. In some way, Rachel herself knew that it was wrong, that the gratitude she felt for her rescuer was no better a thing to base a relationship on than Frank's abuse, but she couldn't help it.

She just found herself *wanting* him. She was sure that with him she'd be forever safe. He'd become an obsession, but she knew she had less chance of finding him than did the police, unless—and this was the thought she kept most secret of all—he really was her guardian angel. She could almost imagine him watching over her, at any moment of the night or day, seeing that she was kept safe from harm. An intimate, invisible presence, forever close and dear.

It was as though by killing Frank, he'd indebted her to him, not just for the obvious reason of having saved her life, but for the endless gift of freedom that had become hers upon Frank's death.

Oh, it was wrong. Wrong, wrong. She knew it was. But her obsession with the man wouldn't go away.

During the days before she went back to work, and in the late evening when Lily or whoever was visiting her had gone, she would go into her studio and paint. She had dozens of character sketches and five completed paintings, all of the same subject. Her guardian angel.

The paintings all had an unfinished, almost ghostly look about them. This was partly due to the fact that Rachel had no clear image of her subject, but it owed something to her medium as well. A finished watercolor could be as finely detailed as a photograph, or, as in the case of Rachel's current paintings, thinly applied veils of color in which objects merged, one into the other, and the absorbent qualities and texture of the paper itself became a part of the final result.

Rachel didn't consider the finished work to be gallery-quality by any means, but she was more than pleased with the paintings, because they represented the first work that she could look upon with any sort of pride since Frank had made her give up her art. And as she considered the reemergence of her talent to be yet another gift from her angel, it seemed fitting that he was a part of each painting.

She sat sometimes for hours in her studio, looking up to where she'd taped the paintings to the wall with masking tape. He, in turn, seemed to watch her back, a partially realized presence ghosting through each scene she'd painted as a backdrop.

He was a face in a crowded street, at a corner, waiting for a light to change, that man's hat blocking part his face, that woman's hair blown in front of him, caught by an errant wind.

He was a phantom standing in a grove of trees along the river by the university common, the trees filled with ravens, mist lying sleepily upon the grass at his feet.

He was a ghost in the Crowsea Market, a motionless shadow, watching from a doorway, when all around him was vibrant with color and motion.

He walked through the drizzle as it fell upon the boardwalk, hat brim pulled down over his eyes, long coat slick with rain, the pier behind him, empty concession stands all closed, the water of the lake turbulent.

He was a face in a car window, caught from the corner of the eye, focus slightly blurred because the vehicle was moving too quickly.

The clearest definition was in the lower face. The lips, the chin. Those she remembered. All else was conjecture. Ghost features waiting to be claimed by her brush when she finally met her angel.

For meet him she felt she would. One day. Life couldn't be that unfair, not to allow her that much. Just to see him, if only from a distance . . .

The studio was changed now; she had reclaimed it from Frank's influence and made it her own. It wasn't so much cluttered as comfortable.

She'd cleaned out all the broken glass, put away the prints and left the walls bare until she could fill them with new work, as she now had. Her drawing table was a litter of pencils and brushes, scraps of paper with half-realized sketches and color samples. The books had been replaced on their shelves, but they were no longer in alphabetical order, but rather in order of preference, the more used volumes closer to hand.

She'd brought the portable radio in from her bedroom, and now when she worked, the room was filled with music, or the sound of voices. Their company was cheering, even when it was just actors selling products in an ad.

She was still lonely, but she was no longer so scared. Because Frank was dead. She was free. She had her art back. Life could be worse—far worse. She knew, because she'd already been there.

The doorbell rang, startling her from her reverie. Still somewhat bemused, she went out into the hall and looked through the peephole to see that it was Rob. She smiled as she opened the door for him.

"How're you doing today, Rachel?" he asked as he came in.

He was wearing a T-shirt that said, "1 out of 10 therapists recommend R&P for their patients who listen to music."

"Pretty good for a change," Rachel told him. "I think I'm going to go back to work on Monday."

"Good for you."

"What's R&P stand for?"

"What . . . ?" Rob asked, then he looked down at his shirt. "Oh. It's Ron and Paul—those musicians I saw when I went to San Francisco last year. Remember I played one of their tapes for you?"

Rachel nodded. "I like the shirt. Do you want something to drink?"

"Well, if you've got a cold beer, I wouldn't say . . ."

His voice trailed off as he paused in the doorway to Rachel's studio.

Oh God, Rachel thought. I forgot to close the door.

But the panic she'd thought she'd feel didn't come.

"I didn't know you painted," Rob was saying. "Can I have a look?"

"Uh . . ."

She didn't feel panicked, but her words still got caught in her throat. In the end, she just nodded.

"These are kind of spooky," Rob said as he moved into the room and looked at the paintings of her angel.

"Are they . . ."

Are they any good? was what Rachel wanted to ask, but she was finding it hard to talk. Maybe the panic wasn't here, but she was still nervous.

Rob took what she had said as the complete question.

"Well, yeah," he said. "The way this guy is in each painting, but he's not really defined. Just a mysterious presence. It's"—he shrugged, turning back to her—"well, I just find it a little eerie."

He stepped closer to the paintings.

"Do you—" Rachel cleared her throat. "Does it make you feel like I'm haunted?"

Rob gave her a brief smile. "Well, the thought did cross my mind, but this guy looks nothing like . . . you know."

Frank, Rachel thought, but they both sidestepped voicing the name.

"How long have you been painting?" Rob asked.

"Oh, ages. I mean, I used to do it a long time ago, but then I gave it up for a while."

Once she started, Rachel realized that it wasn't so hard to talk about it after all. Maybe it was because she always felt so comfortable with Rob. She didn't agree at all with Helen's appraisal of gay men. Without being effeminate, Rob was so in touch with his feminine side, that for Rachel, being with him was just like being with a girlfriend.

"I really like what you're doing," Rob said, as they finally went out into the living room.

He carried a portfolio and a couple of sketchbooks from Rachel's early days in college. Rachel had only relented and let him look through them because he claimed he wasn't going to budge until she did. He sat down on the sofa and started to flip through them while Rachel got them each a beer.

"I know you like the imported stuff," she said as she brought him a can of Coors, "but this is all I've got at the moment. I haven't been out much."

Rob set the art aside to take the beer from her. He studied her as she sat down, a familiar look of concern settling in his features.

"You're really doing okay now?" he asked.

Rachel nodded. "Honestly. I . . . Well, you know I haven't exactly been operating at my best this past couple of weeks, but I don't think I've really been myself for an awful lot longer than that. I'm not even sure who that person is—whether I should even be trying to recapture who I was before I got married, or if I should be concentrating on who I've become now."

"Are they that different?" Rob asked.

"That's just it. I'm not sure. And I think maybe I've been too wrapped up in trying to figure it out to give myself a chance to figure it out—if that makes any sense."

"Perfect sense," Rob assured her. "I think everybody has to go through a period of adjusting who they are with who they think they should be, or who the people around them think they should be."

"That's where I made my mistake in my marriage," Rachel said. "I let Frank—his parents, my parents, everybody from that social circle . . . I let them decide who I should be, but it didn't fit. And now—don't get me wrong—but now I get the feeling that I'm supposed to become someone that, say, Sarah, or Lily, or even Helen thinks I should be, but I'm not sure that's who I am either."

Rob nodded. "I went through a bad time like that," he said. He was looking at Rachel, but seemed to see through her, or beyond her, to another time. "The only man I ever lived with, you know, my only serious relationship, was with John."

Rob's ex-lover had come up in previous conversations, but Rob was never very forthcoming with any details concerning their relationship. Sometimes Rachel had wondered if he thought that by doing so, he might in some way offend her, but she'd never figured out how to tell him that he wouldn't.

"I remember you telling me about him," she said.

"John was a real gay rights activist, and I guess the only arguments we ever had were about how far we should let politics take over our private lives. I believed that our sexual preference was our own business; he believed we had to shout it at the world. Not to shock them—though I think John liked shocking people—but to show that it was natural, as natural as love might be between a man and a woman, just different. He wanted to help others through that confusing period when you're attracted to a member of the same sex, but because you've been taught all your life that it's wrong, you fight it and feel guilty about it and just generally live a miserable existence."

He fell silent, his gaze dropping to Rachel's sketchbooks. He flipped one open and idly turned the pages, but Rachel could tell he wasn't really looking at the drawings.

"Whatever happened to John?" she asked.

Rob wore such a pained expression when he looked up to her that she quickly added, "Never mind. I didn't—"

"There's no reason for you not to know," Rob said. "He was killed—by gay bashers in Fitzhenry Park. It'll be five years, come September."

"I'm sorry," Rachel said. "I didn't mean to pry."

Rob took a sip of his beer. "That's all right," he said. "It's just not something I like to think about, but you couldn't know."

He flipped through some more pages of the sketchbook, before looking up again.

"Anyway," he said. "John's death redefined my own perceptions of self. That's when I got actively involved in the NGLA—the Newford Gay/Lesbian Alliance. I got into it because I realized that John had been right. If those boys—they were just kids—if they'd been educated to see that we're not really that different from them, perhaps he would never have died."

Rachel nodded. "But I don't understand. What you're doing is right, so why would you question becoming involved with it?"

"Because it's not really me. I believe in everything the NGLA is doing—though I draw the line at 'outings'—but I'm still a very private person. Marching in parades, protesting outside of restaurants and bars that have discriminated against gays—this stuff is still all alien to me. But I also know that I have to keep doing it because if everyone who felt the way I do stopped, we'd end up right back in the dark ages again."

He gave her a smile that had no humor in it. "I'm not saying anything's perfect yet, any more than it is with the civil rights or women's movements, but if you look back just twenty years, you'll see that we've come an awful long way."

Rachel thought about Sarah's dedication to feminist principles, Helen's pride in being a lesbian.

"I wish that I believed in something as strongly," she said.

"It starts with believing in yourself," Rob said. He straightened up in his seat. "Listen, I've got to do a little shopping. Feel like going down to the Market with me?"

"How are you going to get there?"

"Well, I was going to take my bike, but we can grab the bus."

"Actually, I want to buy a bike," Rachel said. "Now I wish I'd already done it."

"I've got a friend who works in the Bike Pit," Rob said. "You know that place on Williamson, just a block up from McKennit? I'm sure I can get you a great deal on whatever you're looking for, so why don't we do this: you take the bus down there, and I'll take my bike and meet you. We can go for a little ride, then stop off at the Market on the way home."

"You sure your friend won't mind?"

Rob smiled. "Not at all. We could pretend you're my new girlfriend and really give him a shock."

"Just let me get my purse," Rachel said.

SEVENTEEN

So the queer was there again, Harry thought as he turned away from the telescope. Rob *Car*-ter.

He'd made it his business to get to know Carter. It was through Carter that he was going to make that all-important first contact with Rachel.

Now that he had settled on Rachel as his choice, he had to get as close to her as he could, but without the usual entanglements that arose in a male-female relationship. He wasn't interested in romance, not in its complications, or the questions that arose as such a relationship developed. His interest was far purer than that. But he did need to become a part of her small social circle, because at this stage in the proceedings, absolute verification was needed.

He was certain, or at least as certain as he could be after so many previous failures, that she was perfect, but he'd learned from those same failures.

Check, double-check. Verify.

Since she seemed to prefer the company of queers and dykes, it was as one of the former he meant to meet her. It was only a matter of time—the right time, the right place—and he'd get Carter to introduce him to her. Harry would be charming, sweet. And safe.

Insinuating himself into Carter's confidence had been as simple as Harry had expected it to be. He'd put on his cloak of invisibility, appearing as the liberal man who wore his politics on a T-shirt—protect the environment, safe sex, just say no, have a nice day. A man who, in a city the size of Newford, would never attract a second glance.

To that persona he'd added, for Carter's sake, an overlay of homosexuality—a subtle subtext of movement and speech that let Carter know his sexual proclivity—but without the appearance of availability. He wanted to keep it simple.

Carter had responded cautiously to their first "chance" encounter on Butler U's common, and warmed up on subsequent meetings where Harry manipulated their conversations so that they could "discover" just how similar their tastes were, everything from various aspects of popular culture to the lack of suitable partners.

"Please don't take this wrong, Rob," Harry had confided after a movie one night, "but while I really like you, you're not really my type in terms of . . . well, you know. As a lover. I like you, and I want to be your friend, so I don't want to start off our relationship with any misconceptions."

Carter had understood perfectly, confiding in turn that he felt the same way, but would never have had the nerve to come right out and say it.

Right, Harry had thought. He'd seen those long, soulful glances Carter had sent his way when he thought Harry wasn't looking, but Harry had just smiled and made no response. The only thing he really cared about was that Carter was primed and ready. All that was required now was a window of opportunity.

Harry had wondered why Rachel's friends were all queers and dykes—well, perhaps some of the women weren't dykes, but they were such hard-line feminists that they might as well be. They seemed like such an odd selection of friends. But then, when he got home on the day of the killing and tuned into the news reports, it all became clear.

He still couldn't get over the fact that the man who'd attacked her had been her ex-husband. Her *abusive* ex-husband.

Harry had taped every newscast that day, poring over them with great interest, not so much because of his own involvement—his anonymous participation in his victims' deaths had never held any real drawing power for him—but for what he was learning about Rachel.

The day following Frank Bedley's death, Harry had made his way down to the Ferryside branch of the Newford Public Library and spent a couple of hours going through microfilm editions of old newspapers. He'd never thought to do so when he was first interested in getting background information on Rachel, but then how was he to know that she'd ever had a public history?

The story was there, in far more detail than had been covered on the newscasts following Bedley's death. It made for fascinating reading, when you looked between the lines. What puzzled Harry the most was how a man such as Frank could have had so much beauty in hand, and then just done his best to destroy it.

Harry, himself, wasn't innocent of destruction, but the beauty that died at his hands was never perfect. And it needed to be perfect for him to fulfill what he'd come to realize was his destiny.

Society at large was suffering a mental disorder, and Harry was the one who knew why. North America had lost its mythologies. People wondered why everything kept getting worse, but they never asked him. If they had, he would've told them. Look at yourselves. You're so desperate for avatars that you'll raise up movie stars and singers and talk show hosts to be your royalty. You'll make heroes of traitors and self-serving bureaucrats.

People didn't realize it, but they needed myths to survive, just as much now as when their forebears were alive. Perhaps more. Mythology embodied the world's dreams, helped to make sense of the

great human problems. Just as the dreams of individuals exist to give
subconscious support to their conscious lives, so do myths serve as
society's dreams. They uncover the dark, hidden places where myster-
ies dwell and can turn to nightmare if left untended. They make sense
of injustice in archetypal terms. They give men and women a blueprint
for how they may respond to success or failure, tragedy or joy.

Harry saw his mission in life as a quest to reclaim society's lost
mythologies and return them to their proper relevance. And rever-
ence. And because society was so entranced with the concept of
beauty, it was beauty he meant to capture first. Perfect beauty.

Many photographers seemed to think that they could, or had
already, captured that perfection on film, but they were wrong. Unlike
them, Harry knew that somewhere out in the world the paradigm still
awaited discovery—the living, breathing icon of which filmed images,
no matter how well executed, were but vague echoes. She awaited her
disciple who had worshiped her in secret and from afar, who had preserved on film those aspects of her that he could find in her handmaid-
ens, and never despaired that one day he would find her.

The greatest irony, he had realized a very long time ago, and it was
also the element which would complete her, was that she would be
unaware of the mantle she bore. Like the gods of old, come down
from the heavens to walk among men, she would have forgotten her
destiny. It would be up to him to remind her that she was so much
more than mortal clay. And then . . . then he would give her as a gift to
the world. He would renew the fading mythology that had once
guided mankind. She would be a balm against the merciless onslaught
of actresses and actors, music stars and models who aspired to her station, but cheapened it with their tawdry private lives and blemishes.

She would not be found among them. He'd wasted years searching
through their ranks before he realized that true beauty incarnate
would be undiscovered until he found her. Unrecognized, until he
revealed her existence.

Men saw Rachel Sorensen as desirable; when he woke her divinity, she would drive them mad with her impossible beauty.

Harry smiled to himself in anticipation of the day. This time he had to be right. This time he would make no mistakes.

He had taken the photos of the women in 1216 and 1512 down from his walls, replacing them with more of Rachel. No matter where he turned, he could see her. Her features were revealed from every angle. He lived and breathed her without ever needing to view her through the telescope, but he watched her progress through it as well.

She had yet to disappoint him.

But she might. She might open her mouth and her voice come out all high-pitched and cheap. She might be a moron. She might have a mole on the inside of her thigh where he couldn't see it. A crooked tooth that her smile didn't show.

"Pictures are better than people," he'd told Arnie Norris, a photographer he'd known in Key West. "They don't disappoint you. They give you exactly what they've got, no more, no less."

He'd been feeling the man out, hoping to enlist Norris in his quest, but he'd quickly dropped the idea when he realized that Norris was unable to appreciate even such a simple concept.

"Pictures aren't real" was all that Norris had said, as though that explained everything.

What makes you think people are? Harry had felt like asking him, but he hadn't bothered pushing the matter. He realized then that the journey on which he had embarked was not one that could be shared.

Harry went back to the telescope to see what Rachel and Carter were up to. Sharing a beer. Looking at something—he brought the focus in sharper on what lay on the coffee table between them. Some kind of art portfolio. Carter hadn't mentioned anything about being an artist. Neither had anything he'd found on Rachel, but it would make sense that she would have an interest in more than just the commerce of artwork.

Beauty creates beauty. That was why it was so important to find her and reveal her to the world. Without her ideal to measure against, society was relegated to chasing slickness, sexiness, power. But they were only effects, not the origin.

He raised the telescope's line of sight slightly, frowning when he sharpened the focus and found himself looking at a close-up of Carter's mouth.

He wondered what they were talking about.

"I've met this wonderful man, Rachel; I just know you're going to like him."

Harry smiled as he enlarged his perspective so that both of them were in view.

Not likely.

He watched Rachel for a while as she listened to Carter. She was so endearing. The tilt of her head, the understanding smile, the wisdom in her eyes, the perfection of her proportions, each part of her on its own and taken as a whole. He was amazed that she could have come through so much as she had, through all those years of torment and despair, and appear as unscathed as she did now. So unaffected.

Like Christ in the wilderness, only she had suffered for far more than a mere forty days and nights.

Harry really hoped she wouldn't have to die like the others, the failures.

He thought of Ileandra; she'd been the first.

He should have known not to trust someone who didn't use a surname, but at the time it had seemed so right. This was before Cher had gone from joke to box-office success, when Madonna was still hanging around New York clubs trying to get noticed. Somewhere in his files he thought he still had a photo of her taken on some dance floor, that wanna-be look burning in her eyes.

Ileandra had seemed so different. So perfect. Exotic.

But she had failed him.

She was fresh to the city, delighted that a photographer of his stature would help her with her portfolio, especially since everyone knew that with Harry Landon there were no ulterior designs at work. No hanky-panky. At the time he was making inroads into the worlds of fashion and glamour photography and serious art; in fact, he was just putting the finishing touches on the book in which he brought them all together.

They were up on the balcony of his apartment, the light just right, the city a perfect backdrop for her magnetic appeal. It was almost like witchcraft, she was that captivating.

He'd shot a half-dozen rolls, but was now looking at her through the viewfinder.

"Don't move," he said, when she shifted position slightly.

"But you're not doing anything."

"Don't move."

He didn't want her to talk, didn't want her to change position, didn't want anything to spoil the moment, which was perfect just as it was.

"C'mon, Harry. I'm getting tired."

A bit of a whine in that Midwestern drawl.

"Don't talk," he said. "Just don't do anything."

She was sitting on a high stool that was set on top of a table, the balcony railing just below her knees so that its metal bars wouldn't interfere with the composition of the pictures. He'd chosen the setting because he wanted the height, the angle of looking up to her, which showed her to such good advantage.

He knew models who would have flinched at the somewhat precarious setting—the balcony was twenty stories up from the street—but Ileandra was fearless. It might just have been that she was too young to know fear, since youth believes itself eternal, but privately, Harry believed that it was the goddess in her that allowed her to remain so blithely unafraid.

"No," she said. "You've got enough pictures."

She started to get up, and something in Harry snapped. As he came around from behind the camera, she smiled and held out her hand, thinking he was going to help her down, but he stepped right up in front of her.

"I told you not to move," he said.

"Fuck that. I'm—"

He lashed out, straight-arming her in the chest with both arms, palms slapping against her breasts. She fell back, fingers clutching air, arms flailing, the perfect beauty of her features finally touched by fear. Her calves caught on the edge of the balcony, and over she went.

Harry stepped forward and watched her fall. She just dropped, cartwheeling, trailing a scream that grew fainter. It seemed to take forever before she finally hit the ground. He stared for the longest time at the broken shape her body made on the street below.

A goddess would have been able to fly, he thought.

He put on a mask of shock and went inside to call the police.

It was all so terrible, of course. So tragic. The police were suspicious of him, but that was to be expected. He explained what had happened, his voice numb, stumbling. They confiscated the films he'd shot of her, looking for confirmation of his story, Harry supposed.

They questioned him endlessly.

"Now tell us again, Mr. Landon. How exactly did it happen?"

"I told her to be careful. I knew we shouldn't have taken the chance. . . ."

They wanted him to trip himself up, but he was too good for that. He told the same story, he lost count of how many times, varying how he told it so that it wouldn't seem like it was something he'd memorized just to hide his complicity.

"Have you ever been arrested before, Mr. Landon?"

"I . . . When I was a kid . . ."

He told them that whole story as well, embarrassed, but honest, trying to help, but not being too eager, not eager at all, still numb with shock, after all. But it didn't seem to mean anything to them. The idea of "Peeping Harry" just seemed to give them a laugh.

Eventually they let him go. He'd been just too good for them. But then he'd had all those years of practice at pretense when he was a teenager, playing the repentant, I-want-to-make-things-right son. I'm-so-sorry.

They returned his processed films, but he insisted on having the negatives and prints sent to Ileandra's family, that he couldn't bear to look at them himself. And then he moved to Paris.

Marie-Lise Morisette died there, because now he'd learned that he also had to test them. A goddess wouldn't bleed. Under her skin, a goddess would be made of light. Pure, blinding light.

Marie-Lise hadn't been a model, an actress, or a singer. She'd just been a stunning girl who worked in one of the small bookstores along the Rue de Rivoli that sold every kind of guide to Paris one could imagine—literary, gastronomic, shopping, even cemetery guides.

She'd been charmed by Harry, and he'd been certain that she was the one.

But then she hadn't been made of light. A knife taught him that, before he covered his tracks and fled the city.

Disappointed, he'd returned to North America. His first coffee-table book was published that year, rose up the bestseller lists, and then everybody wanted Harry Landon, from *Life* to *Rolling Stone* and *Playboy*. For a while he was kept busy with assignments, then he got the hefty royalty check for the first book, and a substantial offer for a second book, and he realized that he could escape.

He became a recluse, whereabouts unknown even to his agent. Harry kept up contact on a regular basis to make sure his business interests were being served, and took the assignments that interested him in between his books, but other than that, he simply disappeared into the North American landscape, living under a variety of names, always searching for that one icon of beauty that would give his existence, and all those tragic failures, meaning.

He became inured to disappointment, each failure hanging heavily on his mind until he managed to convince himself that the women in question were as much to blame for wearing the appearance of the goddess he sought, as he was in misjudging them.

He was a chameleon, able to fit into any strata of society, piqued only by chance discoveries such as had occurred a few weeks ago with Buddy Elman, but they were few and far between. He thought as much of the death of someone like Elman as he would stepping on a roach that had invaded his apartment.

No, such deaths were easily forgotten. Incidents like the one with Elman, or when he took a knife to Sherry Jane Palmer so many years before—those were scarcely regrettable. It was only the failures that returned to haunt him, and then only at vulnerable moments such as this, when he had made a new choice. Then ghostly faces would rise up in his sleep, not even accusatory, just watching him. Accusations he thought he could take, for he had the logic and arguments forever ready in mind to validate what he had been forced to do.

But the watching faces, there was no answering them.

It doesn't matter, he told himself, eye pressed to the telescope's eyepiece. This time I won't be wrong. Isn't that right, Rachel?

He sat up straighter. Something was happening at her apartment. Carter was going. No, they were both leaving. This might be the opportunity he'd been waiting for.

He watched Rachel step out of the room, returning a moment later with her purse. Then they left the apartment together.

Neither had a car, so they'd be taking the bus. Harry did have a car, however. If he hurried, he'd be able to follow them.

He left the telescope and went into his bathroom, where he transformed himself into Carter's new friend, the gentle and charming Peter Orlick, by the simple expediency of fitting a dark wig over his short brown hair and adding a false beard and mustache to match. They were of the finest quality, the salesman—"Call me Bob"—in Los Angeles had assured him when Harry stopped in at the man's store on the way out of town, and he'd bought a variety of them.

"Your own mother wouldn't recognize you," Bob had added, probably thinking to himself that neither did he, though it wasn't for lack of trying.

"My mother's dead," Harry had told him, "so I suppose it would be strange if she did."

"Oh, I'm so sorry—" Bob began, then caught Harry's smile and realized it was a joke. He smiled in appreciation, but the strangeness of it had obviously thrown him off. He wasn't nearly as jocular finishing the sale as he had been when Harry first walked in off the street.

Harry adjusted the wig in the mirror, his mismatched eyes looking back at him—one brown, one green—until a brown contact lens made them more uniform.

He got down to the parking garage and had his Rabbit idling in the lot just as Carter and Rachel approached the bus stop, Carter pushing his bike, a safety helmet dangling from the handlebars.

Now what? Harry thought.

He was disappointed at how what had been building up into a perfect moment for his introduction to Rachel was now gone. He almost returned his car to the garage, but when the number 34 stopped and Rachel got on the bus, Carter waving to her before pedaling off himself, Harry decided to follow her anyway.

Since she hadn't been out in days, he was curious about where she might be going.

EIGHTEEN

Lily tried calling Rachel before going out, but the only reply she got was Rachel's answering machine. A male voice, the one from the sample tape that had come with the machine, asked her to leave a message. Lily hesitated. She started to hang up, but then told herself she was just being stupid.

"This is, um, Lily," she said. "I was just, um, calling to see what you were up to. Well, call me when you, um, get a chance."

It's a good thing they don't hand out points for elocution with those things, she thought, because she'd fail miserably. Public speaking had never been her forte, and every time she talked to one of those machines, it felt as though she were confronting a sea of faces, each one hanging eagerly on her every word.

It was funny that Rachel hadn't answered, though.

Lily wondered for a moment if she was home, but just not answering the phone. Maybe she was going through a bad moment and didn't want to talk to anybody. Or couldn't.

No, Lily told herself. If she was in, Rachel would have answered the phone.

"When it gets bad," Rachel had confided to Lily once, "I find myself having long conversations with magazine subscription people and carpet cleaners just to have someone to talk to."

Rachel would definitely have answered. She'd just gone out, that was all. As Lily herself should be doing if she wanted to have anything to eat in the house for the weekend.

It was time she stopped mothering Rachel so much, she decided. Smothering was more like it. But the death of her ex had hit Rachel hard, being there when it had happened and all. It was a wonder she wasn't in worse shape, really.

Lily changed into a pair of black flared shorts and a plain white cotton T-shirt, then walked to the Crowsea Market. When she got back, Tom was waiting for her, comfortably ensconced on one of her landlady's wicker chairs on the front porch.

Tom had the landlady's fat tabby asleep on his knee. He gave Lily a broad smile as she came up the steps.

"Hey there, stranger," he said.

Lily hadn't seen him for a couple of days, but it wasn't Tom's fault. She'd just been too busy with Rachel.

"Hey there, yourself," she said.

Tom set the cat on the floor, where it gave him a disgruntled look then sauntered off as though that had always been its intention. Lily smiled. All animals had their individual personalities, but there was something universal about certain species' traits. Cats just never seemed to lose their cool.

Her gaze returned to Tom, and she realized just how much she'd been missing him.

"Do you want to come up?" she asked.

Tom rose in a lazy stretch from the chair and took the bag of groceries from her. He raised an eyebrow and gave her a comical leer.

"Depends what you had in mind," he said. "I'm just a babe in the woods when it comes to you high-powered money folks, you know, and I've heard you're capable of taking advantage of a simple artist in ways that leave him forever after spoiled for common liaisons."

Lily laughed. "You wish."

Tom tried for a pout, but it came out crooked and he just looked silly. Still, he wasn't one to give up easily.

"Surely," he said, "you're not going to tell me that there's no chance for a little—what did you tell me your mother used to call it? Pillow talk?"

"Help me wash the vegetables and then we'll see."

"I don't know why you don't wash them as you're going to use them."

"I just don't like putting them away in the fridge when they're all full of grit."

"Ah. Something else you learned from your mother?"

Lily was holding the screen door open with one hand and working the key with the other. With both arms occupied, all she could do was aim a kick at his shin.

Tom danced back. "You'll pay for that, you know."

He kept up a playful banter all the way up the stairs and into her apartment. By the time Lily had taken the groceries from him and put the bag on the counter, she was feeling as aroused as Tom obviously was. She looked at the lettuce and carrots poking up from the top of the bag.

"Oh, screw cleaning them," she said.

She made room on the main shelf of her fridge and placed the groceries, bag and all, upon it.

"But what would your mother say?" Tom asked her.

Lily turned slowly to face him. She pulled her T-shirt up over her head. She wasn't wearing a bra, a fact that Tom had no doubt noticed the moment she'd come up the steps with the cotton shirt sticking to her because of the heat.

"What do you think?" she said.

Later they stood in front of the sink, Lily wearing Tom's shirt, held closed by one button, Tom just in his boxer shorts, and cleaned the vegetables.

"So how's Rachel doing?" Tom asked.

Lily smiled. She had to give him credit for this. While she knew he still didn't much care for Rachel, he'd been keeping it to himself as best he could. And he'd been very good about all the time she'd been spending with Rachel lately.

"She's doing okay," Lily said. "I think she went out today, and that's a good sign, and the last couple of times I've been over, she's seemed more and more relaxed. No, that's not quite the right word. It's more like she's been liberated."

"Well, that makes sense. With her husband dead, she's got no reason to be scared anymore."

How to explain to a man that once you've been violated, or treated as Frank Bedley had treated Rachel for all those years, you never got over being scared? Lily was lucky. She was one of that small percentage of women who'd never been abused, but even she got nervous walking down her own street at night.

"I suppose," she said.

"Is she going back to work on Monday?"

"I think so. I hope so. It's not doing her any good staying cooped up in that apartment all the time."

"I thought you said she'd gone out today."

"Well, she did. It's just that I think she's gotten a little phobic about crowds and strangers. I hope nothing weird happens to her while she's out, because who knows how far that'd set her back."

"She should see a shrink."

Lily sighed. "She *is* seeing a therapist. It's just . . ." She paused, turning to him with a handful of leaf lettuce in her hand, dripping water onto the counter. "It's so frustrating knowing that there's this incredibly bright and sweet and, yes, even brave woman locked up behind all those fears. And you can't even tell her they're groundless fears, because she's had to live through what most of us only experience in nightmares."

Tom nodded sympathetically, but while Lily knew he was trying to understand, and had been all along, he really didn't have a whole lot of patience for either Rachel or her problems. Lily was never sure whether it was because of this unfounded dislike he had for Rachel, or because he, like too many men, trivialized Rachel's problems. He was sympathetic—you'd have to be, if you had any humanity in you at all—but he was also of the school that said, Okay, it was bad, but it's done with now. It's in the past. You just have to get over it and carry on.

Lily went back to washing the lettuce she was holding.

Rachel and Tom were her best friends in the world, she thought. What was it going to take to get them to be friends with each other as well?

NINETEEN

"Good lord," Rachel said as she and Rob stepped into the Bike Pit. "I don't even know where to start."

Although she'd taken the bus, Rob had arrived before her. He'd locked his bike to a street sign and was standing in front of the store waiting for her when she came down the block.

Rob smiled. "It's not as bad as it looks."

"Oh really?" Rachel said.

She found the dizzying variety of goods on display more than a little intimidating and was tempted to just back right out of the store again without making a purchase. At that moment, the door closed automatically behind them with a faint hydraulic hiss.

Now our escape route's cut off, she thought.

"Tony will sort it all out for you," Rob assured her.

Rachel wasn't so sure.

"I feel like I did the first time I went to buy a new pair of running shoes after not having any for years," she told Rob. "There must have been a hundred different kinds, and when the salesman asked me what

I wanted them for, my mind just went blank. Then he started to ask, Well, are they for jogging, biking, basketball . . . the list seemed to go on forever."

As did the goods in this store, she thought.

The wall closest to the door was taken up with bike helmets, lights, horns, mirrors and every sort of accessory Rachel could imagine—as well as those she couldn't. Farther along that wall were racks of those stretchy biking shorts along with tops made of the same material, T-shirts and cotton tops. Then all the biking shoes . . .

Rachel didn't even want to think about them.

She turned to look at the bicycles, but their numbers were, if anything, even more bewildering. There were three-speeds, five-speeds, ten-speeds, mountain bikes. A barrage of brand names leapt out at her. Trek. Jazz. Norco. Firoi. Rocky Mountain. Diamond Back.

"I can't possibly sort through all of this," she said, turning back to Rob in dismay.

"That's why I'm here," he told her. "I knew this'd happen, because I went through the same thing last year when I came in to buy my own bike. Before that, the last one I'd ridden was a one-speed CCM that I got when I was fourteen."

"We didn't ride bikes when I was a teenager," Rachel said. "It wasn't considered cool."

Rob's eyebrows rose quizzically. "And cool was important?"

"Of course it was. Except the more you tried, the more it had to seem like you weren't trying."

"I guess some things never change."

Rachel shook her head. "People can change," she said, investing the words with a certainty she wasn't sure was true.

She found herself thinking of her ex. Frank hadn't changed—maybe he couldn't. Maybe it was simply impossible for him. Maybe she wouldn't be able to either.

"I think I'm getting depressed," she said.

Rob gave her a look of sympathy. The easy familiarity of his smile helped her to regain some of the good mood that had started to drain away with the turn their conversation had taken.

"Let me get Tony," he said.

He was back in moments with a short, smiling Italian.

"So you're Rachel," Tony said, putting out his hand. "Tony DiRusso. How're you doing?"

As though to make up for his diminutive stature—he was a couple of inches shorter than Rachel—Tony obviously worked out on a regular basis. And seriously. His white Bike Pit T-shirt was pulled tight against a broad chest and thick shoulders, the dark cast of his complexion standing out in sharp contrast. Thick curly hair, dark as the old-fashioned ducktail he wore, covered his arms, and though it was barely noon, he already had a heavy five o'clock shadow.

Rachel took his hand, but before she could reply to him, he was already talking again.

"Rob's told me all about you. I figure, *he's* got a girlfriend? Well, this I've gotta see."

"But I'm—" Rachel began, glancing at Rob.

He gave her a wink.

"That is—"

"Anyway," Tony said, "I'll be with you guys as soon as I can. We're a little shorthanded today, and I've got a major pain in the ass trying to return a bike that he trashed in a one-on-one with a cab. Says he never had any trouble with his previous bike, so it's got to be the fault of the one he bought here and he wants his money back. Can you figure it?"

"That doesn't seem very reasona—"

"Just give me five minutes," Tony went on, "and I'll be right with you. Meanwhile, why don't you have a look around, see if anything appeals to you."

And then he was off, back to the cash counter, where the irate customer was impatiently waiting for his return. The man towered over Tony, a big hulking figure in blue jeans and a black sleeveless T-shirt. He had a tattoo of a snake curled up around a dagger on one shoulder, black cowboy boots and the sort of grim features that would always be set in a frown.

Rachel turned away when the man looked up and frowned at her.

"Your friend seems nice," she told Rob.

"But he's not what you expected?"

Rachel smiled. "Well, not exactly."

"You thought he'd be gay."

"I guess I did," Rachel said. "It's silly, really, isn't it? I mean, you and I are friends and I'm not gay."

"Not that silly," Rob said. "I mean, everybody tends to hang out with their own because it's more comfortable. Besides, Tony is gay."

Rachel glanced back at the cash counter, where Tony was trying to placate his customer without giving in to the stupidity of the man's claims. At least Rob was kind enough not to mention that assuming a person's sexual proclivity simply by their appearance was a fruitless and, more to the point, narrow-minded enterprise. What difference did it really make? It didn't change who the person was.

She thought she'd gotten past that kind of thinking, but she supposed that society had bred such assumptions into her at such an early age that it might be impossible to eradicate them completely.

Her gaze shifted to the door as it opened, noting the dark-haired man who came in, then turned back to her companion. But Rob's gaze had been caught by the opening of the door as well. A smile broadened across his features as he obviously recognized the newcomer.

"Peter!" he called.

The man returned Rob's smile and ambled over. He nodded pleasantly to Rachel, then turned his attention to Rob.

"Well, this is a nice surprise, Rob," he said. "What are you doing here?"

"Helping Rachel pick out a bike," Rob said. He made the introductions, then added, "How about you?"

Peter patted his stomach. "I've decided it's time to start another exercise regime, so I'm here to buy a bike as well."

He looked, Rachel thought, about as fit as a person could without being a professional athlete. There wasn't an ounce of fat anywhere on his lean frame.

"You seem pretty fit to me," she said.

"Thank you," Peter said. "And so do you. It's staying that way that's the real battle—wouldn't you say? How did a character on the comics page put it a day or so ago? 'The waist is such a terrible thing to mind.'"

They all laughed at the corny play on words, Rob longest of all.

"So," Peter said. "Since you're the only person I know with a bike, Rob, you must be the expert. Where do we start?"

As Rob told Peter about his friend Tony, Rachel explored the faint twinge of familiarity that she got when she looked at Peter. Not the eyes, or the hair or beard or even the build. It was around the mouth, she decided. Only *where* did she know him from?

She also noted how, beside her, Rob had straightened his posture and seemed a bit fidgety. There was definitely an attraction at work here, she thought. For Rob's sake, she hoped it wasn't one-way.

"I just want something that I won't immediately fall off of and make a complete fool of myself on," Peter was saying, when a sudden disruption by the counter interrupted him.

"Screw that!" Tony's irate customer yelled.

"Please," Tony said, still trying to appease the man. He lifted a placating hand between them, but the bigger man just gave Tony a shove, sending him reeling back against the counter.

"Hey!" Rob called over.

"Fuck you, too, faggot," the man said, turning in their direction.

"There's no need to—" Rachel began, but the man cut her off.

"What? None of you are faggots? What the hell else would you call the way the bunch of you are mincing around?" His gaze roved from Peter to Rob, then settled on Rachel. "Hey, the surgeon did a nice job on the sex change, honey. Did he fix the plumbing as well?"

Rachel flushed with embarrassment at being singled out. For a moment she felt like she was trapped in her marriage again, helpless against Frank's cruel barbs. It didn't seem any different. First the words, then he'd start using his fists to drive his points home.

But this wasn't Frank, just some lout, and she wasn't helpless. She had her self-defense training, and she wasn't alone here, either. She had Rob, and his friend Peter, both of whom were stepping forward in her defense.

It wasn't needed. Before the man had a chance to draw them into a physical confrontation, Tony pushed himself back from the counter. With the bigger man's attention distracted, Tony got a hold of his arm and twisted it painfully up behind his back. By that time, the other floor clerk and a man and a woman who'd been working in the rear of the shop had joined Tony and helped him eject the man from the store.

"Jesus," Rob said.

They stood by the window and watched the man yelling back at them through the glass. Peter bent down and retrieved a piece of paper that the man had dropped. It turned out to be a bill of sale.

"Ian Hughes," Peter said, reading the man's name from it. "What a loser." He turned to Rachel and added, "Are you all right?"

Rachel nodded. She was still flushed, the adrenaline rush only just starting to wane. For a moment there she'd been sure that they were going to be caught in the middle of a melee.

"I'm really sorry about that," Tony said when he came back into the store.

He looked mortified, Rachel thought, understanding perfectly what he must be feeling.

"It was hardly your fault," Peter said.

He handed Tony the bill of sale that Hughes had dropped.

"We've never had anything like this happen before," Tony said. He glanced down at the slip of paper he held. "I feel like taking his address from this and putting him on a hundred magazine subscription lists, but"—he crushed the bill of sale into a ball—"that'd just bring me down to his level, I guess."

He tossed the paper ball into a wastepaper basket behind the counter, then wiped his hands on his jeans.

"Okay," he said, turning to Rachel. "Let's see if I can't make it up to you for the damper that jerk put on the afternoon. You're looking for a bike?"

"Two actually," Peter said.

Tony glanced between Peter and Rachel. "Just street bikes, or are you planning to do any long distance or maybe trail riding?"

"Ladies first," Peter said, making a graceful hand gesture toward Rachel.

He's gay, too, she thought and felt oddly comforted. The confrontation with Hughes had brought all her fears about strange men back to the surface. The realization that Peter was gay let her relax again.

"Oh, just for riding around town," she told Tony.

"And what kind of price range are we looking at?"

"Gee, I hadn't really considered that."

"Okay, we'll get back to it later." He took a few steps away and gave her an appraising look. "You've got the leg reach," he said, leading her toward a rack of bikes on the far wall, "so how about one of these . . . ?"

With his easy and friendly way of explaining things, Tony soon had her feeling as though she actually knew something about bicycles, and in no time at all both she and Peter were test driving various models in the long alley behind the store.

Two hours later, her bank account was several hundred dollars the poorer and she was out on the street with a new mountain bike, complete with fenders and a rack on the back. She was wearing the black biking shorts and Bike Pit T-shirt that Tony had thrown in as part of the sizable discount he'd given both her and Peter on their purchases. The clothes she'd been wearing were bagged, along with her purse, and attached to the rack of her bike with a pair of bungee cords. She was holding her helmet by its strap.

Peter had bought a model similar to hers, but he'd forgone the fenders.

"I don't plan to ride in the rain, anyway," he'd said.

He'd passed on the shorts as well, but his free T-shirt was in a bag, hanging from the handlebars of his bike.

"Well," he said, "we're all dressed up—especially Rachel—but we've got no place to go."

"Are you up for a ride along the river?" Rob asked her.

"Sure. Just so long as we take it easy, because I'm not at all in shape for anything too frantic."

"Ditto," Peter put in.

Putting on their helmets, they followed Rob to where he'd left his own bike, then let him lead the way across town to the bike path that followed the river up through Butler University and beyond.

TWENTY

"I ache," Harry said, maintaining his Peter persona, "in places I never even knew existed."

Rachel moaned. "Don't remind me."

"And you're the one who thought I was fit."

The two of them were sprawled on the grass alongside the bike path, just north of the Kelly Street Bridge. Rob, still on his bike, leaned across its handlebars and smiled at the pair of them.

"Wait'll the cramps in your calf muscles kick in around three o'clock this morning," he said.

"I think I'll just die here instead," Harry told him.

"Well, I was ready to stop ages ago, but no. Our intrepid cyclists had to prove their worth."

Harry turned his head until his cheek was on the grass and he was looking directly at Rachel.

"Don't you hate people when they gloat?" he asked.

Rachel laid her own cheek on the grass so that she was facing him as well and gave a weak nod in response.

"Especially when they're right," she added.

The smile she gave him was warm, her whole attitude one of being relaxed in the company of friends.

Oh, she's bought me, Harry thought. Hook, line and sinker. Peter Orlick's another safe homosexual who can be her friend, and she's already completely at ease in his company. And why not? The persona of Peter that he'd created was one whom only the most die-hard of homophobes would find cause to dislike. Rachel couldn't help but feel unthreatened in his presence.

The afternoon had also proved her to be everything he'd hoped for and more. She was bright, vivacious and so beautiful it hurt to look at her. Not a blemish on her skin—at least not on what he could see. Her voice a perfect timbre. Her every movement a step in some sacred pavane.

If *she* wasn't Beauty, then perhaps the paradigm he sought didn't exist at all, and that he couldn't—wouldn't—accept.

There was only the final test, but he was not in any hurry to make it. Light already seemed to shine through her skin. He was certain that she could fly. That she would bleed light. That the revelation of her divinity would set the world back on track once more. Then she would be the lost goddess that society's mythologies lacked and unbeknownst longed for. She would belong to all men, all women.

And have her they would. But after striving to find her, after all the time he had invested in what seemed to be a futile search, he was greedy to have her to himself for just a little longer. He deserved that much for all the long years of struggle.

He imagined licking her skin. She would taste like sunlight. She would . . .

He had to look away.

He let his gaze lift up to the sky. The deep blue stretched in a perfect circle as far as he could see in any direction. A tight drum of sky that thrummed to his heartbeat, filling him with an overwhelming sense of peace.

"You know what I'd like?" he said.

"Uh-uh," Rachel said.

"For this day never to end." He sat up, maintaining the pretense of stiffness, and looked over to Rob. "What say we make an evening of it—just the three of us? We'll go to dinner, maybe a movie after?"

"I'd love to, Peter," Rob said, "but I've got an NGLA meeting tonight."

The goddess was unaware of herself, Harry thought, but surely this was her unconscious divinity offering him a gift for all those years that he'd searched for her. He could feel an invisible presence in the air— her providence, her bounty, reaching out to him.

"So skip it," he said, continuing the pretense to include Rob in his plans for the evening. "Surely they can spare you for just this one meeting?"

"Not this time," Rob said. "I'm chairing it."

Harry sighed. "Now that's depressing." He turned to Rachel. "How about you, Rachel?"

"I . . ."

He saw the momentary uncertainty, the flicker of fear rise in her eyes. He kept his own gaze mild, its focus on her own, but he was aware of every inch of her body lying beside him, the soft mounds of her breasts under the T-shirt, the long length of her perfect legs. She sat up, as though she'd suddenly become aware of the alluring picture she was presenting and was embarrassed by the display.

"I understand," he said. "It won't be the same without Rob. Instead of three brave musketeers, we'll just be a pair of limp noodles, pretending to be people."

Rachel laughed. "No. I'd like to come. It's just that . . . ." She glanced at Rob, but he only shrugged. "I'd want to, you know, go home and have a shower, change."

"It's a bargain," Harry said, and he thrust out his hand. "I want to do the same."

They shook solemnly, as though completing some serious piece of business.

"Honest to God," Rob said. "I don't know which one of you's the goofier."

Rachel and Peter each pointed to the other, then all three of them laughed.

"You'll have to give me your address so that I can pick you up," Harry said, when they'd recovered their breath. "Or we could meet somewhere, if that's easier."

"I live just over in the Sky Towers," Rachel said, pointing away from the river to where the top few floors of the two apartment complexes could be seen. "In the same building as Rob."

She gave him the number of her apartment, then with a grimace slowly got to her feet and mounted her bike.

"I'll pick you up at seven?" Harry said, making a question of it.

"But not on a bike—I don't think I can even face the ride home." She shook her head ruefully. "I can't believe that I paid this much money just to do this to myself. It's worse than aerobics ever was."

"First time's the worst," Rob told her.

Peter got back on his own bike and put on his helmet.

"Are you still up for golf on Sunday?" he asked Rob.

Rob nodded. "But I warn you, I'm not much good at the game. If it's a par-three hole, you can guarantee I'll make it in six."

"Exactly my speed," Harry assured him.

He went with them up the ramp that led from the bike path to Kelly Street, but turned right, back across the river toward downtown, while they made the left-hand turn that would take them to the Sky Towers.

"Until seven!" he called after them.

Rachel turned and waved back, her bike almost wobbling into Rob's before she regained her balance and straightened out again. Harry smiled as he watched them go.

Lines from a Burns poem came to his mind: *But to see her was to love her/Love but her, and love forever.*

If the world but knew my love, he thought.

Not yet, but soon it would. The final decade of a millennium was always a time for great change, and he would bring into the world what hadn't been seen for thousands of years. Divinity wearing mortal flesh.

But first she was his. For an hour. A day. A week. However long he could steal from chance and fate until she must shed her mortal disguise and be revealed for who she was.

Until then, she was his secret. Her divine light shining only for him.

After picking up his car, Harry went back to his own apartment to have a shower himself. He dressed by his window, peering through the telescope in hopes of catching a glimpse of Rachel as she was getting ready, but she didn't come into her living room until just before seven, already dressed.

Pulling up a chair, he stared at her for a long time, comparing the woman in his lens to the one with whom he'd spent the afternoon. Tonight she was dressed in a short black slipdress that seemed to make her hair appear even more golden. The dress had spaghetti straps, baring the lovely curves of her shoulders and neck—he much preferred that to the football linebacker look of padded shoulders. The dress's décolletage was accented with some sort of iridescent fabric that shaped a heart enclosing her breasts, the point descending to her solar plexus. The V of the heart was decorated with fringes that seemed to shiver every time she moved.

She wore very little makeup—another point in her favor so far as Harry was concerned. Too many beautiful women ruined their natural good looks trying to compete with the false imagery to be found in fashion magazine spreads. He could never understand why a truly beautiful woman would still feel it necessary to hide behind a mask.

The only jewelry he could see was a pair of dangling earrings, their shimmering color matching the décolletage of her dress. She walked about in her stockings, but he hoped she'd put on a pair of heels when they went out.

Most people, Harry had long ago decided, were like photographs marred by motion. They posed and vogued, trying to negotiate a three-dimensional world by two-dimensional rules. It was only very few who weren't cheap imitations of a fashion ad. Rachel could definitely be counted among their number, but then she'd have to be, considering who she was.

After a time, Harry switched to his camera and had shot an entire roll of film before he realized that it was time to pick her up. He lingered by the window, watching her for a moment longer, then straightened up. He picked up his car keys and a pair of thin black leather gloves on his way out of the apartment. The gloves went into the side pocket of his sports jacket.

He took her to Zwicker's in the Harbor Ritz. It was a luxurious, five-star restaurant overlooking the lake from its height at the top of the hotel complex. Phillipe Gagnon, long one of the senior aides in Umberto Menghi's restaurant empire, had opened Zwicker's in 1986. He served as his own chef, the house specialities leaning toward an Italian-Californian cuisine. There were no prices on the menu.

"I know it's a bit much," Harry apologized, "but I'm still new to town. This is the only place I knew of where I thought we'd be guaranteed a good meal."

"I'll say," Rachel said. "I've always wanted to come here, but . . ." She glanced down at the menu. "I don't want to sound like a complete hick, but how do we know what anything costs?"

"In a place like this, you're not supposed to even think about it. Besides, it's my treat."

"Oh, no. I'm sure it's far too expensive."

Harry shook his head. "Not at all. And just think of how much fun you'll have telling Rob what he missed out on."

"I suppose."

They returned to studying their menus, until finally Rachel just set hers aside.

"It all sounds so good," she said, "that I can't make up my mind."

Harry pointed to one of the entrées. "I'd recommend the squid-ink fettuccine with baby scallops and fresh basil."

The service was impeccable; the view of the lake, stunning. Their table was by the window, far enough from any other to foster intimacy, but Harry was careful to steer clear of any possible hint of romance. Rachel's presence was enough for him, and it was imperative that she remain feeling unthreatened.

"Rob says you're a photographer," Rachel said as they were sipping their after-dinner brandies.

"I am—or maybe I should say, I was. I'm not really sure what I am anymore, to be honest. The kind of work I was doing in Hollywood didn't exactly make me feel all that proud of my profession."

"You lived in L.A.?"

Harry nodded. "I was a free-lance fashion photographer, but I also played the paparazzo—you can't make your living as a photographer in L.A. and not get caught up in that kind of craziness. I also did a lot of portfolio work for models and actors."

Rachel smiled. "And what is it that you'd *really* like to be taking pictures of?"

"Beauty," Harry said in all seriousness. "Not pretense, not the kind of work that gets airbrushed to perfection, but genuine beauty that doesn't require any embellishment because it simply is."

"Do you mean the intrinsic beauty that every object, every person has?"

"No," Harry said. "Objective beauty that exists, perfect in and of itself."

"I don't think it exists."

Harry laughed. "Well, don't take this wrong, but I'm looking at a perfect example of such beauty at this very moment."

Harry regarded the faint blush that touched her cheeks and wondered if she could really be so unaware of her flawless gift. But that, too, fit with his impression of how the goddess would be until he woke her.

Rachel shook her head. "I appreciate the compliment," she said, "but you know the idea of beauty is too subjective and, so far as I'm concerned, limiting to be classified in that kind of a way."

"What do you mean?"

"Different cultures, at different times in our own culture, have all seen and still see beauty differently. At one time—as recent as seventy-five years ago—the male artistic tradition defined female beauty as lush fertility symbols. From the fifteenth to the seventeenth centuries, it was ripe, rounded bellies; in the nineteenth, it was plump faces and shoulders and generous buttocks and thighs. Look in any gallery; it lasted up into the present century.

"But the last few decades have changed that image, and for the worse. The current epitome for a woman is thinness to the point of anorexia and youth at all costs. Because of the way the media portrays women, in everything from the way photographs of a woman over fifty are *always* airbrushed to look younger to the endless parade of advertising imagery that's impossible to ignore, we've been given this false idea of what being beautiful is supposed to look like and mean, but all it really does is hurt us."

Harry still wasn't sure what she was getting at. "How does that change what's beautiful?" he asked.

"Look," Rachel said. "What happens is that women who are unattractive by those standards become enslaved to the cosmetic and diet industries. The sexual revolution of the sixties was supposed to free us. Suddenly women could be in the workplace, on a par with men, but they end up spending up to thirty percent of their salaries on pursuing the impossible dream that's fed to them by the fashion industry. Instead of being able to feel any pride in themselves, they're constantly barraged with imagery to make them feel inferior.

"And it's not that much better for an attractive woman. Imagine what it would be like to always be judged by your looks—something over which you have no control—rather than by what you're capable of doing. No matter what a beautiful woman does, it's always assumed that her accomplishments are due to her beauty."

"I see," Harry said, though he didn't really.

It was an interesting intellectual exercise, and an intriguing one as well, but when you knew, unequivocally as he did, that Beauty had set aside her godhood to walk among mortals, that she was sitting across from you, how could you possibly take anything else seriously?

"I've never really considered it in those terms," he added, "but I suppose that must have been a subconscious reason for my disenchantment with the work I was doing in L.A. It all seemed so trivial."

"But deadly, too," Rachel said, "because there's no escaping from that awful mythology that's been built up over the past twenty years. Society always prefers its women to be cloistered away where they can't do any harm. In Victorian times, we had the proliferation of women's 'diseases' that kept us in our beds or in asylums. After the Second World War, we were happy housewives, safely trapped in our homes. But every time we try to assert ourselves, be it the suffragettes at the turn of the century or the women's rights movement in the sixties, society finds a way to put us down.

"Today we live in a society where women, for all their so-called freedom, live in a constant state of guilt and fear. We're afraid of our husbands or the stranger who might rape us; we feel guilty because we can't match the ideal vision of what we're supposed to be: impossibly thin and impossibly beautiful."

"Women don't have to follow fashion's dictates," Harry said. "They have the choice to ignore them."

Rachel shook her head. "But that's what's so insidious. We're not given a choice. The image of the ideal we're supposed to attain is instilled in us from the moment we're born. We're not even aware of how desperately we strive toward it, and it's killing us."

"Surely it's not so bad as that," Harry said, genuinely surprised at the quiet vehemence with which she put forth her convictions.

"Not so bad?" Rachel said. "I think it's worse. When we hear so much about the violence toward women in their marriages and relationships lately, it's not *just* because the media has decided it's newsworthy; it's because it's on the rise as well. One in six women have suffered rape, but almost fifty percent have suffered attempted rape. And what we *don't* hear about in the news is how sixty percent of the women in this country have serious eating disorders. The present concepts concerning 'beauty' have given almost all women a compulsive fear and fixation on food."

"Surely not," Harry said.

But Rachel nodded. "The American Anorexia and Bulimia Association says that anorexia and bulimia strike a million American women every year. Each year, 150,000 American women die of anorexia. With five to fifteen percent of hospitalized anorexics dying in treatment, anorexia has one of the highest fatality rates of a mental illness. But you don't *hear* about any of this, do you? We're never told of the toll that's paid to serve this image of the perfect woman that's presented to us every moment of every day in ads and the like. It's not like they're in a pornographic magazine that we can simply refuse to look at; it's there whenever we open a magazine, turn on the TV, look at a billboard.

"'This is what we're supposed to be' is the bottom line of what we're being told. And if we're not, then we're not real women. But real women are as varied in appearance as real men. We come in different shapes and sizes, we get age lines and laugh lines just the same as men do, but instead of our lifetime of experience making us look distinguished, we're told that it makes us look used up."

Beauty was eternal, Harry thought. It didn't get used up. It remained forever unchanged and perfect, because that was inherent in its divinity. But he didn't tell Rachel that. She would learn soon enough when he woke her godhood.

"And do you blame men for this?" he asked instead.

Rachel shook her head. "I blame society. I blame all of us for being blind to the discrepancies that separate men and women. What I blame men for is the power they think they're automatically entitled to wield over the women in their lives, which is partly the fault of the way we're all brought up—you know, women are objects, and there's nothing wrong with imposing your will upon an object. But they have to take responsibility for their part in that horror show as well."

She fell silent and looked out the window. Harry allowed her the moment of contemplation without interruption.

"I'm sorry," she said finally. "I didn't mean to lay all of that on you. It's just that I've been becoming more and more aware of just how serious these issues are, and I can't keep them bottled up inside me."

"I don't mind. I think I've learned something tonight," Harry lied.

"Yes, well." Rachel sighed. "It's just that women are living in this constant state of stress that touches every aspect of their lives: how they look, how they have to constantly prove their worth, how they're always afraid. My marriage was a perfect example—it was like living with a time bomb. I never knew when or what would set it off."

The pain in her eyes woke an odd sympathy in Harry. Why, he couldn't help but wonder, had the goddess allowed such tragedy to infuse the life of this vessel she wore?

"When I first got out of that relationship," Rachel said, "all I wanted to do was to curl up and die. But since then I've slowly been trying to learn how to live as my own person. I realized the unfairness of the way women were always defined by the men in their lives and resolved to change that."

"Amen," Harry said.

"But it's hard. I started reading more and more about women's issues, about what's happening to us, and I realized that it's not that simple. It's not just how men treat us, it's how we treat each other, it's how we buy into the ideal without even realizing it. We're under constant, unrelieved stress.

"Scientific studies have already documented the damage that stress in the workplace creates in an individual; well, women suffer that every day of their lives, except for us it's an invisible illness. Because it revolves around conceptions of beauty and women's need to attain it— a need that's forced upon us—it's not considered valid, but it's just as damaging."

"But beauty still exists," Harry said.

"Subjective beauty," Rachel clarified.

"I'm not so sure," Harry said. "I agree with you that the images that we get from advertising and the like are false ones—and God knows my work in L.A. makes me responsible for perpetuating that false ideal—but I still believe that there exists a paradigm of beauty that simply is. That owes her existence not to the purveyors of the cosmetic and dietary industries, but to her own innate perfection."

Harry watched her carefully as he spoke, but he saw no flickering fire in Rachel's eyes, no sign that the goddess heard him, that she recognized him.

"This paradigm," Rachel asked. "Is she young?"

"She'd be ageless."

"Then don't you see? You're just buying into the same myth."

Harry shook his head. "She would have her origin in the distant past—think of her as an aspect of mother earth."

"But—"

She broke off her next question as the waiter came by to ask if they'd like refills on their coffee. When Rachel indicated that she would, the waiter began to pour the dark liquid into her cup. At that moment, another of the restaurant's patrons, walking by, bumped into the waiter and he lost his grip on the coffee decanter. It slipped from his fingers, shattering on the table, spraying Rachel with hot coffee.

There was a moment of utter pandemonium: Rachel scrambling back from the table, a cry of pain escaping her lips as the scalding coffee splattered her arms and legs. The waiter stunned to immobility, then rushing to help her. Harry rising from his side of the table, a red rage in his eyes. The maître d' and a busboy hurrying over to help. The customer who'd caused the accident offering profuse apologies.

It was all cleared up soon enough. Rachel's burns were superficial—it was the shock of the hot coffee, more than the actual pain, that had caused her distress. But her dress was soaked. While she went into the rest room to try to clean up the damage, the restaurant's owner himself came out of the kitchen to apologize. The meal was free, he assured Harry, and he hoped that the gentleman and his companion would accept a free dinner some other night at their convenience to make up for the unpleasant experience.

Harry was all concern for Rachel and calm in dealing with the restaurant staff, but inside he was seething. The evening was ruined, since Rachel—understandably enough—wanted to go home. She invited him upstairs for a drink—"Just let me change out of this dress"—but he declined politely.

It was all wrong. Everything had gone wrong. Though Rachel wasn't seriously injured, her forearms had become inflamed from where the coffee had struck her. Her legs, somewhat protected by her nylons, had fared better, but not by much, he was sure.

He couldn't bear to look at her like this, but he let none of his anger, or his distaste for her blemished skin, show. When she asked him to come up, he simply begged off with a promise to call soon—"Perhaps we can get together with Rob later in the week"—and beat a hasty retreat.

He kept his mind carefully blank until he reached his car. He sat in it for a long time, hands on the steering wheel, knuckles going white with the tightness of his grip, his gaze staring forward, unblinking, unseeing. Finally, he let go of the steering wheel. He started the car and pulled away from Tower A, but he didn't drive across the parking lot to the underground garage below his own building.

Instead, he headed back downtown.

TWENTY-ONE

Bolting the door of her apartment behind her, Rachel went into the bathroom, where she stripped off her dress and pantyhose. Both could be salvaged; it wasn't as though the waiter had spilled red wine on them. But oh, it had hurt. She lay the dress and hose over the edge of the tub, then sat down on the toilet and smoothed an ointment over the red inflammation on her forearms and thighs.

It had been an unpleasant way to end an otherwise enjoyable evening, she thought. Mind you, the lecture she'd given Peter when he started to talk about beauty might not have been exactly endearing either, but she'd gotten the impression that he'd been genuinely interested in the issue, that he was actually going to think about what they'd been discussing.

He was such a nice man. Too bad he was gay. Not that there was anything intrinsically wrong with his being gay; it was just that he was the first man to whom she'd found herself attracted in a very long time. So of course he *had* to be gay.

Well, at least she'd found herself a new friend.

Wiping off her makeup, she washed up. Thinking back on her conversation with Peter, she frowned at her reflection in the mirror. Yes, it was flattering to be found attractive, but when would people understand that when that was *all* that was seen in you it was just as bad as being plain?

There'd been a time—her last years of high school and as a first-year student in college before she'd met Frank—that she'd gone out of her way to downplay her looks. She'd eschewed makeup, kept her hair shoulder-length and tied back in a short braid, gravitated toward unflattering styles of clothes by only shopping at used clothing stores and garage sales.

But none of that had helped her self-esteem. It was bad enough that by being a woman one was automatically rated as a second-class citizen. Being considered a frumpy second-class citizen only seemed to add to her lack of self-image. And then she'd met Frank. She'd changed to "win" him, bought the beauty lie that was offered up in *Vogue* and perpetuated by her peers.

God, had that been a mistake.

But it hadn't seemed so at the time. Instead she'd suddenly felt free. Liked, desired, loved. She'd won Frank's heart and looked back on old pictures of herself as though they'd been taken of a stranger. She forgot the reasons behind the frumpy clothes and trying to make herself appear plain, forgot how desperately she'd wanted to be accepted for who she was, instead of who she appeared to be.

She didn't remember until Frank turned mean, and by then it was too late.

From the bathroom she went into her bedroom, where she exchanged bra and panties for a long T-shirt that hung to her knees. She felt restless. She wondered how Rob's meeting had gone, she wondered what Lily was doing tonight, but it was too late to call either of them. She wandered out of the bedroom and made herself a cup of Lapsang Souchong tea, which she took into the living room.

She stood in front of the window and looked out at the park, ignoring the bulk of Tower B, which reared up on the left side of her view. If things were different, if life were normal, she could have gone for a walk in the park, followed the path that led through it down to the river and sat there, enjoying the quiet of the evening. But the park was full of strangers who could be anything: lonely soul mates, eager for company, or homeless people, sleeping in the shrubberies and on the benches; but more likely there'd be rapists and muggers, looking for one more victim.

Sighing, she moved away from the window and let her restlessness take her into her studio. She stood in the darkness for a long time, trying to see what she could make out in the half-light before she finally flicked on the wall switch. Her paintings leapt to life in the sudden brightness.

Her guardian angel looked back at her from her half-realized interpretations of him. The face in the crowd, the phantom in the grove of trees, the ghost in Crowsea Market, the solitary figure on the boardwalk, the face in the car window.

For a long moment she stared at the pictures, an odd feeling of déjà vu rising up in her like the slow swell of an incoming tide, until she finally pinpointed the source of her feeling.

No, she thought as the realization hit home. It wasn't possible.

But the more she studied her paintings, the more it seemed to be true. It was all in the mouth. The mouth of her guardian angel was so similar to Peter's that they might as well have been the same.

She tried to imagine Peter killing her husband, tried to imagine any sort of fierceness in him at all, but couldn't. What Peter gave her was the impression of . . . well, softness. It wasn't that she thought of him as a weak person; it was just that she couldn't imagine him taking Frank on, let alone overpowering him.

But still. She wondered what Peter would look like without a beard. Her artist's eye knew how to catch and trap the contour of a jawline, the shape of a lip, or a nose, a brow, a neck, the slope of a shoulder, the musculature of an arm or a leg. She could see it once, and have it forever. She might be terrible with names and dates and the like, but not with what she saw.

Images had always made a magical journey from her mind down through her arm and out her fingers. She was rusty these days, but not so out of practice that she would have gotten wrong the one solid impression she had of the man who had saved her from Frank's attack.

That Peter and her guardian angel had the same mouth was no more than coincidence—she knew that—but all the same, she couldn't seem to stop her mind from getting all snarled up in a tangle of what-ifs.

What if they were one and the same? What if Peter had come into the Bike Pit expressly to meet her, the woman he had rescued? He could have grown a beard, changed his hair color. . . .

And then she had to laugh at herself.

Yes, of course. And he just happened to be a friend of Rob's. Not likely.

The similarity was striking, there was no doubt about that, but she knew that there were two very logical reasons why she was stretching credibility the way she was: she'd been fixated on her guardian angel ever since he'd rescued her from Frank—the proof positive was taped to the walls of her studio; and she liked Peter, liked him an awful lot, and was frustrated that he was unavailable as a lover.

She wasn't at all taken in by the false myth that all a gay man needed was a good woman to set him straight. Gays were gay and heterosexuals were straight because that was just the way they were. It was such a fundamental part of each personality; to change it would utterly change the person.

But her frustration remained all the same. Peter and her guardian angel—both forever out of her reach.

But so were many things, girl, she told herself. Life goes on.

Crossing the studio, Rachel turned on the light over her drawing table and sat down. She set her tea to one side, then tore a new sheet off her pad of watercolor paper and affixed it to the desk with strips of masking tape all around.

She sat there awhile, finishing her tea, letting her mind drift. After a time, she went into the kitchen and refilled her tea mug, then returned to her studio with it and a glass of water. Setting out her paints beside the blank paper, she chose a brush from where they were kept now in an old coffee tin. Then she called up Peter's features in her mind's eye and began to paint, using a dry brush method, the brush barely damp, the paint applied to the dry paper more as if she were drawing, but with watercolor rather than graphite.

Hours later, she straightened up, arching her back to loosen stiff muscles. She glanced at the portrait she'd finished, but was too tired to give it any sort of a critical appraisal. Instead she just stumbled out of the studio and into her bed, where she fell asleep in moments.

TWENTY-TWO

The billboard on top of the Grant-Canty Building at the corner of Williamson and Kelly Street caught Harry's attention as he was about to turn south on Williamson. He pulled over into a No Parking zone and got out of his Rabbit. Leaning on the hood of the car, he craned his neck until he was looking up at the stark black-and-white image that seemed to stretch the whole of the skyline from this perspective.

It was an ad for Guess? Jeans featuring Claudia Schiffer, the darling of first Europe's, and now North America's fashion industry; a beautiful woman whose only claim to fame was her beauty. Schiffer was the new Bardot, necessary now that the old was retired to the south of France, defending baby seals from the fur industry and her neighbor's donkey from castration. But more to the point, the old Bardot was no longer young. No longer beautiful by industry standards, except as a well-preserved older woman. Today's young women didn't want to identify with a well-preserved older woman; they wanted to be Schiffer.

Schiffer was undeniably attractive; fuller of body than the models in current fashion magazines, with a mane of gold hair and that pout. That Bardot pout.

She also didn't seem one bit real.

But how could she be? Harry thought. He knew from his own experience shooting ads that it was the lighting, the frozen pose of promise and sensuality that was so contrived it meant nothing, that transformed her from what she really was into the icon who seemed to assure women that if they wore these jeans, they'd look just like her. That promised men she'd be theirs if they simply made the correct choice in attire.

Rachel was right, Harry decided. Images such as this so pervaded every aspect of society that they made it impossible for real human beings to ever gain any sense of self-worth, because the ideals were unattainable. They would always be unattainable.

But he was right as well. There was only one way to combat the false beauty icons of fashion, and that was by returning true beauty to the world, beauty unsullied by commercial concerns, beauty that was myth in its perfection and so created myth.

It existed and had to be protected, he thought as he got back into his car. It had to be defended.

He drove on.

Harry's eidetic memory easily brought to mind the address he required. All he'd needed was one glance at the slip of paper and he could call it up, picture-perfect, in his mind—now, a week from now, ten years from now. He never forgot a thing he saw.

When he pulled up, a good five blocks away from the building he wanted, he checked his reflection in the rearview mirror. He had stopped in an alleyway after leaving Rachel's place and changed his appearance once more. A familiar stranger looked back at him from the mirror. He'd used this persona in New York City, in Paris, in Miami.

Peter Orlick's beard and mustache were gone. His hair was a dirty blond now, slicked back from his forehead, an obvious dye job, with the roots showing. His skin had a healthy tan that would easily wash off, though that was impossible to tell from a quick glance. Both his eyes were blue.

When he stepped out of the Rabbit, he was wearing hightops and jeans, a white T-shirt with the arms torn off, a package of cigarettes stuffed up under one shoulder, a pair of shades hanging from his neck, one stem stuffed down the neckline of the T-shirt to keep them in place. A pair of thin black gloves were stuffed in the right rear pocket of his jeans.

When he moved toward his destination, he had a swagger in his walk—the cocky don't-mess-with-me attitude that suited this area of run-down tenements where the blue-collar and the no-collar workers lived. Factory men and the unemployed.

He went up the steps of the building. The door was ajar, a drunken man sleeping in the threshold, his limp body keeping the door open. Harry stepped over him. He put on the gloves as he moved up the flight of stairs that led to the second floor.

There was a light on under the door of apartment number 22, where he stopped. He listened. From down either side of the hall came the sounds of TV sets tuned to various stations, stereos playing country-and-western and thrash, an argument two doors down. The sound of televised gunfire came through the door of number 22—a cop show, maybe a movie.

Harry rapped sharply on the battered wooden panel, just under the cheap sticker, gold numbers on black, that identified the apartment. He rapped a second time, then stepped back into the hall as the door was flung open and Ian Hughes glared at him.

"Who the hell're you?" Hughes demanded.

The man wore his tough persona like it gave him courage.

Harry smiled. "You were in the Bike Pit this afternoon?"

Hughes grunted affirmatively, eyes narrowed as he tried to place Harry.

"And you had an altercation with one of the employees?"

"A what?"

"An argument."

"You got a point to this, fuckhead?"

Harry nodded. With a smile, he kicked the man in the knee. Harry's hightops had been customized—he'd done the job himself. Each had a length of steel embedded in the undersole. When that metal-reinforced undersole, driven with the full power of his leg behind it, connected with Hughes's knee, the bone snapped with an audible crack and the man's leg gave out from under him.

Before Hughes could cry out from the pain, before he even hit the floor, Harry had spun around. A second kick caught Hughes in the throat, shattering his windpipe and breaking his neck.

Still smiling, Harry grabbed Hughes by the hair and dragged the dying man back into his own apartment, depositing him in the center of the shabby living room. He closed the apartment door, then went into the kitchen. Rummaging around in a drawer, he finally found what he was looking for and returned to his victim with a steak knife. He ran his gloved thumb over the serrated edge of the blade.

Hughes gave a last rattling breath as Harry knelt beside him.

"Let's see if I can't fix your plumbing for you," Harry told the dead man.

Fifteen minutes later, Harry returned to his car. He glanced at his wristwatch. Just past twelve. Still enough time to make it to the harborfront and pay a little visit to a certain waiter when he got off shift.

Harry had a can of gas in the back of the Rabbit's hatch. He had a lighter in his pocket though he didn't smoke. The cigarette package up under the shoulder of his T-shirt was just a prop, something that neither the gas can nor the lighter was.

An eye for an eye was what the Old Testament said, but that little proverb hadn't originated with Christianity. It had a far older source, dating to a time when the old gods walked the earth. Gods like Beauty. And Revenge.

Harry hummed tunelessly between his teeth as he set a course south toward the lakefront. He remembered a joke that had gone the rounds of his grade school when he was a kid, about how this doctor made a voiceless dog bark. He poured gas over the animal and set a match to it. Woof.

Harry wondered if it worked for waiters, too.

The light ahead of him turned red, and he came to a careful stop. He patiently waited for it to turn green, then put his foot on the accelerator again.

"Woof," he said softly.

TWENTY-THREE

"This city just seems to get worse every day," Lily said, looking up from the newspaper she was reading.

"You don't have to read a paper to know that," Tom said.

"But they report it all so gleefully."

"So why do you read them?"

"I don't know. I just like to know what's going on, I guess."

She had a Sunday morning ritual. She nested in her bed—or in the case of this morning, Tom's bed—plentifully provisioned with cigarettes and coffee, cookies or muffins or croissants, and the Sunday editions of *The Daily Journal* and *The Newford Star*. She stayed there until she'd gone through both papers, front to back, until she'd read every article or column of interest, finished all the coffee and eaten the last crumb of whatever snack she'd had the foresight to buy or bake the night before. She only got up when there was finally no other excuse.

In the short time that they'd been together, Tom had already given up trying to get her out of bed before noon on a Sunday morning. If it couldn't be done in bed—and that didn't just encompass breakfast and the papers; there was always what her mother had so euphemistically referred to as "pillow talk"—then she simply wasn't interested in it.

Sometimes he sat beside her in bed, reading as well, though never the newspaper. The only local periodical in which he had any interest at all was the entertainment weekly *In the City*, which carried all of the city's various concert, art show, theater and club listings. Since it came out on Wednesdays, he'd long finished reading it by Sunday morning.

Today he lounged on the wide hardwood slats of the bay window seat that took up almost a quarter of the wall in which it was set. He was sketching Lily as she played queen for the morning: still nude from their lovemaking earlier, the sheets all tangled around her legs and waist, a flurry of newspaper sheets scattered all about her on the bed, cigarette burning between the fingers of one hand, coffee mug balanced on her stomach while she read a section of *The Newford Star*, which she'd folded up to make it easier to hold. Whenever she turned to the next page, it involved a complicated unfolding and refolding of the section, during which the coffee mug wobbled precariously on her stomach.

This was the only time that Tom ever saw Lily simply let go and relax in a clutter. Within thirty minutes of her finally rising, she'd have the papers all put away in the recycling bin, each section neatly folded and in its proper order, the bed made, the ashtray emptied and the dishes washed. But for now she was as natural as a puppy enthusiastically taking apart a pair of slippers to see what made them work.

He enjoyed the coziness of the setting, the closeness that Sunday mornings seemed to define within the entire spectrum of their relationship. When they spent Saturday night at his apartment, he even went so far as to stumble out of bed early and fetch her the Sunday papers from the newsstand down the street.

"Now I know it's true love," she'd told him the first time he went out before she woke and came back with the papers, coffee and fresh croissants.

The word "love" had woken an uneasiness in him until he realized that love was exactly what he felt for her.

"Did you *read* this?" Lily was asking now.

Since he'd glanced at the headlines of both papers on the trip back from the newsstands this morning, Tom knew what she was referring to. There'd been two rather gruesome deaths reported this morning.

The first was a waiter who'd been burned alive on the lakefront near the Harbor Ritz; he'd just come off shift from Zwicker's, where he worked, and was headed for home when he'd been attacked. According to the paper, police had no leads, no motive.

The second was in Midtown, where a suspected cocaine dealer had apparently been bludgeoned to death, his genitals then removed and stuffed into his mouth. In this case, while the police still had no leads, they suspected the killing was drug-related or possibly part of a sado-masochistic homosexual relationship gone bad. The Newford Gay/Lesbian Alliance had already taken the chief of police to task for the statement.

Those weren't the only deaths in the city last night, by any means. There had also been a shooting and a knifing—separate incidents—in the Combat Zone, a hit-and-run on the strip where Williamson turned into Highway 14, a confrontation between two teenage gangs in Fitzhenry Park that had left one of the combatants dead and a second shooting outside a club in Upper Foxville. But all of these had been bumped from the front page of both papers by the exotic nature of the deaths suffered by the waiter and the drug dealer.

"That's why I *don't* like to read the papers," Tom said. "Except for the entertainment pages and the funnies, there's nothing *but* bad news in them."

"It's so sick," Lily went on, as though she hadn't heard him. She paused to light another cigarette. "I don't know about this drug dealer—if you deal with criminals, I guess you've got to know that you're taking your chances—but this poor guy who worked at Zwicker's. He was just going home from work. How could somebody *do* something like that to another human being?"

With the newspaper no longer blocking his view of her face and upper torso, Tom began quickly to add in the details he'd been missing in his sketch.

"The kind of person who would do a thing like that," he said as he drew, "is so far beyond my comprehension that I can't even imagine how his mind works. I don't think he'd be a person that has any feelings whatsoever."

Lily shivered, goosebumps rising up her arms.

"Maybe your friend Isabelle is the smartest one of us," she said. "There's things I'd miss if I left the city, but living out on an island where the worst thing that happens is your cat gets fleas looks pretty good to me right about now."

"You'd go mad living in the country," Tom said with a smile. "No dance clubs, no shopping malls."

"I don't shop *that* much."

"Only because you can't afford to."

She gave him a perfect moue, which he filed away in his memory for another drawing.

"And I'd miss my friends," she added.

"That's true."

Lily looked down at the newspaper she was holding, then tossed it aside.

"Are you still getting together with Leroy this afternoon?" she asked.

Leroy Johns was a young black musician who specialized in sampled sounds and synthesizer work. He'd approached Tom a few weeks ago about composing a soundtrack to accompany Tom's next show, and the two had been getting together on a regular basis over the past couple of weeks, listening to endless hours of Leroy's music and making plans.

Tom nodded, worrying over the discrepancy between the slope of

Lily's shoulder as it really was and how it appeared in the drawing he was working on.

"Then I guess I'll go see Rachel," Lily said.

"Wait a sec," Tom said as she butted out the stub of her cigarette and started to get up. "Just let me get this last line right."

Lily pulled a face, then assumed the exaggerated pose of a *Playboy* centerfold. She held it for a long heartbeat before she collapsed on the bed, laughing, arms crossed over her breasts.

So long as she wasn't really aware that he was drawing her, she was fine, Tom had realized right from the beginning of their relationship, which was why he usually didn't ask her to pose, just snatched the opportunities when they arose. But this piece was going so well that he really wanted to finish it—from life, not memory.

"Just give me a couple more minutes," Tom said.

"Do I have to?" Lily asked. "I feel so stupid doing it. And besides, it makes my nose itch whenever I have to pose."

"One minute, that's all."

Sighing, Lily raised herself up until she was leaning back once more on the pillow propped up against the headboard.

"This isn't going to show up in one of your shows, is it?" she asked. "I don't know if I'm all that keen on having nude portraits of myself on public display—especially not if you're putting my face in it. Knowing my luck, Cameron'll buy it and hang it up in his office, where everybody I work with will see it whenever he calls them in to give them one of his boring lectures."

Tom just kept working.

"Well, you're not, are you?" Lily asked.

"Not if you don't want me to." He finished the sketch off quickly. "There. I'm done."

Lily wrapped a sheet around herself and came to stand beside him. She looked down at the drawing.

"Actually," she said, "that's really nice. I mean, your art's always good, but I don't look too bad in it." She lifted a hand to her nose, running a finger down its short length. "Is my nose really that small? I always feel like I've got such a big schonz."

Tom laughed. It never failed to amaze him how a woman as attractive as Lily could only focus on what she perceived as her flaws.

"You look better than this," he told her.

"Flatterer."

"Tell you what," Tom said. "Let me add a little more detail, and then I'd like you to have it."

"Really."

"Really. We can have a private showing of it in your bedroom."

Lily's response to that was to take the drawing from his lap and set it aside. Then she dropped the sheet she'd wrapped around herself and got up onto his lap. Tom leaned back against the window.

"People are going to see," he said.

"So tell 'em to get their own lover," she said as she wrapped her legs around his waist, her arms around his neck. "Or do you want to share?"

"Not a chance."

Tom cradled his hands under her thighs. Standing up, he carried her back to the bed. He'd be late meeting with Leroy, but he didn't really care.

TWENTY-FOUR

Rachel arose late on Sunday morning. It was almost noon before she was standing at her kitchen counter brewing a pot of coffee, impatiently watching the water seep through the Melitta filter into the glass decanter below. A watched kettle never boils, she thought blearily, and the same seemed to hold true for the process of brewing coffee. It seemed to take forever before she could finally pour herself a mug and take it over to the table.

She'd slept longer than she'd intended, which always left her feeling a little groggy. It wasn't until halfway through her second cup that she remembered the small portrait of Peter that she'd painted the night before, and that, in turn, reminded her of the fiasco that ended their dinner at Zwicker's.

She looked down at her arms and ran a finger lightly over the red inflammations. They looked worse than they felt. She'd been lucky that the waiter hadn't spilled boiling water on her instead.

That poor waiter. He'd looked so mortified, even when she'd assured him that she was all right, that she didn't blame him at all for what had happened. If anyone was at fault, it was the customer who'd done a quick fade after bumping into the poor guy. Zwicker's was such a classy place. She hoped the waiter hadn't lost his job or something over an incident that hadn't even been his fault.

His boss had seemed so mad—all solicitous toward her, to be sure, but she'd seen that he wasn't one bit happy about this stain on the restaurant's reputation.

She was the one who'd gotten burned, but in some ways, she felt that she'd been the least affected. Even Peter had seemed more upset over the whole thing than she'd been. Maybe it was because of how bad the inflammation on her arms had looked last night—an ugly red smear across her forearms.

It was funny, the ideas he had about beauty, she thought. Somehow she hadn't expected him to buy into that whole fashion-as-holy-icon lie, though she couldn't have said why.

With her thoughts returning to him, she found herself wanting to look at the result of her late-night endeavors, to see if the painting was really as good as she'd thought it was when she finally stumbled off to bed last night. She topped up her coffee and took it into the studio.

She hadn't been mistaken. The portrait really was the best thing she'd done since taking up her brushes once more. It wasn't just that it was a good likeness, or even that she'd managed to catch in its lines and hues the odd paradox of warmth and distance that seemed to make up his personality—she'd realized in retrospect that, for all his immediate charm, Peter spoke very little of himself or his past. The painting seemed to say something beyond mere portraiture, which was what she'd been striving for. The watercolor was at once specifically Peter and Everyman.

Not bad, considering how just a few weeks ago she had had trouble making proportions properly coordinated.

Looking from the new painting to the ones of her guardian angel where they hung on the wall, she had to laugh at how she'd let her imagination get away with her last night. Yes, there was certainly a similarity between the mouths of the two men—ghostly memory caught in watercolor and paper, and Peter as she knew he was—but the idea that Peter could be her guardian angel appeared ridiculous in the reasonable light of day.

What she needed, Rachel realized, was a real man in her life. Not a ghostly fantasy, nor an attractive but gay friend. What she needed was a flesh-and-blood heterosexual male with whom she could have both an emotional as well as a physical relationship. That would put to rest all these odd yearnings and strange fancies that had been troubling her for the past few weeks.

It had been over a year since she'd left Frank, and there'd been no one in all that time. She hadn't *wanted* anyone to get close to her because she couldn't get past the fear that ran like ice through her veins at the very thought of intimacy.

She thought that perhaps she could deal with it now. Considering the frustrated attraction she felt toward Peter, it seemed obvious that she was ready, that it wasn't simply Peter's safeness that had attracted her to him, but the need to be physically close to another person, to have a sexual partner in her life once more, one that cared as much for her as she did for him.

Only where did you find one?

She remembered all those conversations she'd had with Lily before Lily met Tom. Rachel had been merely paying lip service during many of those sessions where they'd complained about how all the good men in the city seemed to be either married or gay. She'd still been too scared even to think of entering another relationship, but she had wanted one for Lily.

The endless unresolved circling of those conversations came back to her now. Where *did* you go to meet a nice man? And how could you be assured that he really was nice, that he wouldn't start out charming and sweet, and then turn mean the way Frank had?

A sudden image leapt into her mind—Frank hitting her so hard that she fell to the floor; Frank sitting on top of her in the corner of their kitchen, the gun pressed up against the soft underside of her throat. Her pulse started to quicken with remembered fear that seemed too immediate to be simply memory. She could almost feel the weight of him, the cold press of the gun's muzzle against her skin, the crazy look that came into his eyes when he stopped taking his medication—

Stop it, she told herself.

Frank was dead.

She turned to the paintings of her guardian angel and let their soft-focusing mystery work like a balm against the sudden terror that had gripped her. She took a deep breath, then slowly let it out.

"You can't hide from what your husband did to you," her therapist had told her, "because that just gives the memories power over you. Be aware, remember and be cautious, but try not to dwell on it."

That was true, she reminded herself. And it had to be true that relationships didn't have to be adverse. Just look at how Lily and Tom got along. There didn't have to be violence and anger. If she stayed strong, if she didn't *allow* it to happen to her, then it wouldn't.

But how could she *know*?

We're all strangers, she thought, locked in our flesh. We only let others see the parts of us that we want them to see. Where was the test to assure you that a monster didn't lurk behind a charming smile and kind eyes? How did a person get brave enough to try again when they'd been hurt so badly in the past?

There didn't seem to be a middle road between the anonymity that kept one safe and literally throwing oneself out among the wolves and hoping for the best—or at least not one Rachel had ever been able to find.

The phone rang then, and Rachel went into the living room to answer it, grateful for the interruption.

"You went to Zwicker's?" Lily asked as Rachel was telling her about how she'd met Peter the day before.

Rachel nodded. They were sitting out on Rachel's balcony, where the smoke from Lily's cigarettes could simply drift away, rather than pervade Rachel's draperies and furniture.

"I've never been in a restaurant *that* classy before," Rachel said. "The food was unbelievable."

Lily tapped the ash from her cigarette into the saucer that Rachel had provided for her.

"Wasn't it awful what happened last night?" she said.

Lily's question gave Rachel a momentary sense of dislocation. She thought Lily was referring to how the waiter had dropped the coffee on her, and she couldn't figure out how Lily could have known.

"The waiter that died," Lily explained when she saw the confused look cross Rachel's features. "He worked at Zwicker's."

"Died?"

"It was all over the papers—just an awful thing. He'd gotten off work and was going home when someone dragged him out onto the beach, poured gasoline over him and set him on fire."

"My god!"

Lily nodded. "I don't know how something like that can even happen in a supposedly civilized society." She ground her butt into the saucer. "Wouldn't it be creepy if it was your waiter who died?"

The features of the young man who'd served them last night leapt into Rachel's mind. He'd been in his mid-twenties, had a kind face, gentle eyes. His smile had been warm and genuinely friendly when he came to their table with the wine list and menus.

"What . . . what was his name?" Rachel asked. "The man who died."

She felt a strange stirring, as though something had just woken up inside her. It was a kind of fear, but not the sort with which she was familiar, not like the fear she'd retained as a legacy from her marriage. This had an almost supernatural eeriness about it.

"Uh, Nanes, I think," Lily said, brow furrowing as she thought back to the news report. "That's right. Timothy Nanes."

("Hello," the waiter had said as he laid Rachel's menu on the table in front of her. "My name's Timothy. . . .")

Rachel thought of the inflammation on her arms and thighs. She'd been burned; the waiter had died by fire. What she was thinking wasn't possible, but that sensation of being watched over returned. The strange fantasy that somewhere, somehow, the man who had rescued her from Frank was watching over her. Her guardian angel.

The fantasy didn't seem nearly so romantic or comforting anymore.

"Rachel," Lily said. "Are you all right?"

"Our waiter's name was Timothy," Rachel replied. "He seemed like such a nice person."

"I'm sorry. I didn't mean to—"

Rachel waved off her apology. "No, it's not your fault. It's just unsettling, that's all."

There was no such thing as guardian angels, she told herself. And if there were, they wouldn't exact such a dire punishment for what had only been a simple accident. It was coincidence, nothing more. An unhappy coincidence.

But the feeling inside her wouldn't go away.

"Our evening there kind of ended in a disaster," Rachel explained. "Just as the waiter was giving me a refill of coffee, someone bumped into him and he dropped the pot onto the table. It broke and I got scalded."

She rolled back the sleeves of the sweatshirt she was wearing to show Lily the inflammation on her forearms.

"Oh, yuck. Does it hurt?"

"No, it just looks bad."

"But—"

"Oh, I know this is stupid," Rachel said, "but I can't help feeling weird about the fact that I got burned because he spilled the coffee on me, and then he died because someone set him on fire."

Lily gave her a look that Rachel recognized all too well. It was part concern, part walk on eggshells so Rachel doesn't get upset.

"But surely you don't think there's a connection," Lily said finally.

Rachel couldn't bring herself to take it any further because that would have entailed telling Lily about her guardian angel fantasies and that would have been just too embarrassing. As it was, the whole idea made her feel crazy; she didn't want to add to her own discomfort by having other people thinking she was, too.

"No," she said. "Of course not. It's just . . . I don't know . . . eerie, that's all."

"Well, I can certainly understand that," Lily said. She swished the remainder of her iced tea around in the bottom of her glass before taking a sip. "So tell me more about this Peter," she added. "What makes you think he's gay?"

"It's just the way he carries himself," Rachel said. "Plus he's a friend of Rob's. Actually, I think Rob's got a major crush on him."

"But has he come right out and said he's gay?"

"Well, no."

Lily thrust a defiant finger straight up into the sky. "Then there's still hope!"

"No," Rachel said. "He's definitely gay."

"Are you going to see him again?"

"He said he'd call this week."

"Well, I think you should just come out and ask him," Lily told her.

"I couldn't do that."

"Why not?"

"It's just not something I could do," Rachel said.

The turn the conversation had taken was beginning to make her feel uncomfortable, so she changed the subject.

"Come with me for a moment," she said. "I want to show you something."

Lily had too much of a sense of curiosity not to take the bait that was offered.

"What is it?" she asked, Peter's sexual inclination already relegated to a back burner in her mind.

"You'll see," Rachel said as she led the way back into the apartment.

"Is it bigger than a bread box?"

"Sort of."

"Well, is it . . ."

Lily's voice trailed off as Rachel opened the door to her studio and ushered her friend in. Lily stood looking at the paintings for a long time, a big smile on her face.

"Oh wow," she said finally and turned to Rachel. "Did you do these?"

Rachel nodded.

"They're fabulous. How long have you been painting?"

Each time she told it, Rachel found, the story became easier to tell—so much so that it was beginning to be difficult to remember why she'd found it necessary to keep her art hidden away in the first place.

"I know exactly how you feel," Lily said when Rachel was done. "I used to write poetry—no, I'm not being honest. It's confession time, isn't it? I still write poetry, but I never show it to anyone because the same thing happened to me. Everybody thought it was a lovely hobby, but they belittled my seriousness until finally it got to the point where I couldn't think of it as anything more than a hobby either.

"I went from fantasies of being published—you know, like in those lovely little editions produced by the East Street Press—to totally stopping for almost two years, until one day I was going back through a folder of my old poetry and realized that while my poems might have little value to anybody else, they defined *my* life. Reading through them was like reading a journal—all the bits and pieces of my life through the years were captured there. I could remember where I was when I wrote them, what was happening to me, what had *meaning* for me.

"I might not have that little fantasy of having them published anymore, but that day I vowed that nothing's ever going to stop me from writing again."

"I'd love to read any that you might want to share with me," Rachel said.

Lily wouldn't meet her gaze. "Yeah, well, they're not that great."

She pointed to the small portrait still taped to the drawing table. "Who's this?"

"Peter."

"If this is true to life, he's some good-looking guy, isn't he?"

"But gay. About your poems, Lily."

"Honestly. They're really not that great. Not like your paintings."

Now it was Rachel who was discomfited.

"My work's hardly gallery quality," she said.

"You're just too close to them, that's all," Lily told her. She brightened suddenly. "I know. We should get Tom to look at them."

"I don't think Tom much likes me."

"He just doesn't know you, that's all. You'd respect his judgment, wouldn't you?"

"I respect his work."

"Even if Tom didn't like you," Lily said, "which I'm not saying is the case, he'd still give you an honest appraisal of your work."

"I suppose."

"Oh, come on, Rach. What've you got to lose?"

What little pride I've got left, Rachel thought.

"This'll give you and Tom some common ground," Lily said. "You guys are my best friends in the world, and I really hate not being able to share the two of you with each other."

"All right," Rachel said, relenting with obvious reluctance. "But only if you let me read some of your poems."

"You won't show them to anyone else?"

"And you want me to show Tom my paintings."

"But this is different. I know your paintings are good. You haven't read my stuff yet."

Rachel smiled. "I won't show them to anyone else."

Lily picked up Rachel's art portfolio. "Can we take this out onto the balcony? I want to look through it again, but I'm dying for a cigarette."

"Sure."

What have I done? she asked herself as she followed Lily back outside. I'm going to die when Tom looks at my work. He's going to hate it.

"I love this pen-and-ink stuff," Lily said.

She had the portfolio open to a series of landscape studies that Rachel had done at Butler University—autumn scenes from the wooded hills that rose up behind the western side of the campus. She'd loved to watch the seasons change in those woods, finding it easy to forget that just beyond their crest were the estates of the Beaches, the million-dollar homes of Newford's rich and powerful, nestled in tamed forest and lawn.

The university side of the hills was like a lost part of wilderness, hiding in the city; a small, heartwarming counterpoint to all the square miles of concrete, steel and glass that surrounded it.

"When did you do these?" Lily asked.

"My first year at Butler U," Rachel said.

As she started to talk about them, she realized that art was as much a journal for her as poetry was for Lily. Maybe it was a good thing that she hadn't done any painting when things got bad with Frank. It was hard enough to forget that nightmare time without having artistic journal entries to further fuel her memory.

TWENTY-FIVE

Harry watched the two women on Rachel's balcony through his telescope. The woman with the slightly Oriental cast to her features would be Rachel's friend Lily. He had seen her at the apartment on a number of occasions but hadn't known her name until yesterday afternoon when Rachel and Rob had been speaking of her.

Lily Kataboki.

She was very attractive, but not Beauty. She was somewhat too exotic. Her eyes an unnaturally bright blue. Her skin so very pale.

He focused back on Rachel, taking his gaze from the telescope when she pushed up the sleeves of her sweatshirt to show Lily the inflammation on her forearms.

He'd have to wait until she was healed now. And he'd have to watch over her more carefully than ever before, because it was patently obvious that anything could happen. If she was hurt too badly, if she was scarred . . .

That oaf he'd eliminated, the man from the Bike Pit. What if in the midst of their altercation, Hughes had hit Rachel and broken her nose? Or if the burns she'd sustained last night had been worse? Any-thing could happen if he didn't keep careful watch. But he'd been right there, across the table from her, and he hadn't been able to do a thing to stop her from being hurt.

Last night had been an error. Instead of thinking of himself, instead of enjoying her company as he had, he should have tested her while she was still unblemished, while *he* could control the situation. Now he had to wait until the inflammations died down. How long would that take? A few days? A week?

When he began to consider what could happen to her while he waited—the sheer diversity of stupid, pointless accidents that could befall her if she was in the wrong place at the wrong time—it gave him a chill. Goosebumps marched up his arms.

He considered simply snatching her and taking her someplace secluded and safe until she healed, but immediately dismissed the idea. He'd have to bind her, and that would just create more bruising and chaffing of her perfect skin. But waiting like this was going to be so hard.

Harry took a deep breath, let it out slowly, then took another. His nerves were all on edge. He had the sense that things were unravel-ing—not just in terms of his quest, but within himself as well. The pressure had been building up through all the long years of his search-ing. He'd been aware of it, but he'd kept it in check. He'd remained in control. So why was the pressure so strong now? Why did it have to come to a head at this time, when he was so very close finally to realiz-ing the fruits of his labor?

Because this time he had found her, he realized. Really and truly found her.

He looked through the telescope again.

It was just a few days more, that was all. Her skin would heal and he'd make the final test and then all the pressure would be gone because he'd be vindicated. The goddess would stand at his right hand as he confronted the world with her beauty.

Until that moment, he would protect her. From accident and from abuse and from all the dangers that lay in wait for the innocent and the beautiful. He would be true of heart. He would be her shadow. No threat to her, no matter how slight, would be allowed to harm her.

"I promise you," he said softly, his gaze locked on Rachel's beauty.

The telescope brought her up so close that he had to fight the illusion of being able to just reach out and brush an errant lock of hair away from her smooth brow. He could almost see her divinity shining out from the pores of her skin, surrounding her like a nimbus of golden light.

"No one will ever harm you again."

TWENTY-SIX

"Orlick," the homicide detective repeated.

Brian Corsaro, the maître d' on the evening shift at Zwicker's, nodded. He was a slender, dark-haired man in his early forties, obviously upset over what had happened last night to the young waiter on his shift. Fidgeting on the couch in the spacious living room of his apartment, where the interview was taking place, the maître d' wouldn't quite meet Freeman's gaze, but Freeman didn't think it was because of guilt.

"Yes," Corsaro said. "Peter Orlick. There was an unfortunate accident late on the shift. Ti-Timothy dropped a coffee carafe on the gentleman's table, and the contents spilled over his companion. She wasn't seriously hurt, I assure you, but I'm sure it was painful."

Corsaro's gaze darkened. He's thinking of burns and pain, Freeman thought. You're right, pal. Last night, Timothy Nanes suffered a lot more pain than having a little bit of coffee spilled on him.

"And this Orlick," Freeman asked. "How did he react when it happened?"

"Well, he was upset, naturally."

It was really starting to hit home for Corsaro, Freeman thought. He'd probably reamed the kid out once he got him alone after the incident, and now, with the kid dead, he felt like a shit.

He glanced over to his partner, but Stone was looking idly out the patio doors, which led onto a balcony overlooking Battersfield Road and the river. He leaned a bulky shoulder against the frame of the patio doors and didn't appear to be paying any attention to the conversation in the room behind him. Freeman returned his gaze to the apartment's owner.

"Do you have an address for this Orlick?" he asked Corsaro.

The maître d' shook his head. "There was no charge for the meal, of course, and I simply gave him a voucher for another dinner that he could use at his convenience. I noted his name, but there was no need to ask for further information."

"He's a regular?"

"I hadn't seen him before." He hesitated for a moment, then added, "Surely you don't think Mr. Orlick was responsible for . . ."

His voice trailed off as Freeman shook his head.

"We're just covering the bases," he said. "Routine—that's all."

Stone finally turned from the view.

"What kind of a man was Mr. Orlick?" he asked the maître d'.

"I'm sorry?"

"How would you describe him? Quick-tempered, meek, ordinary Joe?"

"I . . ." Corsaro hesitated again. "To be honest, he seemed somewhat effeminate. If he hadn't been in the company of such a stunning woman, I might have thought he was gay."

Stone pushed away from the wall and joined the other two men in the middle of the room.

"Thanks very much for your time," he told Corsaro. "If we think of anything else, would it be all right for us to drop by again or give you a call?"

"Certainly."

Freeman stood up beside his partner, which brought Corsaro to his feet as well.

"So what do you think?" he asked Stone, once they were alone in the elevator.

"Orlick interests me."

"What're you seeing that I'm not?"

Stone shrugged. "Damned if I know. The victim was so squeaky clean it's like he couldn't have made an enemy if he'd tried. This business with Orlick's the first thing that's come up that's even remotely close to a motive."

"Waiter spills coffee on Orlick's date, scalding her, so he torches the kid?"

Stone smiled. "Sounds pretty farfetched when you put it like that. But I'd still like to see his hands."

Freeman didn't need to ask why. He'd been there for the autopsy with Stone. Nanes had been beaten to death before he'd been set on fire.

Freeman pulled out his notebook and glanced over their agenda. "So who do you want to hit next?"

"I want to call in first," Stone said.

Freeman raised his eyebrows questioningly.

"I'd like to have Sandy run a make on Orlick," Stone explained. "See what comes up."

"And then?"

"Then we'll see if that busboy's home yet."

TWENTY-SEVEN

Rachel went downstairs with Lily when it was time for her to leave. They took the elevator down to the underground garage, where Rachel fetched her new bike from her storage locker, then they walked together to the bus stop.

"Nice wheels," Lily said. "When you told me you got a new bike, I didn't think it'd be this classy. It must've set you back a small fortune."

"But it's worth it," Rachel said. "Except if I keep spending money at this rate, I'll be going through my savings in record time."

"You could always move."

Rachel glanced back at the apartment building. Lily was right. Without the threat of Frank hanging over her anymore, she could get herself a little studio apartment in Lower Crowsea at half the rent. Not only would she be saving money, but living in one of those old buildings was far more her style than the Sky Towers.

Frank, she remembered, had hated the idea of owning anything that someone else had owned before him. Car. House. Furniture. Antiques.

"I don't want somebody else's garbage" was the way he put it.

But Frank was dead.

"Maybe I'll do that," Rachel said.

"I'll let you know if I hear of an apartment," Lily told her, "but you'd better start looking quickly. This time of year is when the university students start coming back, and they'll snap up all the decent places."

"Does your landlady have anything coming up?"

"Not that I know of, but I'll ask. Hey, wouldn't that be great if we were neighbors?"

"It'd be fun," Rachel agreed. "I don't need much. Even just a bachelor would do."

She leaned her bike up against a sidewalk bench when they reached the bus stop.

"So Tuesday night's okay?" Lily asked.

Rachel sighed. "I suppose."

Showing her work to Rob and Lily was one thing, but Tom. . . . They didn't much get along in the first place—though it wasn't from lack of her trying to make nice. He'd just taken a dislike to her as soon as he found out that she worked at the LaBranche Gallery, for all that he denied it to Lily.

It was little wonder that she felt anxious, Rachel thought.

Having heard him go on at length about the dearth of decent contemporary art far too many times only added to her anxiety. What would he say when he saw her work?

So much for self-esteem, she thought wryly.

Still, she'd made the commitment, and the portrait of Peter she'd painted last night was good. Maybe the "showing" would be fairly painless.

"I'll make sure he stays on his best behavior," Lily assured her, as though aware of what was going through her mind.

Rachel shook her head. "No, if he's going to look at my work, I want him to be honest, otherwise what's the point?"

Yes, what was the point? It wasn't as if she were ready to show her work in public anyway, so what difference would Tom's opinion make? She knew how far she still had to go—not just to regain the style she'd lost when she'd put her art aside, but to improve upon it as well.

But Tom's opinion of her art wasn't the real reason she'd agreed to Lily's suggestion. As Lily had said, she and Tom were the most important people in Lily's life. Rachel wanted to get along with Tom as much as Lily wanted them to be friends—it was for Lily's sake. There was nothing worse than having a relationship with only one half of a couple.

"If you're sure," Lily said.

She seemed to be having second thoughts herself.

"I'm sure," Rachel told her. "Here's your bus."

"After eight's okay?"

Rachel smiled. "After eight's *still* okay. Tuesday."

She waited until Lily was seated and they'd exchanged waves through the window, before putting on her helmet. The bus pulled away in a cloud of noxious fumes. Trying not to breathe until the exhaust had blown away, Rachel followed along on her bicycle, turning off at the little confectionery at the corner of Kelly Street and River Road.

Since she'd only be gone a moment, she didn't bother locking up her bike while she went inside. She started to lean it against the window, but the store owner rapped on the pane and waved her away from the glass, so she put it up on its kickstand instead. His frown changed to a smile when she came in.

"I didn't recognize you with that helmet on," he told her. "It's the kids, you see. They're scratching the glass, always leaning their bikes up against the window."

"I'm sorry," she said. "I wasn't thinking."

"Ah, that's okay."

He turned back to the magazine he was reading as Rachel stepped over to the magazine stand. The newspapers were in a wire rack beside the magazines.

It wasn't morbid curiosity that had her here, picking up copies of the city's two dailies, but if pressed she couldn't have exactly said why, either.

It was to look at the picture of the victim, she realized as she reached for the top copy of *The Newford Star*. To drive home the fact that it really *was* the waiter who'd served her last night who had died. But when she glanced at the front-page photos, it wasn't the small candid shot of Timothy Nanes that drew her attention. Her gaze froze on the photo that was just under another headline: "MUTILATED CORPSE DISCOVERED IN MIDTOWN APARTMENT."

The man in the picture was familiar.

Hey, the surgeon did a nice job on the sex change, honey.

She could almost hear his voice.

Did he fix the plumbing as well?

Her hands trembled, making the newspaper shake. Her head started to hurt as her mind leapt to make the connections. Frank, the waiter, the man from the Bike Pit.

"My god . . ."

The guardian angel. *Her* guardian angel. He hadn't just rescued her from Frank's attack. He was still watching over her, only now he was meting out lethal justice for the smallest offense.

It was a crazy thought, but as sure as she was standing there, she was certain it was true.

Her stomach churned with nausea. The paper slipped from her fingers and fell to the floor, various sections scattering around her feet. She was barely aware of the mess they made on the floor. Staring at the magazine rack, she saw not the latest issues of *People* and *Newsweek* and the like, but a blurring, dizzying image of the man who had killed Frank. Eyes hidden behind sunglasses, but she remembered the mouth, the smooth, pantherlike grace with which he had carried himself.

The little fantasies she'd had of him died inside her, mutated into nightmares. What watched over her was no guardian angel, but a dark angel. A dark, unforgiving monster.

And Peter had the angel's mouth.

Peter had been at the Bike Pit.

Peter had been at the restaurant last night.

"Miss?"

She started from her reverie to find the store owner at her elbow.

"Are you all right?" he asked.

She managed to nod. "I've just . . . just had a shock. . . ."

She bent down to pick up the newspaper and put it back into a rough semblance of order. Tried not to look at the accusing photos on the front page.

Your fault, they seemed to be saying. We died because of you.

"Someone you knew?" the store owner asked, indicating the picture of the waiter.

Rachel nodded.

"I'm sorry."

"I . . . I didn't know him that well," Rachel said. "It's just . . . I . . ."

She'd just known him well enough to cause his death, that was all.

Somehow she managed to purchase both papers and escape from the store and the solicitous sympathy of its owner. She fastened the newspapers to the rack of her bike with the bungee cord, then walked the bicycle across the small parking lot, not trusting herself to ride it.

She looked nervously around herself, feeling very exposed. Was he watching her now? She could *feel* a gaze, the sure sensation that she was being closely observed, but couldn't pinpoint its source.

The helmet seemed to cut off too much of her peripheral vision, so she took it off and hung it from the handlebars. When she studied the few people she could see, no one seemed suspicious. No one seemed to be paying any particular attention to her.

Not the woman walking with her two toddlers, one of them laboriously pushing a double-seated stroller but insistent upon doing it himself.

Not the two kids sitting at the edge of the parking lot, listening to M. C. Hammer on their boombox.

Not the college-age kids playing with a Frisbee over on the lawn between the road and the river.

Not the three joggers, or the other bicyclists, or the man who pulled into the convenience store's parking lot and gave her an appreciative once-over, then concentrated on getting his car into a parking spot.

But then none of them had the look, the stance, the mouth of the man who had rescued her from Frank.

None of them was Peter.

She got as far as the grass border that lay between the parking lot and the street and then had to lay her bike down on the grass and sit. Feeling faint, she hung her head between her knees until the weak, shaky feeling passed. But the nausea remained. And the headache was getting worse.

Think, she told herself. Be reasonable. It can't be true. There's no such thing as guardian angels. When the man had saved her from Frank, that had been pure chance. The deaths of the other two men were simply coincidence.

And if they weren't?

At least he meant her no harm.

No, not at all. He'd just kill anyone who looked at her the wrong way.

Jesus.

Logic told her she was building this far out of proportion, but her heart told her it was true. She had to do something, but she didn't know what. Contacting the police with what she knew seemed the natural thing to do, but they knew her as the woman who'd been trying to escape from her ex-husband, who'd been there when he died, who'd been uncooperative during the investigation of Frank's death, who'd demanded protection, who'd been a constant nuisance.

They'd think she was crazy. God knows, she did. But with what she knew . . .

What she knew. What did she know, anyway? She had no proof. She had nothing but this certain feeling that made her head ache and was tying her stomach up in knots.

She looked around herself, fruitlessly trying to find him—the monster, Peter, whoever he was.

What did he *want* from her?

She could feel panic rising up in a wave.

Don't, she told herself. Think. She practiced the slow breathing taught to her by the instructor at the defense course that she and Lily had taken.

"The worst thing you can do is panic," he'd said. "No matter what happens, no matter how scared you are, you've got to fight the panic. Because if you don't, then your assailant has already won."

Think.

Peter had been there at the Bike Pit and the restaurant. He had a mouth that reminded her of the man who had saved her from Frank's attack. His hair was the wrong color, but hair could be dyed. He could have grown a beard.

Okay. But she'd met him purely by chance. There was no way that meeting could have been planned because the decision to go buy a bike yesterday had been completely spur of the moment. Not unless she wanted to include Rob in the conspiracy.

No, that was pure paranoia. And why would Peter want to kill anybody over such slight incidents? He barely knew her.

But if it wasn't Peter, then who was it?

She lifted her head as a man came by, walking his dog. He gave her a friendly smile, but Rachel shivered and had to stifle a new wave of panic. The man gave her a curious look, but then shrugged and continued on his way.

Rachel watched the man's receding back, her panicked feeling waning with every step he took. But the fear remained. Constant. Drumming against her temples. Roiling in her stomach.

It could be anybody.

Once, she would have given anything to feel safe. Now, with her unseen, manic protector watching over, she felt smothered by safety. What if that man with his dog had gotten into an argument with her?

Would he be dead by tomorrow morning? Or if the owner of the convenience store had shortchanged her? Would he be dead, too?

She felt that she had to go home and bar the door and never venture out, never have anyone over, in case they might have an argument over something, or someone might bump into her, or spill something else on her. . . .

I'm going insane, she thought.

TWENTY-EIGHT

"Jesus, Lily," Tom said. "You're really putting me on the spot."

Tom's apartment was in its usual state of disorder. Lily picked up the handful of pens and a sketch pad that lay on the pillow between them and somehow found room for them on the coffee table, which was already buried under a clutter of books and papers. Then she scooted closer to him on the sofa.

"Come on," she said. "It won't be that bad."

"What if I don't like her work?"

"Well, then you'll have to tell her so—but constructively." When he frowned, she added, "You do it in your classes all the time."

Tom sighed. "But those people are paying to have their work critiqued. They've come to learn. This is different. When someone wants you to have a look at their work outside of a classroom situation, what they're really saying is 'Reassure me. Don't tell me what's wrong, tell me how good I am.'"

"Well, if you want to know the truth, Rachel was uncomfortable with the whole idea herself. I'm the one who brought it up, and then

I had to convince her to agree." She paused for a moment. "Besides," she added, "maybe it'll give the two of you some common ground."

"Now we get to the nitty-gritty of what this is all about."

"I can't help wanting the two of you to be friends."

"I don't dislike Rachel."

"But you don't really like her either—do you?"

"It's not a question of liking or disliking," Tom said. "There's just something about her that makes me uncomfortable. Maybe it's because she's so obviously a born victim. I try to feel sympathetic toward her, but mostly I just want to give her a shake and tell her to assert herself and get on with her life."

Lily couldn't deny—at least to herself—that she'd had similar feelings, but when she heard them from another, she immediately rose to Rachel's defense.

"That's not fair," she said.

"But what you're asking me to do is?"

When it was put like that, Lily realized that she *was* being unfair. Friendships couldn't be forced; people either got along or they didn't. The way she was going about trying to get them together was probably just making things worse.

"Oh, never mind," she said.

She'd call Rachel and tell her it was off. Considering how much work it had been to convince Rachel that it was a good idea in the first place, she was sure that Rachel would just feel very relieved. But then Tom surprised her.

"How long has she been painting?" he asked.

Ha, Lily thought. I knew he'd be intrigued.

"Since she was a kid," Lily told him. "She took fine arts as well as art history in college, but her husband and her family belittled her work so much that she finally just put it all away. She told me today that she hadn't touched a brush, hadn't even *thought* about her art until she left Frank for that last time. She started it up again as a kind of therapy, but then she discovered that it was through her art that she used to define herself and was surprised to find that she wanted to be able to do that again."

"Sounds like she's got the right attitude at least."

"The trouble is, until just a few weeks ago, she hadn't been able to paint anything she thought was worth keeping. Now, she says, it's all she thinks about."

"And you never knew?"

Lily shook her head. "Weird, isn't it?"

"What's her work like?"

Lily thought about that for a moment. She didn't have the terminology to professionally convey Rachel's style and medium, but that wasn't really what Tom was asking.

"I like it," she said finally. "She's like you, working mostly in watercolor and inks. Her early stuff's kind of tame—you know, landscapes and still lifes and that sort of thing—except for her people. She's really good at people. And her new stuff's wonderful. It's all kind of mysterious and strange. Very contemporary—street scenes around the city, mostly—but they've all got this odd recurring element about them."

That mysterious figure, not quite scary, but not quite safe either. It was like when Lily saw a wolf or one of the big cats in the metro zoo. She always wanted to pat them, but knew if she stuck her hand in between the bars, the animal would probably take her fingers off with one quick bite. Not because they were evil, but because that was simply their nature. They weren't good or bad the way humans defined the terms; just amoral.

Like Rachel's mysterious figure seemed to be.

The man who haunted Rachel's paintings had left Lily with an uneasy feeling. It wasn't Rachel's ex—in fact, if anything, the man reminded Lily more of the portrait that Rachel had done of this Peter Orlick, but Rachel had only just met Orlick yesterday; the paintings had been done over the past few weeks before she'd ever met the man.

The figure wasn't well defined, not like Orlick's portrait. When you looked at the portrait, you immediately felt like you knew the subject.

The figure in the paintings only hinted at definition. It was like a familiar stranger. You caught a glimpse of him, felt you knew him, but knew you couldn't possibly have seen him before. Except maybe in a dark dream.

Lily had found the figure in each of the recent paintings that Rachel had shown her, but when she'd asked Rachel about it, her friend had only shrugged.

The nonchalance hadn't fooled Lily. That figure meant something to Rachel. Its presence in every recent painting was more than just an artistic quirk.

She might have put it down to simple need—after all, Rachel hadn't had a lover in over a year. Longer, really, when you considered what a monster her husband had been. But Lily didn't think it was merely a matter of Rachel's libido. The figure wouldn't have been so . . . spooky if that was the case. If it were just Rachel's sexual drive being kindled in her art, then she'd probably be doing life studies of handsome young men. Tom had once confessed to her that he used to paint attractive young women when he got to feeling that way and had no lover.

"There's art," he'd told her, "and then there's need. The best art grows out of compulsions and obsessions."

Well, there was certainly something both compulsive and obsessive about Rachel's paintings.

"Actually," she told Tom, "there's something about her current work that kind of scares me."

She tried to explain the odd mix of feelings that the mysterious figure awoke in her, but couldn't find the right words. In the end she had to just give up.

"Now I'm really intrigued," Tom said.

"Well, you'll have to wait until Tuesday night to see for yourself."

"But speaking of obsessions," Tom said.

He dug under a stack of art magazines to come up with a small package wrapped in brown paper, which he gave to her. The shape was flat and rectangular.

"For me?" Lily asked.

She loved getting presents; it didn't matter how small or silly they were. In fact, something small and personal attracted her far more than something costly.

She turned it over and over in her hands, carefully feeling through the paper to try to guess what it was. A picture frame. Obviously a small one. Now what—

"Would you just open it," Tom said.

He wore an exasperated expression that made Lily laugh, but she decided not to torment him any longer and tore the brown paper away. Her mouth shaped a silent "oh" of pleasure as she looked down at what she held. It was the drawing that Tom had been doing of her this morning, finished now, matted and framed.

"Do you like it?" he asked.

"I *love* it. I usually hate pictures of myself, but I *love* this one."

She wrapped her arms around his neck and gave him a kiss, then held up the picture behind his back to look at it some more.

"It's so delicate," she said into his ear. "How can you do that with just a pencil?"

"It's the artist's touch," Tom said.

His hands began to roam over her shoulder blades, then traveled down her spine before squeezing up between their bodies to each cup a breast. Lily pulled back a little so that she could put the painting down in a safe place. When it was safely stowed away, she lay down on the couch and pulled him down on top of her.

"I love an artist's touch," she told him.

TWENTY-NINE

"Well, that's it for me," Freeman said.

He went through the procedure of closing the file he'd been working on and shutting off his computer, then pushed his chair back from the desk. Standing up, he stretched the kinks from his back, then walked the few short steps over to Stone's desk.

Norm Freeman wasn't a large man. While he stood at six-one, he only weighed in at a hundred and sixty pounds, giving his partner an inch in height and thirty pounds over him. His was a boyish face, which didn't show the cynicism that both men had acquired over the fourteen years that they'd been with the NPD. But he still laughed easily and seemed able to shed the job when he left Homicide Division's offices in the Newford Police Headquarters at the end of his shift.

Not so Stone. He carried each case with him until it was solved. Considering the percentage of unclosed files that were an inevitable part of the job, that made for a lot of excess weight. With his dark eyes and brooding features, Stone was like a shadow to Freeman's light. When they played good cop/bad cop, Stone was always the latter.

"How're you doing, John?" Freeman asked, perching on the edge of his partner's desk.

Stone shrugged. It was a quiet night so far, which would allow him to catch up on his paperwork. He'd been working for close to twenty hours straight, just as Freeman had, but his second wind still hadn't run out.

"I'm going to get a jump on organizing the rest of these files," he told his partner.

"Better you than me."

Stone watched Freeman leave, then slowly turned back to the work at hand, but the interruption had distracted him. He found himself thinking of Timothy Nanes, instead. Twenty-four years old. Beaten to death. Body set on fire.

Why?

That was the million-dollar question. Nanes hadn't been robbed, and he was so clean, he squeaked. Raised in the burbs, A-student, no record. He had a scholarship at Stevenson U; the job at Zwicker's was to pay for books, pocket money, living expenses.

Nice-looking kid, from the pictures Stone had seen. No enemies. According to the various family, friends and colleagues they'd managed to track down to date, Nanes just naturally got along with everybody in his life.

So why'd he die?

He hadn't just been murdered, Stone thought. It was like the killer had wanted to erase Nanes from the face of the earth. The beating might have been spur-of-the-moment, but the burning meant there'd been some planning involved. You didn't just happen to find a gas can on the beach.

Motion in his peripheral vision dragged Stone from his brooding. He smiled at Liz Brauman's approach.

She was a slim woman in her mid-thirties, dark-haired and brown-eyed, with a heart-shaped face. Her slenderness was deceptive. She might look like a good wind would just blow her away, but she could also bench press more weight than half the guys who also used the gym in the basement of the NPD's main Headquarters.

Stone knew her as a strong, attractive woman, but it wasn't her looks that made him smile with approval. It was the extra cup of coffee that she was carrying.

"You look like a dog worrying a rat, John," she said as she set the coffee in front of him.

They were old friends, a friendship that dated back to the Police Academy where Stone's career had first started to parallel hers. They'd both come out of the same class at the Academy, both made detective third grade in the same month and were both transferred to Homicide within two weeks of each other.

"A dog?" Stone said.

Brauman nodded. "Bull terrier, I'd say. Just caught himself a whiff of a Tombs rat and now he's digging through the garbage to get at the little sucker."

"Lovely image," Stone told her.

He popped the plastic lid from the foam cup and took a gulp of the coffee, not caring how it burned his throat going down.

Brauman laughed. "Jesus, you're just a real he-man with that stuff. You planning to inhale the rest of it?"

"Anybody ever tell you you've got a mouth on you?"

"Yeah, you do—every chance you get."

She perched on his desk, skirt riding up her thigh as she crossed her legs. Stone appreciated the view, but only in the same way he might appreciate the musculature of a male athlete. Brauman was too much like a sister for him to look at her as a potential sexual partner.

"So what's eating you?" she added when he didn't carry on with their usual good-natured jibing.

Stone stabbed a finger at the Nanes file.

"The waiter that got burned?"

Stone nodded wearily. "I've got nothing. No motive. No suspects. Zip."

"Hey, count yourself lucky. The Loot's got me working the Hughes case. I've got more people who wanted Ian Hughes dead than I can even start to deal with."

"Dealer?"

"Dealer, misogynist, self-proclaimed hardcase, all-round asshole. Loser with a capital L. If anybody ever deserved to die with his own dick in his mouth, it was this guy."

Stone understood where she was coming from. She'd do her best to crack the case, but it was hard to get worked up over the death of a lowlife like Hughes. For every petty criminal like Hughes who went down, there were a half-dozen others clamoring to take his place.

Nanes was a different matter.

Brauman agreed when Stone said as much.

"Maybe those Old Testament guys had it right," she added. "I'll bet we'd see a drop in serious crime if we were still running with the punishment fitting the offense—you know, all that eye-for-an-eye shit they used to go on about."

She wasn't the only cop Stone knew to feel that way. There were days he'd gladly embrace the credo—like every time some asshole who should have been put away years ago took down an innocent victim.

"Still wouldn't help a guy like Nanes," he said.

"I suppose."

Stone sighed. "I just hate the idea of his death being random."

He didn't have to explain why. If it was random, that meant it might happen again.

A half-hour later, after Brauman had returned to her own desk and Stone was just getting ready to pack it in, Lieutenant Takahashi came out of his office and entered the squad room. He looked about the room and crossed over to Stone's desk when his gaze found the detective.

"Good thing you're still here," he told Stone.

"What's up?"

"Your torcher's back in action. Got himself a dealer in Fitzhenry Park this time."

The sympathetic glance that Brauman threw him didn't deflect the sinking sensation that grew in Stone's stomach.

"I hate this shit," he muttered as he followed the lieutenant out of the squad room.

THIRTY

It seemed to take Rachel forever just to make the short return trip back to her apartment. She walked her bike in a daze along the street that led to the Sky Towers. Her fingers fumbled with the combination of the lock on her storage locker as she put away her bike. It took her four tries to get it open. When she finally took the elevator upstairs to her apartment, she closed the door firmly and engaged all the locks, as well as the safety chain, but she still didn't feel at ease.

The sense of being watched remained until she crossed the room and pulled the living room drapes closed.

She kept trying to argue with the unreasoning fear that had taken hold of her, but it didn't do much good. She'd seen no one paying any attention to her, either in the convenience store's parking lot, or on the way home, but she knew she was being watched. She had enough locks on her door to keep out an army, but they all seemed flimsy. She knew she was on the fourteenth floor; no one was going to come peeking in her windows. But if he had a telescope? He could be watching her from one of the apartments in the other apartment tower.

He wasn't. She knew that. It was all coincidence. She knew that too. But what if . . .?

She sat in the gloom that shrouded her living room, with that end-less circular conversation echoing in her head. She couldn't read, couldn't paint, couldn't do anything but sit on the sofa, staring at the wall across from her and listening to her thoughts as the argument went back and forth.

Either she was going crazy, or a crazy man was watching over her. A very dangerous, lethally crazy man.

She didn't know which was worse: that he existed or not.

In the end, it all boiled down to the fact that she was trapped here as surely as she'd been when Frank was still alive. No, it was worse. She didn't dare go out; she couldn't have anyone in. She didn't even dare *call* someone, because what would they say? Lily, Rob, Helen—she couldn't call any of them. They'd know something was wrong and they'd want to come over. What if one of them accidentally dropped something on her, bumped her . . .?

Until this moment, she had never felt more clearly the dichotomy between the two women who made up her personality—the woman in control of herself, who made things happen, and the victim to whom things just happened, who in some twisted way believed that she deserved the ills that befell her. There had to be a way to make peace between the two, to meld the strength of the former with the experi-ences of the latter, but if there was, Rachel didn't even know where to begin to find it.

She'd been strong as a teenager and in college—until she met Frank. From then on, as though she'd acquired an addiction, she'd become a victim. Whatever had carried her through her adolescence was lost. Stolen away. Trying to recapture that lost strength seemed an impossible task.

Twice she stood up and made to go into the bathroom, where the last of Dr. Caley's prescription waited for her in the vanity. Each time she forced herself to ignore the siren call of the pills. She was numbed enough as it was; all sedatives would do was make it worse.

At last she could stand it no more. Still unable to concentrate on anything productive, she picked up the remote from the coffee table and switched on the TV. Voices and incidental music filled the room. She let herself get stolen away by the small dramas being enacted within the twenty-inch screen—comedies, commercials, a special on wolves, they all merged into one blessed distraction that allowed her finally to shut down the argument in her head.

Until the news came on at eleven.

She meant to switch the TV off, but found herself ready to watch the news with the glum fascination of someone approaching the scene of an accident.

The first story was about the burning.

No, she realized, as she paid closer attention. It wasn't about the waiter who'd died last night, but another man, who was killed in Fitzhenry Park.

Utter panic came roiling up inside her until the victim's likeness flashed on the screen. She only dimly heard the newscaster mention something about him being a drug dealer and totally missed hearing the victim's name.

I don't know him, she thought. I never saw that man before in my life.

The newscaster mentioned the death of the waiter last night, linking the two deaths by the obvious.

The waiter's death and that of the man who'd harassed her in the Bike Pit . . . they *had* just been coincidence.

The relief she felt was a physical balm. The man who'd died tonight. His death was tragic, of course, even if he was a criminal, but she'd never been happier to hear such news.

She'd gotten a little out of control, a little crazy, imagining conspiracies where there were only coincidences. That was disturbing, but she felt she could deal with it. What had been impossible to deal with was the idea of her guardian angel turned rogue. That out there, somewhere, was a man killing other people for trivial slights against her, imagined or real.

She turned off the TV, then made her way through the darkness to open the drapes. Stepping out onto the balcony, she opened herself up to the sensation of being watched.

It was still there, but she could deal with it now. It was nothing but her imagination. Her overworked imagination. Weird, disturbing, but she *could* deal with it.

She had to.

She forced herself to stand out there for a long time before she finally went back inside. Her hand reached for the cord to pull the drapes closed, but she forced it to stay at her side.

You're going to fight this thing, she told herself. You're not going to let fantasies rule your life.

The skin at the nape of her neck prickled as she switched on a light and then turned her back to the window.

Don't turn, she thought. Don't give in.

She went into the kitchen to make herself a late dinner—not because she was hungry, but to give herself something constructive to do. She surprised herself at how quickly she finished the meal when it was ready.

After she was done, she washed up, spending an inordinate amount of time cleaning not only the dishes, but the counters, the stove, the outside of the refrigerator. She knew she couldn't sleep—not even knowing she had to get up early for work tomorrow. Whenever she stopped concentrating on not thinking, she'd find herself dwelling on the manic mood swings.

Finally she went into her studio and surprised herself a second time when she found that she could actually paint. And not only could she paint, but the longer she worked, the more she concentrated on the images that her brush woke on the paper, the further her fears fled.

THIRTY-ONE

Something was wrong, Harry decided.

He'd followed Rachel and Lily out to the bus stop, one more yuppie jogger in dark green shorts and an Earth Day T-shirt, white sweatband and $195 running shoes. He had brown hair today—a short, bristly look—trimmed mustache, a dark brown contact in his left eye. Cotton padding in his mouth gave him a slight overbite; tape under the wig pulled the skin at his temples, changing the shape of his eyes.

I'm just like the invisible man, he thought as he jogged by the two women where they waited for Lily's bus.

Neither of them paid him any attention at all.

". . . were neighbors," Lily was saying when he came abreast of them.

"It'd be fun," Rachel said. "I don't need much. Even just . . ."

Because he had to keep moving, he lost the last part of what Rachel said. Ten yards past them, he paused on the sloped grass border that followed the street and began a series of stretching exercises which he continued until Lily left on her bus. Rachel got on her bike and went past him, pulling a face in the wake of the bus exhaust.

He started jogging again once Rachel was far enough ahead of him, and returned to his stretching exercises when she went into the Speedy Mart on the corner.

Harry didn't like convenience stores. They were too personal. You couldn't be as invisible in them the way you could in a large supermarket.

As soon as she stepped inside, Harry lay down on the grass, casually turning his head so that he could watch Rachel through the Speedy Mart's window. He sat up when he saw her drop the newspaper. The distance was too great for him to be able to make out her features, but her body language told him that she was upset.

What had happened? Had the store owner or some customer done something to bother her?

But no, Harry could see the store owner now, obviously concerned as well about whatever was causing Rachel's distress.

Something in the newspaper.

Harry had read both of today's papers himself and could think of nothing unpleasant in either of them. There were the accounts of the deaths of the two men he'd killed last night, but that was scarcely worth being on the front page, let alone upsetting anyone. Unless . . . Had Rachel known one of the men more than she'd let on at the time?

He thought back to how she had reacted to the incidents in the Bike Pit and later on in the restaurant.

No, he decided. She hadn't known either of those two men. She probably wouldn't recognize either of them if she were to see them again. But even if she did, surely, after all they had done to her, she couldn't be sympathizing with them, could she?

When she came out of the Speedy Mart, he put aside the nagging puzzle of it and immediately pretended to be interested in absolutely anything but her. There was a look about her, the way she stood, the way her gaze scanned the parking lot and beyond, that told him she was looking for someone.

Looking for *him*, he realized.

Had he made a mistake? Had she noticed him following her?

Impossible. He was the invisible man. No one was aware of him unless *he* allowed it.

He remembered Buddy Elman, but shook his head. That had been an anomaly, a simple coincidence, nothing more. Except hadn't he heard somewhere that coincidence was the name given to something by people who couldn't see the connections?

A ridiculous conceit.

Besides, Harry had dealt with the problem. He always dealt with the problem.

Surreptitiously, he turned his attention back to Rachel. He watched her stow the newspapers she had bought onto the back of her bike, but instead of riding off, she walked the bicycle across the parking lot. She seemed unsteady on her feet, and when she reached the grass, she sat down, face buried in her arms.

What was *happening*?

He was tempted to simply approach her and ask, but he wasn't Peter Orlick today, just a brown-haired stranger whose concern would probably upset her even more than she already was. All he could do was watch, frustration building in him. When she finally sat up and looked around herself again, he ducked down behind the sloping crest of the grass and pretended to be resting.

A few moments later she passed by him, still walking her bike. She glanced in his direction, but he had closed his eyes, watching her through only the faintest of slits. Her image was blurred by his eye-lashes.

You can't see me, he thought. I'm the invisible man. Just another yuppie jogger who bit off a bit more than he could chew with his exercise regime, and now he's too exhausted even to make his way back home.

Rachel's gaze didn't linger on him. As she went past where he lay, her gaze slid right over him, past the grass to the Speedy Mart. She looked carefully back the way she'd come, then swept her gaze ahead, back and forth, from one side of the street to the other, searching, but finding nothing.

Harry opened his eyes when he considered her to be far enough away to make it safe to do so, but he didn't change position. Sure enough, from thirty yards on, she looked back, gaze sliding over him once again before she went back to studying the landscape in front of her and on either side of the street.

It's not me, personally, Harry thought. She just knows that *someone* is watching her.

Interesting, but perhaps not all that surprising. Her hidden divinity would be aware of him. Perhaps that explained what had happened in the Speedy Mart.

He grew excited at the thought.

Perhaps her divinity was waking of its own accord, with no need for him to test her. Such an occurrence would disturb anyone. To be half-asleep like every other drone walking the planet, then suddenly be barraged by the vast spectrum of sensory input to which a goddess would naturally be subject—such an influx of awareness would be enough to stun anyone.

If anything, Rachel was handling it admirably.

He was so proud of her as he returned to his own apartment, but there, bringing her up close in the sights of his telescope, he felt his theory crumble. The woman who entered her apartment was not touched by awakening divinity. She just looked numb. In shock. Not more aware of the world around her, but completely shut down from its influence.

Then she closed the drapes of her living room, something she never did during the day.

Harry's agitation deepened as the afternoon dragged by. The drapes remained closed. When evening fell, no lights came on in apartment 1414. Nothing stirred.

She's just gone out, he told himself, but he knew it wasn't true. He could still *feel* her in there, locking herself away from the world.

From time to time his hand inched toward the telephone, but he never called her. The same sixth sense that told him she was still at home in that darkened apartment also told him that to call would be a mistake. He was supposed to be with her friend Rob this afternoon, playing golf. How was he supposed to explain his being free to call her, when he was the one who'd called off the game?

But he wanted to call her. What was she *doing* in there? What had happened in the Speedy Mart to set this off?

The sun had almost set when there was finally a change in 1414. Light flickered through the drapes, puzzling Harry until he realized it was just that she had turned on her television set.

Again it was so unlike her. Rachel rarely watched TV.

The evening dragged by even slower than the afternoon had, punctuated only by the flickering glow of Rachel's television behind the draped windows. Harry's agitation had grown to such an extent that he was almost ready to don his Peter Orlick persona and go over to the other apartment tower, for all that he knew it would be a mistake.

He knew he wouldn't be able to hide the turbulence of his thoughts. But if something *happened* to her . . .

He was taken by surprise at the sudden darkness in Rachel's apartment as the TV set was turned off. He sat up straighter, eye pressed to the end of the telescope. He was still focusing on the drapes, trying to find some crack to peer through, when they opened and there she was.

She seemed changed to Harry as he focused in on her face, but he had trouble exactly pinpointing the difference. She almost seemed to be looking directly at him, her eyes wide, almost luminous, and then he had it.

She looked at peace.

There was almost always a tension in her eyes, even yesterday afternoon, when she seemed so relaxed, even last night in the restaurant before the unfortunate incident with the coffee carafe. That tension was now gone. Her body language still showed a certain wariness, but her eyes spoke of a release from the mild state of stress she always seemed to be in.

He tracked her with the telescope as she went back into her living room, almost losing her in the dimness that lay inside the apartment until she flicked on a light. He watched her make dinner, eat, clean up—the mundane activities all transformed into something meaningful because of the serenity he now sensed in her.

Perhaps her divinity *had* woken in her. Perhaps Rachel had found herself and managed to come to terms with the marvel of the goddess's presence inside her.

He continued to watch her, not letting her move out of the eyepiece of the telescope until she finally went into another room. He kept the telescope focused on the empty hall for another fifteen minutes, before he finally moved away from it.

He sensed an eerie undercurrent to the day, as though hidden tides had moved beyond his understanding. As though the goddess, by awakening on her own, was slipping from his grasp.

But would Rachel's divinity awake in an imperfect body? There were still those inflammations on her arms and thighs, and Harry couldn't conceive of the goddess awakening when the vessel that held her was marred with even the smallest blemish.

No, the divinity slept. She had to be sleeping. She was waiting only for his touch before she finally woke, and that had to wait until Rachel was fully healed.

He realized suddenly that he was exhausted. He hadn't had anything to eat or drink since noon. But while his stomach grumbled and his mouth had the grating texture of sandpaper, he refused to bow to the weakness of his body. The day's agitation, the vague unsettling laughter of the voice deep in the back of his mind, the endless mental turmoil and questioning . . . they all told him something: he was weak.

The goddess had tested him today, and he couldn't help but feel that he'd been found unworthy. Nothing had happened to Rachel in the Speedy Mart—he'd been watching her the whole time. No, it had to have been a test, and he had failed it.

He needed to purify himself.

He spent the next two hours running through a rigorous series of physical exercises, ranging from simple t'ai chi forms and more complex aikido techniques to strengthening his hands by plunging them repeatedly into a wide-brimmed vase filled with coarse sand.

Not until his body felt aflame with a white-hot glow, until his mind was utterly at peace with his *tan t'ien,* the physical center of his body, did he allow himself a bowlful of cold rice and a glass of water.

He did not look through the telescope again, but he did stand before his favorite portrait of Rachel for a long time, following the familiar contours of her features, which had long ago been committed to memory.

"Now we are both at peace," he said.

He had been tested. Perhaps both he and the physical vessel that held the goddess had been tested today. When Rachel's hurts were completely healed, he would see how well each of them had fared in that testing. Perhaps when he called to her, the goddess would be ready to speak to him through Rachel. Or perhaps he'd need the knife. . . .

He trembled, imagining the light bleeding from Rachel's perfect skin when he freed the goddess from her mortal prison.

Soon. Very soon.

But first he would allow himself to rest.

Eschewing his bed, he lay down on the floor, and fell immediately into a dreamless sleep.

THIRTY-TWO

Stone exhausted his second wind, and a third didn't seem to be forthcoming. At midnight, he was standing with Lieutenant Takahashi and Detective Brauman inside the police barricade that had been set up around the scene of the crime in Fitzhenry Park, watching Forensics swarm over the site now that the medical examiner had finished with his preliminary investigation.

Neither the lieutenant nor Liz seemed tired, but of course Takahashi had just come on shift a few hours ago, while Liz never seemed to need more than a short catnap before looking as refreshed as if she'd had eight hours of blissful, uninterrupted shut-eye.

Stone shook his head. It got bad when you started fantasizing about sleep.

"No way it's the same M.O.," his partner said as he joined the three of them.

Freeman had been taking Polaroids of the scene for Stone and him to use as reference until they got the official shots back from the police photographer.

"You mean torching the guy's not similar enough for you?" Brauman asked.

"It's the knife," Stone said wearily.

Freeman nodded. He shot a wary gaze toward the various members of the press, each jockeying to get a better angle for his or her broadcast. Only a few free-lance photographers were left, and the film crews. Staff photographers for the dailies had all rushed off earlier to have their films developed, once they realized nothing new was forthcoming. A handful of print reporters were still on the job. They stood to one side of the TV crews, sharing cigarettes and coffee.

"Plus there's the identity of this victim, Liz," Freeman said, "which puts it closer in line with your case."

"You've got an I.D.?" Brauman asked.

"Tentative. Does Grover Jenkins ring any bells?"

"He's a pimp," she said.

"And a dealer."

"Okay," Brauman said. "I see the connection. But my stiff didn't get a knife used on him until *after* he'd been beat to shit."

Something nagged Stone about what she'd just said, but he was feeling too foggy to pick up on it.

"The Nanes kid was squeaky clean," Freeman went on. "He never even had a parking ticket. Whoever killed him took his time to break every one of his ribs before he torched the poor bastard. We're going to have to wade through a lot of shit trying to find somebody who even liked Jenkins."

Yeah, Stone thought. You handle it, Norm. You at least had a couple hours of sleep before you got called back in.

"Tell me about it," Brauman said.

"I think it's a copycat killing," Freeman added, turning toward the lieutenant.

Takahashi nodded. "I think I'm in agreement. But let's wait to see what the M.E.'s got to say before we jump to any conclusions."

The press, of course, was already riding on the serial killer tag, despite Takahashi's earlier statements that it was still too soon to tell if the cases were connected or not.

Stone didn't know which was worse. The only thing that really made him nervous was the thought of Nanes's killer getting pissed about somebody else stealing a piece of his glory. The psychologists had all kinds of pretty ways to put it, but Stone knew these killers for what they were: amoral creatures who, once they were discovered, gloried in their infamy. Far too many of them kept clipping files and videotapes of the ongoing investigations for him to feel that wouldn't be the case here as well.

The city didn't need a pissed-off pyromaniac loose on its streets—especially not one who got his jollies beating innocent people to death and then setting them on fire.

Men had already been assigned to pull in the usual arsonists, but there was a big difference between torching a building and a person, enough so that Stone doubted any of them was responsible for what had happened out by the Pier last night or tonight. He agreed with his partner—this was the work of a copycat. Somebody was using last night's killing as a cover for a hit.

"Are we about wrapped up?" he asked the lieutenant.

Takahashi nodded. "Go home and get some sleep, John. I need you back downtown first thing in the morning." He turned to Freeman, adding, "I've got both your shifts covered for tonight."

The Loot could be a ballbreaker when he had to be, Stone thought, but at least he had some heart.

"Eight o'clock," Takahashi said.

But not a lot, Stone amended, stifling a groan at the thought of the meager six hours he'd be able to catch before having to fight the traffic back downtown in the morning.

"Eight o'clock," he confirmed, then left with his partner, trying not to stumble as various cameras turned in their direction.

"No comment," Freeman told the reporters, the phrase falling from his lips with easy familiarity as they made their way through the crowd, ignoring the questions.

"What do you think our torcher's going to do when he hears about this?" Stone asked his partner once they were in the car.

"I don't even want to think about it."

"Because he's nuts and who the hell knows what a guy like that's going to pull next, right?"

Freeman nodded.

"Waiter spills a pot of coffee on your date," Stone went on. "You'd have to be pretty nuts to take it out on the waiter by torching him, right?"

"You think Orlick looks good for it?"

Stone shrugged. "I don't know what to think. You saw what Sandy came up with when she ran his name. Zip. No priors. Department of Motor Vehicles has got nothing on him. He's not on the voter rolls."

"Out-of-town visitor?"

"She was working on the airlines, hotels and the like just before she left for the day, but I've got a feeling they're going to come up blank as well."

"He could have driven into town," Freeman said.

Stone shook his head. "It's all computers now, Norm. When she runs a check, it feeds right across the country. If he drove, he doesn't own a car, and we've got no record of him renting one."

"Maybe somebody else drove him. Maybe he's staying in town with a friend."

"Maybe. Or maybe he's using an alias, and you know what that makes me wonder?"

"Give," Freeman said.

"What's he got to hide?"

"You're reaching, John. A place like Zwicker's is pretty classy."

"All you need is money to get in. And don't forget who used to own the place."

Freeman nodded. The Harbor Ritz had been part of Mickey Flynn's empire before his own lieutenant cut him up into little pieces and was caught trying to smuggle him out the back of the hotel. That was the way the Irish mob worked: without a body, there could be no charges laid.

"You think it was a mob hit?" he asked.

Flynn's organization had fallen to pieces, but that hadn't ended organized crime in Newford. They still had Chinese triads tripping over the Caribbean posses. Yakuza. South Americans. Not to mention the good old Italian and Sicilian social clubs, which were so much a part of the criminal landscape by now that they might as well have been considered homegrown.

"No," Stone said. "The kid was too clean. I'm just trying to keep an open mind on this."

"Yeah, but . . ."

Stone knew. Some guy killing Nanes because the waiter spilled coffee on his girlfriend was a long stretch.

"I'm so tired," he told his partner, "that everything makes sense and nothing does."

"Want to crash at my place?"

Freeman had a bachelor in Midtown, about a third the distance from police headquarters that Stone's own apartment in Upper Foxville was.

"I thought you'd never ask," he said.

THIRTY-THREE

She was simply going to ignore the news from now on, Rachel decided as she biked to work Monday morning. TV, radio *and* newspapers. It was all too depressing anyway.

Which was how she missed the police statement that was issued mid-morning, announcing that Grover Jenkins's death the previous night in Fitzhenry Park had been a copycat killing and not related to the death of Timothy Nanes. A suspect had been arrested, euphemistically described by the police as a "business associate" of Jenkins. There were still no new leads in the Nanes case.

With Rachel in a more communicative mood, Helen didn't bother with the radio. Instead the two women spoke of their weekend. Helen had gone out to the Islands to stay the weekend with her new lover— "You wouldn't believe the place she's got. It's heaven." Rachel only talked about the bike she'd bought and then told Helen about her art.

She'd done three new paintings last night, not one of them with a mysterious figure in it. She'd taken the other work down from her walls, embarrassed now by the weird infatuation she'd had with her "guardian angel." The scare she'd had yesterday made her want to just put it all out of her mind.

She was good at ignoring the bad things that happened to her, pretending that they'd never occurred. She couldn't have lived with Frank's abuse all those years otherwise.

The three new pieces came from memory, but from a happier time—her first year at university, before she'd met Frank. She and her roommate had hung a bird feeder in the old oak tree outside their dorm window, and Rachel had spent many hours through that first winter away from home watching the birds the feeder attracted. Last night's paintings celebrated the sparrows that had always been her favorite regulars.

She was smiling as she painted their brown bodies against the white snow. There was one painting of a small flurry of feathers landing on the feeder, a second of another perched on the peak of the roof, regarding her with a cocked eye. The last was a long shot from below: the tree, the feeder, the sparrows flocking around it like so many feathered gossips.

When Rachel had stopped in her studio before leaving for work this morning, she was just as happy with the new work as she'd been when she finally got to bed. Standing back to look at them, she'd been surprised to realize that she wasn't at all scared about Tom coming to see her work anymore. In fact, she was rather looking forward to getting his opinion of her art. And who knew? Maybe Lily was right. Maybe this would help her and Tom to find some common ground.

She wondered if she should bring the paintings into work tomorrow and mount them during her lunch hour.

"Boy, talk about keeping secrets," Helen said when Rachel finished telling her about her painting. "Most people I know that're involved in the arts, that's all they can ever talk about, but you never said a word about being an artist."

Rachel just shrugged. She didn't want to get into explaining the whys behind her secret.

"So are you going to bring something in to show me?" Helen asked. "Have you taken any pictures of them yet?"

Rachel had pretty well decided that she was going to mount her latest work, so Helen could see them then, but she found herself wanting to share her older pieces with Helen as well.

"Why don't you come over tonight and see them yourself?"

"Can I bring Linda?"

Linda Chalmers was Helen's latest lover, the one with the heavenly cottage in the Islands. Rachel didn't even hesitate before replying.

"Sure," she said.

She actually felt normal, Rachel realized. It was an odd sensation, but a good one. Maybe she was actually on the road to recovery.

"We'll bring a bottle of wine," Helen said. "This'll be fun."

Rachel smiled in agreement as they both went back to the prints they were mounting.

THIRTY-FOUR

Late Tuesday afternoon, Lily finally got through to Tom's studio.

"You really should get an answering machine," she told him when he picked up the receiver at his end.

It was a familiar complaint that had lost any pretense of seriousness after the first couple of weeks of their relationship.

Tom laughed. "Sorry, Lily. I was picking up some new supplies at Condon's and ran into Leroy, so we went for a coffee."

"And here I thought you were just too caught up in a new piece to answer the phone."

"I wish. I've been tidying up the studio all day."

"Ha."

"No, really."

"Well, I'm just calling about tonight," Lily said.

"And I haven't forgotten. Do you want me to meet you after work?"

"That's just the problem. Cameron's gone and called one of his stupid staff meetings for after work and obviously I can't not go."

"So tonight's off?" Tom asked.

"Actually, I was hoping you'd go on ahead and I could just meet you there."

"Ah . . ."

"Oh, come on. You make it sound like Rachel's some kind of ogre."

Tom looked out the window of his studio and tracked a pigeon skimming along the rooflines of the buildings across the street. He hadn't been looking forward to tonight, but now that he thought of it, if he had to do a critique of Rachel's work, maybe it'd be better to get it over with before Lily arrived.

"No," he said. "I can do it. Have you called Rachel?"

"I thought maybe I wouldn't."

"Because *she* might call it off?"

"Well, something like that."

"Don't worry, Lily. I'll be gentle."

"Yes, but—"

"Honest, but gentle."

He heard her sigh on the other end of the line.

"I guess I just worry too much," she said finally.

"If Rachel's work's half as good as you say it is, then there's nothing to worry about. And if it's not, I'll be a study of diplomacy."

"You're good at that," Lily said.

"At what?"

"Diffusing worries. Maybe you should have been a diplomat."

Tom laughed. "I'd be fine until somebody said something stupid. Then I'd probably cause a war."

He could feel her smile over the line.

"Yes, there's that, isn't there? Well, I'll try to get out of here as soon as I can. Apologize to Rachel for me, would you?"

"Chicken."

"*Bruck, bruck, bruck.*" Lily followed up her bad chicken imitation with a kiss that she blew into the phone. "Thanks, Tom. I'll see you at Rachel's."

Tom smiled as he cradled the receiver. He swiveled his chair from

the window and surveyed his studio. Half of it was tidy, the other half
in its usual state of disarray.

"Screw it," he said.

He picked up the bag of new brushes that he'd bought at Condon's
and dumped them on the table beside his easel. He could tidy up any-
time. Right now he wanted to paint.

Ever since he'd done that quick sketch of Lily yesterday morning,
he'd been wanting to redo it in watercolors. With any luck, he'd have
time to get the basic composition down before it was time to go.

But don't be late, he told himself. If he were, Lily would never for-
give him.

So he set his alarm clock, then shut out the world and let the act of
creation take him away.

THIRTY-FIVE

It was almost seventy-two hours now since the body of Timothy Nanes had been discovered, and Stone realized that the case was dead in the water. The first forty-eight hours were the most important. Every hour after that, especially in a case like this, where they had nothing to go on, made the trail colder.

The line on Peter Orlick had dead-ended, and there were no other leads. Other news had swallowed the front pages and Stone knew it would probably stay that way. The only thing that would change that was for the torcher to strike again, and that wasn't something Stone was particularly hoping for. It might open the case up wide, but the cost wasn't worth it.

He looked up as his partner entered the squad room.

"You get a chance to pull Gould's sheet?" Freeman asked him.

Kevin Gould looked good for a rape/mugging that had turned into a homicide late last night on a side street running out of the Combat Zone. Stone tapped the file folder that lay over on the side of his desk.

"Well, the Loot's ready to see us now," Freeman told him.

Stone sighed as he closed the slender folder that held all they had so far on the Nanes case. He picked up Gould's file and followed his partner into the lieutenant's office.

The Nanes case wasn't closed, but the workload was rapidly pushing it into the nonactive file cabinet. But it wouldn't get there. Not if Stone could help it.

He was still carrying a double image of the victim in his mind—clean-cut school picture and the charred corpse that had been found on the beach.

Stone carried all his failures around inside him until a conviction could put them to rest.

THIRTY-SIX

Early Tuesday evening found Rachel fussing about her apartment in anticipation of Lily and Tom's arrival. The first order of business had been to clean up the mess from Helen and Linda's visit the night before, which she'd been too tired even to consider tackling after they left. They'd stayed up so late and she was still so tired when she got up, that it had been all she could do just to get ready for work, let alone tidy up.

Wouldn't the mess have driven Frank crazy? The living room had been littered with a scatter of glasses and wine bottles—they'd gone through two—coffee mugs, the plates on which Rachel had served cheese and crackers, and the usual detritus of a relaxed evening. Then there were her paintings, portfolios, sketchbooks and the examples of her earlier work, all spread out on the floor where Linda and Helen had been looking at them.

Rachel had thoroughly enjoyed herself last night. Linda had turned out to be a striking woman in her late twenties who worked for the city's water department. She was a stylish dresser, easy to feel comfortable around, and she had an appreciation of art to match Helen's. Their praise for Rachel's work had bolstered her confidence for tonight, even if they hadn't liked the paintings of her mysterious angel. But they hadn't liked them for all the right reasons.

"There's something menacing about this figure," Linda had said, pointing the angel out in the crowd scene set in Crowsea's Market. "Everything else appears to be in motion, to have a purpose, except for him. He's just so . . . so . . ."

"Predatory," Helen put in.

"Exactly," Linda went on. "If the painting wasn't so beautifully executed, that figure probably wouldn't bother me as much as it does, but I can almost *feel* his presence." She shivered, shooting Rachel a quick grin. "Almost like he's watching me right now."

"I get that feeling, too," Rachel said.

"He really gives me the creeps," Helen put in. "Where did the idea for him ever come from?"

"I don't really know," Rachel replied truthfully. "I fell into a frenzy after Frank's death, and it seemed like I just *had* to do that whole series of paintings."

"What I like is the sweetness of these," Linda went on, indicating the studies of the sparrows that Rachel had just completed the night before.

Helen nodded. "All the 'serious' artists"—she put the word in quotations by lifting her arms and making quote marks with the first two fingers of each hand—"are afraid that they'll be considered too commercial if they do this kind of thing. Like they're immediately going to get relegated to being an Audubon artist, no matter what else they do."

"But that's wrong," Linda added. "It doesn't matter what the subject matter is, what technique an artist uses, so long as they work from the heart."

That was something that Rachel agreed with entirely, but she wasn't so ready to dismiss contemporary artists who shunned simple nature studies.

"Who's to say that the more experimental artists *aren't* working from the heart?" Rachel asked.

A lively discussion had followed, and they'd finally ended the evening with the promise of continuing it next weekend at Linda's cottage. Rachel had made a mental note to herself to mount one of the sparrow paintings and bring it to Linda as a present when she and Helen went out there Friday night after work.

God, it was so nice to feel normal again, she thought. She wasn't even nervous about Tom coming over with Lily this evening. They were just people, and people could be as good for her as Frank had been bad.

She was almost completely prepared by the time eight o'clock rolled around. The apartment was tidy once more. Since Tom was more of a beer drinker, Rachel had a six-pack chilling in the fridge, along with a bottle of wine for herself and Lily. She'd also prepared another tray of cheese and crackers. What to wear had kept her at her closet for the better part of twenty minutes until she'd finally opted for comfortable and pulled out a pair of jeans and her favorite sweater. The only makeup she put on was a touch of lipstick.

But now she couldn't decide what to do with her art. Leave it in a pile in the living room where it would be so obvious the minute Lily and Tom walked in through the door, or put it back in the studio, which would be a little cramped for all three of them to stand around in comfortably?

The buzzer from the lobby went off then, and she realized it was too late. The art would just have to stay where it was.

She went into her hallway and pushed the button on the intercom that let her talk to the guard downstairs.

"Yes?" she said.

"There's a gentleman here to see you, Miss Sorensen. A Mr. Tom Downs."

That seemed odd.

"Just the one person?" she asked.

"That's right, Miss Sorensen. A Tom Downs."

Tom? What about Lily?

"Shall I send him up?" the guard asked when she didn't reply.

"What? Oh, yes. Of course."

Rachel distractedly regarded her reflection in the hall mirror, trying to make sense out of Tom coming here on his own. She was *sure* that Lily had said they were both coming. Maybe they were planning to meet there?

She could feel her self-confidence ebbing at the thought of being alone with Tom. Without Lily there as ballast, she felt far too vulnerable. It was stupid, and she knew it, but there it was all the same.

The doorbell rang, and she hesitated before answering it.

Get ahold of yourself, woman, she told herself. Nothing bad is going to happen unless you let it happen. Just be yourself. Your new strong self.

She took a deep breath, fixed a smile on her lips and opened the door. Tom stood out in the hallway, looking handsome, and as awkward as she herself felt.

"Uh, hi. Lily had to work late, so I came on ahead."

"She never said . . ."

Tom shrugged. "Well, you know Lily."

Yes, Rachel thought. Lily, who was always so organized and punctual that you could set your clock by her.

"Can I come in?"

"I'm sorry. Of course."

Rachel stepped aside to let him in, then closed the door. Lily had probably planned this all along, she realized. She could almost hear Lily rationalizing it to herself: throw the two of them together and suddenly they're going to be friends.

Tom still looked awkward. He shuffled from foot to foot, then peered down the short hallway that led to the living room.

"Nice place," he said after a moment.

"Thanks."

Come on, Rachel told herself. You're the one that's making the weird vibe. Relax. Just go with the flow.

She gave Tom a bright smile, but he obviously saw through it to the discomfort she was feeling.

"Look," he said. "Lily really is working late tonight. She said she'd be along as soon as she could get away from the meeting her manager called."

Rachel started to relax. Okay. Be cool. Lily will be along soon and everything'll be fine. Just fill in the time.

"Would you like a beer?" she asked.

"Sounds great."

He followed her down the hall to where the entrances to the kitchen, living room and bedroom met. Suddenly Rachel felt embarrassed at the way her art was so obviously stacked up on the coffee table.

"I had some friends over last night, looking at my stuff," she explained, "and I never got around to putting everything away."

"Mind if I have a look?"

Well, that's what you're here for, isn't it? Rachel thought, but she amended the cattiness of the thought. She shouldn't prejudge him, and he did seem genuinely interested. It was part of being an artist, she supposed. You couldn't *not* be intrigued with another's work.

"Please do," she said and escaped to get his beer.

When she returned to the living room, Tom was sitting on the sofa, one of her portfolios open on his lap. He thanked her for the beer and took a sip, before placing it on the coffee table in front of him.

"Is this some of your earlier work?" he asked.

Rachel nodded. She'd brought herself a beer as well and knew she was clutching the glass too tightly, but she couldn't make her fingers relax.

"Those are all from the summer before I started my first year at the university," she told him.

At least her voice sounded normal.

"They're really quite remarkable—especially the compositions. This perspective here . . ."

He pointed to a watercolor sketch of the old Stanton Street Bridge, viewed from a helicopter side view that she'd had to imagine based on the perspectives she could actually see of the bridge.

"Considering your age at the time," he added, "there's a great maturity in this work." He glanced up. "Had you had any formal training up to this point?"

Rachel shook her head. "Just art classes in high school."

"That'd be in the late seventies?"

"'79–'80."

"Mmm."

It felt like a job interview, and she wished it didn't.

You're doing this to yourself, she thought. *There's nothing that he's doing to make you feel this way.*

Well, yes. She knew that. But knowing why she was feeling the way she was and stopping were two different things.

Tom studied all three of her portfolios, the various sketchbooks, new and old, and finally her more recent work. He spent the longest time with the five paintings she'd done while infatuated with what she'd perceived as her mysterious guardian angel.

"I just did those a couple of nights ago," she said when he picked up one of the sparrow paintings.

"I see."

What do you see? Rachel wanted to shout at him. Except for those few comments about some of her earlier work, he hadn't said a thing for over half an hour. It was enough to drive her crazy.

"So what do you think?" she asked finally.

Tom laid the sparrow painting down. Picking up his beer, he leaned back into the sofa.

"Well, let me ask you something first," he said. "What is it that you want to do with your art?"

Rachel gave him a puzzled look. "I'm not sure what you mean."

"Do you consider it a hobby, or is it something you want to get serious about?"

Rachel pounced on the words "get serious." Didn't he think she was serious already?

She'd known it all along, she supposed. Her friends might think she was good, but the first real artist she showed her work to could see right through her, knew she was a pretender, knew she had no talent. Wondered if she wanted to "get serious," as though she hadn't been beating her head against a wall for the past year, since separating from Frank, trying to do just that.

She'd finally felt she'd made some progress—with the angel paintings, the portrait of Peter, and especially the studies of the sparrows—but he wanted to know if she was planning to "get serious." What she wanted to do was whack him on the side of his head with her beer bottle.

"I already am serious," she said, keeping her voice level.

"Well, yes," Tom said. "I can see that you're certainly putting in the effort. Your technique's a bit rough, but you've only been at it again for—what?"

"A pretty short while."

"Exactly. Given the level of proficiency of your earlier work, it'll just be a matter of time before you regain your technical skills. But what I don't see in any of this later work is the unique sense of vision that it's apparent you once had."

"What do you mean?"

Tom sighed. "Do you want an honest opinion?"

Rachel's heart sank at those words. In her experience, they inevitably led to some devastating critique.

In for a penny, she told herself.

"Sure," she said. "That's what you came for, right?"

Tom gave her an odd look, his discomfort obvious.

Oh shit, Rachel thought. Now he's going to think I can't take criticism. But if he knew what it took just to get the courage to pick up a brush again . . .

But that didn't matter, did it? When it came down to it in the end, the art had to stand on its own. It didn't matter how handicapped she was when she did it, her art had to answer for itself. It either worked for what it was, or it didn't, and all the sad histories concerning its creation didn't matter in the final crunch.

"I'm sorry," she said. "I didn't mean that to sound the way it probably did. I really appreciate your taking the time to come over and look at my work. So yes, I do want your honest opinion."

Tom nodded slowly. "Okay," he said. "It's just . . ."

"Not very good?" Rachel asked when his voice trailed off.

"No. It's that it's not there in this later work—that spark, that unique frisson of uncommon perspective and exuberant spirit that made your earlier work so remarkable." He touched a finger to the edge of one of the sparrow paintings. "Anyone can do something like this with varying degrees of skill. As a hobby, I would think it would be most satisfying to its creator; as art, it tells me nothing."

"But—"

Tom leaned forward, and Rachel could almost imagine him at one of his lectures, earnestly putting forth his views. He spoke the way people do when they won't hold with contradiction—not necessarily because they're closed-minded, but because they can't possibly conceive of anyone disagreeing with them. What they have to say isn't an opinion, but simply the way things are, period.

"Art is communication," he said. "It speaks from the deepest places inside you and somehow translates the untranslatable into something that makes sense to another person."

He gave her an earnest look.

"Island communicating to island," he added. "Do you understand what I mean? We're forever separated from one another—literally islands set apart on a great sea. The only thing that connects us is how well we communicate with each other. The glory of art is how it can reach across all that open water and, for a brief moment in time, bridge the gap between our islands."

"But that painting *does* have meaning to me," Rachel said. "It does speak from inside me."

"Maybe it does," Tom said, "but it isn't telling me anything. To me it's just a pretty picture."

"Well, that's just subjective, isn't it?"

"I'd like to think I'm being objective. Tell me. What does this painting mean to you? What are you trying to tell me with it?"

I was trying to recapture what I've lost, Rachel thought. I was reaching for a time when not only did my art mean something to me, but I was good at it as well. I saw everything with a sense of not only what it was, but what it *meant*. But, confronted with Tom's self-assurance, that all seemed inadequate.

"If I could put it in words, I wouldn't have done the painting," she told him.

"That's a cop-out and you know it."

"I don't think so," Rachel said. "My responsibility as an artist is to paint from the heart. If what I'm communicating doesn't get across— whether it's because I didn't express myself clearly enough or due to some lack of insight in the viewer of my work—that doesn't invalidate the creative process."

Tom shook his head. "If it doesn't work, it's a failure."

"*You've* never done a piece that was misinterpreted or that someone didn't get at all?"

"Certainly. And I consider them failures. If I have to explain what I was trying to do, then I haven't done my job properly."

"What I learned," Rachel said, "what I believe, is that anything done from the heart is valid. Maybe sometimes one's technique doesn't quite match the inner vision, but that does *not* negate the work."

"Who told you that?"

"My art history professor during my first year at Butler. Professor Dapple."

As she spoke his name, Rachel realized that his classes were responsible for much of the way she viewed art, even today. All her arguments last night with Helen and Linda, as they discussed the merits of various mediums of expression, had had their origin in what the professor taught her. It wasn't that she was parroting his theories; rather he had given her the background so that she was informed enough to form her own.

Dapple. She hadn't really thought of him in years, except in passing. It was amazing how people could be so important to you at one time of your life and then just be forgotten. The process was so gradual that you didn't even realize the void until you met them, or thought of them again.

If she closed her eyes, she could see him as though it were yesterday. The small wizened features, the cloud of hair, the slight frame always dressed in rumpled tweed, and those bird-bright eyes behind the wire-framed glasses that he wore, not because he needed them to see properly, but to give his hands something to do—constantly adjusting and cleaning them.

Tom's mocking laughter dragged her out of her reverie.

"Dapple?" he said. "God, the man was a joke. If he hadn't had tenure, he would have been out on his ear years before they finally got him to resign."

"He—"

"I'll grant he was liked by his students, but the man was a lunatic. Do you know what he does these days? He studies what he terms as 'oddities and marvels.' What the rest of us read about in tabloids while we're waiting at a supermarket checkout, he thinks are valid phenomena."

Rachel couldn't bear to hear this.

"Don't you mock him," she said.

She remembered a gentle, kind, *generous* man. She remembered . . . A flush of embarrassment touched her cheeks as she recalled the last time she'd spoken to him. It was during her second year at Butler, when she'd become less serious about her art, after she'd met Frank, after she'd begun dressing to please Frank.

The professor had approached her on the common outside the library. He'd looked like a wizened little mole, blinking in the sunlight, and seemed completely oblivious to everyone around them.

"I know you don't want to hear this," he told her, "but it's something I have to say and I'm hoping you'll listen to me, if not with understanding, then at least with the same respect you gave me when you were in my class.

"You're a beautiful woman, and I see nothing wrong in expressing your beauty with more fashionable clothes and hairstyles and makeup. But cliché though this will sound, beauty is not how you appear, but who you are. Beauty has given you a great gift—not so much your attractive appearance, but that artistic spirit that the body holds.

"You will touch more people, you will retain a more generous and loving spirit to share with others if you use that artistic gift, rather than ignoring it. Don't give up your art, Rachel."

Rachel had always perceived the professor as quiet and soft-spoken, coming alive only in class when he would rampage across the front of the classroom, or grip the podium as he made his points, as though he were a drowning man and it a life buoy. She had never spoken to him outside of class before.

"That's all I wanted to say," he told her, and then he walked away, across the common and out of her life.

Something had stirred inside her at his words. She had wanted to call out after him, to tear off the trendy clothes she was wearing and give it all up, but then Cindy, a friend of Frank's who was standing with her, spoke and broke the spell.

"What a weird little man," she'd said.

"He's—"

Not, she'd meant to say. He's a good man.

"A total loser," Cindy finished for her. "C'mon. Judy's waiting for us."

To go shopping. For new clothes, new lipstick, eyeliner, new blush. With the professor's words ringing in her ears, it all seemed so trivial. But then she thought of Frank, how he always told her she looked so good, smelled so good, how he held her and woke feelings inside her that art never had.

She'd lost her chance then. She could've walked away, after the professor, regained what she'd lost, but instead she'd laughed with Cindy at the funny figure the professor cut, walking across the common, and she'd gone shopping.

Now, years later, she remembered and mourned, but now it was too late. Her real downfall, she realized—the exact moment when she'd changed from being someone she was proud to be, to being another person's shadow—might well have happened, not with meeting Frank, as she'd always thought after the separation, but with her complicity in that mockery.

She'd lost her chance to defend the professor once, but she wouldn't do it again.

"Don't you *ever* mock him," she repeated, eyes flashing.

"Jesus," Tom said. "Dapple exists to be mocked. The man was a disgrace to his profession. He had a responsibility to his students, to impart an objective understanding of art, but he just ignored it. Instead he filled their heads with New Age psycho-babble like a person thinking their art's not a failure just because they don't believe it's a failure."

"You don't—"

"Know?" Tom asked, the volume of his voice rising slightly. "I've had a number of his old students in my classes. I know all too well the damage he's done. It's because of people like Dapple that the current art scene is so riddled with mediocrity."

"How can you dare blame him for something like that?"

"Because of things like what he told you about failure. The whole point of what an artist does is to communicate. When a piece of art doesn't work, when it *fails* to communicate, it's a failure. That's *it*, plain and simple. To pretend otherwise, well, you might as well just be masturbating."

Rachel was so furious that she had to grip her knees to stop her hands from shaking.

"I can't believe what a closed mind you've got," she told him.

"Oh? Well, what would you call it then?"

"Expressing oneself. If you're truly working from the heart, then you're expressing yourself and it has meaning, no matter what anybody else thinks."

Tom shook his head. "That's what failures tell themselves to feel good. A real artist keeps on working until he gets it right."

"So does the kind of artist *I'm* talking about."

"No, you're talking about masturbation. I'm talking about a learning process."

"Listen. You can't just—"

"No, *you* listen," Tom told her, his voice rising above hers, cutting her off. "Your Professor Dapple was a weird little shit who fucked up the heads of a lot of potentially very good artists—yourself included— because he taught them not to look past their limitations, but to revel in them."

Rachel gave him a long, hard stare.

"Jesus, Rachel," Tom said. "You told me to be objective. Why don't you take off those rose-colored glasses he saddled you with and—"

Rachel stood up. "I think you'd better leave."

Tom looked confused.

"Did you hear me?" Rachel said, her anger barely kept in check.

Tom rose as well. "Aren't you overreacting a little?"

It was Tom's voice, Tom's face she was looking at, but it was Frank that Rachel heard and saw. Frank, constantly belittling her arguments with those same few hurtful words.

"I'm serious," Rachel said. "If you're not out of here immediately, I'm calling Security."

"But we were just—"

"I don't have to listen to what you've got to say. I'm not *interested* in hearing any more of what you've got to say. Will you please just leave?"

Tom took a step toward her. It was a nonthreatening movement, but Rachel flinched and backed up as if he'd raised his hand to her.

Don't let him intimidate you, she told herself, but she felt as if she were going to pieces inside. Her stomach was in sour knots, and all she wanted to do was cry, but she was determined to stand her ground, not to give in.

"I'm sorry," Tom said.

Sure he was. Frank used to say that all the time as well. First he'd mock her, then he'd beat her, then he'd say how sorry he was. Tom wasn't Frank, but he was proving to be different only in degree. Where did he come off assuming that only what he had to say had any validity?

"Please," she said. "Just go."

He nodded and left.

Rachel waited until she heard the front door close behind him, then she sank onto the chair she'd been sitting in. She took hold of the portfolio that held some of her work from her first year at college. She started to open it, but then just held it to her chest.

You were right, Professor, she thought. All those years ago, you were right. I could have saved myself so much heartache and grief, if only I'd listened, *really* listened, to what you told me.

Maybe you do believe in all that weird stuff that Tom was talking about, but that doesn't change the things that you were right about. It doesn't change them at all.

Hugging the portfolio, she began to weep. Her tears weren't so much for herself, but for the girl she'd been before she'd met Frank, for how bad this was going to make Lily feel, and for how she'd let herself forget one of the few men in her life who'd ever treated her with genuine decency and respect.

THIRTY-SEVEN

It was in his Peter Orlick persona that Harry watched the argument take place in Rachel's living room. He'd put on the wig and the beard and the brown contact lens in anticipation of dropping by Rachel's apartment for a visit. Just in the neighborhood, thought I'd drop by, I want to apologize again for the unfortunate ending to our dinner on Saturday night, yes, terrible what happened to that poor waiter, wasn't it?

Instead, he discovered that for the second night in a row she was having guests over.

He'd watched her bustling about, cleaning and tidying, saw the red-headed man arrive to have a beer and look through her artwork. They didn't appear to be doing much of anything, and he was rapidly losing interest when he realized that the conversation Rachel and the red-haired man were having had turned into an argument. Her distress woke a dull ache behind his temples.

"Don't," Harry said softly, as though the red-haired man could hear him. "Don't make it worse."

But of course the man couldn't hear him.

Harry watched it all unfold, the harsh words going back and forth, obviously upsetting Rachel, until finally the man left and she was alone, weeping in her living room.

What had it all been about?

It didn't really matter. All Harry knew was that Rachel's eyes were already red and swollen, the perfect flesh around them puffing up, her beauty being stolen away. As he focused in on her profile, a dark rage swept over him. Forgotten was the headache. Forgotten was caution.

Without bothering to change, he headed out of his apartment. He pushed the down button at the elevator but was too impatient to wait for it to arrive. He entered the stairwell instead, taking the steps two and three at a time. When he reached the entrance to the lobby, he stood for a moment before the door, ran a finger through his wig, then stepped out into the lobby, not even breathing hard.

The security guard looked up as he crossed the lobby, and Harry gave him a pleasant smile and a half salute.

"Have a nice evening, sir," the guard told him.

"Thanks. You, too."

Outside, he was walking briskly toward Rachel's building when a sudden thought struck him. What if the red-haired man had driven over to visit her? He'd be able just to drive off, unopposed, leaving Harry standing behind on the pavement. Harry's anger deepened at the thought of the man getting away, of feeling ineffectual, his anger unappeased.

I should have brought the .32, he thought. Blow out his tires, his windshield, his damned smirking face.

But then the man exited from Rachel's building and headed toward the street.

Gotcha, Harry thought.

He angled across the lawn, meaning to catch up with the man in the relative darkness in between streetlights. From out of the side pocket of his jacket, he pulled a pair of thin black leather gloves and put them on as he closed the distance between himself and his target.

THIRTY-EIGHT

Way to go, Tom told himself as he rode the elevator down from Rachel's apartment. *Lily's going to be real proud of the way you handled yourself in there.*

Tom wasn't all that proud of himself either.

He slouched to one side of the door and regarded his reflection in the mirrored wall on the opposite side of the elevator. Usually he felt invigorated after an intense discussion concerning the arts, but right now he was just tired. He *looked* tired.

What the hell was he going to tell Lily?

The truth, he supposed.

He hadn't set out to upset Rachel. The truth was he'd made a deliberate effort to keep the chip from his shoulder that always seemed to be there when he was around her. This afternoon while he worked, he'd thought about what put it there and realized that it was only partly the fact that Rachel worked on the business side of the field, ranked up there in Tom's mind with all the agents, gallery owners, investors and other no-talents who got rich off artists while the artists themselves so often just had to make do.

No, being honest with himself, he'd admitted that Rachel's victim mentality also rubbed him wrong. The way everybody had to pussyfoot around her so as not to upset her, the way she was always leaning on Lily for support. Sure, Rachel had had it hard, but so did other people. The thing was you had to pick yourself up and carry on. You didn't drag everybody who happened to be around you down as well.

He'd worked hard at meeting Rachel tonight with a clean slate in his mind. He'd been determined to treat her as he would one of his students—honestly, sparing no punches, but pointing out the good that was there in the work as well. And he'd been doing fine, he thought, until the business with Dapple came up.

Professor Dapple was a real sore point with Tom.

He'd seen too many mediocre artists come out of Dapple's classes—students with no sense of real art history, who never strived to overcome their limitations because they'd been taught that the best they felt they could do was good enough. And then there were the ones that had bought into all his mystic mumbo-jumbo. It enraged him to see an artist such as Jilly Coppercorn, who was capable of producing some of the most powerful work he'd seen in years, utilizing her considerable talents on work that was really no more than illustrations for supermarket tabloids.

A rumpled Elvis pushing a shopping cart full of bags of clothing and old wine bottles. Victorian flower fairies living in a garbage dump. Punk elves. Bigfoot driving a cab.

Real life as seen through the spaced-out spectacles of Professor Dapple. Lunatic Art 101.

It was such a waste.

But Tom knew he shouldn't have come down as hard on Rachel as he had. He *knew* how fragile she was—God, hadn't he listened to Lily talk about the woman's problems for months?

The elevator reached the lobby, and the doors hissed open. Tom hesitated for a moment, wondering if he shouldn't just go back up and apologize, but he had the feeling that might just make things worse, because he couldn't take back what he'd said about Dapple. No, he'd walk down to the bus stop and wait for Lily, tell her what had happened and see what she thought he should do. She knew Rachel better. He'd just have to face the music with Lily and hope that she could see a way out of it.

As the elevator door started to close, he used his hand to stop it and stepped out into the lobby.

People like Rachel Sorensen just complicated the lives of everyone around them, he thought as he left her building. And they never saw it. Weren't even vaguely aware of it. He wondered if Rachel knew just how good a friend she had in Lily.

He smiled, thinking of Lily. He couldn't help it. From the first day he'd met her, he'd realized that with her his life was finally complete. They'd only been together for a few months, but he knew, without question, that he just wouldn't be able to function without her. They'd only had the one fight, and he'd felt like such a shit that he didn't ever want them to have another one.

Which meant, he realized, that if Lily asked him to take back what he'd said about Dapple, he'd probably do it.

His smile broadened. So much for integrity. But he doubted that Lily would ask that of him anyway. She wouldn't be happy about what had happened tonight, but she wouldn't want him to compromise his ideals either.

She was the first woman he'd ever met who hadn't tried to get him to clean up the constant state of mess that was his apartment—which, when you considered the rigid organization of Lily's own lifestyle, was something of a miracle.

Maybe he should ask her to marry him.

He'd almost brought the subject up Sunday night when he gave her the small portrait of her that he'd done, but he'd lost his nerve.

Wouldn't that make his friends laugh? Tom Downs, who had about as firm an opinion as you could imagine on any subject you were likely to bring up, who never backed down from anything or anybody, losing his nerve.

But it happens. It had happened to him Sunday night. He'd felt so vulnerable, unable to face the idea of Lily saying no.

He thought of Rachel then, of her vulnerability, of what it must be like always to have to deal with it, and for the first time since he'd met her, he had more than a momentary sympathy for her.

What a way to live. And it wasn't that Rachel had chosen such a life, or that she wasn't strong enough to overcome it. Lily had told him a little of the circumstances of Rachel's marriage, explained how that kind of situation built up, to where the only person with whom they could bond was the person abusing them.

It wasn't a matter of not being brave or strong enough to leave the abusive relationship, but rather that the choice wasn't there at all. The victim was seduced into seeing her abuser as her only friend. The abuse she received was justified punishment for what she had done "wrong."

Tom wasn't stupid. He'd understood what Lily was telling him when she explained all of that, but it had never seemed quite real before. When you saw the world as he did—challenges that you overcame through tenacity, or experience, or just plain common sense—it was hard to relate to the kind of situation in which Rachel had found herself. It took the chance connection of what he knew about Rachel, with his own moment of vulnerability on Sunday night, to really drive it home.

He tried to imagine that indecision and, yes, fear, projected through every aspect of his life—just there, coloring every moment— and it left him in awe of what Rachel had survived. He could take the horrible details that Lily had given him now and clothe them with new flesh. When he considered Rachel actually escaping the horror of her relationship with her husband and trying to remake her life, when he thought of all the emotional baggage with which she had to deal, every day, maybe every hour . . .

Tom felt like a heel all over again.

He paused and turned around, almost ready then and there to go back and apologize to her, but he was closer to the bus stop now than to Rachel's building, so he kept on going. He was definitely going to make it up to Rachel, but he really needed Lily's advice on the best way to go about it.

Heading on, he noticed the man angling across the lawn toward him, but he thought nothing of it. It wasn't that he was fearless; it just never occurred to him that he might have something to fear. Especially not when, looking ahead, he saw Lily approaching him from the bus stop.

He knew it was her immediately. No one else had that unmistakable sway to her hips when she walked that Lily had. It wasn't in the least contrived, and only partly due to her heels; it was just the way she walked. He remembered the first time he'd seen her, at the gallery, crossing the floor with that walk. He'd had to stick a hand in the pocket of his jeans to try to hide the unmistakable swelling that she'd woken with just that walk and the blue fire in her eyes.

Tom smiled and quickened his pace, moving aside to give the man approaching from the lawn some room on the sidewalk.

"Excuse me," the man said.

A quiet, undemanding voice.

Tom paused. "Sure," he said. "What can I—"

It didn't feel like a fist that hit his chest, but rather a steel rod. He heard snapping sounds that he realized were ribs breaking, but he was already falling to the ground, balance gone, pain roaring in his ears, before the realization made its way through his mind.

The man hit him again as he was falling, his collarbone breaking under the blow. Blood filled his mouth even before his face smashed into the pavement.

As though from miles away, he heard Lily screaming.

Run! he wanted to yell to her. For Christ's sake, Lily, get out of here!

But broken ribs had punctured his lungs, and his throat and mouth were too full of blood.

The toe of the man's shoe lashed against the side of his chest, and he felt more ribs give, but he was too far gone now to feel the new pain.

The man bent down toward him, face suddenly highlighted by an approaching car.

Why? Tom wanted to ask him.

Even through his pain, the question seemed important.

Then the iron rod that was the side of the man's hand smashed across his windpipe and there was only the pain.

The pain. And the swelling darkness. And there, in the dark, a pin-prick of light that seemed to swell as though it was rapidly approaching, or he was falling into it.

Lily, he thought. Please don't hurt Lily.

The light suddenly flared around him, swallowed him. He could see nothing now, feel nothing.

Lily, he cried.

But there was only the light.

THIRTY-NINE

Harry had a moment of exquisite joy, as pure and sharp as an orgasm, as his gloved fist smashed into the man's chest, bruising flesh, breaking ribs, dropping the man where he stood. In rapid fire, Harry hit the man again, then lashed out with his foot, the rubber-encased steel hidden in the sole of his running shoes breaking more ribs.

He went down beside the man to strike him yet again, and suddenly there were a car's headlights bright on his face, blinding him. Panic washed through him even as he delivered the killing stroke.

What am I *doing*?

He staggered up and back from the man's body, still half-blinded by the headlights. He heard a woman screaming, a car screeching to a halt, and he knew he was lost.

He'd been seen. Caught in the act like some fourteen-year-old homeboy taking down a member of an opposing gang—some little punk who *wanted* to be seen, wanted the world to know how big a man he was.

Maybe he could kill the woman if he could just clear his sight long enough to find her, but he'd never get to whoever was in the car—not in time.

What in god's name had possessed him?

Not god, he told himself. But rather goddess. She was punishing him for his allowing her to be hurt, for his stealing a few hours of her company for his own selfish reasons when he should have woken her from the perfection of her body. For his plans tonight to steal a few more.

"I'm sorry," he said.

Not to the dead meat lying on the sidewalk in front of him, but to the goddess.

"I'll do it—I'll do it right. I promise you, I will."

If she only gave him the time. If she only kept the authorities away from him long enough. If she let him think, instead of filling his head with this red rage.

"I promise," he whispered.

And then he fled.

FORTY

The number 3 bus running from downtown Newford to Ferryside broke down on the east side of the Kelly Street Bridge. Sitting at the front near the driver, Lily heard the whole of his radio conversation with Newford Transpo dispatch. The reason for the mechanical failure went in one ear and out the other. All she retained from what she overheard was that this particular bus wasn't going anywhere and that a replacement bus was being sent.

Lily had never been on a bus that had broken down before. And of course it had to happen tonight. It wasn't an experience she would recommend.

After waiting ten impatient minutes, she finally gave up on the replacement and decided to exit the bus, which started a general exodus. Out on the pavement she tried to flag down a cab, but the three that passed all had fares.

Looking across the bridge to where the tops of both the Sky Towers apartment buildings could be seen, she decided to walk the rest of the way. She was wearing heels, and her legs were already killing her from being on her feet most of the day, so it wasn't something she was looking forward to.

But that wasn't the only reason for her reluctance. It was also a long way to walk at night on her own.

She'd tried to explain it any number of times to male friends, but they never could seem to understand how the city at night was two separate worlds—one for men and one for women. They thought she was overreacting when she talked about it, but all you had to do was check out the statistics, or just read the newspapers, to understand. Alone, at night, women were at risk.

It wasn't so bad on the bridge itself since there was plenty of traffic and even a few of her fellow female passengers from the bus for company. But once they got to the other side, the other pedestrians turned off or waited at the number 34 bus stop, leaving her on her own. Surely somebody else was heading for the Sky Towers, she thought, but if they were, they were keeping a secret of it.

Count yourself lucky, she told herself. If somebody was going on the same route, he'd probably turn out to be a rapist. Still, it was a long walk on her own through far too much open space between her and the paired apartment complexes that were her destination. Pulse beating at a rapid rate, she started off.

It got worse when she was well away from the bus stop and making her way through the dark pools of shadow that gathered in between each of the streetlights. Her imagination peopled the shadows with every sort of deviant she'd ever read about on the front page of a newspaper. Then her nervousness kicked into overdrive when she saw figures approaching her—one on the sidewalk and one cutting across the lawn at an angle that would have him join the man on the sidewalk.

She almost fled. She was ready to kick off her heels and make a run for it, but there was something about the loping walk of the man on the sidewalk that tweaked a sense of familiarity in her. Then he passed momentarily under the glow of a streetlight and she felt herself relax. It was Tom. She didn't know what he was doing out here when he was supposed to be with Rachel, but she didn't much care either, she was so relieved to see him.

She had started to call his name when the man angling across the lawn reached him. He said something to Tom, stopping him, and then the nightmare began.

Lily froze as the first blow was struck. This wasn't real, she thought, numbness spreading through her limbs. This only happened in movies or on TV. It didn't—*couldn't*—happen to someone she loved.

Then Tom went down, his attacker kicking him, and Lily's paralysis broke. She screamed Tom's name. Kicking off her heels, she started to run toward the pair. She swung her purse in an arc above her head, remembering what the instructor at the Ferryside Women's Co-op defense course had told her: "If you need to use what I'm teaching you, it's not a game. There won't be any rules; there won't be any umpire to cry 'foul.' You use whatever's at hand because the bottom line isn't winning, it's survival."

Tom's attacker lifted his head and was caught in the light of an approaching car's headbeams. He stumbled to his feet, the light seeming to trap him. Tom lay so still, so very, very still.

Lily realized that she was still screaming—no longer Tom's name, just a long wordless cry that encompassed all of her fear and anger. She ran harder, her purse humming above her head. But before she could use it on the attacker, he had fled. The car screeched to a halt at the same time as she reached Tom's side.

She let the purse fall and dropped down beside him. Crooning his name, she lifted him up, but his head hung at an impossible angle. Blood surged from his mouth, splattering her skirt and thighs. Behind her, she could hear the occupant of the car approaching.

"Jesus, oh Jesus," the man was saying in a shocked voice.

Lily never turned around. She stared at Tom's face, lit by the headbeams, and knew that she was never going to hear him say her name again. He was never going to paint another picture, never going to argue art with his pals at one of the Crowsea cafés, never going to turn to her with that quirky look in his eyes and the big welcoming smile. . . .

She held him tighter to her chest, her head bowed over his bloody features, tears streaming from her eyes. More cars stopped, the police arrived, soon followed by an ambulance, but Lily paid no attention to any of them. She held onto Tom and kept murmuring his name, hoping against hope that she could bring him back from wherever his spirit had fled, knowing it was impossible, it was too late, far too late, but unable to stop.

When a police officer gently tried to pry her away, she turned a snarling face toward the woman—lioness protecting her young.

"Easy," the officer said. "We've got paramedics here. We just want to help you. Please, just remain calm. Let us have a look at your friend."

The woman's voice was soothing and pitched low. She put a comforting hand on Lily's shoulder.

Lily shivered. The officer's concern didn't help—it couldn't even start to help—but she let herself be drawn away from Tom's body. Someone draped a blanket over her shoulders. The officer stood at her side, an arm around her, holding the blanket in place. Lily could barely feel the woman at her side. All she could do was stare numbly at Tom's body as the paramedics gently lifted him onto a stretcher.

She moaned when they covered him with a blanket as well, folding the fabric over his face.

"I'm so sorry," the officer holding her said.

Lily shivered again. She closed her eyes and froze the image of Tom's killer in her mind's eye—bearded features caught in the car headlights, eyes startled, blinded.

I know that face, she realized.

She opened her eyes and searched the crowd that had gathered, but the murderer wasn't among them. No, he'd be long gone by now. But she'd find him, and when she did, she was going to kill him.

She started to look away again, away from the faces, anywhere but at the stretcher that held Tom's body, the blanket folded over his face, and then she saw Rachel approaching from the back of the crowd.

Rachel would know where to find Tom's killer. Hadn't she painted the bastard's portrait?

But no. Peter Orlick was the big mystery man. Dropped Rachel off without leaving a phone number, or an address. Maybe Rob would know. Maybe . . .

The pressure around her shoulders eased as the police officer stepped away. Lily clutched the edges of the blanket to stop it from falling. Her hands shook where they gripped the rough fabric.

"Can you talk?" the police officer asked.

Lily nodded dully. She looked again to where she'd spied Rachel, saw her friend's eyes widen with shock when she recognized Lily. Rachel pushed through the crowd as the police officer led Lily away to where the cruiser waited; she joined them just as they reached the vehicle.

"Lily!" Rachel cried. "What . . . what's happening?"

Lily started to speak, but the words wouldn't come up her throat. She swallowed painfully and tried again.

"It . . . it's Tom," she said.

Rachel's gaze traveled to where the paramedics were lifting Tom's body into the back of the ambulance. Her features were white when she turned back to Lily.

"T-Tom . . . ?"

Lily nodded dully.

"Perhaps you could both have a seat in the cruiser," the police officer said.

Neither woman paid her any attention. Rachel turned again to the ambulance. The paramedics were shutting the rear doors. The clang as the lock closed had such a final sound that Lily shivered again.

Oh, Tom, she thought.

"It's all my fault," Rachel said.

The words slowly penetrated through the roiling confusion that held Lily's mind. She turned in Rachel's direction. She'd never seen her friend looking this screwed up before, but she didn't have the patience to deal with Rachel's problems right now. Not with Tom dead.

Tom. Dead.

His name went through her with a wave of sorrow so deep that she could barely stand.

"Don't . . . please, don't start with that," she told Rachel. "Not now. I haven't got the strength."

She could barely stand. Any moment now she was just going to collapse. Maybe they'd lay her down in the ambulance, beside Tom's corpse. They could hold hands—dead man, and woman who might as well be dead.

"But—"

Lily turned an angry gaze on her friend. "Would you just give it a break? Yes, Tom was here because he was seeing you, but this could have happened anywhere."

But it had happened here. Tom, murdered right before her eyes. If she'd been just a little closer, maybe she could have hit Orlick with her purse, kicked him in the balls, torn out his throat with her fingernails.

Oh, Christ. When she finally did get her hands on him, she'd do all of that and worse.

She shuddered, closing her eyes.

"But we had . . . we had this argument," Rachel was saying. "And I know he must have been watching me, he's *always* watching me. . . ."

The face from Rachel's portrait swam up before Lily's closed eyelids again. She opened her eyes.

"*Who's* watching you?" she demanded.

The police officer stepped in between them.

"Please," she said. "Could you wait with this until the detectives arrive?"

Lily looked at her, then at the crowd pressing close, eager to hear every word that was said, savoring the real-life drama that was playing out like a TV show in front of them. She nodded slowly and let herself be led toward the backseat of the cruiser. Rachel entered behind her.

The two women looked at each other for a long moment. Words rose up between them, needing to be spoken, but instead they just held onto each other and waited for the homicide detectives to arrive.

FORTY-ONE

Rachel hadn't cried for very long after Tom left her apartment. She forced herself to stop, then went out onto the balcony to get some air. It was hard to do, but she was proud of herself when she managed to win just that small victory. She still felt unbalanced, but the sensation wasn't so overpowering anymore. The air helped. She'd needed to clear her head. She needed—

A new life, she thought. I should just move away from this city and start over again somewhere else.

And would running away make a difference?

It hadn't seemed so with Frank. Her therapist had always told her that she would eventually need to face up to him. Now that they were separated, she could no longer let him control her life. Until she confronted her fear of him, she'd never be able to recover.

But she hadn't been strong enough. Somebody'd had to kill Frank before she'd been able to really feel as though she were starting over again.

But even now, even with Frank dead, she still felt so vulnerable. The argument with Tom Downs was a perfect example. He'd been expressing an opinion—strongly, it was true, but it was just his opinion. She'd taken it as an attack. She'd taken it all so personally, just as she always did.

And yet, it *was* personal, wasn't it? He'd been calling her judgment into question, telling her she was a fool. What she had to learn to do was accept that she was going to have differences of opinion with people and leave it at that. She had to stand by what she believed, and if someone like Tom thought she was a fool for doing so, well, that was his problem, not hers.

More advice, courtesy of Dr. Caley. If only it were as easy to follow as it was to hear.

Rachel sighed. She leaned on the balcony's railing, looking out across what she could see of the park, what wasn't hidden by Tower B. The sudden flurry of sirens and the commotion down on the street past the Sky Towers' parking lots caught her attention. A shiver of dread went through her, a premonition that stalked up her spine on sharp claws.

She'd never been one to rubberneck at accidents, never been drawn to the bad news that was endlessly paraded across newspaper headlines and TV screens, but she found herself leaving her balcony now, hurrying from her apartment to the scene of confusion she'd seen from her balcony.

The sense of foreboding followed her all the way down the sidewalk to where the crowd was gathered, blossoming into full-blown dread when she saw Lily, the blanket wrapped around her, the police officer with her arm around Lily's shoulders.

And when she saw the body, when she realized it was Tom lying there with the blanket over his face, she almost lost it again.

He's real, she thought, panic sending an adrenaline rush through her. Her perverted guardian angel, the angel of death, was real. Tom had argued with her; now Tom was dead.

It took every bit of courage she had not to just turn and flee. It would have been so easy to do. Run for the Kelly Street Bridge and throw herself over the railing and let the river swallow her. That way no one would ever have to be hurt because of her again.

But that was Lily there. Lily, who would need a friend to stand by her now, as she had so often stood by Rachel. And the madman was still out there, somewhere.

This time she had to tell the police everything she knew. It didn't matter how crazy they thought she was. She had to tell them. She couldn't let anyone else die because of her. If she killed herself, who was to say that the monster wouldn't simply fixate on some other woman and start all over again?

She had to tell them what she knew. She had to help them catch the madman.

Holding onto Lily in the back of the police cruiser, she told herself that, over and over again.

It was all that gave her the courage to carry on.

HARRY

FORTY-TWO

Liz Brauman caught the Tom Downs case, but as soon as the connection was made between it and other ongoing homicide investigations, she brought Stone in and they took what they had to Takahashi. When the lieutenant heard them through, he immediately set up a six-man task force with Stone and Brauman at the head of it. It was the first time Stone and Brauman had worked together.

Brauman had asked Takahashi once why he'd never partnered the pair of them.

"So what'd he say?" Stone asked when Brauman told him about it.

Brauman smiled. "We think too much alike. He says the secret to a good partnership is the difference that each officer brings to the relationship."

"We're too much alike?" Stone had repeated, then grinned. "I don't know if I should feel complimented or insulted."

"Yeah, up yours, too."

The other detectives assigned to the task force included Freeman, Brauman's partner Josh Draycott, and the two detectives who'd originally investigated the death of Rachel Sorensen's husband: Mike Kirkland and Rufus Snipes.

Stone sat now at a table in one of the small conference rooms at police headquarters, with Lieutenant Takahashi, Brauman and Sarah Taylor, the assistant D.A. Across the table from them were the two women. On the table between them, amid a clutter of papers, file folders and paper coffee cups, was a tape recorder.

Sorensen seemed to be in the roughest shape, Stone thought, even though it hadn't been her boyfriend who'd been killed. She was jittery, but Stone didn't think her case of nerves had anything to do with guilt—at least not the kind of guilt he normally had to deal with in this kind of a situation. She also seemed embarrassed. Listening to her story, Stone could see why.

Both she and Kataboki had refused medical attention, though it was safe to say that they were both suffering from shock. Neither had asked for a lawyer to be present.

"How do you know somebody's watching you?" Stone asked Sorensen, backtracking, now that they had the basic gist of the story down.

The woman shrugged. "I don't *know*. It's just a feeling I've had, ever since Frank—my ex-husband—was killed."

"And you think it's this Peter Orlick who's been watching you?"

Always go with your gut instinct, Stone thought as he asked the question. Just as Sorensen knew she was being watched, he'd *known* that something wasn't kosher with Orlick from the first time the maître d' at Zwicker's mentioned the man.

"He . . . he was there," Sorensen said, "both at the Bike Pit and the restaurant. And then he—God, it sounds so stupid—but I think he resembles the man who saved me from Frank's attack."

Stone nodded. "Because of the shape of his mouth, you said," prompting her when she fell silent.

"That and . . . well, just a feeling."

"Why didn't you bring this to our attention earlier?"

The anguish in her eyes wasn't put on.

"Oh, God. If only I had." Sorensen shot Kataboki a look. "Then . . . then Tom would still be alive."

Though Kataboki was obviously hurting, she laid a comforting hand on Sorensen's arm. Sorensen gave her a grateful look, but Stone could see that the guilt she'd taken on because of Downs's death still lay like a raw wound inside her.

"I just . . . didn't think you'd believe me," Sorensen went on. "And then, when I heard about the other man being killed in Fitzhenry Park, I was relieved. Not that someone had died," she added quickly, "but that I was wrong. I thought I was wrong. I thought I'd just imagined the . . . the connection."

"You weren't aware of the statement we issued the following day?" the lieutenant asked.

Sorensen shook her head. "I decided to just cut myself off from the news. It's all so depressing . . ."

No kidding, Stone thought. You should try living with it from my perspective.

"I don't know why we're going through all of this again," Kataboki suddenly said. "I told you what I saw. The man who killed Tom was the same man in Rachel's portrait: Peter Orlick. Why don't you just arrest the bastard?"

Stone could understand her frustration. It was her boyfriend who'd been killed. She'd been able to identify the killer—her description corroborating that of Ralph Moran, the man whose headlights had caught Orlick in the act of committing the murder. The trouble was, knowing who did it, and finding him, wasn't proving to be as simple as they'd all have liked it to be.

"I'd love to," Stone said, "but Peter Orlick doesn't seem to exist." He raised his hand at their protests. "He doesn't exist on paper," he went on to explain. "We've got nothing on him, no way to find him—yet. Your friend, Mr. Carter, couldn't provide either a phone number or address and every other line of inquiry has run into a dead end so far."

They had been talking to the maître d' from Zwicker's again, to the clerk from the Bike Pit, to Ian Hughes's neighbors, to the street people on the waterfront where Timothy Nanes had been killed. They were showing around Xeroxed copies of Sorensen's portrait and car dealers' photographs of a Rabbit to match the description of Orlick's car that Rob Carter had been able to give them. Copies of Orlick's portrait had been faxed to New York and L.A.—the two places that Orlick had told Carter and Sorensen he'd lived.

Net result to date: nada.

"This isn't a fruitless exercise," Brauman told the two women. "The more we talk it through, the better chance you'll remember something else that might be able to help us."

"I understand," Kataboki said. "It's just . . . hard."

Kataboki's features didn't give much away, Stone thought. He hated to fall into stereotypical observations, but she really did seem inscrutable. Beyond her sorrow, and the occasional flash of impatient anger, he couldn't read her at all.

Beside Stone, Sarah Taylor looked up from her notes.

"Did he ever offer to photograph you?" she asked.

Sorensen shook her head in response to the assistant D.A.'s question.

"And he made no advances?" Taylor went on.

"I thought he was gay," Sorensen said. "He never came out and said he was, but I was so sure he was gay. Rob thought so, too."

Which jibed with what Stone had learned from his partner, who had conducted the interview with Carter.

"This guy's on the level?" Stone had asked when Freeman called in from Carter's apartment.

"I'd say so. I'd also say that he had the hots for the guy—though he didn't actually come out and say so. I don't think he's faking his shock."

"Yeah, well, bring him in anyway," Stone had said. "I'd like to talk to him myself."

Stone didn't want to let even the smallest bit of information slip by.

They had a witness, they had circumstantial evidence tying Orlick to four homicides, but they also had Orlick as an invisible man.

Right now, Carter was in another conference room with Freeman, waiting for Stone and Brauman to finish up in here.

"I just don't understand why," Sorensen was saying. "Why did he pick me?"

Stone just looked at her. When no one else spoke, he said, "Maybe this is stating the obvious, Ms. Sorensen, but you're a beautiful woman."

"So that makes it okay? The way I look gives him license to terrorize me, to kill people?"

"I didn't say that."

"A guy like this," Brauman put in, "doesn't get off on ugly women."

"This is a sick society," Sorensen said, staring down at the paper coffee cup on the table in front of her.

"You're not going to hear any argument from us on that," Stone told her.

He glanced at the clock on the wall across from him. Coming up on one A.M. Both Sorensen and Kataboki looked beat, and he didn't think they were going to get anything else from either of them tonight. He exchanged a quick glance with the lieutenant and then with Taylor. They'd all been through this so many times before that there was no need for words. The two just nodded, each in turn.

"Will you be staying together tonight?" Brauman asked the women.

Sorensen glanced at her companion. Kataboki put her hand on Sorensen's arm again and left it there.

"We'll stay at my apartment," Kataboki said.

"That'd be for the best," Brauman told her. "Ms. Sorensen's apartment would be too dangerous."

The way Sorensen looked, Stone didn't think she ever wanted to go back to her place again.

"We'd also like to assign an officer to accompany you," Brauman said. "Preferably someone who can stay in the apartment with you, rather than watch from the street, if that's all right."

When the women hesitated, Brauman added, "The officer will be a woman."

Liz had read that well, Stone thought. Considering Sorensen's history and what Kataboki had just been through, he didn't think either one of them was particularly enamored with members of his own gender tonight. One of them had killed Kataboki's lover; others had made Sorensen's life a living hell. If they were going to be guarded, they wanted it to be by one of their own.

"We'll be in touch with you tomorrow morning," Stone told them. "I know it'll be hard, but try to get some rest. In the meantime, we'll be doing all we can."

Pushing back his chair, he rose to his feet.

"I saw Diane Cruz in the squad room," Brauman said as she stood up as well.

"Give her the assignment," the lieutenant told her. "And have her take them out the back. We've got press crawling all over the front steps of the building."

Brauman turned to the two women. "If you'll come with me."

Stone accompanied Brauman as she led the women from the room to meet Detective Cruz.

"We've still got your apartment keys, Ms. Sorensen," he said. "If it's all right with you, I'd like to go back to your place and look around a little more."

Whatever has been keeping the two women going up to this point was rapidly wearing off. They seemed dead on their feet.

"Why?" Sorensen managed to ask. "He was never there."

"Not *in* your apartment," Stone agreed. "But if he was watching you, it had to be from one of the apartments in Tower B. I want to check the angles, see how much I can narrow down the choices."

"Do whatever you have to do," Sorensen told him.

"We'll get him," Stone said. He looked from her to Kataboki, keeping his voice confident. "I know that doesn't change what's happened, but I promise you this, Orlick's going down. It won't bring your friend back, but maybe it'll help you deal with things a little easier knowing that there's no way we're going to let him get away with what he's done."

Sorensen nodded, but made no reply.

"Thank you," Kataboki said.

Stone watched them follow Brauman out to the squad room, then headed back to where Takahashi and the assistant D.A. were still sitting. They all still had a long night ahead of them.

"I don't want any part of this investigation screwed up," Taylor said when Stone sat down again. "When this goes to court, I want a conviction."

"You got it," Stone told her. "Every move we make is going to go by the book."

FORTY-THREE

Diane Cruz was a dark-haired, statuesque Hispanic who looked as though she'd been poured into the tank top, miniskirt, net stockings and heels she was wearing when Brauman introduced her to Rachel and Lily. She didn't look like a police detective so much as a hooker, Rachel found herself thinking.

"I've been working a co-op investigation with Vice," Cruz explained in an apologetic voice, as though reading Rachel's mind.

Rachel felt an immediate embarrassment for her snap judgment.

"Just give me a chance to get changed," Cruz added, "and I'll have you out of here."

Five minutes later, she reappeared in casual jeans and a T-shirt, the excessive makeup washed off. She wore a shoulder holster under her left arm that disappeared from view when she put on a light cotton jacket.

"You'll be spelled at eight hundred hours," Brauman told Cruz before turning to Rachel and Lily to add, "Please do us all a favor and give us an hour or so's notice if you're not planning to stay together anymore."

"We will," Rachel said.

"And I don't think either of you should even think about going to work tomorrow. Don't follow any of your regular routines. The best thing you can do right now is just stay put at the apartment."

Rachel and Lily nodded.

"Is this just a baby-sitting gig," Cruz asked, "or are we expecting trouble?"

"I doubt you'll see any trouble," Brauman said, "but it doesn't hurt to be prepared for the worst."

"Gotcha." Turning to Rachel and Lily, Cruz gave them a quick smile. "Well, ladies, what say I get you out of here?"

An hour later, Rachel and Lily were sitting on the bed in Lily's bedroom, with Detective Cruz keeping watch in the apartment's living room. Lily was holding the small portrait that Tom had recently given her. She had a pillow between herself and the bed's backrest, the portrait clutched tightly to her chest. Though her eyes were shiny, she wasn't crying.

Rachel sat farther down toward the end of the bed, cross-legged, facing Lily. She tugged at a loose thread on the hem of her jeans and didn't know what to say.

"Are you going to be okay?" she finally asked.

She knew it was a stupid question, but she had to say something. The silence, Lily's pain, her own fears—they were all building up into the approach of another panic attack. She had to get out of her own mind, even if it meant sharing the pain that filled Lily's.

Lily shook her head. She brought the portrait away from her chest and looked at it.

"This is the way he saw me," she said in a soft voice. "Like I was special."

"You were special," Rachel said. "You *are* special."

"And Tom's dead."

Everything came around to that, Rachel thought. For a long time, it always would, and there was nothing she or anyone else could do to take away the pain, except to be there for Lily. To give her whatever she needed—be it comfort or space.

"Do you want me to leave you alone for a bit?" Rachel asked. "I could go sit with Diane in the living room. . . ."

Lily shook her head, hugging the portrait again. After a few moments, Rachel moved up beside her and put her arm around Lily's shoulders. Lily burrowed her head against Rachel and wept.

It was an awful thought, Rachel realized, but being strong for Lily was all that was keeping her from dissolving into a panic herself. When she thought of the madness that Peter Orlick had brought into her life, of all the people who had died at his hand because of her, she just wanted to crawl away and die.

She held onto Lily long after the tears stopped. Finally Lily sat up and accepted the tissue that Rachel offered her.

"You know what hurts the most?" Lily said after she'd blown her nose.

Rachel shook her head.

"Right now, what hurts the most is knowing he's out there, alive, and Tom's dead."

"The police'll catch him," Rachel said, though privately she had her doubts.

They hadn't been able to catch him after he'd killed Frank. But then, they hadn't had anything to go on with that investigation. The police tonight had said as much.

When she thought of the fantasies she'd had about him in the weeks following Frank's death, she wanted to throw up. How long had he been watching her, following her?

"Do you think he knows where we are right now?" she said.

Lily gave a tired nod. "Probably."

I won't let you get hurt, too, Rachel vowed. She only hoped she'd be able to keep that vow.

FORTY-FOUR

Harry removed his gloves as he ran. Once he had rounded the side of Tower B and was out of range of vision of the gawkers gathering around the man he'd killed, he slowed down to a quick walk. He removed his wig and the contact lens, then peeled off the beard and mustache, stuffing them all in the pocket that held his gloves. Using his key-in card, he opened the garage door to the underground parking and safely made his way back up to his apartment.

The first thing he did when he got back was check Rachel's apartment through the telescope.

The drapes were open, the living room lights were on, but there was no sign of Rachel.

She was in the bathroom, he decided, or lying down. He'd wait until she came back in to turn off the living room lights before he went over to get her.

Because it was all over now. He knew that. He—Peter Orlick—had been seen. The police would soon have his description, and an artist's sketch would be appearing on the TV and in the papers before morning.

It wouldn't take long for someone in his building to remember seeing Peter Orlick, for the security guard to point the police up to Harry's apartment.

He switched on his set, but the murder hadn't been big enough news to interrupt regular programming. He'd have to wait for the news at eleven to see what the police had told the press, unless there was something on the radio. Going into his bedroom, he switched on the alarm clock radio and moved across the channel bands until he came to a station covering the murder. The details they had were sketchy.

He began to pack a small traveling bag. He put a copy of his favorite picture of Rachel in it—a small version of the poster-sized photo hanging on the wall of his living room. His makeup kit went in as well, along with a change of clothes, toiletries and a high-powered set of binoculars. Lastly, he took from his sock drawer a small .32-caliber automatic, a spare clip of rounds and a stack of twenty-dollar bills held together with elastic, and placed them inside the bag as well.

Returning to his telescope, he found no change at Rachel's apartment.

He couldn't do a thing until he was certain she was there.

The hour and a half he had to wait until the eleven o'clock news passed slowly. He sat by the telescope, peering through it at regular intervals. Just before the news came on, he spied the uniformed policeman enter Rachel's apartment.

He watched the police officer go through the artwork that Rachel and the red-haired man had been looking at, choose one item, then leave the apartment. He turned the lights off when he left, plunging the room into darkness.

Rachel wasn't home.

She must be at police headquarters—perhaps because she'd been the last person to see the red-haired man alive—but how had the police made the connection so quickly?

The eleven o'clock news gave him his answers. The situation was worse than he'd thought. They had a portrait of Peter Orlick—an uncanny likeness that had been done in watercolors. Rachel had painted that, he realized. That was what the policeman had taken from her apartment.

The woman who'd seen him was Rachel's friend, Lily, lover of the man Harry had killed. No wonder Rachel was involved. News footage showed Rachel and Lily at the scene of the murder, a uniformed policewoman ushering them into the backseat of a cruiser. Now the screen filled with an on-the-street interview with the man who'd been driving the car, the other witness.

Ralph Moran was the man's name, the computer-generated script that ran across the bottom of the screen helpfully told Harry.

They were both going to have to die.

Ralph Moran and Lily Kataboki. A simple problem of being in the wrong place at the wrong time.

They wouldn't be able to identify him, because Peter Orlick was now as good as dead, the persona likely never to be used again, but Harry didn't care for loose ends, just on general principle.

The police would be interviewing both of them. For how long? Hours. So Harry would just have to wait for the early hours of the morning, while the police were running around into dead ends and Ralph Moran and Lily Kataboki finally were allowed to go home and sleep.

He looked up their names in the phone book and found addresses for both of them.

He'd screwed up, but that was all right. It was just the goddess, forcing his hand. She'd protect him. She had to because no one else knew what he knew, no one else could wake the divinity in the mortal vessel she'd chosen to wear.

He'd stop by the Moran and Kataboki households and bid them each a tender, if rather permanent, good night, and then he'd go get Rachel. Yes, everything was working out just fine.

Around one-thirty, he saw the light go on in Rachel's apartment again. Good. Now he knew where she was. The police had probably sent Ralph and Lily home as well. But when he looked through the telescope, it wasn't Rachel he saw in the apartment, but a complete stranger. A tall man with a wide chest and broad shoulders, wearing a rumpled suit and a tie. The top button of his shirt was undone, and his tie hung slightly askew.

A policeman, Harry thought. What was another policeman doing in Rachel's apartment?

He watched the stranger leaf through Rachel's artwork, then walk over to the patio doors. He stepped out onto the balcony and leaned on the railing, studying Tower B.

He can't see me, Harry told himself.

His own apartment was dark, his telescope was invisible, but that didn't stop him from feeling the weight of the man's considering gaze, boring in on him, on him alone.

They know, Harry realized. They know about me. They know everything.

Then why weren't they knocking down his door?

Who was to say that they weren't about to? How did he know that they weren't already in the lobby, SWAT team surrounding the building, men in bulletproof vests creeping down his hallway at this very moment, converging on his door?

Harry, always so in control of any situation, never one to panic, had, in that moment, his first real brush with fear. It wasn't for himself, though, that he was afraid. It was for his mission. His calling. For the goddess that he'd spent his whole life trying to wake.

It couldn't end before he'd completed his task.

He wouldn't let it.

FORTY-FIVE

Stone leaned on the railing of Rachel Sorensen's balcony and studied the dark bulk of Tower B that stood almost directly across from him. There was somewhat of an angle in the placement of the two buildings, Tower B standing a little off to one side to allow the residents of Tower A a view of the park, but that didn't make a whole lot of difference in terms of what Stone was looking for. All that the peep freak would need was a good pair of binoculars or a telescope and he'd have a front-row seat looking into Sorensen's living room.

Peter Orlick. Didn't matter what his real name was, he had to live in Tower B. It was just going to be a matter of checking out the side of the building that faced Tower A, apartment by apartment.

Stone suddenly stepped back inside the apartment and shut the patio doors and drapes.

Now that hadn't been too bright. Orlick could be looking at him through a telescope right this minute. The last thing Stone wanted to do was spook him.

Pretending an indifference he didn't feel, Stone took another look through Rachel's artwork before he casually made his way to the front door. There was nothing more to do here. They had to concentrate on Tower B. In one of those apartments facing this tower . . .

Jesus, Stone thought suddenly. Had *anyone* thought to show Sorensen's sketch to the security guard in Tower B?

He went back into the living room to use the phone. A quick call downtown confirmed his fear. In a typical fuckup, everybody had thought that someone else had done it. Bottom line: if the guard could put a real name to him, they could have the peep freak in custody within the hour.

Stone hurried from the apartment, pulling a photocopy of Sorensen's sketch from his pocket.

The security guard on duty in the lobby of Tower B was very impressed with Stone's ID and badge. He was a large man in his late thirties, grossly overweight, with pasty white skin and a hairline that had receded to leave behind a prominent widow's peak. He introduced himself as Seymour Whitley.

"I was going to be a cop myself," he confided to Stone, "but my mom thought the work was too dangerous. What do you think? Is it dangerous?"

Stone put the photocopy of Sorensen's painting on the desk between them. "Ever seen this man before?"

"Sure," Whitley said. "He's been around lots lately. He's a friend of Mr. Kennedy's in 1462."

"Do you have a first name for Mr. Kennedy?" Stone asked.

"He told me to call him James, but management doesn't like us to refer to our residents on a first-name basis—even if the resident himself asks us to."

"James Kennedy," Stone repeated.

The guard nodded.

Stone put his finger down on the photocopy. "When was the last time you saw this man?"

"He left just before all the excitement started up—you know, down the street where that man was killed. Has this got something to do with—"

"But he hasn't come back?"

Whitley shook his head.

Stone's disappointment didn't show in his features.

"Is Mr. Kennedy in some sort of trouble?" the guard asked.

Well, he might be a peep freak, Stone thought. And he just might be responsible for at least four deaths over the past four months. What do *you* think, Seymour?

Take it easy, he told himself. None of this was the guard's fault.

"I just have some routine questions for him," Stone said.

"Oh, sure," the guard said, nodding with a look of sage understanding that Stone decided came from having watched too many cop shows on TV.

He ignored the guard for a moment as he tried to think things through. Though he had a gut feeling that Orlick and Kennedy were one and the same, he couldn't afford any assumptions at this point in the investigation. Not with how badly they'd already screwed it up.

"What about Mr. Kennedy?" he asked. "Is he in his apartment at the moment?"

Whitley reached for his phone. "Just a minute," he said, "and I'll—"

Stone reached over the desk and put his hand on the guard's, stopping him from lifting the receiver.

"I'd like to make a call first," he said.

The guard shook his head. "I'm sorry, sir, but management doesn't allow lobby phones to be used for personal calls."

"Remember the badge I showed you?"

"Well, sure. But I don't see—"

Stone pulled the guard's hand from the receiver. "You're interfering with a police investigation, Seymour. How do you think management would take it if I ran you downtown on an obstruction charge?"

"They . . . they wouldn't like it very much at all."

"Exactly. So just relax and let me make the call."

Whitley slumped back in his chair as Stone punched in the number for police headquarters. A quick transfer of the call and he had his partner on the line.

"Nothing new yet," Freeman started to say, "but—"

"Drop everything," Stone told him. "I want you to wake me a judge and get a search warrant for apartment number 1462, Sky Towers, Tower B."

Stone's own inclination was to go up to the fourteenth floor and kick down Kennedy's door, but if the D.A.'s office wanted this to play by the book, then that's how he'd do it.

"What've you got?" Freeman asked.

"Maybe Orlick. It's not a hundred percent, but it feels real good. Tell the lieutenant we're going to need a SWAT team out here immediately, but ask him to keep it low-key. No sirens, no circus shit. We don't want to spook the freak."

"They'll be on their way as soon as I hang up," Freeman told him. "Plus the Loot's had a judge waiting in his office just in case something like this came up."

Nice to see someone was thinking ahead tonight, Stone thought.

"Have somebody run a James Kennedy of the same address for priors," he told Freeman.

"Will do. Anything else?"

"No. Thanks, Norm."

"I'll be there in twenty minutes with that warrant."

"Make it ten," Stone said, then he hung up.

He looked around the lobby.

"That stairwell," he asked the guard. "Is this the only place it exits to the outside?"

Seymour shook his head. "It goes all the way down to the parking garage—same as the elevator does."

He pointed to the television monitors on his desk. They showed various closed-circuit views of the building. One was of the garage door, viewed from the inside.

"Have you seen Mr. Kennedy go in or out today?"

"No, sir."

"What about Orlick? Could he have come back in through the garage?"

"No, sir. He'd need a security card to operate the garage door."

"But if he had one?"

"Well, sure. But residents aren't supposed to lend them out."

Right, Stone thought. Like that'd stop anyone. And it certainly wouldn't stop Orlick if he and Kennedy were the same man.

"Has Mr. Kennedy got a car?"

Whitley pointed to another monitor, which gave a long view of the parking garage. "It's that Rabbit there, parked beside the two Toyotas."

Bingo, Stone thought. Orlick drove a Rabbit.

"Did you recognize everyone who came in through the garage door tonight?" he asked.

"Yes, sir. I know all the cars."

"Anybody on foot?"

If Orlick, Kennedy, whatever the hell his name was, liked to play with disguises, Stone thought, who knew how he might have been disguised after he killed Thomas Downs.

"No, sir. Just . . ."

"Just what?" Stone asked when the guard hesitated.

"Well, there was a malfunction with the garage door earlier this evening. It opened and closed, but I didn't see anybody using it."

Stone leaned over the desk to check out the monitor that showed the garage door. From the angle it gave, a person on foot could easily have slipped by without being seen. Orlick could've slipped back in. By the same token, if he and Kennedy weren't the same person, it could also have been Kennedy taking a hike.

"Just that one time?" Stone asked.

"Yes, sir. It wasn't long after Mr. Orlick left the building—maybe twenty minutes, tops."

"The door's electronically controlled?"

Whitley nodded.

"Can you shut it down from here?" Stone asked.

"Yes, sir. But I'll get into a lot of trouble with management if I—"

"Just do it," Stone told him.

"But—"

"I'll take full responsibility for it, Seymour, so do it."

"I—"

Whatever Whitley saw in Stone's face shut him up.

"Yes, sir," he said and hit the appropriate switch. He looked up to Stone. "Now what?"

Stone sat on the edge of the guard's desk. He looked at his watch. The SWAT team would be there within fifteen minutes; Freeman would probably make it a little earlier—say within ten.

"Now we wait," he said.

And then the building's fire alarm went off.

"Oh my god!" Whitley cried.

He started to rise, but Stone was blocking his way from behind the desk.

"Where's it originating?" Stone asked.

"I . . . I . . ."

Stone looked around the guard to see a red indicator light flashing on the security console. Beside it was the number 200.

"Shut off the elevator and seal the front doors," Stone told the guard. "Don't let anybody in or out unless they show you a badge."

"But I can't—"

"Just do it, Seymour, or you can guarantee I'll have your ass."

Stone drew his gun and ran for the stairwell. With the elevator out, there was only going to be one way down. The freak was going to have to go through him to get out of the building.

A good plan, Stone thought, until he'd got as high as the door to the second floor. As it crashed open, he swung the muzzle of the weapon toward the door. There were a half-dozen people there in their bed-clothes and bathrobes.

Already panicking from the fire alarm, they fell over themselves to get back into the hall behind them when they saw the gun in his hand.

Christ, he thought. The Loot's going to have my balls on this one.

Other doors were clanging open above him, and the stairwell filled with the sound of voices as the building's residents responded to the fire alarm.

"Police!" Stone cried, brandishing his ID in his free hand as he con-tinued up the stairs, but he already knew he was defeated.

In all the mess and confusion, there was no way he'd be able to find Kennedy. He didn't even know what the man looked like—and con-sidering the freak's ability to disguise himself, it wouldn't have made much difference if Stone had.

Before the crowding got too insane in the stairwell, Stone headed back down to the lobby. Behind him, people were shouting, crying, asking one another in panicked voices what was going on. It was going to be hell sorting it all out.

The security guard was just letting Freeman in through the front doors when Stone got back to the lobby. Holstering his gun, he turned to the people crowding out of the stairwell behind him.

"Be calm," he told them. "Everything's under control. There isn't a fire—it's just a false alarm."

"I've got news for you," Freeman said, coming up behind Stone. "You've got smoke billowing out of a window halfway up the building. This ain't no false alarm."

"Oh Christ," Stone said. "He didn't just pull an alarm—he torched his apartment."

"We can't keep anybody in here," Freeman said.

Stone noted the walkie-talkie attached to his partner's belt.

"Okay," he said. "Call in the SWAT team. We'll let the people out, but nobody gets away without us IDing them first."

"It's going to be messy."

"It's totally fucked," Stone told him, "but I'm not losing the chance of picking the freak up. He's got to be in this crowd."

With the guard's help, they herded the panicked residents out the front door in a somewhat orderly fashion. When Stone finally got outside, he could hear the fire trucks approaching. The quiet night that he'd left behind just a half-hour ago when he went to interview the security guard had turned completely chaotic. It was now filled with jostling crowds, the noise of sirens and the panic of the building's residents when they saw the members of the SWAT team surrounding them.

At that moment Stone just wanted to walk away. As it was, he could barely think straight in all the confusion.

"John," Freeman said.

Stone sighed. He rubbed his temples, trying to ease the headache that was starting up.

"Yeah," he said. "I know. Let's try to organize this mess."

They had to clear a way for the firefighters. Have the SWAT team maintain a perimeter so that nobody got out. Set up an area where the residents could be IDed, but their needs looked after as well.

It was going to take them the better part of the night to do all of this, Stone realized with dismay.

He looked up the side of the building where the smoke poured out of the apartment that he knew had to belong to Kennedy.

The freak was smart. Stone would give him that. Real smart. But Stone was still going to bring him down.

"And you can bank on that," he said softly as he went to help Freeman bring some semblance of order to the surrounding confusion.

FORTY-SIX

Harry waited by the window until he saw a figure emerge from Rachel's apartment building. Swinging his telescope around, he brought into close focus the same man he'd seen rummaging about in Rachel's apartment. Everything about him, from the way he carried himself to the far too competent set of his features, told Harry the man was a cop. A plainclothes detective. And what was he investigating?

Expect the worst, Harry told himself as he watched the man approach his own building.

He stood up from the telescope and looked about the room. He could get away. That wasn't the problem. And they had nothing on him, couldn't prove a thing. Except for what was to be found in this room.

He could fix that.

Tearing off the sheers from in front of the windows, he tossed them onto the carpet in the middle of the living room. He dumped the contents of his dresser drawers upon them—clothing, photographs, negatives—until he had the makings for a good-sized pyre. A funeral pyre for Peter Orlick and James Kennedy.

He pushed the sofa up against the heap of flammable material, then the telescope and his cameras. Bringing a large jug of cooking oil from the kitchen, he slopped its contents over the whole mess and the surrounding carpet. He trailed the oil back into the kitchen, where he pulled the newspapers from his recycling bin and tossed them all over the linoleum floor. These he soaked with the last of the cooking oil.

That should do it, he thought.

He collected the bag he'd packed earlier and slung it to his shoulder. At the front door of his apartment, he paused to look back at the chaos he'd created. Rachel looked down at him from the poster-sized photograph taped to the wall.

All the photos of her would burn, but that was fitting. This was a funeral not only for his Orlick and Kennedy personas, but for Rachel Sorensen as well. She had to die so that the goddess could be born.

He lit a match and tossed it onto the paper, shutting the door just as the oil-soaked carpet erupted in a huge *whoof* of flame.

For the second time that night he went down the stairwell, but this time he exited at the second floor. He walked down the hall as far as the elevators, then pulled the fire alarm. Within moments its Klaxon wail had the occupants of the surrounding apartments filling the hall in a disorderly confusion.

He walked slowly down another hall, waiting until its residents were all ahead with their backs toward him, before stepping through a door left open by that apartment's fleeing occupant. He closed the door quickly, bolting it shut behind him.

Crossing the living room, he flung open the patio doors and moved out onto the balcony. He stood there for a long moment, looking for signs of the police, but he couldn't see anything yet. The night was filled with the sound of approaching sirens.

Still time then, he thought.

Putting his arm through the strap of his bag so that it hung at his back, he swung over the railing and let himself drop from the balcony to the ground. He landed like a cat, knees slightly bent to absorb the shock. In moments he was strolling away from the building.

On the far side of Tower A, he came across a SWAT team preparing to move in on his building. He stopped in his tracks and feigned shock.

"Wh-what's going on?"

He was approached by a man who was obviously in charge. The beam of a flashlight shone on his face.

"Could I see some identification please, sir?" the man said. It wasn't a request.

"Cer-certainly," Harry said, playing the part of the frightened innocent to the hilt.

He took out a wallet and handed over a driver's license identifying him as Ron Templeton. It had a Foxville address. The flashlight rose from the picture on the driver's license to Harry's face.

"Where are you going, Mr. Templeton?" the policeman asked him.

"I was just over at my buddy's watching some videos," Harry told him. "He lives behind the Texaco station down on River Road. I was taking a shortcut home. I didn't mean to, you know, cause any trouble or anything."

Harry put just the right nervousness into his voice—the amount that most people would have, confronted by a well-armed policeman in the middle of the night like this.

"What's going on anyway?" he added.

"I'm going to have to keep this," the policeman said, pocketing Harry's driver's license.

"But—"

"It's just routine, sir. We'll have it back to you soon. In the meantime, I'd appreciate it if you'd wait with this officer."

Harry wanted to smash the man in his officious face, but he kept a bland expression on his own features, colored with just a touch of a citizen's righteous indignation.

"I don't understand—" he began.

The officer looked away from him. "Byrne!" he said sharply, calling another officer over. "Escort Mr. Templeton outside our perimeter and stay with him until we get back to you."

"Yessir. If you'll come with me, Mr. Templeton?"

Harry let the man lead him away. From his vantage point where the officer had him wait, he could see the SWAT team fanning out across the lawn in their approach to the building. They moved with military precision—well-trained, competent men. No one was going to get through their lines.

Good luck, Harry thought. He turned to the officer.

"So what's going on, anyway?" he asked. "You got yourself some big-shot criminal holed up in there?"

The officer made no reply.

"You mind if I get myself a smoke?" Harry asked.

The SWAT team was closing in on Tower B. The air was still full of sirens. From where Harry stood, he could see smoke billowing out of the apartment complex, about halfway up the side of the building, where the window to his own apartment must have blown out.

"Help yourself," the officer told him.

Harry reached into his pocket, then let his penknife fall to the pavement.

"Shit," he said.

As he bent to pick it up, he managed to give it a kick that sent it skidding across the concrete. His guard's gaze flicked to track it. Before he could look back, Harry had stepped in close, turning as he moved, foot rising, powered by all the weight of his leg and the turn. The side of his shoe caught the man in the throat and broke his neck.

Harry caught him as he collapsed and eased him to the ground, then headed quickly off, away from the apartment buildings. Twenty minutes later, he was driving a stolen car toward one of the addresses he'd taken from the phone book after he'd seen the eleven o'clock news.

FORTY-SEVEN

Up until that moment earlier in the evening, when his headlight beams had caught the man in the act of murdering another human being, the most exciting thing that had ever happened to Ralph Moran was winning a thousand dollars in a lottery. About the only people to pay any attention to that brief moment of fame had been his family, and Gary Crawford, the office mooch, who immediately tried to hit him up for a hundred-buck loan.

Moran knew his coworkers thought of him as a loser, but he hadn't been so much of a loser to lend Crawford even a dime. And things were really going to be different now. Being on the news and all—this was going to change everything. The whole city was going to know his face.

As soon as Moran had gotten back from the police station, he'd put a new tape in his video machine and started flicking through the stations, taping every segment he could find related to the killing. He looked pretty good, he thought, whenever his own face flashed up on the screen, his name right there for everybody to see.

Ralph Moran. Concerned citizen.

No, more than that. He was a frigging hero, Christ, because if he hadn't shown up when he had, the killer would've gone for the woman next. No question. And what a piece of work she was. Dressed to the T's, perfect legs, great tits.

Now that the main excitement with the killing had died down, Moran had time to play back the segments he'd taped. He hit the Pause button when the woman was on the screen, then slow-moed frame by frame as she got into the cop car. Christ, you could almost see right up her dress as she slid in.

He'd like to slide it into *her*, he thought. Oriental women were supposed to be the best. They were frigging trained from when they were just kids to make a man feel good. Do anything for you, anything you wanted.

His free hand slid down from his thigh and closed itself around his crotch as he played back the video so that he could watch her get into the car again. Slow-mo. Those legs. He could feel them wrapped around him. He could—

His doorbell sounded, and he guiltily hit the Stop button on his VCR.

Who the hell could that be? he wondered as he shifted his bulk up from the sofa. Then his features brightened in anticipation. Probably more reporters.

He stopped by the hall mirror and checked himself out. Looking good. He glanced down at his crotch, but his penis was already shrinking, no longer pressing so tightly against his chinos. Running a hand through his thinning hair, he stepped over to the door and opened it.

He couldn't hide his disappointment. No cameras. No fancy network news babe come to do a follow-up. Fact of the matter was, the man standing there with the black gloves on didn't look much like a reporter at all.

"Hey, Ralph," the man said as though they were old friends.

Moran peered a little closer at the man. "Do I know you?" he asked.

"Just moved in down the hall," the man told him. "Caught you on the news. Hell, that must've really been something."

Moran straightened up, drawing in his gut.

"Yeah, well, you know," he said. "I just wish I'd got there a few minutes earlier."

The stranger smiled. "You would've showed him. Well, say, I just came by to borrow a tablespoon. Sorry it's so late and all, but what can you do?"

Moran wasn't sure how it happened. One minute the man was standing out in the hall, the next he was in the apartment, standing in the middle of the living room, looking like he belonged there and Moran was just visiting.

"A tablespoon of what?" he found himself asking.

"Just a tablespoon." At the blank look on Moran's face, the man added, "Seems like that'd be the best tool for what I've got in mind."

"What're you talking ab—"

His voice died in his throat as the man pulled a small gun from his pocket.

"I'm talking about people being where they shouldn't be, seeing what they shouldn't be seeing," the man told him.

He picked up a pillow from the sofa and stepped toward Moran.

"Please," Moran said, all thoughts of heroism fleeing. "I never meant—"

"Too late, Ralphy."

The man backed Moran up against a wall. He shoved the pillow up against Moran's trembling stomach, the gun into the pillow. The sound as it was fired sounded like just a couple of muffled pops to Moran, but the pain . . . oh, the pain . . .

The man stepped away, and Moran slid to the floor, clutching his stomach. Blood poured out between his fingers. He looked at it in disbelief.

The man moved into his kitchen, came back in moments with a tablespoon in his hand.

"It's in the eyes," the man said as he bent down beside Moran. "That's what they say, you know. It's all in the eyes."

Moran tried to lift his arms, but there seemed to be no strength in them. He passed out as the man placed the spoon under his left eyeball and began to press.

FORTY-EIGHT

Sam Porter had an obsession with the doings of his neighbors. Little could go on in the neighborhood, night or day, without his being aware of it. He'd known that Judy Frazer was dating a white boy weeks before her parents had, that the Goldmans had sold their confectionery a full month before the "Under New Management" sign appeared in the store window, that Bobby Thompson had lost his job at the Jordan Carpet Factory, that the Griersons were divorcing, that Martha Friel had bought a new fridge—and where *did* she get the money for that, being on welfare as she was?

Porter knew that as well.

There were few secrets in the neighborhood to which he was not privy, a fact that irritated as many of his neighbors as it amused.

The late movie was still on that night when he decided to make himself a cup of cocoa. Waiting for the water to boil, he stood at the living room window in his undershirt and skivvies and peered idly through a crack in the drapes. It was late enough on a weekday night that he doubted anything of interest was unfolding outside, but the act of observation was second nature to him. He could as little stop snooping as he could give up breathing.

The street was empty except for parked cars and an alley cat sniffing around the two bags of garbage that the Frazers had put out for pickup a full day early. There were a few lights on in the windows of the tenement across the street. In all but one of the lighted windows televisions, probably tuned to the same late night movie he was watching, flickered blue white against curtains. The one anomaly would be Jackson Pierce, snatching a few extra hours of studying for his mail-order auto mechanics course before he had to leave for his job as a driver with Newford Transpo.

From the kitchen behind him, Porter could hear the water in the kettle beginning to boil. He was about to turn away from the window to deal with it when a sleek dark-blue Ford Tempo pulled into the empty parking spot on the street below him. The blond-haired man who stepped out was a complete stranger.

Now what would his business be here? Porter found himself wondering as the man approached Porter's building. It was late for visitors—even considering Martha Friel's "business."

He went over and listened through the thin front door of his apartment as the man climbed the stairs. The stranger came all the way up to Porter's floor and knocked on a door close to the landing. He was at Moran's or Mrs. Willerton's apartment, Porter decided. When he heard a man's voice respond to the stranger's knock, he knew it was Moran. Unfortunately, he couldn't make out what either man was saying.

Porter had run across a book not so long ago in which a man had installed hidden closed-circuit cameras and microphones in every apartment of his complex when he had built. That was what *he* should have, Porter had thought at the time—and in every instance such as this, when his curiosity couldn't be appeased because the walls of his building, thin as they were, simply weren't effective enough conductors of sound. Not in the fine detail that Porter required.

He went into his kitchen and took the kettle off the stove, then returned to his post by the door. A faint murmur of conversation still wound down the hall from Moran's apartment, but it was more muffled now. The door was open, Porter decided, but both men were inside the apartment.

He remembered seeing Moran on the news earlier this evening—he'd been witness to a murder over in Ferryside. Probably while he was driving back from a visit to his mother, Porter had decided at the time, knowing that Moran's mother lived in the older part of Ferryside—the area that had once housed most of the workers in the old canning factory. So . . . was Moran's visitor a reporter, perhaps? Or a policeman?

Porter took the chance and cracked open his own door in time to hear an odd sound that he just couldn't place—a kind of muffled pop that came once and then was immediately repeated. This was followed by what sounded as though something was being shifted about—a sofa, perhaps, or a large chair. From the few glances he'd had of Moran's apartment, walking by when the door was open, he knew Moran owned both.

The stranger spoke again, conversationally, but Porter still couldn't make out what was being said. He didn't hear a response from Moran.

He waited a few moments longer, but there were no further sounds at all. Then some sixth sense warned him, and he silently closed the door of his own apartment. He heard Moran's door shut, then the stranger going back down the stairs.

Porter hurried over to the window and peered down at the sidewalk through the crack in his drapes. He saw the stranger emerge from the building and return to his car, but then he did the strangest thing. He retrieved a shoulder bag from the car and walked a little farther down the block, where he bent over the driver's side door of Jackson Pierce's old Dodge sedan.

When the door opened under the stranger's administrations, Porter realized what he was dealing with here. The man was a thief, because

Pierce always locked his car doors before he went up to his apartment. If Porter had seen Pierce do it once, he'd seen him do it a thousand times.

He quickly crossed the living room and called the police. When he'd given them the details of what he'd seen on the street below, he put on his trousers and a shirt, then left his apartment and walked down the hall to Moran's door. He hesitated at the door, feeling momentarily foolish. Moran was one of Porter's neighbors who wasn't the least amused at being constantly spied upon. Porter could just imagine what Moran would say when he came to the door.

But what if he needed help? What if the stranger had robbed him—though what Moran could have that anyone would want to steal was beyond Porter's realm of painstakingly acquired knowledge.

There was only one way to find out.

Straightening his shoulders, Porter rapped firmly on the hollow paneling of Moran's door. When there was no response on his fourth knock, Porter hurried back to his own apartment to call the police again.

FORTY-NINE

As soon as the firemen had put out the fire, Stone, Brauman and their lieutenant entered James Kennedy's apartment. Stone surveyed the mess with a critical eye. The air reeked of smoke and wet ash, burned plastic and smoldering fabric. The apartment had obviously been stripped, all of its furnishings piled in a heap in the middle of the living room to feed the fire. While Brauman and the lieutenant fanned out to either side, Stone picked his way to the middle of the room and stood over the remains of a high-powered telescope.

"This was the guy," he said softly.

Over on her side of the room, Brauman reached down and picked through the remains of a half-dozen photographs. She was wearing thin plastic gloves and held the prints gingerly so as not to smudge any possible latents.

"Look familiar?" she asked, offering the photographs up for her companions to see.

Stone came to her side. The shots were all of Rachel Sorensen in her apartment.

"Taken with a telephoto," Brauman said.

Stone nodded grimly. "He was here when I was in her apartment. We were *this* close to getting him."

Outside the building, the residents were still being checked out against the hope that Kennedy was among them, but Stone already knew the man was gone. Somehow Kennedy had known that they were onto him. He'd hadn't known by much, but he'd *known*. Enough to get out of here in time.

"Looks like," Brauman said.

She looked up as her partner joined them in the fire-gutted room.

"Forensics is on the way," Draycott told them.

Information was already filtering up from the investigation that was being conducted throughout the building and around it. Reports of a stranger on the second floor. An open patio door found in one of the apartments there. Then they learned about the man who'd been stopped by Sergeant Davis's SWAT team and the death of Officer Byrne.

They had detectives and patrolmen combing the streets, and they'd come up with nothing until Dispatch called in a report of a stolen car a few blocks over from the Sky Towers. There was a citywide APB in effect now for both Kennedy and the car.

But Stone was sure that the man had already slipped beyond their reach. To be so close . . .

The only object on which he could vent his anger lay at his feet. He kicked savagely at the debris.

"Stone!" Takahashi said.

The lieutenant didn't have to say more. Stone nodded in weary acknowledgment of the unspoken admonishment. What they had in here was all they had to go on to find Kennedy.

"He's just playing us," he said when Brauman laid a hand on his arm and drew him back into the hall. "Leading us around by our dicks like the idiots we are."

"Take it easy, John," she said.

"How can I? The death count's hit five now, and my gut tells me it's going to get worse."

The arrival of a breathless patrolman soon paid weight to Stone's instinct. The report he gave the members of the task force held all the improbability of a TV script, but the only part of it that Stone zeroed in on was that they were being given another chance to nab their killer. He didn't care how much luck or coincidence had been involved in having a busybody stumble upon Kennedy's latest victim only moments after Moran had died. What was important was that they not only had a make on the new car he'd stolen, but also a damned good idea as to his current destination.

"If he's killed the witness . . ." Brauman began.

"He's only killed *one* of them," Stone said. "But what he doesn't know is that we're on to him."

The M.O. was slightly different from the previous killings, but no one on the task force had any doubt that Moran's killer was the same man they were looking for. This time he'd used a gun—then spooned out Moran's eyes and left them sitting on top of his chest. When he heard that, Stone was certain. It fit the twisted sense of "justice" that had led the killer to burn the waiter who'd spilled hot coffee on Rachel Sorensen, to mutilate Ian Hughes because of his remarks to her in the Bike Pit.

Ralph Moran had had his eyes removed because he'd seen what the killer hadn't wanted him to see.

"He's going to go after Kataboki next," Stone added.

"Makes sense."

Stone grinned. There was no humor in the expression.

"Only this time," he said, "we're going to be there, waiting for him."

As Brauman nodded, the lieutenant began issuing a rapid-fire series of orders. He wanted Cruz to be informed that it was likely the killer would be making an attempt on Lily Kataboki's life and that they would be sending her immediate backup. He wanted unmarked cars covering every possible route between Kataboki and Moran's apartments, with squad cars and the SWAT team kept on standby. He wanted all radio lines cleared of everything except for this business.

Takahashi was still issuing orders when Stone and the other members of the task force headed for the elevators that would take them down to their own vehicles.

"This time we're going to get him," Stone said as he and Brauman jogged past the police lines to where they'd left their cars. "I can feel it."

"I don't know," Brauman replied. "He's a wild card—not only smart, but luckier than any man has a right to be."

Stone nodded. "Yeah, well, this time his luck's run out. Our team's finally up to bat."

FIFTY

Officers Joe Kita and Nelson Foster were in the middle of a friendly argument when the dark blue Dodge sedan went by. Kita straightened up in his seat as Foster was speaking, his attention diverted by the sedan, which had now paused for a red light farther down the block.

"You catch the plate number on that Dodge?" he asked, interrupting his partner.

As Foster shook his head, Kita started up the squad car and pulled out onto the street behind the sedan, cutting off a cab. The squeal of the cab's brakes mixed with that of the squad car's tires as it set off in pursuit of the Dodge. The light for which the car had stopped had already changed, and the Dodge now had a two-block lead on them.

"Call it in," Kita said. "I think we've found ourselves a cop killer."

Foster hooked free the radio microphone and called their dispatch receiver.

"This is Charlie-car," he said into the mike. "We're in pursuit of a dark blue, late-model Dodge sedan, license number—what'd you say that number was, Joe?"

Kita told him, and Foster relayed the information into the mike.

"Copy, Charlie-car," the dispatcher said. There was a moment's pause, filled with radio static. "Can you give me verification on that number?" she added.

Foster repeated the plate number.

"Jackpot time, boys," the dispatcher told them. "You've got Paul Byrne's killer. Stay on his tail. Keep the line open and update your position as the pursuit progresses."

"Heading south on Flood Street, about to cross Stanton."

Kita hit the lights and siren and put some more weight on the accelerator. The cruiser leapt forward, momentarily closing the two-block lead that the Dodge had on them. Then the Dodge started to pull ahead once more.

"What's he got under that hood?" Kita muttered.

As they crossed over Stanton, they could see another cruiser and an unmarked car with a cherry on its dash pull across the intersection at Bunnett, to cut off the Dodge. The sedan headed right at them until the last possible moment, then the driver cut his wheel rapidly to the right.

The Dodge bounced up on the sidewalk, showering sparks when its back end bounced against the curb. It sideswiped a newsstand and roared down the sidewalk, scattering a half-dozen late night pedestrians. Siren blaring, Kita followed the Dodge up onto the sidewalk.

"Jesus Christ, man!" Foster cried as, even buckled in by their seat belts, the two men bounced against each other on the front seat.

Kita made no reply, his attention entirely focused on the Dodge ahead of them. Once the sedan had circled around the makeshift blockade made up of the two cars at the Bunnett-Flood intersection, it returned to the street, fishtailing when it took a sudden right on Walker Street. The rear end smashed into a parked Mazda, then bounced off. The driver never slowed.

"Vehicle is now traveling west on Walker," Foster said into the mike.

"Copy, Charlie-car."

Kita and Foster had a half-dozen other squad cars trailing behind them now, filling the night with their cherry lights and the sound of their sirens. Two intersections farther on, more cruisers pulled across the Dodge's path again. The driver of the Dodge never braked.

He went up on the sidewalk again, this time to the left of the road-block. The side of the Dodge howled with another shower of sparks as it careened off the side of a squad car. Kita slowed down their own vehicle and made it through the narrow gap between the end cruiser and a light post without touching either.

Ahead of them, the Dodge took a sharp right, rear end fishtailing, tires screaming.

"Vehicle heading north on Yoors," Foster informed the dispatcher.

He used one arm, braced stiffly against the dash, to keep himself in place, the other to hold the microphone.

"Hang on," Kita told him.

To Foster, it seemed as though they took the corner on two wheels and a prayer. As soon as they were around, they had to dodge an oncoming streetcar, then slow down for a stalled Buick that was block-ing their lane. Once the streetcar was out of the way, Kita shot their squad car through the narrow gap it left in its wake. The wide, fright-ened eyes of the Buick's driver stayed with Foster for the whole next length of city block.

Ahead of them, the Dodge now had a three-block lead that seemed to be widening. The Dodge's driver didn't seem to care if he lived or died, Foster thought. He drove on whatever side of the street had an opening, never letting his foot off the gas. The only thing that was let-ting him get away with it was the fact that the traffic was so light at this time of night. Still, it was a wonder that no one had been hurt yet.

No sooner did he have that thought, than he saw the Dodge clip a man who was just that one fatal second too slow getting out of the way. The Dodge just kept right on going as the man was flipped high into the air and thrown against the windshield of an oncoming car.

"Civilian down just south of Grasso," Foster said into the mike.

"Copy, Charlie-car."

Kita swerved the squad car around the scene of the accident and stayed in pursuit of the Dodge. Turning in his seat, Foster saw one of the cars following them pull over to deal with the situation. The rest remained on their tail, a long, speeding snake of flashing lights and sirens.

"I think the stupid fuck actually thinks he can make a run out of the city," Kita said.

"It's that," Foster agreed, "or he's going to die trying."

Yoors Street could conceivably take the driver of the Dodge right out of Newford, but the man was never going to get the chance. There were just too many cars mobilized against him and not nearly enough room for him to maneuver a way out of the tightening police web.

Then, just past the estates lining the west end of Stanton Street, the Dodge took a sudden left on McKennit that would take him into the tangled lanes and narrower streets that made up Lower Crowsea.

"Shit," Kita said as they reached McKennit themselves. "It's a fucking maze in there."

"Vehicle traveling west on McKennit," Foster informed the dispatcher.

"Copy, Charlie-car."

While Kita negotiated their cruiser through the narrow twists and turns in the wake of the Dodge, Foster listened as Lieutenant Takahashi's voice replaced that of the dispatcher. The lieutenant ordered various cars to block the streets leading into this part of Lower Crowsea.

"I think we've got him boxed in now," Foster said.

"Yeah?" Kita said. "Well, I just lost him."

Foster radioed in their position as Kita slowly cruised down the last street onto which they'd seen the Dodge turn.

"Too many damn old sedans around here," Kita said.

Foster nodded in agreement. Then he caught a glimpse of a red taillight down an alleyway they were passing.

"Down there!" he cried.

Kita braked and threw the cruiser into reverse with a suddenness that made the transmission groan. He barreled down the narrow alleyway, knocking over a half-dozen garbage cans in his haste. They burst out of the end of the alley just in time to see the rear end of the Dodge vanish around another corner.

"Vehicle's on Quinlan, heading west toward Lee Street," Foster told the dispatcher.

"Copy, Charlie-car. We have three cars now on Lee."

"*Now* we've got him," Foster said.

They rounded two more corners, then Kita took a chance and shortcutted through one of the old horse-carriage lanes that still ran behind the area's older buildings. They saw the Dodge go by the front of the lane as they sped down its length. When they turned onto the street after the sedan, they were only a half block behind it.

"Okay," Kita said.

He put his foot down on the gas, hard.

This was a long block. At the far end of the street, they could see a cruiser pull up to block the exit onto Lee Street. At the speed the Dodge was now traveling, it could no longer turn off onto another carriage lane. As though realizing this, the Dodge leapt forward, heading straight for the cruiser.

"Jesus!" Foster cried. "He's going to ram it!"

The two officers from the cruiser had taken up defensive positions behind their vehicle, handguns out. But the Dodge was moving so fast that neither had a chance to fire a shot before both officers were sprinting out of the way of the coming impact.

Just before it ran headlong into the cruiser, the Dodge's brakes flared red. The car skidded, tires burning rubber on the pavement, now bearing down on the cruiser at an angle. At the last moment before impact, the driver of the Dodge hit the gas and his car shot for the small break between the cruiser and the building at the corner of the street.

The Dodge hit the cruiser, metal screeching against metal as the sides of the two cars smashed into each other. Because of the angle of the impact, the Dodge sustained only a battering of the metal on the driver's side of the car. It shot through the gap it had made in side-swiping the cruiser and was out on Lee Street. Caught in its beams for a long moment was one of the officers from the cruiser.

The driver of the Dodge turned his wheel enough to hit the officer, throwing him through the plate-glass window of the jewelry store on the corner, then the vehicle was racing up Lee Street.

"Officer down! Officer down!" Foster shouted into the mike. "Corner of Lee and Waterhouse. Vehicle now heading north on Lee Street."

Contrary to police shows on the television, inner-city police rarely dealt with prolonged car chases. Chases that did take place, this deep in the heart of the city, were inevitably over in minutes.

As this one should've been, Foster thought.

But every time they thought they had him, the driver of the Dodge managed to pull another rabbit out of the hat and get away. Foster was beginning to get the sinking feeling that the cop killer was actually going to get away—especially when they reached the Kelly Street Bridge and the driver of the Dodge finessed his way through yet another roadblock to actually get onto the bridge.

With a skill Foster hadn't realized his partner possessed, Kita duplicated the other driver's maneuver, although at a much slower speed. They were just beginning to accelerate again when they saw an unmarked car, cherry flashing on its dash, cross the double lines in the center of the bridge.

For a long moment the driver of the Dodge and the unmarked played chicken, then the Dodge pulled suddenly to the right. It crashed through the railings, popping the metal poles from their concrete moorings as it went over the side and plunged into the river.

Kita brought the squad car to a screeching halt, no more than a few yards from where the unmarked car came to its own sliding stop. Foster hit the release on his seat belt. Snagging a powerful flashlight from under his seat, he jumped from the car to join the driver of the unmarked police car, who was staring down at the river below.

Together they watched the car sink. Foster played the beam of his light across the water. Moments later, they were joined by Kita and other officers. The bridge filled with cruisers and unmarked cars. Officers closed off either end of the bridge. A SWAT team disembarked from their van and fanned out along either side of the river, following the shoreline.

Foster looked up as an attractive woman approached. She had a detective's ID pinned to her lapel.

"Was that him, John?" she asked of the driver who'd forced the Dodge from the bridge.

The other detective turned to Foster. Foster recognized him now. It was John Stone, a Homicide dick from downtown. The man looked beat. The woman, he read from a quick glance at her ID, was Liz Brauman, also from Homicide.

"There was a blond Caucasian behind the wheel," Foster told him. "The car and plate number matched the one from the APB."

"If we're lucky, he'll be dead," Stone said.

Brauman regarded the sixty-foot drop to the river below. The water had swallowed the vehicle. Both sides of the shoreline were lit up with police spotlights. Members of the SWAT team could be seen patrolling the shoreline. As they watched, another van pulled up and three German shepherds and their handlers issued forth.

"I doubt anyone could've survived that drop," Brauman said.

"I didn't get here in time to see it hit the water," Stone told her, "but both doors were still closed as it sank."

"The Dodge took a couple of solid hits on its driver's side during pursuit," Foster offered. "The door was probably jammed shut."

"Good," Stone said. "I hope the fucker drowned and I hope his dying was hard."

"Amen," Brauman said.

FIFTY-ONE

There were two sets of visitors to Lily's apartment the following morning. The first to arrive were Detectives Stone and Brauman, who came to the door of the apartment just before eight. They met with Lily and Rachel in the living room, grateful for the coffee that Diane Cruz made for them while they related the events of the past night. Brauman passed around photocopies of some of the half-destroyed photographs they'd found in James Kennedy's apartment.

"He'd been watching you for some time," she told Rachel. "Taking pictures with a telephoto lens."

Lily had changed from her nightgown into a sweat suit; Rachel was wearing one of Lily's terry-cloth bathrobes. Rachel hugged the bathrobe closed about her chest and sat beside Lily on the sofa while the detectives spoke.

"Forensics came up with a match for the prints we found in James Kennedy's apartment," Stone was saying, "and it's a real miracle they got them as quickly as they did. Kennedy's real name was Harry Landon—you've probably seen the coffee table photography books he's done."

"Harry *Landon*?" Rachel said in disbelief. "But he . . . he's . . ."

"We may not arrest as many big shots as we do ordinary Joes," Stone told her, "but they're just as capable of committing crimes."

"But still . . . There's got to be some sort of a mistake."

Rachel didn't know very much about the reclusive photographer— no one did, really—except that his work was stunning. He was a true artist, showing an astonishing sensitivity even in his more commercial work. It seemed inconceivable that this was the man she'd known as Peter Orlick, that he was a killer.

"We pulled Landon's sheet," Brauman said. "There wasn't much in it, but what there was proved telling. When he was still a juvie, he was picked up on a peeping charge. Later, when he was working in New York, he was involved in the death of a young model. She fell from his balcony during a photo shoot.

"He was never charged—there was no evidence to make the incident seem like anything more than the accident he claimed it was at the time—but when you start to put that together with the profile we've been building of the man you knew as Peter Orlick, it all begins to make sense."

Lily took Rachel's hand as Rachel slowly shook her head in shock.

"But why?" she asked. "It's so crazy that I find it almost impossible to believe. A man like Harry Landon could have had anybody in the world he wanted to be his model."

"Maybe he just liked to do it on the sly," Stone said. "Remember, he was a peeper once. Just because he never got picked up again doesn't mean he ever stopped. It just tells us that he got more careful."

"And one thing we know for certain," Brauman said. "The man we were looking for was careful. No witnesses—until last night; nothing left behind at the murder scenes. He knew how to cover his trail. And from what you've told us, he was a consummate actor as well."

Rachel was only half-listening. Her mind had returned to the Saturday she'd spent with Landon—when she'd still known him as Peter Orlick. He'd told her he was a photographer. She also remembered his odd views on beauty. She shivered, and Lily gave her hand another squeeze.

"But he's dead now?" Lily said.

"We saw the car go over the bridge," Stone said. "No one was seen jumping from the vehicle before it hit the water, and it's unlikely that anyone would have survived the impact, let alone come out of it undamaged enough to simply swim away. The trouble is there wasn't a body in the car when we pulled it out of the river."

"Divers are still trying to recover the body," Brauman added. "It's not an easy process. With the current running the way it does in that part of the river, it's conceivable that it could have been pulled out into the lake. If that's the case, it may get washed up on shore sometime over the next couple of weeks. Or we may never find it."

For a long moment no one spoke. Diane Cruz leaned against the windowsill, sipping her coffee. The other two detectives appeared exhausted—especially the man named Stone. His face had a haggard, drawn look to it, and exhaustion crawled around in his eyes.

"What do you think?" Rachel asked him. "Is Peter Orlick, I mean, Harry Landon—*is* he dead?"

Stone sighed. "I was there. I watched the car go over; I didn't see anybody get out."

"That's not really an answer," Lily said.

"You're right. I guess what I'm saying is, I can't be absolutely, positively sure—not until I see him laid out on a steel tray in the morgue."

"He didn't survive," Brauman said firmly. "No one could have. It's just a matter of time before we find the body."

But Rachel felt like Detective Stone: she wanted to know, without a shadow of a doubt, that Harry Landon was dead. She didn't want educated guesses, or to be told that no one could have survived the plunge he'd taken off the bridge. She, too, wanted to see the body—*needed* to see it—to be sure.

"Since you won't be requiring protection any longer," Brauman went on, "Detective Cruz will be returning to her previous assignment. We would like to have you come by Headquarters later today to read over and sign your statements. Do you think you can make it in?"

Rachel and Lily both nodded, Rachel more reluctantly than Lily, and Brauman rose to her feet.

"I know what you're feeling," Stone said as he rose from his own chair to join Brauman, "and I wish we could do more. Landon's death won't bring back your friend, or make up for what you've gone through yourselves, but at least you have the satisfaction of knowing that justice of a kind was served."

Lily nodded, but remained seated when Rachel rose to let the police out. When Rachel returned to the living room, her heart broke to look at her friend. Lily seemed so small, all drawn into herself and lost on the sofa. It was as though Tom's death had stolen her own will to live. Without makeup, her normally pale skin seemed completely washed out, as though she were one of those porcelain statues that her grandmother kept sending her from Japan.

Rachel sat down again and put her arm around Lily's shoulders.

"I . . ." Lily began in a small voice. "I thought that know . . . knowing that the man who killed Tom is dead, would make it feel better. But it . . . it doesn't."

"The police knew that," Rachel told her. "They were just trying to help."

"It doesn't help." Lily's voice was muffled as she spoke against Rachel's shoulder. "It doesn't help at all."

She began to cry, and all Rachel could do was be there for her. She held Lily, rubbing her back, and wondered at the strange role reversal that had come about. Now Lily needed her. Now she was the one who had to be strong.

That responsibility, Rachel realized, was all that was keeping her from falling apart herself.

The second set of visitors came about mid-morning. Lily was lying down when the doorbell rang, so Rachel went to see who was there.

Before she opened the door, she looked through the peephole to find a nondescript middle-aged couple standing out in the hall in front of Lily's door. Leaving the chain on, she opened the door to the length of the chain.

The woman's features were lined in a permanent frown. Her sense of fashion was expensive, but basic: plain skirt, the hem of which came to just below her knee, a white blouse buttoned to the throat, sensible walking shoes, a bulky purse hanging from her shoulder. The entire outfit must have set her back some seven hundred dollars, but for all the effect it had, she might as well have bought it at a thrift shop.

Her companion had a receding hairline and friendlier features. He was wearing a shirt and tie and a dark blue tailored suit. Looking at him, Rachel couldn't help but feel that she'd seen him somewhere before.

"Can I help you?" she asked.

"I was under the impression that you were one of those Orientals," the woman said.

"I beg your pardon?"

"I'm Harold Downs," the man said, "and this is my wife, Jennifer."

Of course, Rachel thought. That's why the man looked familiar. These people were Tom's parents.

"We're looking for a Lily Kataboki," he added.

"Just a moment," Rachel said.

She closed the door and undid the chain, then let the pair in. The woman immediately began to look about the apartment as though searching for something.

"I'm so sorry about what happened to Tom," Rachel said.

"Thank you," Mr. Downs said. "It was . . . quite a shock."

Rachel nodded sympathetically. "I'll go tell Lily that you're here."

When she returned with Lily, it was to find Tom's father sitting uncomfortably on the edge of one of the sofa's seats. Mrs. Downs was going through the tidy stack of magazines and letters that Lily kept piled up on top of the TV set until she'd had a chance to deal with them.

Tom's mother turned when Rachel and Lily entered. Her frowning features, if anything, deepened with displeasure when her gaze fell on Lily.

This was not a pleasant woman, Rachel thought, remembering the condescending tone of voice that Mrs. Downs had used when she spoke of Orientals while she was still out in the hallway. The woman's presumptive nosiness, combined with her general disagreeableness, had Rachel wishing she'd never let the pair in—especially with the way Mrs. Downs was currently regarding Lily.

She glanced at her friend, but Lily didn't even seem to have noticed.

"We . . . we've never met," Lily began, "but Tom often—"

"Yes, it's because of Thomas that we're here," Mrs. Downs broke in. "We will be, as is only proper considering the circumstances, the executors of Thomas's estate."

Rachel was sure that the confusion on Lily's features mirrored her own.

"I . . . I don't understand what you mean," Lily said.

"Thomas was a very talented and popular artist," Mrs. Downs went on in a tone of voice that plainly said she had no patience for what she considered to be their obvious stupidity. "His work, therefore, is of considerable value."

"Well, yes," Lily said. "But I still don't understand . . ."

Maybe Lily didn't, but Rachel could see where this was leading. The ghouls. Tom wasn't even dead a day, and here his parents were out sniffing after a profit.

"Since the two of you were conducting some sort of a *relationship*," Mrs. Downs said, "it stands to reason that you might be in possession of some of his artwork. We have come to collect it."

"But I don't . . ."

"Oh, yes," Mrs. Downs said. "I'm sure you're about to tell me that he never gave you anything, but I know better. Thomas was always too generous for his own good. Come along now. Let's have a look through your apartment."

While Lily was still digesting this, Rachel stepped in front of the woman.

"I'm afraid you'll have to leave," she said.

Mr. Downs immediately stood up. His wife shot him a frown.

"Oh, sit down, Harold," she told him. Turning back to Rachel, she added, "I'm afraid I must insist that you—"

"If you're not out of here immediately, I'll call the police and have you charged with trespassing," Rachel told the woman.

"I can get a court order."

"Fine. Then get one. But right now, either you're leaving of your own free will or you can discuss this at the police precinct while you're waiting to make bail."

"Young woman. You have no right to—"

Rachel stepped over to the phone. She picked up the receiver.

"Out," she said. "Now."

Mr. Downs rose again, and this time he ignored the hard look his wife gave him and headed for the door. Reluctantly, she followed after him.

"Thomas could never have been serious about you," she told Lily just before they left the apartment.

Lily just stared at the woman, her eyes swimming with tears.

"What the hell are you taking about?" Rachel demanded.

Mrs. Downs regarded Rachel as she might a bug. "Well, she's not exactly white, is she? Fine for a dalliance, but—"

She never finished. As Rachel clenched her fists and stalked toward her, the woman stepped out into the hall and closed the door quickly behind her—but not before giving Rachel a self-satisfied smile. She might not have gotten what she came for, it said, but by God, she'd put them in their place.

Rachel shot the bolt on the door. Turning, she found Lily standing in the middle of the living room, tears streaming down her cheeks. Quickly, she closed the distance separating them and enfolded Lily in a comforting embrace.

"I . . . I can't understand it," Lily said when the flow of tears finally waned into sniffles.

They had moved to the sofa again. Freshly brewed tea sat on the coffee table in front of them, along with a box of tissues. Lily had a wad of the latter clenched up in a ball in her hand.

"How can they be like that?" she asked Rachel. "How can such a sweet man as Tom have been raised by such a monster?"

Rachel remembered how Tom had been at her apartment before he died, or at other times, when she'd seen him arguing with his friends. Yes, Tom could be sweet, but he could also be arrogant and oblivious to anybody else's opinions or feelings. She could see the resemblance between Tom and his mother all too clearly, but she didn't say anything. Now wasn't the right time. It would never be the right time to tell Lily something like that.

"They won't get a thing from you," Rachel assured Lily. She was thinking of the lovely portrait that Lily had shown her last night. "If worse comes to worst, you can hide anything you have at my apartment."

Lily shook her head. "I'm not going to hide anything. I'm not—Oh, Rachel. How can I go to the funeral with them there?"

"Your friends will be there, too," Rachel told her. "And Tom's. They all know how much you cared for each other."

And none of them are money-grubbing racists either, she thought.

Lily nodded, but she was still plainly unhappy.

"I'll come with you," Rachel assured her.

"I know you will. I—"

Lily looked away, but Rachel saw the shine of tears in her eyes again. Lily took a deep breath.

"Don't take this wrong," she finally said, "but I think I need to be alone for a little while."

"I understand," Rachel said. "Maybe . . . How about if I go home and freshen up, then come back in a couple of hours?"

"You . . . you don't mind?"

After all Lily had done for her? Rachel thought.

"Of course I don't. Can I bring you anything back?"

Lily shook her head.

Rachel hesitated for a long moment, but then rose and went into the bedroom to change back into the clothes she'd been wearing when she came over last night. Returning to the living room, she found that Lily hadn't moved. Her eyes had welled with tears once more. They spilled down her bone-white cheeks, moving with the slow inevitable drip of an icicle, and she didn't even seem to be aware of them.

How could she leave Lily like this? Rachel thought.

"Please," Lily said, not looking at her. "I just . . . I just need some time. . . ."

"Call me if you change your mind," Rachel told her. "Otherwise I'll be back in a couple of hours."

Lily nodded.

Her own heart breaking for what Lily was going through, Rachel moved slowly to the door. She didn't want to go, but she also knew that some grief was private. What Lily had lost when Tom died couldn't be replaced by however many condolences and well-meant intentions. Sometimes it could only be faced on one's own.

Not for always. Grief wasn't something that anyone should have to deal with on their own. It took time, and it took the support of one's friends and family, to be sure; but part of it also took being alone, just to come to terms with the very existence of the loss.

She paused at the door to look back.

"I love you," she said.

"That . . . that helps," Lily said.

Rachel tried to find a smile, but without success. Finally she just said, "I'll see you in two hours," then closed the apartment door softly behind her.

FIFTY-TWO

When Rachel reached the street, everything seemed wrong. So much had happened to her and Lily in the last twenty-four hours that the ordinary scene that confronted her from Lily's porch left her feeling out of step with the rest of the world. It was all so ordinary, so untouched by the monstrous shadow of Harry Landon.

Lily's street, and the busier street it crossed a block-and-a-half down from where Rachel stood, had only the usual traffic, vehicular and pedestrian, people just going about their business as though it were nothing more than another day. Two doors up, a cat lay stretched out on the short walk leading up to an old Victorian-style house that was a twin to the one that Lily's landlady owned. Across the street, a woman with a stroller stood talking to the postman. A little past them, a thin old man in chinos and a T-shirt sat on his front porch, smoking a cigarette.

The sheer normality of it all gave Rachel a momentary sense of vertigo. She leaned a hand against the post by the porch steps to keep her balance.

But then how else should it be? she realized. For most people, nothing had changed. The world went on, as it always did, the sheer volume of its diversity making insignificant one's personal story, no matter how tragic.

After a few moments, the dizziness passed and she was able to walk down the street to the bus stop. She checked the bus schedule on the side of the pole against her watch, then sat down on the bench when she saw that she had a ten-minute wait.

Too bad she didn't have her new bike, she thought. In ten minutes she could already have been home.

She watched a dark blue Ford Escort pull up by the bus stop. Nervousness flickered through her when she saw the man's beard. His eyes were hidden by sunglasses, and he was wearing a black baseball cap. The first person she thought of was Peter Orlick, and how Detective Stone had told her that there hadn't been a body in the car.

But then the driver leaned across the front seat and called to her through the passenger's window, asking if she could tell him how to get to the ferry that would take him to Wolf Island. His voice carried the light burr of a Scottish accent.

Peter Orlick is dead, she told herself. But just for a moment there, she hadn't been able to shake the feeling that it was him in the car.

"Can you help me?" the man asked.

"Sure," she said, getting up from the bench to approach the vehicle. "You just keep going straight down . . ."

Her voice trailed off when the gun appeared in the man's hand. He held it low, in a position that gave him a clear shot at her through the open window, but left the weapon invisible to anyone except for her.

"Get in the car, Rachel," he said.

It was Peter Orlick's voice. Except, no. That wasn't his real name, was it? His real name was Harry Landon, the world-famous photographer, and, oh yes, incidentally, he was a multiple murderer as well.

Panic reared up in her—a hot white flood of fear.

"Please," he went on. "Don't do anything foolish."

Rachel had been about to flee. Her fear was so profound that she was barely able to register the simple fact that if she tried to run, he would shoot her.

"I don't want to hurt you," he said.

She should have trusted her instinct, that first flash of fear that this was Peter—she still had trouble thinking of him by his real name. It was all so obvious: the beard, the shape of his mouth and nose . . .

"Just get into the car, Rachel. Please."

The advice of the instructor from the defense course she'd taken with Lily at the Ferryside Women's Co-op returned to her as she faced Peter: "The one thing I don't want any of you to do once you've finished this course is get cocky," he had told the class. "What you've learned here will help you in many of the situations you might encounter out on the street, but the bottom line is this: if your assailant has a weapon and there's no way you can disarm him without risking your own life, *don't* make the attempt.

"It's a terrible piece of advice to give you, and I hope to God none of you ever finds herself in such a situation, but if your assailant's holding a gun on you, or has a knife at your throat, just do what he says. Give him your money. Don't fight off his physical advances. What you should do is memorize his features and anything distinctive about him so that you can give the police the most effective description possible.

"But also keep your wits about you, because if the opportunity does arise where you can utilize what you've learned here in the past few weeks, you must be ready to take it. In such a volatile situation, you won't get a second chance."

Peter opened the passenger's door, the muzzle of his small automatic never wavering. With her every nerve screaming for her to just run and damn the consequences, Rachel slowly got into the car and sat down beside him.

"Shut the door," Peter said.

The fake accent was gone now, but there was still something odd about his voice. It sounded strained—as though he were in pain.

For God's sake, Rachel told herself. Don't worry about him. Think. There's got to be a way out of this.

She looked out the window for help, but all around her, business went on as usual. A cab went by, but the driver never even glanced in their direction. Two high school–aged girls, obviously skipping class, stood by a shop window, sharing a cigarette. Three doors down from them, a man was sweeping the sidewalk in front of the pharmacy. A Quicksilver Messenger Service van pulled up on the opposite side of the street.

"What . . . what do you want from me?" Rachel asked.

She remembered Tom, dead at this man's hands. The detectives telling her about how he'd killed the witness to Tom's murder, how they'd intercepted him en route to Lily's place, where he'd obviously meant to kill Lily as well.

He was supposed to be *dead*.

"I have to talk to you," he said.

A year ago, a few months ago, perhaps only weeks ago, Rachel would have fallen to pieces in a situation such as this. But something had changed in her. Whether it was the freedom that Frank's death had given her, or having to be strong for Lily last night, or maybe just that the process of learning to cope had finally kicked in—she wasn't sure. But her panic had ebbed.

Fear was still a steady pulse, drumming through her veins, but she could think beyond it. If she were going to die, she realized, she would not die begging for mercy. She was never going to beg a man again, not for anything. Not even for her life.

She swallowed thickly and hoped her voice wouldn't break.

"So . . . so talk," she said.

The Escort was an automatic. With his left hand on the steering wheel, the right holding the muzzle of the gun against her, Peter waited for a station wagon to go by, then pulled out onto the street. He grimaced as he turned the wheel, as though the simple movement had hurt him.

"Someone's trying to kill me," he said.

It was the last thing in the world that Rachel had expected to hear. She had no idea what form Peter's madness was going to take—having killed as many people as he had, for the reasons he had, she could only think of him as insane—but this caught her completely off-guard.

He shot her a quick look, then took the gun away and laid it on her lap.

"I think I'm going crazy," he added, "because what's happened to me in the past twenty-four hours couldn't possibly happen in a sane world."

Rachel stared at the gun in her lap but made no move to pick it up. Her thoughts were reeling. *He* thought he was going crazy?

"What . . . what are you talking about?" she asked.

"I was leaving a bar last night," Peter told her, "when a man grabbed me and pulled me into the alleyway behind it. He had a gun in his hand—the one that's in your lap—and he pushed it up under my throat when we got to the end of the alley."

Rachel couldn't suppress a shiver. She knew the feeling of cold metal on the soft flesh of her throat. Frank's gun.

"'You're going to die right here, fag,' the man said, 'but before I kill you, I want you to know why you're going to die.' Then he told me it wasn't because I was gay, it was because I knew you."

Again he shot her a glance. Rachel shook her head. She didn't want to hear this.

"He said that he was your protector, that anyone who hurt you had to die.

"'I never hurt her,' I told him.

"'Not yet,' he says. 'But you will. That's the problem when people get close to each other—somebody always gets hurt. Well, no one's going to hurt Rachel, not ever again.'

"I don't think I was ever more scared in my life than I was at that moment. I felt so . . . . so helpless. The guy had forty pounds on me and it wasn't fat. And he had that gun. I could hardly breathe, he had it pushed up so hard against my throat."

Rachel gripped her hands together, fingers knotting nervously as she listened to a story that was all too familiar. She didn't want to believe any of this.

"How . . . how did you get away?" she found herself asking.

Don't be stupid, she told herself as she realized that she was swallowing his story. It's all a lie. He's just making it up.

Maybe. But maybe he wasn't. Maybe Harry Landon and Peter weren't the same person. After all, he'd given her the gun.

She hated the weight of it on her lap.

"I got lucky," Peter said. "While he was going on about how he'd first met you and realized how special you were and how the only way he could keep you from being hurt was to remove anybody who could possibly get close to you, the pressure on the gun at my throat began to ease. I was scared, all right, but I also knew I was going to die if I didn't do something, so I kneed him in the groin."

He gave Rachel a tight, humorless smile. "It's funny. You see that kind of thing in the movies, but you never realize how effective it can be until it happens right in front of you. He just buckled over. The gun went off, but he wasn't aiming at me anymore. The bullet hit the side of the building behind us and went ricocheting God knows where.

"Before he could recover, I kicked him again. This time I knocked the gun out of his hand. Then I kicked him some more. When he was lying on the ground, I picked up the gun and I ran.

"I've been trying to get hold of you ever since, but there was never an answer at your place. I was sure the guy had gone completely over the end and kidnapped you or something. Then I remembered you telling me about your friend Lily, so I looked up her address. I was just on my way to her apartment when I saw you sitting at the bus stop."

Rachel shook her head. What he told her fit within the framework of other events that had happened during the night, and her previous liking of him made her want to believe what he'd just told her, but it all seemed too surreal.

"Why the gun?" she asked. "Why did you point the gun at me?"

"I was scared—and feeling crazy. I started to think, What if she's in on it? What if she *knows* this guy? I know it's a terrible thing for me to say to you, but after what happened, nothing really made much sense. See, I heard about the waiter from the restaurant, and I saw the picture of that guy from the Bike Shop in the paper. I didn't really think about it until this guy started bragging to me about having killed them, but suddenly it all fit. I knew that, crazy as it seemed, it was true."

"Why didn't you go to the police?"

Peter shot her an anguished look. "Didn't I tell you? This guy in the alleyway—he *was* a policeman. He first met you when you were looking for protection from your husband. He said that ever since then, he just couldn't get you out of his mind. He's been following you around, trying to figure out a way to make you his. Then he just happened to be there when your husband attacked you, and that's when he said he realized how he could do it—he'd protect you and then you'd just naturally go to him because you'd be so grateful.

"The man was out of his fucking mind, Rachel, but he was dangerous."

"And what about the car chase?" Rachel asked. "What about going over the bridge?"

"What are you talking about?"

When Rachel explained, Peter shook his head. "I don't know anything about that."

"Lily saw you kill Tom."

"What?"

"Last night," Rachel said. "On the street running by the Sky Towers."

"I was in a bar last night. I can take you there, and the barman will prove it."

Rachel didn't know what to think. All Lily had seen was a bearded man—she'd never met Peter. She just recognized him from the portrait that Rachel had done. But it had happened at night, she'd been upset, and even in a car's headlights, all bearded men looked somewhat the same.

"What about Harry Landon?" Rachel asked.

"What's he got to do with anything?"

"Do you know him?"

Peter shook his head. "Not personally, but any photographer worth his salt knows *who* he is. He's a genius. God, what I wouldn't give for a quarter of his talent."

"The police think he's you," Rachel said, and then she went on to tell him what she knew of last night's murders, the car chase and Harry Landon's death.

Peter had been driving aimlessly the whole time they spoke. By now they were out past the Tombs, driving along Williamson Street where it was about to turn into Highway 14, which wound into the hills north of the city.

"Jesus," he said when she was done. "This is insane."

Rachel was beginning to think so as well. She looked down at the gun lying in her lap. If Peter were guilty, she thought again, why would he have given it to her? That was the point when she realized that she actually believed him. With all one heard of police corruption, it was all too easy to accept that both of them had gotten caught up in some weird delusion headed up by one rogue policeman.

In many ways, Peter's story made far more sense than the idea that the famous photographer Harry Landon was responsible for all of this. A rogue policeman was so much easier to swallow. She could see how his protective instincts might go out of whack until he took the whole "serve and protect" concept too far—it would be just an unhappy coincidence that he'd fixated on her. A policeman would have the tools and ability to kill and get away with the murders. Where would someone like Harry Landon have learned such dubious skills?

God help her, but she believed Peter.

"What do we do?" Rachel asked. "How do we get out of this? If we can't go to the police . . ."

"They can't all be crooked," Peter said.

"But how do we know which are and which aren't?"

Peter shook his head wearily. "I'm falling asleep behind the wheel here. The first thing we need to do is find a place to hole up—I have to get some sleep. Then—God, I'm too tired to think about what we'll do after that. My head hurts, and I just can't seem to think straight."

Rachel had developed a monster headache of her own, trying to sort through it all. She needed time to think as well.

"We'll have to find a motel," she said.

"This guy's a cop," Peter said. "He'll be able to track us down if we register at a motel."

"Not if we pay cash and use fake names. We can give them the impression that we're just looking for a place to . . . you know. They won't know you're gay."

Peter smiled and nodded. "I'm glad one of us is thinking clearly. That's a good idea. We'll need a place with cabins—some place off the road where the car won't be seen. I—" He shot Rachel an embarrassed look. "This isn't my car," he admitted. "I couldn't get to my own, because I was afraid that the man who attacked me was right on my heels, so I just took the first one I could find."

"Someone left their keys in their car?"

Peter shook his head. "No. It's a trick I learned from my brother— he's a mechanic in New York. I'd never actually done it before. To tell you the truth, I was surprised that it even worked."

They drove on north, through the suburbs that had collected around the city over the years, until they were well into the hills. The dark green of the pine forest that was now on either side of them was a welcome relief from the barrage of lights and cars, billboards and the like that they'd been driving through before they hit the suburbs.

"Do you remember the names of the policemen who were present when you first went to them for protection?" Peter asked after a while.

Rachel shook her head. "Just the faces."

"Well, it was one of them. If we could narrow it down, get his name . . ."

"And then?"

"Christ, I don't know. There's got to be a way out of this."

A sign came up on the right of the highway.

"Pine Mountain Cabins," Rachel read. "That sounds promising. Do you think it's far enough out of town?"

"I guess."

A half-mile later they came up on a log cabin structure with a dark forest-green roof, set back from the road, surrounded by pine forest on all sides. Leading away from it into the forested hills was a narrow track.

"It looks perfect," Rachel said. "That little road must run to the cabins."

Peter nodded. Pulling in near the log building, he brought the Escort to a stop and killed the engine.

"Here," Rachel said, gingerly picking up the gun. "I don't want this." Just the touch of it gave her the creeps.

"Jesus, I don't want—"

"Please. I can't stand to hold it."

Reluctantly, Peter accepted the weapon and stuck it in his pocket. He got out of the car.

"Ready to play the young lovers?" he asked.

Rachel nodded. She just hoped there wouldn't be any trouble.

There wasn't. The woman behind the registration desk in the log building seemed totally disinterested in the fact that they were paying cash or in what their names were. Peter signed the register Mark and Polly Mawson, and the woman handed over the cabin's key.

"It's number eight," she said. "Just go down the road, and take the fourth turn on the right."

There was a door behind the registration desk. From the room beyond came the sound of an afternoon soap opera.

"Have a nice stay," the woman added, then headed back through the door.

"Friendly, wasn't she?" Peter said.

Rachel shrugged. "I've got to call Lily," she said. "She'll be starting to get worried about me. I told her I'd be back in a couple of hours, and it's been over three."

"Sure," Peter said. "But why don't you do it from the cabin?"

Number eight was set far enough back from the dirt track that when they parked the Escort beside it, the car couldn't be seen. It sat under a canopy of enormous pines that dwarfed the small structure. Peter pulled a small carryall from the backseat, then led the way inside.

The cabin proved to be a one-room affair. One whole wall was taken up by a fieldstone fireplace with a battered old sofa set in front of it. There was a queen-sized bed in one corner, covered with a quilt. In the other was a small kitchenette—fridge, stove, a small pine table with four mismatched chairs, a sink with one cupboard above it and a small stretch of counter. There were two other doors—one leading to a small bathroom, the second to the deck out behind the cabin. The phone was on a nightstand beside the bed.

"I'm going to call Lily," Rachel said.

Peter closed and locked the door behind him, pocketing the key. He laid the carryall down on the floor, then took the revolver from his pocket.

"I don't think so," he said.

Rachel stopped on her way to the phone and slowly turned.

"Peter. What are you—?"

But she already knew. Stupid, she was so damned stupid. Not only had she believed him, but she'd willingly gone along and helped him bring her here to this place where no one could possibly help her.

"You're very trusting," Peter said.

He took off his sunglasses, and she saw the two black eyes that they'd hidden. Of course, she thought. The police saw him go off the side of a bridge. She didn't know how he'd survived, when the detectives were sure he had to be dead from the drop, but he had survived. And he was hurting.

She remembered him wincing when he turned the steering wheel a certain way, how he'd seemed to favor his left side. She'd thought it was from the beating he'd told her about. Now she knew the truth, little good though it did her.

But perhaps he'd broken a rib or two—that would slow him down some, wouldn't it?

Perhaps he'd do them both a favor and just drop dead.

"You," she said. "It's all true, isn't it? What the police told me?"

Peter shrugged. "I'm not sure what all they told you, but if you mean what you related to me on the drive up here, then yes. That much is true."

"You really *are* Harry Landon?"

Peter—no, Landon—nodded.

"And you . . . you killed all of those people?"

" 'Kill' is such a harsh word, though I will admit that's how I did deal with some of them. But not the women. I never killed them. I just had to . . . to test them."

All of Rachel's strength ebbed from her. She sat down on the edge of the bed, her legs no longer capable of holding her upright. She wished that she had a guardian angel now—a real one, not a madman such as Landon. Someone to protect her, someone to—no. Look where that kind of thinking had gotten her before. She didn't want anybody else hurt because of her.

But it was hard, having no one but herself.

"What do you mean, 'test them'?" she asked.

"Their beauty," Landon explained. "I needed to test the perfection of their beauty, to see that they were without blemish, and then it was necessary to see if they bled or if it was light that poured forth when their skin was punctured."

He was utterly insane, Rachel realized. To stand there, discussing women he'd murdered in such a calm, reasonable voice, how could he be anything but?

He made a motion with the gun.

How could she have been so stupid as to give him back the weapon?

"Please," he said. "I'd appreciate it if you would remove your clothes."

"There's no such thing as perfection in the human body," Rachel said. "Don't you understand? That's what makes us all human—individuals."

"But I am searching for the divine. The Goddess of Beauty has hidden herself in a human vessel, and only I know how to wake her divinity. That's why I'm here, Rachel. That's why you're here. Together we will make history—myself for having the courage to find the goddess and you for harboring her spirit in your flesh.

"We stand on the threshold of a new world, you and I. Together we will strip the banality and self-interest from a soulless society and return to it the gift of its soul."

Rachel shook her head. "You're wrong. What you're saying is crazy. How can—"

"No more discussion, please. Remove your clothes, Rachel."

She shook her head again. "No. If what you say is true, then you can't shoot me, because I won't be perfect anymore, will I?"

It was rhetoric, and Rachel knew it, but she had to make the effort. If she could keep him talking . . .

Oh, who was she kidding? She should have just let him shoot her as soon as he pulled out the gun again—just gotten it over with. But that would have meant that he had won. He and Frank and all the other monsters that preyed on women.

Where—*when*—did it finally stop?

She knew that she'd do what he wanted in the end. Wasn't that the way it had always worked with Frank?

The advice of the defense course instructor rang in her mind.

If your assailant's holding a gun on you . . . just do what he says. Give him your money. Don't fight off his physical advances.

But how far could you go and still retain a shred of self-worth? At what point did it no longer matter if you lived or died, when you wouldn't be able to look yourself in the mirror because of what you'd let someone do to you? If she took off her clothes—then what? If he tried to rape her, if he started to beat her . . .

Where was she supposed to draw the line?

Something Landon had said earlier came back to her, when he first started to talk about testing. . . .

To see if they bled . . .

She knew what he meant now.

. . . or if it was light that poured forth when their skin was punctured.

He was insane. And she was supposed to let him cut her?

She could almost picture the defense course instructor in her mind. Where did it stop? she wanted to ask him. Where do I draw the line and say, no more, even it means I have to die?

Landon touched the carryall with his foot.

"I have other methods at my disposal," he said, "but I don't like to use chemicals unless it's absolutely necessary. Now, I will ask you for a third and final time, would you please remove—"

The phone rang.

Rachel turned, startled at the jangling interruption. When she looked back at Landon, he was frowning, indecision plain in his features. But it didn't last. He crossed the room and crouched down beside her, wincing as he lowered himself down. Before Rachel could think of some way to take advantage of his hurt—smash him in the side with an elbow, kick him—he had the gun jammed painfully against one breast.

"Pick it up," he said.

The weapon added all that he left unsaid: Don't let on that there's any trouble.

The message was plain, but she knew she should ignore it and take the chance. There might never be a better moment than now, with him so close to her, his attention half on the phone, rather than all on her. But she couldn't find the courage to move. All she could do was lift the handset from its cradle.

As she brought the receiver to her ear, Landon bent close so that he, too, could hear.

"H-hello?" Rachel said into the phone.

FIFTY-THREE

For a long time after Rachel was gone, Lily simply sat on the sofa and stared blindly at the floor, tears coursing down her cheeks. Her mind was empty except for a simple phrase that spiraled through the bleakness in an endless circling loop.

Tom was dead.

Those three simple words were like one of her brother's meditative mantras, but she gained no peace from them. All they did was explain the vast emptiness inside her, the grief of her loss. They brought no relief.

Tom was dead.

Tom was dead.

Tom was—

"I know!" she cried suddenly.

She swept her arm across the top of the coffee table, knocking tea mugs and the box of tissues to the floor. One of the mugs hit the leg of the sofa, and its handle broke off on the way to the ground. Lily stared at the residue liquid in the mug as it dripped out onto the rug.

"I know," she repeated.

Her voice was softer now, but it carried a world of pain.

She rose slowly to her feet and went into the bedroom. From where it lay on the dresser, she took the portrait of her that Tom had drawn and sat down on the bed. When she looked at it, she didn't see her own features, only the hand of the man who'd drawn it. Tom, sitting by the window, brow slightly furrowed as he worked to get the lines just right. Tom with his rumpled hair and clothes, and his sweet smile.

"Oh, Tom," she murmured, new tears coursing down her cheeks.

She lay down on the bed and hugged the portrait to her chest. Her pillow was wet with tears before she finally fell into an exhausted sleep.

When she woke, it was after only a few hours' sleep. Setting the portrait aside, she went into the bathroom and washed her face. The grief was a cold ache now, hidden behind a blank mask, just the way intense emotions were always hidden in her family. She stared at her reflection in the mirror. Her pale skin was almost white. With her red-rimmed eyes, she looked like a ghost. Haunted.

She stared at herself for a long time before finally turning away, unable to bear the reflected features of the woman who looked back at her from the mirror. That woman seemed too much like a stranger.

But the whole world felt strange, because Tom was no longer in it. The unfairness of his death left her feeling detached, and she didn't think she ever wanted to reconnect with a world that would let such a thing happen. How could anyone live in such a world? She'd found the love of her life—a gift that only came to a very few, she was sure—simply to have him taken away from her. All those years they could have been together had been stolen in the few short minutes it had taken Harry Landon to beat Tom to death.

She knew what she should do: cherish the time that they *had* been together. But that didn't ease the pain. Remembering just made her feel worse.

When she realized that she was wandering aimlessly around the apartment, she paused in front of her TV set and looked down at the digital clock on her VCR. It was just past four. She remembered then that Rachel had said she'd be back in a couple of hours. It took her a few moments to figure out when Rachel had left. Once she had, she realized that Rachel should have been back a couple of hours ago.

This wasn't like her, Lily thought with a twinge of uneasiness.

The face of the man who'd killed Tom flashed in her mind. She remembered what the police had said about Harry Landon, how he'd been following Rachel around for months, secretly taking pictures of her, "protecting" her, *obsessing* on her.

There'd been a car crash, she remembered. Landon's car had gone over the side of the Kelly Street Bridge. The police said that he had to have died.

But they hadn't found a body.

Really starting to feel nervous now, she tried calling Rachel's apartment, but there was no answer.

She just got tied up, Lily thought. She's probably on her way back right now.

She got up and took her cigarettes and lighter from her purse. She smoked one cigarette after another, staring out the window to the street below. When another half-hour had gone by and Rachel still hadn't arrived, and there was still no answer at her apartment, Lily tried phoning Rob and then Rachel's friend Helen at the framing store. All she succeeded in doing was worrying both of them.

She considered calling Rachel's parents, but Rachel had had nothing to do with them since they'd sided with Frank in the breakup of the marriage, so there was no point. Rachel was hardly likely to go see them now.

Who else? With a sense of shock, Lily realized that there really wasn't anybody else. Rachel had no other close friends—and even Helen was a recent addition to her life.

What an awful way to live, Lily thought as she drifted toward the window to look out on the street.

Friends meant everything to Lily. She couldn't imagine being close to only a couple of people.

When she looked both ways down the street and still didn't see Rachel coming, she returned to the phone. But who to call? She tried Rachel's apartment again—no response. Then she had a sudden idea. She pulled out the phone book and looked up the number to call the security desk in the lobby of Rachel's Sky Towers building.

What the guard told her confirmed her growing fear.

"No, I'm sorry," the guard said. "Ms. Sorensen hasn't entered or left the building since I came on shift at eight this morning."

"Thank you," Lily said and slowly cradled the handset.

Rachel had never made it back to her apartment. Something *had* happened to her.

Lily picked up the phone and dialed again.

"I'd like to speak to, uh"—it took her a moment to remember the name—"John Stone," she said when the police switchboard operator took her call.

"I'm sorry, but Detective Stone is off-duty."

"Can you tell me where I might be able to reach him?"

The switchboard operator apologized again, adding, "We don't give out the personal phone numbers of any of our staff. I'm sure you understand why."

"Yes, but—"

"Is there someone else that might be able to help you?"

Lily tried to remember the names of the two women detectives, but her mind went blank. She just remembered that the detective staying with them last night had been Diane Something-or-other.

"I'm not sure," she said.

"Can you tell me what this is in relation to?"

"Well, it's my friend, Rachel. Rachel Sorensen. She's missing and—"

"Just a moment and I'll connect you with Missing Persons."

"No, I'd rather—"

But it was too late. She was already on hold as the operator transferred her call. She lit a new cigarette while she waited. A moment later the new connection was made, and a woman's voice replaced that of the man who'd first taken her call at the switchboard.

"Missing Persons, Sergeant Pearson speaking. Can I help you?"

Lily told the woman her name, then spelled it out for the officer.

"It . . . it's about my friend, Rachel," she said. "Rachel Sorensen."

"Could you spell that for me as well?"

Lily did.

"And when was the last time you saw Ms. Sorensen?"

"About four hours ago. She—"

"I'm sorry, Ms. Kataboki, but we don't normally consider a person to be officially missing until twenty-four hours have passed."

"But—"

"Is your friend mentally deficient or not in full possession of all of her faculties?"

"No. Of course not. It's just that she said she'd be back in a couple of hours, and it's been at least three hours now and I'm getting really worried."

"That's understandable, Ms. Kataboki, but if your friend isn't mentally or physically impaired, there's not really much we can do at this point. What's usually the case in a situation such as this is that your friend will prove to have been unavoidably delayed—a flat tire, say. She's probably on her way as we're speaking."

"No, you don't understand," Lily said. "She's involved in . . . That man last night, who killed all those people. He was looking for her."

Lily shivered as she spoke. According to Detective Stone, Landon had also been planning to kill *her*. He'd been on his way to her apartment when his car was spotted by a police officer in a cruiser.

"Do you know the name of the detective in charge of the case?" Sergeant Pearson asked her.

"John Stone. I tried calling him first, but the switchboard operator said he wasn't in. Then she transferred me to you."

"If you'll stay on the line, Ms. Kataboki, I'll see if I can find someone to help you."

While she was on hold, Lily glanced nervously toward the door. The chain was off and the upper lock—the one you needed a key to lock behind you when you went out—wasn't engaged.

What are you thinking about yourself for? she asked herself. Rachel's the one who's missing.

But the half-locked door bothered her. She was about to get up and engage the other lock when a male voice came on the phone.

"Ms. . . . ah . . . Kataboki?" he asked.

"Yes."

"This is Detective Draycott. I was part of the task force set up to deal with the killings last night. I believe my partner, Elizabeth Brauman, spoke to you earlier today?"

That was the name of the detective who'd come with Stone. Brauman. It came back to her now. And Diane's last name had been Cruz.

"Yes," Lily said. "Yes, she did."

"Sergeant Pearson indicated that there's a new problem relating to the case?"

"It's my friend Rachel, the one that . . . that Harry Landon was so fixated on. She was supposed to be back here over three hours ago, but she never came back and she doesn't answer her phone. The security guard in her building says she never arrived there."

"She said she was going home?"

"Yes. To change. And then she was coming right back."

"People don't always do what they say they're going to do," Draycott said. "They get distracted and—"

"*Has* Harry Landon's body been recovered?" Lily asked.

"No, but I don't see the relevan—"

"Rachel always does what she says she's going to do, especially at a—" Her throat got tight, vision blurring.

Oh, Tom . . .

"Ms. Kataboki? Are you still there?"

Lily cleared her throat and managed to finish her sentence. "At a time like this. I think something's happened to her, and if something has, then it's got to do with the so-called dead Harry Landon."

Landon should be dead, not her Tom. Landon was the monster, and monsters should never be allowed to live.

"Please," she said. "Won't you help me?"

There was a moment's pause.

"Hold tight, Ms. Kataboki," Draycott said then. "Give me your address and I'll be right over."

Lily did.

"I'll be there in fifteen minutes, tops," Draycott told her.

"Thank you."

Lily cradled the phone, then wrapped her arms around herself. She knew something terrible had happened—was happening—to Rachel. Logic told her this was true, instinct confirmed it. There was no other explanation for Rachel's not returning.

But the relief Lily felt at having convinced the police to look into Rachel's disappearance was short-lived, for instinct also told her that both she and the police were already too late to help Rachel. They couldn't possibly find her in time.

Wherever she was, Rachel was alone with a madman.

Lily bowed her head. The weight of it all was too much for her. Tom's death, now Rachel's disappearance, the *knowing* that Harry Landon had Rachel, that he might have already killed her . . .

But she had no more tears left. When her doorbell rang and Detective Draycott identified himself by holding his badge and ID up to the peephole, she met him dry-eyed. She knew she looked terrible, features haunted, red-eyed, but none of that mattered. All that mattered was Rachel.

"What can we possibly *do*?" she asked the detective when he came into her apartment.

"Let's take it from the top," Draycott said.

His voice was calm and steadying, but all Lily wanted to do was scream with frustration. She knew they had to take it step by step, follow the logical path. But somewhere, right now, if she wasn't already dead, Rachel was in terrible danger, and Lily couldn't see how anyone could possibly help her.

"What was Ms. Sorensen's state of mind, the last time you saw her?" Draycott asked.

Lily lit a cigarette with trembling hands.

"I . . . I don't know," she said, blowing a wreath of blue-gray smoke into the air. She fiddled nervously with her lighter. "I was . . . upset myself, and I wasn't really paying attention. But I know she said she'd be back in a couple of hours—she made a *point* of telling me that, and so when I woke up and found that she still wasn't back . . ."

FIFTY-FOUR

"Mrs., um, Mawson?" a stranger's voice asked after Rachel spoke her "Hello" into the phone.

Rachel's mind went blank. She started to turn to Landon to tell him that it must be a wrong number, but then she recognized the voice—it was the woman behind the check-in counter. That made her remember the fake names Landon had used when they were checking in. Mark and Polly Mawson. A hysterical urge to laugh rose up inside her, coupled with a need to weep for her own stupidity at allowing herself to be so taken in by her captor.

Landon drew the gun back from her breast, then rammed its muzzle hard against her.

"Answer her," he mouthed.

The ice in his gaze sent a chill traveling through her.

"Y-yes?" she said.

"Since you're just passing through," the woman said, "I thought I'd tell you that the only decent restaurant in the area is the Lakeview— it's about two miles up the road—and it closes at eight o'clock sharp.

After that, all you'll find is a truck stop north, just outside of Kinnley, or the all-night diner south on 14. You must have passed it on your way up from the city."

Why was the woman telling her all of this? Rachel wondered. Had her soaps finished and was she so bored she decided she had to call somebody?

She looked at Landon. He pulled his face away from the receiver, wincing at the movement.

"Thank her," he said in barely audible voice.

Thank her? Rachel wondered. For what? For being safe while I'm about to die?

The gun rammed against her again, a painful impact against the already bruised flesh.

"Th-thank you," Rachel managed.

"I wouldn't bother you normally," the woman went on, "but we don't get much traffic through the week, and those we do get are usually passing through and don't know the area. I would have told you when you checked in, but I was in the middle of one of my stories—as you might have noticed—and it clean went out of my mind."

I'm going to die, Rachel thought. He's going to degrade me, make me do God knows what else once I've stripped for him, and then he's going to kill me.

"Well, I won't keep you any longer," the woman said, completely oblivious to the silence on Rachel's end of the line.

Rachel panicked at the idea of the woman hanging up. So long as the woman was on the line, Landon wouldn't hurt her. Landon. . . .

She looked at his face, so close to hers that his features were a little blurry, doubled. This close, she could see that the beard was fake. It was the best quality—enough so that if you weren't looking too closely, you could never have told it wasn't real—but this close she could see a little of the adhesive he'd used to apply it . . . there, by his upper lip where the mustache was attached . . .

"Say good-bye," Landon whispered through clenched teeth.

He's going to kill me and he's going to get away with it, Rachel realized. It's really going to happen.

I can't let it happen.

I can't let him kill me without putting up a fight.

She thought of all those years when she was at the mercy of Frank's moods, trying to please him, begging him not to hurt her, hiding her cuts and bruises from the prying eyes of the outside world. This was just more of the same.

Harry Landon had never been her protector.

He was just another monster.

"Tell the woman," Landon began.

"Th-thank you Mrs.—what's your name?" Rachel asked.

Landon frowned and jabbed her with the gun again. The pain almost made Rachel cry out, but she bit the sound back. She felt a sudden dissociation from the situation she was in. Unlike all those times she'd been at Frank's mercy, she now discovered a primal core of courage that was blossoming inside her. She could stand back from her pain, from her fear. She could plan.

"Arnold. And it's Miss, more's the pity. Moira Arnold."

"Moira?" Rachel repeated, putting a question into her voice.

Landon started to pull the gun back to ram her with it again.

"I'll bet you're wondering where *that* came from," Moira said with a chuckle. "Well, my granddad was Irish, you see. He's the one that first started this place up after he retired. Anyway, he . . ."

Rachel wasn't listening. She waited just long enough for the gun to be about six inches away from her, as far as Landon had pulled it back before, then she suddenly twisted violently aside and brought her elbow down upon Landon's wounded side.

His cry of pain and the gunshot merged into one sound. The bullet missed her torso; it creased the top of her shoulder and took the tip of her earlobe away as it went by. Blood sprayed over the side of her face and the front of her shirt, but she ignored it, ignored the sharp pain that came in its wake.

She heard Moira's voice—asking, as though from miles away, "What's going on?"—as she slashed the handset across Landon's face. He'd been bringing up the gun for a second shot, but the blow stunned him and threw off his aim again.

Rachel's ears rang painfully with the second shot, so much so that she could no longer hear the small voice coming from the phone's receiver.

"Hello? Hello?"

Rachel kicked out with one of her running shoes. The toe caught Landon's wrist, and he lost his grip on the weapon. It went skittering across the wooden floor. He started to reach for her, but she kicked him again. When her shoe connected with his wounded left side, she actually heard something snap inside.

A cracked rib, broken now.

Landon went white and buckled over from the pain.

That was all Rachel needed. She got around him and bolted for the door, turned the knob and gave a tug. It wouldn't open. She looked for a lock release, but there wasn't one. It would only take a key—the key that Landon must have pocketed when they came in.

She turned around to find that he was on his feet again. He'd moved from the bed and gone to the fireplace. As she turned, he pulled the iron poker from its holder to the left of the hearth.

"Look at you," he said through tight lips. "You're a lie. You bleed, just like all the others."

Rachel's earlobe and shoulder felt as though they were on fire. Her shirt was soaked with blood. The hair on the right side of her face had matted and was stuck to her neck and cheek.

She looked around the room, searching for a weapon. Hurt as he was, Landon was still stronger than she. And with that poker . . .

"Where's the light?" Landon cried. "Where's the goddamned light?"

Rachel edged toward the kitchenette, where she snagged a chair and held it protectively in front of her. She thought of the woman on the other end of the phone—Moira. She couldn't hear Moira's voice anymore.

Please, she prayed. Don't come looking on your own. Call the police.

"Maybe there is no goddess," Landon said. He sounded confused, disoriented. "Maybe it's always been a lie—all of it."

But would the police even get here in time? Rachel asked herself.

Disoriented or not, Landon was still set on killing her. He stepped closer, the poker upraised in his hand.

"You have to kill lies," Landon told her. "You have to wash away their blood."

His gaze roved back and forth across the room, as though looking for something, or someone, but it always returned to her.

"It's just a test," he said. "That's right, isn't it? I'm just being tested again. But I'll come through. I always win. I'm pure, that's why. I win, because I'm *pure!*"

He screamed the word and lunged at her. She brought the chair up, and the poker smashed through a wooden rung. Her hands stung with the impact, and she almost lost her grip on the chair. As it was, she staggered backward, unbalanced.

"Beauty knows I'm no lie!"

He swung at her a second time—a wild, unaimed blow which she again managed to deflect with the chair. But she didn't know how she was going to keep it up. Her right shoulder—the one that the bullet had creased—was aching something fierce now. Every movement she made brought a new wash of blood. Her bra and shirt were soaked, and she was starting to feel dizzy from the loss of blood.

"I'll kill you," Landon said, stalking her. "I'll prove my worth by killing you. And then I'll find her, my sweet goddess, and she'll kiss me and she'll touch me with her healing hands and she'll put her lips around my cock and drink the sweet nectar . . ."

His eyes were mad. He was shaking with rage. But he spoke now in a voice that sounded as if it issued from the lips of a dead man. It was flat, emotionless. Cold as the air in a sealed tomb, suddenly opened.

The gun, Rachel thought, searching the room for it while trying to keep her gaze on Landon as well.

"But first I have to kill the lie," Landon said, moving toward her.

Rachel lifted the chair between them with arms so weak she could barely keep it aloft. She knew now that the police, even if Moira had called them, would never get here in time. She was on her own with Landon.

That's the way it had been with Frank, too, but this time she wasn't submitting to his superior strength. This time she'd die before she let another man treat her the way Frank had.

The gun, she thought. Where did the gun go?

FIFTY-FIVE

Dan Hautala had been a member of the Newford Police Department for fifteen years before it all finally got to him. He was a great, hulking man—two forty, six-three—but when he went into the Foxville apartment to break up a domestic, his last day on the force . . . when he saw the baby lying dead inside the oven and its parents screaming at each other, oblivious to the tiny corpse, he just couldn't take anymore.

Working as a State Trooper over the past three years had still brought him face-to-face with death, but even the worst accidents he had to deal with, he could handle. They could be messy, Christ, they could make you lose your lunch, but they weren't the same, because nobody planned them. They weren't deaths that one human being had deliberately wrought upon another. They weren't husbands staving in the heads of their wives with a hammer, or three-year-olds found in dumpsters with telephone cords wrapped around their necks.

He was parked in the lot of the Lakeview Restaurant, cruiser set back a little from the road so that he could work his radar without giving the speeders coming over the hill too much of a chance to slow down when they spotted him. A red Camaro had just topped the hill, hitting eighty-five according to the readout on the radar, when the call came over the radio.

"Car 4, we have a four-fifteen at the Pine Mountain Cabins that was just called in. Over."

Hautala unhooked the mike from its holder and thumbed the transmit button.

A disturbance, he thought. Right. Probably Moira was just bored. Glumly, he watched the Camaro flash past, having appropriately slowed down once the driver saw the cruiser.

"Car 4 to HQ," Hautala said as he made a note of the Camaro's license plate number on his notepad. "What's Moira's problem this time? Another skunk got into her root cellar? Over."

"She's reported gunfire in one of her cabins," the dispatcher said. "She sounds serious, Dan. Do you copy? Over."

"I copy. I'm in the lot of the Lakeview and on my way. ETA three minutes. Over."

"Car 12 has been dispatched as well, ETA twelve minutes. Watch your ass, Dan. Do you copy? Over."

"I copy. Over and out."

Hautala tossed the radio mike onto the passenger seat of the cruiser and started up the car's big engine. Moments later he was pulling out of the lot, rear tires spitting gravel, and heading south on Highway 14.

He was traveling at ninety-five, but he never did catch up to the Camaro before he was turning into the Pine Mountain Cabins. Moira was waiting outside for him, looking nervously to where the dirt road went back into the forest.

"It's cabin eight, the fourth on the left," she said when he slowed to a stop beside her. "Be careful, Dan. They've got a gun."

Hautala nodded. "I will. Now, you go on inside, Moira, and let me do my job."

He took out his service revolver and laid it on his lap before he eased the cruiser down the little dirt track.

FIFTY-SIX

Landon came at Rachel, swinging the poker in a wide arc, the full force of his unhurt side behind the blow. Her hands went numb when the poker smashed into her chair. A wooden leg snapped and the chair dropped from her hands. Landon brought the poker up for a second blow, but Rachel kicked the wreckage of the chair toward him.

His feet got tangled in its three remaining legs, and he went down, hitting the floor hard. The poker fell from his hand, but when it came to rest, he was between her and the makeshift weapon. Rachel dodged behind the small kitchen table as Landon rose up on one knee. She looked desperately across the room.

Where was the gun?

Landon's fingers closed around the poker. He put a hand on the other side of the table and started to hoist himself back to his feet. Rachel gave the table a tug toward her, and it threw him off-balance again. Before he could recover, she rammed the table into his hurt side.

The gun.

As he went down again, face white with pain, she looked behind him to where they'd first started struggling.

Where was the—

And then she saw it, lying on the floor, between the bed and the hearth. She grabbed another chair and held it protectively toward him, as though she were a lion tamer and he the lion. When he started to get up again, she threw the chair at him and ran for the gun.

She was so weak that there was no real force behind the chair as it came at him. He easily batted it aside, but be wasn't fast enough to stop her from reaching the gun. She crouched down and scooped it up. Turning, she knelt there on the floor beside the fireplace with the weapon in her hands and aimed toward him.

"No—no more," she said.

The gun trembled in her hands, and Landon just laughed.

"I can't die," he told her as he started toward her. "Don't you understand that yet? Beauty won't let me die. We have an appointment. We—"

She fired. The small gun kicked up in her hands, throwing off her aim, but she hit him. High in the chest. His mouth shaped an O of surprise that was almost comical, and he staggered back under the impact of the bullet.

But he didn't go down.

The gun was so small, Rachel realized, the caliber of its rounds such that it would take more than one bullet to stop him. Biting at her lower lip, she tried to steady her aim.

As he stepped toward her, lurching now, the poker no longer upraised but hanging at his side, she fired again, and again, four shots in all, until her ears rang, until he finally went down, until he lay still on the floor barely five feet away from her with blood soaking his shirt and his lifeless eyes staring at her.

A wave of dizziness came over her, and she bent over, arms hugging her stomach. She shook as though from a fever. Her stomach roiled, and then she threw up, vomiting until there was nothing left to bring up.

She remained like that for a long time, bent over, hugging herself. The stink rising from the puddle of vomit made her feel sicker. Her head whirled and spun.

She had . . . had to . . . get out.

Fresh air. She needed . . .

Slowly she focused on Landon's body. The thought of touching him made her feel still more nauseated, but she knew she couldn't remain inside with him while she waited for help. Gathering the last remnants of her courage, she crept forward, the gun held out before her in case he was only pretending to be dead.

He had gained an almost supernatural stature in her mind. The police had seen him go over the side of the bridge in a car, but he'd survived, survived to come back and hunt her down. She could see he was dead—knew he was dead, his body riddled with bullets—but she still half-expected him to sit up, lifting that poker to attack her again.

When she was close enough, she nudged him with the muzzle of the gun. He didn't move.

Her relief was brief and not strong enough to cut through the spinning stew of shock and remorse over what she had done.

Dead. Oh God, he was dead. He deserved to die, but she . . . to think that she had killed him . . . another human being . . . no matter how much of a monster . . .

Choking back an onslaught of dry heaves, she moved closer still until she could put her hand in the side pocket of his jacket. She could have cried with relief when her fingers closed around the key to the cabin door.

She pulled it out of his pocket and scuttled back, still half-believing that he could rise up again. When she got to the door, she slowly hauled herself to her feet. She was still shaking so much that it took her three tries to get the key into the lock. Then, just as she turned the key, she heard a voice call to her from outside the cabin.

"You, in the cabin. This is the police."

With her ears still ringing from the gunshots, the voice was vague and faint, but she'd never been more happy than she was at this moment, hearing that voice.

The lock disengaged and she opened the door. As she stepped out, she had a brief glimpse of a large man in a State Trooper's uniform, hunkered down behind the open door of his cruiser, handgun out and pointed toward her.

It's all right, she wanted to tell the officer. He's dead.

But a shaft of sunlight came down through the trees, and she lifted her hand to block its glare, forgetting about the gun in her hand. The last thing she heard was the thunderous boom of the trooper's revolver, then the bullet struck her. It lifted her onto her toes and slammed her back into the doorjamb.

The little automatic slipped from her fingers. She slid down the door toward the ground. She tried to talk, but the words caught in her throat.

"Wh-why . . . ?"

Then darkness washed over her in a great comforting wave, and she let herself fall into it, aiming for the small pinpoint of light she thought she could see, just there, far off in the distance, but growing in size as she fell, rushing closer, ever closer toward it.

AFTER

FIFTY-SEVEN

It was the wrong kind of a day for a funeral. The sky was so pure, a cloudless blue that it hurt the eyes. The mid-morning sun beat down on the small crowd gathered in the graveyard, its bright light glittering on jewelry and buttons.

Lily stood by the open grave and stared down at the coffin. She looked like a still print, cut from the reel of an old pre-color film, dressed all in black, her skin so very pale, features drawn. Her red-rimmed eyes were hidden behind sunglasses.

It hurt so much, but whenever the pain swelled up in her to the point where she knew she just couldn't bear it any longer, she'd think of how Rachel must have felt, alone in that cabin with a madman. Alone and helpless. And then, when she'd actually managed to kill Landon, to be shot by that stupid State Trooper. . . . .

The priest's voice droned on. Lily tried very hard to listen to what was being said, but all she could think of was that the words meant nothing. Words wouldn't bring life back into the body that lay within the coffin. Nothing could.

Behind her sunglasses her eyes welled with tears. She bowed her head, wishing the sun would go away, the blue sky, the priest, the crowd. Grief came rolling up inside her, a great drowning swell that threatened to swallow her.

She felt a touch at her elbow, then an arm went across her shoulders. She turned and gave Rachel a grateful look.

Her friend had her other arm in a sling, and she looked almost as pale as Lily's natural pallor. She was still supposed to be in the hospital, but she'd refused to let Lily face Tom's funeral without being there with her.

With all Rachel had gone through, Lily had thought that her experience with Landon would be the finishing blow, that she'd never recover, but Rachel had emerged stronger and more assured of herself than Lily had ever known her to be. Some of it, she knew, was for her sake, but Rachel had changed as well.

Whatever else became of her in this life, Rachel would never again be a victim.

Lily reached up and gave Rachel's hand a grateful squeeze, then turned to watch Tom's coffin as it was lowered into the grave. A part of her went down into the ground with him. Without Rachel being there for her, she might just as well have thrown herself down into the grave with it, because without that friendship and comfort, she didn't know how she'd ever be able to carry on.

"Good-bye, Tom," she whispered under her breath.

Rachel's arm tightened across her shoulders.

There was only one person present when Harry Landon was interred in a pauper's grave at the city's expense. The family had refused to take the body; none of them attended the funeral. There was only Stone.

He stood and watched until the gravediggers threw the last shovelful of dirt onto the grave, his compulsion to see that Landon could no longer hurt anyone else finally satisfied. He stood a moment longer, while the workmen put away their tools, then he slowly walked away.

He had work to do.

In his job, there was always more work to do.